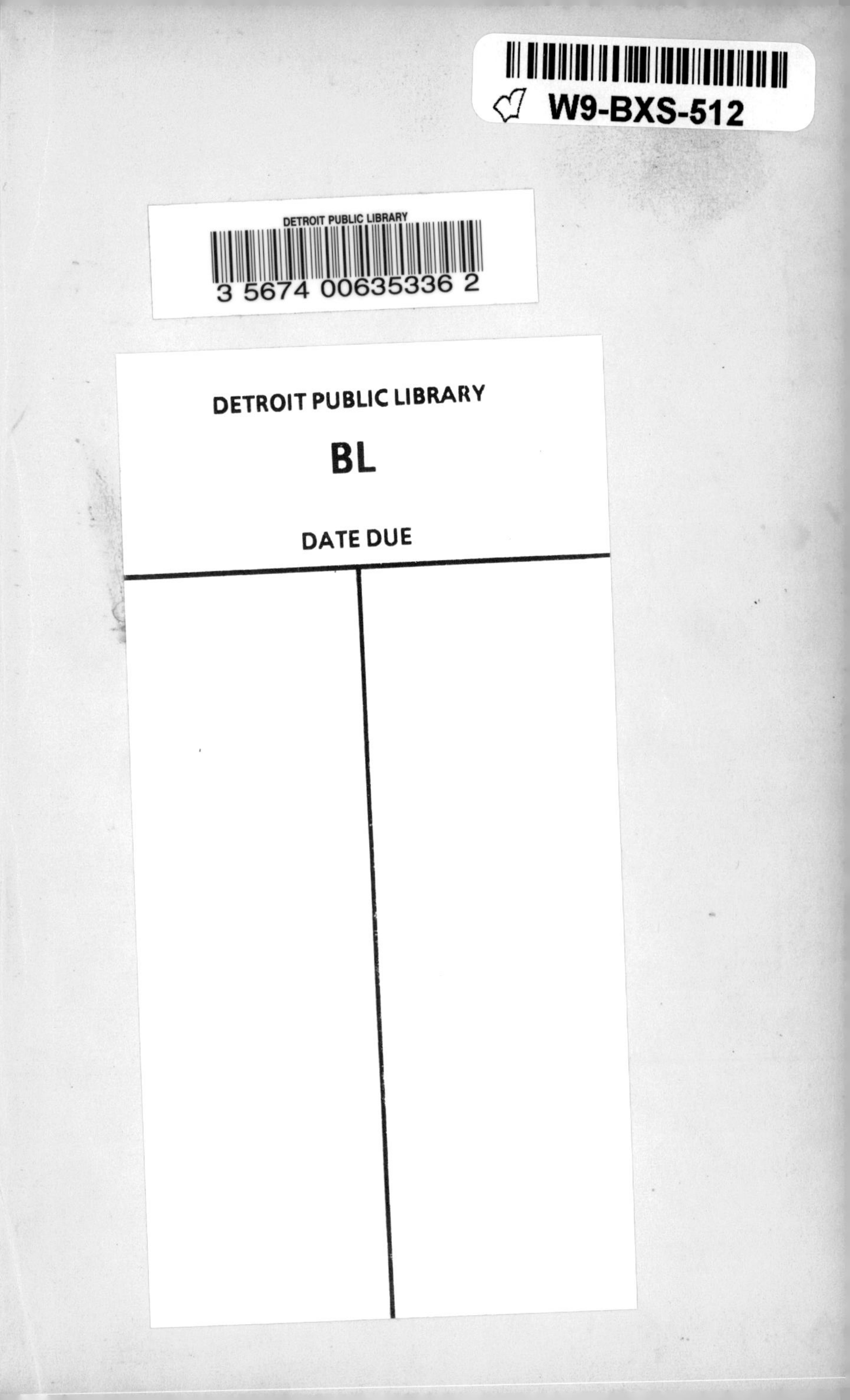

The Other Elizabeth

BY JESS GREGG

The Other Elizabeth

RINEHART & CO., INCORPORATED

NEW YORK

TORONTO

PUBLISHED SIMULTANEOUSLY IN CANADA BY
CLARKE, IRWIN & COMPANY, LTD., TORONTO

PRINTED IN THE UNITED STATES OF AMERICA

LIBRARY OF CONGRESS CATALOG CARD NUMBER:52—5575

FOR DEAN B. AND MIZ EDNA

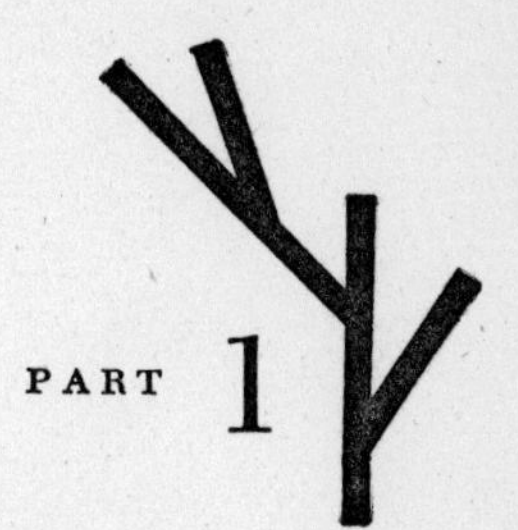

PART 1

Elizabeth Deveny

THE OTHER ELIZABETH is one of the strangest love affairs of fiction: a tale of mounting suspense and eerie psychological fascination. Not since Daphne du Maurier's REBECCA has there been anything like it.

CHAPTER 1

As the Baroness entered, Elizabeth arose. The room was long, permitting the two women to appraise each other before their finger tips touched.

"Miss Deveny, isn't it?" The Baroness' intonation was skillful, designed to put the young woman at ease without letting her forget this was not a social visit.

Elizabeth passed her tongue over dry lips in preparation to say something and then only nodded self-consciously. She tried not to make her scrutiny apparent, but close range forced an immediate revision of her first impression. Madame von Schillar was not young. Her skin was youthfully tinted, but fine linear webs entrapped the cool green eyes and bracketed the scarlet mark of her mouth. She was fashionably emaciated and her hair had been reddened; yet her artfulness, far from hiding her age, merely attested that vanity had outlived youth.

"Harry Mellett seemed most enthusiastic about you," the Baroness was saying. "Frankly, I was in favor of having a man help me. I don't get along too smartly with other women." She flicked a glance at the girl's drab tweed suit, at the hang of her dark hair. "I feel we'll get along, however." She motioned for Elizabeth to sit down. "Tell me about yourself. I gather you've been published before."

"Yes. A book of sonnets."

"Love poems?"

"Well—yes."

Madame von Schillar smiled. She could not quite visualize this quiet creature giving any authority to a love sonnet; but her pallor did make her eminently suitable for a ghost writer.

"How long will it take?" she asked, abruptly. "This book. How long will it take us to write?"

"That's hard to say," said Elizabeth. "Some books take years."

"Well, this one won't," Baroness von Schillar assured her with a dry laugh. "I don't have forever, any more. A few months. That's all I can give it."

"Then we'll have to work hard," Elizabeth warned.

"Mornings, too?"

"Probably."

Mocking martyrdom, Madame von Schillar rolled her eyes heavenward. "I can't work Wednesday afternoons," she added, suddenly. "My hairdresser comes, then. And Thursday is my day at home, so I can't work then, either. So how about evenings? Couldn't we work evenings, instead? Or are you involved with someone?"

Elizabeth glanced away. "No," she said, too quickly.

The Baroness smiled lazily and tapped the girl's wrist. "My dear," she reproached, "think of all the personal questions you're going to be asking me!" Still smiling, she leaned back in her chair. "In the meantime, do we argue about money?"

"That's all been settled. I'm satisfied with the terms."

"Now there's a pity," said the Baroness. "If there's one thing I dearly love, it's to bargain. Haggle, Flix used to call it." She tugged at her pearls restlessly. "Well, let's get you settled. You'd probably like to see your room before we do anything more."

"My room? Oh, I've already taken one," said Elizabeth.

"Indeed? Where?"

"Down the block. A boardinghouse, three doors away—" Fearing she had implied the growing shabbiness of the neighborhood, she quickly added, "But your house is magnificent."

"Then why do you want to live in a run-down boardinghouse?"

"It's just it never entered my mind you'd want me here—"

The Baroness studied the girl's clean-cut features. "Deveny," she mused. "I used to know someone in Rome by that name. Or was it Di Vanni? Yes, a sweet little—" She was about to say croupier, but adroitly changed it to banker. "But despite your black hair, I fancy you're not Italian."

The young woman shook her head. "Irish, I believe."

"Oh, what a shame!"

By habit, Elizabeth's face betrayed no surprise. "A shame?"

"I'm sorry." The Baroness smiled apologetically. "Old Boston prejudice. But I've been away from here so long, I suppose all that has changed now. Incidentally, what am I to call you?"

"Elizabeth."

"Well now, that does present a problem, eh?"

"How so?"

"Two in this house would be confusing. I'm also Elizabeth, you see." Idly, she flicked the garnet pendant swinging from her ear. "I shall refuse to call you Betty or Liz, or that kind of tosh. So I think I'll just call you Miss Deveny and pretend it's really Italian, after all."

Elizabeth laughed. "Or French. Surely I had a French ancestor, somewhere."

Madame von Schillar tipped her head. Abruptly, she held out her hand for Elizabeth to come and take. "I like you. So I really must insist you stay here. I'm fond of company. Besides, we can work the easier. Close harmony, and all that!" Without awaiting Elizabeth's reply, she quickly added, "Oh, if it's privacy you want, take the whole second floor. Or the third. Or both, if you want, I never go upstairs. Besides, you'll be my first guest since my return to these"—she snorted—"delightful shores, so you really daren't refuse."

"Then I'd be delighted to stay," said Elizabeth.

"*Bon!* I'll send in Worth to fetch your luggage." She pushed open the double doors to her own suite of rooms, still speaking. "Dinner will be at seven and quite informal, so . . ." The doors swung shut, obliterating the rest of her words.

Elizabeth stared after her in bewilderment. Not knowing what was expected of her now, she sat down and waited. Restlessness soon forced her up again, and she wandered about, inspecting the ornate parlor.

It was a room laid out in state. Even the flowers had the arid perfection of floral tributes. In other days, this parlor had been closed off except on special occasions, and it still retained an air of fastidious seclusion. Heavy drapes prohibited the intrusion of sunlight. A fan of folded paper replaced fire in the hearth. The chairs were so delicate as to discourage relaxation. The piano was locked against any tampering musician. Here only silence was welcome, and, mutinously, Elizabeth considered singing aloud or shoving awry one of the stiff, gilded chairs.

A door slammed, and she jumped guiltily as if apprehended in her revolt. The stout, elderly woman who bustled into the room was the one who had first admitted her to the house.

"I'm Worth," she said, patiently, as if it were Elizabeth's fault for not knowing. "The Lady told me to fetch your bags."

Elizabeth gave her the address, adding, "There's only one bag, Mrs Worth."

She eyed Elizabeth shrewdly. "The Lady says you're a writer. Does that mean from the newspapers?"

"From Chesterton Yard," the girl answered. "A publishing house. I'm to help the Baroness with her memoirs."

"Are you planning to ask me questions, too?"

"I don't think it'll be necessary, Mrs Worth."

"The Lady calls me just Worth, Miss."

"Do you prefer that?"

"The Lady calls me Worth," the woman repeated, stolidly. As she reached the hall, however, she paused and added more gently, "Maybe I ought to show you around the house first, Miss, so you can choose your room."

Elizabeth hesitated. "I can manage alone, thanks."

"Well, suit yourself." The servant moved on.

Fearing she had offended, Elizabeth hastened after her. "It's just that I don't like to be any extra bother . . ." But without replying, Worth closed the door on her.

Sighing, Elizabeth climbed the steep stairs and wandered through the shuttered twilight of the rooms. Somewhere a clock chimed five. Moments later, a grandfather clock ponderously reiterated the same announcement as if, until then, the hour had not been established with any authority. A strange conceit, Elizabeth thought, to keep clocks going in these deserted rooms where time had ceased to matter. She hastened on, oppressed as much by the heavy elegance as the isolation. Wealth had been enshrined here for over a century, and the devotional offerings of each generation produced an airless clutter very much like a museum.

Thus it was with relief that she found one room decorated by little but the fading sunlight. Its high, whitewashed walls were free of the gilded tiers of pictures, and the floor was barren plank like the deck of a frigate. There was nothing to distract her, nothing either to admire or avoid. With symbolic acceptance, she took off her scarf and hung it in the empty wardrobe cabinet.

On the oak panel of its door, she noticed a smudged crimson fingerprint. "Blood," she thought, but without actually believing it was more than ancient paint. Impulsively, she put her finger to the red mark and nodded her head, as if this were a formal introduction to whatever memories still lingered here.

"Sure now, you don't want this room!"

Elizabeth whipped around. It was only Worth, carrying the shabby valise.

"The back rooms are nicer," the servant continued, "and second room front on the third floor is cozier. Has the Winslow collection of glass shoes."

There was a personal pride in her voice, and Elizabeth, eager to make amends, asked, "You've been here a long time, haven't you?"

"Yes, Miss. I used to work for old Mr Winslow, and when he deeded this house to the Lady on her first marriage, it's almost like he deeded me with it." She ran her palm over the desktop, testing for dust. "Sure I can't show you a nicer room?"

"I like this," Elizabeth said, shyly. "It's so simple and—without fuss."

"It would be," said Worth. "It was his."

"Whose?"

"Mr Wrenn's."

"Marius Wrenn?"

The servant nodded, and Elizabeth studied the room with fresh interest. "Was this his studio or bedroom?"

"Both. Painted here, slept here too. And sometimes ate. Anyway, his last months alive, he did."

"And died here?" Elizabeth asked, glancing at the narrow cot.

"No." Mrs Worth set down the valise. "He drowned."

"How did it happen?" Elizabeth asked.

Worth opened the door. "Most likely she'll tell you about it, when the mood strikes her, Miss."

"Her?"

"Mrs Wrenn," the servant said. "The Baroness."

Alone again, Elizabeth opened her valise. Her possessions were sparse, but she unpacked them with meticulous care. Upon the desk, she placed a scarred leather box which served no purpose, but it had been her father's, and so gave each of the many barren rooms she had inhabited an identity more personal. Beside the box, she stacked three books: Keats, Shakespeare and a sheaflike volume, slender as its own shadow, called *Dark Pantomime;* this, her lone venture in print.

"And very rare," she thought, with rueful irony. "I may be the only one in the world who actually owns a copy." Absently, she flipped open the cover and glanced at that name on the dedicatory page. Her jaw tightened. Quickly, she laid the book aside.

There was still darning to do on her other blouse, but the light was fast fading, and for the first time she noticed this room had not been wired for electricity. There was only a hanging lamp, whose archaic mechanism challenged and defeated her. Unresisted, darkness descended, and she lay down to rest until dinner. Sleep did not come, but instead that vacuousness in her stomach, always induced by strange surroundings. Idly, she lit a match and held it up, watching the shadows creep back. Her eyes were drawn to her book, open on the desk, and she found sudden comfort in seeing his name printed there in dedication: "For Harry Mellett."

The match burned out, but the darkness was no longer empty. In her thoughts, she once more stood beside Mellett that afternoon a week ago; but her memory was not exact. She did not feel now that brief hostility which always accompanied each meeting with the young editor; no panic that, by some trick of speech or silence, she might betray her feelings. She sensed only pleasure, for it was over now. In memory, the unexpected could no longer happen, and she was safe, mistress of the situation.

He had not summoned her to his office at Chesterton Yard, as usual. This had been a special invitation. Chatting, they strolled down the galleries of the Modern Museum in New York, and she felt the drumming of her heart even in her finger tips. As he spoke, she watched him intently, not to flatter him, but because it was always necessary to accustom herself to his appearance, to memorize his face again, before she could forget it and really listen.

In judging him, Elizabeth made a common mistake. Mellett was not extraordinary looking. His hair was only brown, cropped short, and his face, lean, tan, lined with white from squinting in the sun. His animation, however, and the directness of his eyes easily persuaded one he was handsome.

"I'm worried about you," he said.

"Why?" she asked, happily.

"Because you haven't gotten back to work yet. No new poems for me." She lowered her eyes. "You know, Elizabeth," he continued, "when you fall off a horse, it's best to get right back on and ride again."

"Do you think it's because my book was a failure that I'm not writing any more?" she demanded.

"Isn't it?"

"Certainly not!"

"Why, then?"

She pretended to study a scene by Lautrec, and her answer was barely audible. "I don't know."

"Don't you want to write any more?" he asked, gently.

"Yes." She faced him now. "Oh, very much!"

"Good." They resumed their stroll, stopping again before a powerful portrait of a girl reflecting her nudity in a cracked mirror. "I suppose this is my favorite picture here," he said.

" 'Study of Emma'?"

He nodded. "Like it?"

She hesitated. "Why, yes, as a matter of fact, I do. Only I've seen it reproduced so much, I never really stopped to think."

"Know much about him?" he asked. "Wrenn?"

"Not really."

"Neither does anyone else," Mellett mused. "Everybody knows his work, but nobody knows him. Curious chap. A hero without a legend. I've been crazy to put out a book on him since his work's gotten so popular. But no luck. There just haven't been enough facts to go on. He didn't leave anything. Oh, paintings, sure; but no diaries, no letters. Nothing, except what the newspapers printed during the scandal, and that's mostly nonsense."

"What scandal?" she asked.

"Well," he laughed, "maybe it isn't so scandalous today, but it was too much for Boston, early in the century. Wrenn ran off with some Senator's wife. It resulted in the messiest divorce case of the decade, but the two of them braved everything to be together and get married. I've always thought it would make one hell of a book, if I could get hold of the real facts. But only his widow can give those, and she's always refused to share any part of him with the world."

Elizabeth was immediately, almost indignantly, defensive. "You can't blame the poor thing for wanting privacy—"

"Well, she never got it," Mellett said. "She was always in the headlines. The darling of the tabloids. Had all the ingredients for it —great beauty, rich, old Boston family, and a genius for getting involved. Besides all that, she married three times, always spectacularly and quite in the tradition of the American heiress—a statesman, an artist, and, inevitably, a nobleman." Then he added, casually, "She returned to this country about four months ago."

Elizabeth glanced at him sidelong. She was less clever than highly intuitive. Schooled by loneliness, she had learned to reach into other lives, to borrow their motives and reactions and to play them against her heart. So she did now, and Mellett's offhandedness rang false. Suddenly, she knew that it was for business, after all, that he had invited her out, this day.

"What is it, Harry?" she asked, quietly.

"What is what?"

"What you have up your sleeve."

"Oh!" He grinned. "Well, I went up to see her, last week. Scarcely mentioned Wrenn. It was her I emphasized. The glamour, the excitement of her life. I proposed putting out a luxury edition of her life and times, written in her own words."

"What did she say?"

"Ordered me out of the house. But—she called me back."

"Vanity?"

"Not just that," he said. "But look—most of her life, she's fought for obscurity, struggled to live down all the gossip and scandal. Well, now that she's succeeded, my bet is she misses the challenge, the drama, the prestige of notoriety. The world's passed her by. She's forgotten, and I think she's lonely. And that's what I played on. This book would remind the world just who she is—but, for once, sympathetically. Of course, it'll mean printing a lot of nonsense, but well worth it, if we can get her to uncover even a portion of her life with Wrenn."

"Go on," she prompted, resignedly.

"Well, naturally, she has no knack for writing. So I had to promise her someone first-rate to ghostwrite the autobiography for her. But who?" He watched her face carefully. "Got any suggestions?"

"Can't think of a soul." Her voice was toneless.

"How about yourself?"

"Why me?"

"I need a poet," he replied, gravely. "I need the insight and sensitivity of a poet and a woman. Unless the material is handled delicately, the Baroness won't let us publish. She's had enough of the other kind of reporting. This book can't be tabloid fare. It has to have heart."

"But why me?" she persisted. "Surely you have other writers on the string, more successful—"

"But I believe in you," he said.

She flushed and, nervously, snapped her purse open and shut. "I'd have to live in Boston, wouldn't I?" she said, at last. "I'd have to leave New York."

"For a few months, yes."

"Well, I—couldn't. I just couldn't, right now."

"Why not?"

"I just couldn't, that's all."

"Is there someone here, who . . . ?"

"No!"

"Then what's holding you here?"

Her voice tightened with anger. "Is that why you asked me out today? To cross-examine me? Because I've said all I'm going to say about it. I don't want the assignment, and I don't feel obliged to explain."

He met her defiant eyes, then shrugged. "Okay," he murmured. They moved on down the gallery in silence.

"Are you angry with me now?" she finally asked.

"No. Just a little surprised at all that passion."

"If you think I'm so cold," she said, "how could you imagine I'd be competent to work on a love story?"

He turned on her sharply. "You certainly have a point there!"

Although she had goaded him into it, Mellett's remark rankled Elizabeth and challenged her. Grudgingly, she returned to the museum alone the following afternoon and once more paused before Wrenn's powerful study of Emma. The brushwork was bold, masculine, and the colors were raw, persuading the casual spectator that the portraiture itself was harsh; yet as she gazed into the face of Emma, she became aware of the tenderness exercised here, the delicacy and understanding, as in a clumsy, but infinitely loving, caress.

She approached a guard. "Can you tell me anything about this man? This Wrenn?"

He shook his head. "Don't think anything's known about him much."

She moved on to another of Wrenn's paintings, a dark sea storming a bleak but resistant wharf. The scene so precisely reflected her own turbulence and obstinacy that she stood fascinated before it, peering as if into a mirror.

She left the museum that afternoon with curious exhilaration and returned the next day to replenish it. On the fourth day, she called Mellett.

"I don't know why I want to do the book," she said, "or even if I'll be able to work at all. But I'd like to try—"

Dinner was no triumph of conversation, Madame von Schillar being too absorbed by thought. Occasionally, and with exquisite grace, she would punctuate her silence with questions about Elizabeth, but the answers usually quite escaped her attention.

Elizabeth was not offended. From childhood she had been familiar with such oversight. Her parents' passionate concern for each other had overshadowed everything else in their lives, even their child. Overlooked on her own ground, Elizabeth had early learned to borrow attention by invading their domain. It was a simple enough trick: her mother could be lured into vivid conversation if the topic Elizabeth broached was her father; and when the subject discussed was Mama, her father's immediate and gallant interest was sunshine for the child to bask in.

Recalling her success with this method, Elizabeth tried to ease the Baroness into conversation by discussing the man she had so loved.

"Before I left New York," she began, "I went to an exhibition of your husband's—"

The Baroness arched her brows. "An exhibition of my husbands? A waxworks, perhaps? 'On display, for today only, the collected husbands of the Baroness von Schillar'?" With faint amusement, she measured the girl's confusion. "Tell me—which of them did you find the most attractive?"

"I mean, I went to an exhibition of Mr Wrenn's work."

"Ah!"

These were not the reactions Elizabeth had foreseen. "He had such a wonderful eye for color . . ." she blundered on. The Baroness watched her with a little smile. Wisely, Elizabeth retreated to silence.

"Are you quite through now?" asked the Baroness. "With your dinner, quite through?" Elizabeth nodded, and Madame von Schillar tinkled her spoon against a goblet. Worth appeared at the pantry door. "I think you might serve coffee now, Worth. Perhaps in my room, eh?"

Madame von Schillar's suite was in itself a miniature biography, cluttered with footnotes to each phase of her extravagant career. A collection of painted fans covered one wall; a baronial crest emblazoned on worn red velvet, another. Upon tables, desk, and mantel were nests of silver-framed photographs: friends and celebrities from Washington, Paris, Rome. Dominating all, and reflected in the several mirrors about the room, was a superb portrait of a young titian-haired beauty rising in the smoke of tulle and the ice of satin. With a rush of recognition, Elizabeth glanced from it to the Baroness. Unconsciously, Madame von Schillar assumed the pose of the portrait.

"But surely Mr Wrenn didn't paint this," Elizabeth said.

"Sargent, my dear. John Singer Sargent. I thought we could use it as a front-piece in my book." She stretched out on a chaise longue and lifted an obese black spaniel onto her lap. "Theo Carver—my first husband—fell in love with me from seeing that picture," she mused, "even though we'd never met, and he wasn't much for art."

Elizabeth quickly noted this statement in her booklet, then waited attentively for the Baroness to continue. Madame von Schillar, however, was preoccupied by her dog, a wheezing, brown-toothed odalisque.

"Her name is Jabot," Madame von Schillar announced. "Because her has a patch of white under her chin . . ." Then, with that charming indolence she employed to soften her habitual bluntness, she demanded, "What have you found out about me?"

"Why, nothing—"

"No research? No checking old newspapers and tabloids?"

"Not yet."

"Then don't waste your time. Not an ounce of truth in the lot."

She touched some perfume to her ears and wrists. "I haven't read a book in years, so I don't know the fashion in confessions today. But tell me what you want to know, and you shall have it."

Elizabeth answered gravely. "I want to know you."

The Baroness laughed and fanned out her hands. "Don't you now?"

"I mean—to know you as—you know yourself," Elizabeth replied. "I want to remember what you remember, so when I finally write a word, it will be the word you might choose and not I."

Madame von Schillar studied her. "What a curious child you are," she mused. Then, shrugging, "Where shall I begin?"

"Why not at the beginning?" Elizabeth suggested. "You were born . . . ?"

"So I am told," drawled the Baroness. "Here in Boston—well, at the turn of the century." She noticed the girl's furtive glance at the portrait which was signed Sargent, 1905. Dryly, she added, "I was big for a five year old, eh? Well, suppose we gloss over my birth and begin with *ma famille.* Father was Asa Winslow, whose ancestors practically invented glass—"

With that irreverence possible only to pride, she outlined her forebears' shortcomings, soon interrupting this to recall how, in Paris, people used to stand on chairs to see her enter a ballroom. This, in turn, inspired some data about her debut party, and then of her disastrous fondness for gambling. Yet, as she spoke on, she began to falter, swerving away from events like one crossing the street to avoid acknowledging a former friend. Her eyes grew dull, and her voice sank until, at last, the uneasy recital lapsed into silence. She lay back with eyes closed, and when she spoke again, it was with freezing courtesy.

"Good night, Miss Deveny."

"Aren't you well?" Elizabeth arose in alarm. "Can I do something?"

"Just go away," the Baroness whispered. "Just leave me alone."

She did not open her eyes again until the door had long been shut. Frowning, she stared into the fire. Now and then, brief as the flame itself, cunning would brighten her face, only to flicker out, suffocated by the despairing frown. Abruptly, she bowed her head and pressed her knotted fists against her eyes. The sigh which swelled within her escaped her lips in silence.

At last, she arose and tugged the bell cord. By the time Worth appeared, Madame von Schillar's face was once more impassive.

"Tell the girl I shan't need her any more. I've decided not to do my memoirs, after all." She was not used to explaining her actions to anyone, so the urgency of her words could only be to convince herself. "It's rather too taxing, and—my heart, you know . . ."

Worth nodded stolidly. She knew Madame von Schillar's heart. "Ought I tell the young lady now?" she demanded. "Probably's gone up to bed."

"Tomorrow will do. I shan't want to be disturbed, so she needn't feel obliged to say good-bye. Tell her I'll write her a letter." She glanced out the window and did not answer when Worth, withdrawing, murmured good night.

It was the ticking of the little silver clock which roused her. She crossed to the mantel and stayed the pendulum. A few minutes later, she started it again, so time would pass the quicker and bring an hour more conducive to sleep. Then, sighing again, she laid out a spread of solitaire.

Near midnight, the shrill ring of the telephone jarred her from concentration. She arose quickly, spilling the cards onto the floor, and snatched up the receiver. Then she silently counted to five so as not to seem eager.

"Hello," she said, glancing toward the mirror. Her smile was arch and her voice interesting, vibrant.

"Hello." It was a man's voice. "May I speak to Mr Morgan?"

Madame von Schillar frowned. "Who? Who do you want?"

"Mr Morgan?"

"No Mr Morgan lives here." Her voice rose sharply. "And it's a perfectly ridiculous hour to telephone anyone—" She slammed down the receiver.

Her face was tight-drawn with disappointment. "Ought to have that damn thing disconnected," she muttered. "Fat lot of good it does. No one ever calls me . . ." She shoved aside the telephone as if it were to blame and returned to the littered cards. She knelt down, but did not pick them up; merely stared at them, and for a long time. "There was a game in Berlin," she had told Elizabeth earlier, "when I was literally down to my last seventy dollars, and I bet it, every cent, on the turn of a card—"

Gravely, she picked up a card from the floor. "Red," she predicted, and turned it face up.

Red it was, the three of hearts.

For a moment, she drummed her fingers meditatively. Then she arose. The prospect of so great a gamble brought the color to her cheeks. "Ladies and Gentlemen," she said, "place your bets!" Grasping a flashlight, she hurried through the dark corridor to the foot of the stairs. "Miss Deveny," she called. "Miss Deveny!"

There was no answer. She despised stairs, but too impatient to wait for morning, she climbed up to the girl's room. Elizabeth was asleep. The Baroness, breathing hard from her exertion, encircled her with the wavering light until she sat up in confusion.

"What is it?"

"I've changed my mind," the Baroness said. "I want you to stay."

Not having been informed of her dismissal, Elizabeth stared at her in bewilderment. "I don't understand—"

"But how can I say it more clearly? I've decided to go on with my memoirs after all," the Baroness said, excitedly. "And I'm in the mood to work now. Don't bother dressing, just throw on a robe—"

She did not wait for the girl, but left at once, her footsteps echoing up the stairwell, bespeaking her difficult descent.

Extracts from Elizabeth's notebook:

"Although Madame von Schillar still clings to such courtly phrases as 'Pray be seated' and 'I fancy—,' she occasionally makes great show of bad grammar: he don't, they was, etc. I suspect she flaunts these mistakes as a minor challenge to convention—to prove she can get away with what would condemn as uneducated any lesser person. In the same way, a debutante may chew gum, but an ambitious shopgirl daren't. And only the rich can afford to wear rags."

"She told me of the continual conflict with her father. At the age of seven, for instance, she developed an unreasoning appetite for the lace collars on her dresses. In moments of contemplation she chewed them, and in times of stress. At first, his reproof was gentle, parental. She chewed on. Next his method was mockery; announced he would send her all his old shirts to chew on. She acknowledged this with a fresh attack on her collar. His consequent wrath had no more effect. 'My unhappy collars became a badge of honor,' she told me, 'but I reckoned without his genius for punishment. When all my dresses became unwearable because of their raggedy collars, he announced I would henceforth wear boys' coveralls to school.'

" 'And the following morning, that's how I was dressed. As I left my room and stood at the top of the stairs, I knew only a miracle could save me. And if the hand of God was not willing, I would help Him along. The stairs were steep and I was afraid of them. But even more afraid of humiliation. Quite coldly, I put my hands over my face and fell forward.'

"She did not go to school that day, nor that week. When finally she did, it was in a new dress her penitent father had given her. It had a lace collar. 'I knew I was free to chew it if I chose,' she told me, 'but it was no longer necessary. I had won this battle.' "

"She hates Boston; longs to return to Europe, but cannot, due to what I suspect is a ruinous gambling debt."

"In 1907, when Senator Carver was courting her, he invited her to grand opera, procuring as was customary, three seats, one for the chaperon. When he arrived to fetch them, however, she appeared with an enormous doll, introducing it as her best friend, Dorothy, who simply loved opera and would keep a careful eye on them. The Senator, aghast, flatly refused to be party to this whim. Whereupon, she haughtily announced that if her friends weren't good enough for him, he might as well go and never come back.

"Senator Carver finally persuaded her to leave the big doll at home, but she would not consent to take her maid along to chaperon her. 'She always hums during opera,' she told him. 'And besides, if your intentions are so wicked that I need a chaperon, then you're not fit company for a pure-minded woman like Worth.'

"The third seat at the opera remained unoccupied that night. 'And I've always felt sure that's why Theo proposed so soon after,' the Baroness told me. 'He felt that by escorting me in public without a chaperon, he had compromised me.'"

"Her only child, born in her second year of marriage to Carver, lived only a week. The Baroness went into mourning for an entire year."

"This is a woman who can organize a charity bazaar with ease, but creates chaos trying to run her own home; who has disdain for the masses, yet allows them to be her judge and jury; who prizes her Yankee common sense, yet rummaged through all Monte Carlo for a certain hunchback to touch for luck before entering the casino; who talks in terms of guests and gaiety, yet receives no one at her home; who longs for convention, yet constantly catapults into scandal."

There was page after page of such notes. Once more, Elizabeth leafed through them, and at last, with a sigh of discouragement, added this notation in her book:

"A fool came upon a pool of water whose surface, reflecting the sunlight, was gilded over. 'I have found a lake of molten gold,' he thought, joyously, for he was poor. Yet when he dipped forth some to sell, his cup held only water. Being a fool, he persisted, day after day, skimming his cup over the surface, wasting his energy, and profiting himself nothing.

"I am that fool. For two weeks now, I have talked daily to the Baroness, taking pages of notes, trying to understand this woman's motivations, and so interpret her actions. But I can find neither motivation nor meaning. There is no gold here. Nothing but a glittering surface of whim and caprice. . . ."

And yet surely, Elizabeth thought, lifting her pen, there must be warmth, depth, and sensitivity in this woman to have attracted a man like Wrenn. "But how am I to learn about it?" she demanded, aloud. One could not simply go up to the Baroness and say, "Confess what you really are! Open your soul to me!" It was not as in a dissection where the heart and brain could be lifted from the resistless body, the symptoms analyzed, and the causes laid bare.

"And yet, that's little excuse," she abruptly wrote in the notebook. "The creative mind is less dependent on fact than on intuition. The humblest object may inspire complete understanding. From the suspension of dust in a shaft of sunlight, a poet can reconstruct the universe. From a falling apple, a scientist can deduce the law of gravity. The jab of a needle can acquaint a writer with the fiercer pain of a dagger. A mustard seed can intimate to the prophet the kingdom of heaven. Only a hint is needed and creative imagination does the rest. I have many pages of hints, but the creative imagination has been asleep. The fault then is not with Madame von Schillar. It is with me."

She stared at these words for a long time, then shook her head. Turning the page, she wrote, "Dear Harry—I've tried, but it's useless. I can't get back to work again, can't seem to concentrate—"

"Why?" he would probably demand. "What's the matter?"

And would she dare to answer? "You're the matter! How can I

write, or do anything, when all I can think of is you? If I could just settle my mind, just know, one way or the other, if you could ever care for me—" Could she write that to him?

Her mouth tightened. Ripping the page from the notebook, she crumpled it, flung it into the fireplace. Once more, she tried to study her notes, but the room seemed stifling. Rising abruptly, she grabbed her coat and hurried downstairs, out into the dark street.

She walked without destination. A brisk wind sent the dry leaves scuttling alongside her, pacing her rapid steps. It was not until she had crossed the dark expanse of the Common that she began to shiver from cold. A sign, swaying in the wind, caught her attention. Tarnished gold letters proclaimed the George Washington Tavern. The place was shabby and not too well lit, but the name gave Elizabeth a sense of security. Entering, she sat down in a dark booth by the window. She was out of reach of the wind now, but, hearing its drone, still shivered.

A drink of brandy warmed her, seared a channel through her consciousness. "Maybe if I drank enough of these," she mused, "I'd have the courage to write that letter—"

Undermined by desperation and weariness, she was easier prey to the suggestion this time; for even if he answered, I do not love you, at least she could rest in the knowledge and be free to think of other things.

Abruptly, she signaled the waiter and, in ordering another drink, asked for a sheet of paper.

"Not that I'll ever send this to him," she assured herself.

As she looked at the blank sheet, it was no better than standing before Mellett himself; the words she longed to say hid behind a hundred excuses. To break this spell, she wrote, "My dear Harry—" But what then? She tapped her pen against the table in a regular beat. Rhythm sometimes helped release her feelings in words.

She stared unseeingly into space, at last realizing her eyes were resting on someone: a man at the bar who was staring back at her.

Quickly, she glanced down at her letter. Yet she looked up again to see if she were still being watched. Alert to her action, the man yawned and stretched, a slow, animal movement for her benefit.

"I wonder if he thinks he's being attractive," Elizabeth thought. For all her scorn, she inched back into the shadows of the booth where she could watch unobserved. He was probably, she decided, a stevedore or truck driver. Beneath his scarred leather jacket, his khaki shirt opened around a powerful neck, and his trousers of coarse blue denim adhered tightly to his flanks and the cleft of his buttocks. He squinted slightly as if trying, by force, to penetrate the shadows about her. His nose was broad and his lips the color of meat. It was an animal face, not handsome and not needing to be.

She tightened her lips contemptuously and returned to composing her letter.

A shadow fell across the page. She looked up. The man stood beside her table. She lifted her eyes no higher than his hands, numbly noting the blue ring tattooed on one of his thick fingers. He sat down across the table from her, but did not speak. In panic, she glanced sidewise for the waiter. He was not in sight. Haltingly, she met the man's eyes. He studied her face, but still without speaking. For an endless moment, they looked at each other. At last, he glanced away with contemptuous ease and, rising, left her.

In surprise and relief, she stared after him. The fool had obviously mistaken her scrutiny as an invitation. "Fool, fool!" she mocked. Yet beneath her contempt, the familiar self-doubt was stirring. Remembering his near-sighted squint, she narrowed her eyes and looked at her reflection in the windowpane. That was how he had seen her face—pale, too civilized, over-refined; her eyes and the hollow of her cheeks deeply accented with shadow, like a death mask. Nothing there to provoke passion. No wonder he had rejected her.

She laughed to herself a little sharply and glanced down at her letter. For a moment, her pen poised above the paper and idly, she scanned the salutation, "My dear Harry—" Then she lowered her pen, capped it, put it away.

"I'll write him tomorrow," she decided.

But she knew she would not. There was no need to write the letter any more. She knew now, knew in her heart. Mellett would never care for her. His would not be the crude dismissal of the man here, but for all its grace, charm and friendliness, it would be substantially the same. She was not the type men wanted.

Mechanically, Elizabeth put some money on the scarred table and left the tavern. She hastened down the dark street, absently tearing the sheet of paper. Caught up by the wind, the white shreds danced after her.

The Baroness paused for breath, then began afresh.

"I was thrown out of finishing school, y'know," she said, almost defiantly. "Not because I was a bad student. Actually, I spoke better French than Madame Fabre, who had a horrid Belgian accent. And I was naturally gifted in mathematics and debating. But the poor and the plain think intelligence is their special compensation, and it infuriated my teachers that I should have brains as well as beauty and wealth." She selected an aspirin from a little snuffbox and reached for her glass of water.

In the interval of silence, Elizabeth could hear the whisper of wind outside, and she stirred the fire. The flames licked at the log experimentally, rather, she thought, like a child trying its tongue over dubious candy. Then the Baroness laughed, and Elizabeth looked up defensively.

"I was thinking—oh, it was funny!" Madame von Schillar explained. "Every spring, the Misses Matson, who ran the school, let us have a ball and, my dear, it couldn't have been more funereal. Everyone said the punch was spiked with embalming fluid. And the place but crawling with chaperons, absolutely saber-toothed. They made us waltz so far away from our partners, it looked as if we were playing London Bridge. Decency, y'know. Oh, dear yes, decency! We girls done up to the chin in pastel organdy. Nudity was not encouraged at the Misses Matson's. And, *hélas!* I had a new black gown from Paris which uncovered my shoulders and arms. Well, being a thrifty New Englander, I couldn't see wasting all that, so I told Kitty Leighton—she was my roommate—I was going to wear the black, anyway. Kitty said I wouldn't dare. So did everyone.

"Well, that night, I entered the ballroom, all prim in pink silk. Oh, such a pretty little dress, and oh, such a pity, I had to go spill punch all over it. Such woe! The Misses Matson immediately ordered me to go upstairs and change. I protested that my other ball gown was not as nice, but they snapped that I must learn to obey.

"So I did. As instructed, I slipped on the other gown, the black one, and just for good measure put a heart-shaped beauty mark on one bare shoulder. Well, my dear, if I climbed to a new high with the boys that night, my popularity with the Matson sisters thudded to a record low. Although I explained my only crime was obedience, they took a dim view of the whole matter. So did Father, and the following week I was carted off to Europe."

A draft shuddered faintly through the room and she drew the old spaniel closer to her. "I don't fancy he'll want me to detail the voyage."

"Who?"

"Mellett."

Elizabeth heard his name without any plummeting of the heart. Having reconciled herself to Mellett's indifference, mention of his name no more shattered her concentration than the sound of the log falling apart in the hearth. If she had known little joy of late, at least she was now free from torment. Her love, like the log in the hearth, had gone through fire and been reduced to ashes; but its energy, remaining undestroyed, had escaped into a new form: work.

"Not much to tell about the trip, anyway," Madame von Schillar was saying. "Father considered traveling part of my education, so it wasn't allowed to be fun. There was nothing for me to do. At least Father could attend to business matters over there—he manufactured glass, y'know. 'The Glass King.' And it would have been so easy for him to let me help him—be his secretary and sit in on conferences—"

"You?" Elizabeth said, with an incredulous smile.

"Why not? I knew all about glass. As much as Father did; and much more than him about management. Once I drew up a plan for distribution that would have saved him thousands, but he just laughed. Business wasn't for anything so soft as a girl; he never tired of telling me that. And besides, nice women didn't think. Not in Boston!"

She leaned back in her chair studying her rings. "Maybe I had delusions of grandeur," she added, ruefully. "I just took it for granted, from childhood on, that someday I'd be a titan like Father. He helped to shape worlds, and that's what I always expected to do." She shrugged. "Maybe that's why I married the Senator . . ."

As she listened, Elizabeth's eyes fixed on a glass dome which sheltered an arrangement of jewellike flowers on the mantel. Noting her scrutiny, the Baroness explained, "That's from my father's collection. They're glass."

"They look almost real," Elizabeth mused.

"Oh, I hope not," said the Baroness. "Their whole virtue is in being artificial. Real plants would die under there, y'know." Suddenly, the girl turned and looked at her piercingly. "What's the matter?"

"I was just thinking," Elizabeth said, slowly, "of a plant powerful enough to finally shatter the glass bell and burst free—"

"What an idea!" the Baroness laughed. She chattered on, but Elizabeth continued to gaze at her as if, for the first time, she were seeing the Baroness.

It was no wonder, she thought, that this woman had been considered a *fleur de mal.* Under the glass bell of convention, young ladies were expected to be mere ornaments, their artificiality a virtue; but the Winslow heiress, fed by deep-rooted executive drive, and with no outlet provided her vitality, had been impelled to break through the invisible restriction. There had been no authority she had not challenged, no convention she had not defied, until, at last, she burst free. For a moment, Elizabeth glimpsed the woman as Wrenn must have seen her—forceful, impetuous, rebellious. It was inevitable that he, who had burst from a similar prison, the orthodoxy of art, should recognize and adore her.

She stood up abruptly. "Will you excuse me?"

"Where are you going?" the Baroness demanded.

"To work," Elizabeth said, vibrantly.

Through the night and into the next day, she kept to her room, studying the notes and trying to visualize events through Madame von Schillar's eyes. All the data she had dismissed as superficial caprice now had meaning, viewed through the lens of her new understanding. And, at last, chameleonlike, she began to assume the rich hue of the material she touched, so that when she set down the first chapter, it might have been the quintessence of her own girlhood rather than Madame von Schillar's.

CHAPTER 2

Haltingly, Elizabeth opened the door to the attic and, after listening apprehensively for mice, ventured in. The darkness was but faintly relieved by a stuttering gradation of light which filtered through the shuttered window. The air, long imprisoned here, was stale, hot, searing her lungs. Gasping, she wrenched open the window. At the sudden influx of light and air, the shadows cringed back as before sacrilege, and there was the silent sifting of dust in retreat across the floor.

"The Winslows were true Yankees," Madame von Schillar had warned. "Never threw away anything."

It was on this statement that Elizabeth counted. Intently, she opened trunk after trunk, rummaged through each chest and valise, until she came upon the heavy hamper spilling with dusty papers. It could only be termed a documental cemetery—correspondence, legal records, ancient invitations, yellowing newspaper clippings, even laundry lists, indiscriminately heaped together; but she bent to her task eagerly, hoping to find some letters from Senator Carver for her chapter on his courtship.

Even with the windows open, there was scarcely enough light in the attic, and soon her eyes were aching. Nor did the hamper yield much in compensation. She found several letters from Carver, but they little revealed the man. Sincere he undoubtedly was, but it seldom escaped the stricture of formality. More provocative was a note without salutation and signed only "Q" which, in its entirety, read: "Have you completely lost your mind?" She found also some tumultuous letters from the Baron, each, without exception, headed "Liebchen," but saved from monotony by the extreme variety of his spelling.

And then, as she opened another letter, the yawn she had been suppressing was cut off. Unbelievingly, she tipped the letter toward the light. There could be no doubt. It was signed by Wrenn. She held her breath as if in fear it would disintegrate the brittle paper before she knew its contents. Then, as she read, her body stiffened. The lines were addressed to herself.

> Elizabeth, Elizabeth,
>
> I can not say how many times a day I repeat your name, summoning you, commanding you, conjuring you. Elizabeth, Elizabeth. It is my prayer and my penalty, exalting me one moment, punishing me the next. Sometimes, when I say your name enough, I can bring your face to my mind. I suppose this should be enough for me, but it isn't. I want to see you, talk to you. I know this would be unwise just now; but if we dare not speak openly yet, at least let me see the form of your words. A letter, Elizabeth. Even one word to refresh my hope that your thoughts are secretly saying
>
> Marius Marius Marius.

Turbulently, Elizabeth read it a second time, and only then remembered that the Baroness shared the same name as herself.

Abruptly, she pursed her lips contemptuously at the unabashed romanticism of Wrenn's letter; but this did not quite counteract the loneliness which had come back upon her. Words of love were no new thing to her. They were a poet's stock in trade. But it was the first time she had ever held in her hand a love letter with her name upon it.

"No," she corrected, sadly. "Not my name. Hers!"

Slowly, she arose and stared out the garret window, blind to the little park below, blind to its barren trees. For a moment, she was shaken by a desire to crumple this letter, destroy it, and so punish the Baroness for having so much love, and herself none. And yet, she realized, Madame von Schillar was no better off than herself. Love long past and love that never had been were of the same stuff, leaving both women equally alone now.

Deliberately, carefully, she laid aside the letter and, kneeling again, continued to sift the papers, seeking more of Wrenn's letters to Elizabeth. They would be such brilliant additions to the book, she assured herself; yet when she found nothing more from him in the hamper, her disappointment was not entirely that of a scholar.

Frowning, she again studied the letter. An attempt to visualize Wrenn made her acutely conscious that, as yet, she knew nothing about him. Not once had Madame von Schillar shared a detail of him in her discussion.

"What was Mr Wrenn like?" she asked the Baroness, at luncheon.

Madame von Schillar fixed her with reproachful eyes and, at last, said, "He was tall."

"But I mean, what kind of man was he?"

"Have you finished the chapter on the dear Senator already?"

"Not yet."

"Well, when you have," the Baroness said, quietly, "we can start discussing Marius."

Chastened by the gentleness of this admonition, Elizabeth withdrew into silence; but more and more, she found this difficult to maintain. As she now knew every word of the letter by heart, she was impatient to read the rest of his letters. Yet she hesitated to ask openly if she might be allowed to see his correspondence. The Baroness, with her lingering possessiveness for Wrenn, would only refuse. The invitation would have to come from Madame von Schillar, herself. Somehow, that idea would have to be instilled in her mind.

At dinner, that night, masking her motive with an attitude of indifference, Elizabeth led up to the matter with trivial questions. Who, for instance, was "Q"?

The Baroness lifted her brows and looked at her blankly. Then she shrugged; no one she knew. Elizabeth teased with an extravagantly arch manner: was Madame von Schillar in the habit of receiving such terse notes from perfect strangers? The Baroness frowned thoughtfully and murmured the initial over and over, as if fitting it into the various locks of memory. Did this "Q," she finally demanded, sound like an admirer or a relative?

"All the note said was, 'Have you completely lost your mind?' "

"That," said the Baroness, "could be either an admirer or a relative! But I don't recall ever knowing any Q." Then, briskly, "Why do you ask?"

"It's helpful to know all these details." Elizabeth was very glib. "Never can tell what we'll be able to use in the book."

"And did you find anything usable amongst my papers?"

"Some letters from Senator Carver—"

"That must have amused you."

"No," said Elizabeth, "but it gave me a fair idea of the man. Letters can clear up so much, you see. Sometimes I think if I could get hold of more letters, I wouldn't have to bother you with so many questions . . ." As Madame von Schillar did not reply with the offer Elizabeth had been angling for, she was forced to add, "So I'm hoping you'll let me read the rest of your letters."

"Those are all I have. In the box in the attic."

"Oh." Elizabeth moistened her lips. "I thought maybe you might keep your more precious letters separately."

"Precious letters from whom?" the Baroness demanded.

"Oh—the Baron. Or Mr Wrenn."

"The Baron never wrote precious letters," Madame von Schillar said, dryly. "And as for Wrenn, I don't believe he ever wrote to me. Or if he did, I burned his letters."

"Burned!"

"Of course."

"But why?"

"Why do you think? The dear Senator was collecting evidence to divorce me. Thought he'd ruin me, y'know," she added, bitterly. "But as it turned out, he only ruined himself. What with the scandal he let loose, he never got re-elected."

"But you couldn't have burned all Mr Wrenn's letters," Elizabeth insisted, vehemently. "I'm sure you have some left."

"Why are you so sure?" The Baroness eyed her shrewdly. "Did you happen to find one?"

Elizabeth's hesitation was almost imperceptible. "No," she said.

Ordinarily, Elizabeth was governed by a desire for perfection in her work, but since discovering Wrenn's letter, her curiosity drove her forward with untidy haste to finish the chapters on Senator Carver. Yet if the resultant work was not first-rate, it did catch something of the impatience the Baroness once must have felt to be done with the uninspiring statesman and begin with the artist.

To Elizabeth's exasperation, however, Madame von Schillar would not be rushed. For the first time in her life, the Baroness admitted, she was actually enjoying spending time with the Senator. The autobiography served her as an arena where, at last, he was at her mercy.

"Read aloud the part where I describe his *faux pas* at the British Embassy," she would say; or "Don't forget to put in how he was afraid of the dark." And once, she directed, "Let's suggest I could never keep a maid for long in Washington. Not that his familiarity took form in pinches. Lectures, my dear! He lectured them on the tariff by the hour, and when they couldn't stand any more, they quit! Which gave them considerable advantage over the members of the Senate—"

"Do you really think we should?" Elizabeth ventured, gently. "I mean, the man's dead now. It just isn't necessary to jeer at him—"

"You think I'm being petty?"

"I think it isn't worthy of you."

Abruptly, Madame von Schillar jerked her head away so Elizabeth could not see her face; but her voice, authentic in its emotion, betrayed her. "I don't care! I don't care! At least I've waited till he was dead. He said worse things about me while I was alive. Was that necessary? Was it necessary to do what he did to me? Was that the good taste he was always sermonizing about? Oh, Christ, Christ!"

She shook an aspirin from her snuffbox. "To see your whole life and all you love spattered with filth and ripped up and down in front of everyone . . ." She made a desperate effort to control herself. "Maybe I am being petty, but—" Flinging away the aspirin, she burst out again, "If there's a library in hell, I hope he reads my book and learns just how much I hated him. And laughed at him. I want everyone to know that, so they'll understand that when I finally met a man who was really fine and good, I had to fall in love with him, whatever the cost. . . ."

It was the moment Elizabeth had been waiting for. "Where, actually, did you meet Mr Wrenn?"

"At a friend's house." Her voice became expressionless again. "I'll tell you about our meeting when the time comes."

"But—"

"When the time comes," the Baroness repeated, sharply. Then, patting Elizabeth's hand: "But, to please you, we won't jeer at the dear Senator. Only not you or anyone will ever make me forgive him."

In her craving for information about Wrenn, Elizabeth turned hopefully to Mrs Worth. If the woman knew anything about the artist, however, she kept it to herself; or if asked a direct question, neatly effaced herself as a servant, not in a position to know. Yet, once, she unwittingly contributed something. It was by no means the key to the story, but it was to help Elizabeth pick the lock.

Tidying the room, this day, Worth indicated Elizabeth's few books with her dustrag. "You don't read much for an author."

"I don't have much time when I'm working," Elizabeth said.

"That's the way with you artistical people I guess," Worth stated, running her cloth over a chair. "Like with him. Books stacked up on the floor and under his cot. Awful dust-catchers. I'd say, 'Mr Wrenn, let me put them downstairs in the liberry.' But he'd never let me, just in case he got the time to read. Only, like yourself, he never left himself time for much but work."

Elizabeth recalled one of Wrenn's early paintings, "The Long Room, Morning," in which he had depicted a stack of books on the floor. "I wonder what sort of things he read?" she mused.

"Couldn't say, Miss. Never had the notion to look." She cast another glance at Elizabeth's volumes as she left. "Myself, I'm partial to the New Testament."

The conversation lingered with Elizabeth. A person's taste in books being a competent guide to character, she felt that, until the Baroness provided richer details, it would be possible to obtain a concept of Wrenn through the books which had influenced his thought.

To obtain this basic information, however, required the familiar challenge—maneuvering Madame von Schillar into a position where speaking of the artist seemed like her own idea.

"You know, it's funny," the girl began, perhaps too casually, that afternoon, "you've never asked to see the work I've been doing."

The Baroness stroked her spaniel indolently. "Mr Mellett recommended your work. I trust his judgment. Anyway, reading hurts my eyes."

"Would you like me to read aloud to you, sometime?" she asked.

"I don't necessarily mean the manuscript. I could read you some novels, for instance—"

"Don't have any." She indicated the bookshelves which housed nothing but glass knickknacks and ivory toys.

"But you have an enormous library across the hall," Elizabeth persisted. "Surely we can find something good there."

The Baroness lifted her scented hands in horror. "Nothing but lawbooks, my dear. And God save me from them. The Senator used to be a lawyer, and that's all he ever talked about."

"But your other husbands read, didn't they?" Elizabeth continued. "And surely they must have left some interesting books."

Madame von Schillar uttered a high-pitched sound, a fragment of laughter. "Flix—that's the Baron—I don't think he ever cracked a book in his life. And Marius never kept his for long. He was always loaning books. They were mostly from the public library anyway, but he'd loan them just the same. Or mutilate them!"

"Mutilate!"

The Baroness repeated her little laugh. "Funny, isn't it? If you so much as touched a finger to an oil painting, he'd lose his mind. But he scribbled notes all over book margins or tore out leaves so he could carry around in his pocket something he wanted to study."

While Elizabeth was weighing the advisability of asking a direct question now, the Baroness changed the subject, making it impossible for the girl to continue without utterly betraying her motive.

Acting on the one wisp of evidence she had salvaged from the conversation, Elizabeth went directly to the north study. The walls were lined with volumes long untouched except by a dustrag. Methodically, she selected a book, quickly leafed through it, replaced it and repeated the process with its neighbor. Although she could not imagine Wrenn's being tempted by such gems as *The Merry Art of Lawn Tennis* or *Orations of Judge Wilkins Tyler,* there was always the chance that she would find a page he had annotated, or even a letter lodged as a bookmark.

By midnight, however, she had found nothing more enlightening than a copy of Dante, whose flyleaf proclaimed it the property of Kitty Leighton. The name was curiously familiar to Elizabeth, although she could not identify it. In her disappointment at finding no clue of Wrenn, however, she soon forgot the inscription. Not till some days later was the name again brought to her attention.

"It used to make me scream," the Baroness said, so lazily one could imagine her screaming at nothing, "people forever criticizing me, and then they'd do just as bad or worse and get away with it. Like Kitty. Always telling me I was going too far, and then she upped and married *un juif*—"

"Kitty?"

"Kitty Leighton. She's Kitty Wallach, now. My roommate in school. Back in town again, I've heard, though I haven't seen her in absolute years. Why do you smile?"

"I came across one of her books the other night," Elizabeth said. "A copy of Dante."

"Dante, Dante—" Madame von Schillar murmured.

"The Italian poet," Elizabeth prompted. "The *Inferno*."

"I know, silly," she laughed. "I read the bloody thing!"

"You did!" Knowing Madame von Schillar's reluctance to read anything, Elizabeth could not keep the amazement from her voice.

"Yes, I did. Not from choice. Anyway, I don't think it was from choice. But it was one of—" She broke off abruptly. Her jaw tightened and she flung Elizabeth a fierce glance. "Again?" she said, coldly.

"I beg your pardon?"

"You know what I mean!"

"No, I don't, Madame, I—"

"Oh, you're clever, all right. Clever!" Indignantly, she drummed her nails against the tabletop. "It's this prying, prying, prying," she lashed, suddenly. "This endless trickery. Don't think I haven't noticed it before. Always trying to jockey me into blurting out something." She slapped her hand against the table. "Leave me alone!"

White-lipped, Elizabeth marched upstairs. Her face remained expressionless as she packed her bag; it was only when she drew Wrenn's letter from concealment that she faltered at all. Moodily, she read it and, several times, feinted at putting it in her valise. Abruptly, she sighed and began to unpack. Whatever the humiliation, she knew she could not yet leave this house.

Within an hour, she was summoned back to Madame von Schillar's suite. Pridefully, Elizabeth waited for the woman to turn away from her dressing table; but she did not, even when she began to speak. Her voice was gentler than Elizabeth had expected, and her words more startling.

"Have you ever said 'I love you' to a man?"

"No, Madame."

"Neither have I." She turned now to the astonished girl. "That does not mean that I have never loved a man, for I have. But even so, I could never tell him 'I love you.' It was as if, by putting it into words, I'd have let something out of me. Something I didn't dare lose. Like as if . . ." She stumbled into momentary silence, then held up the cut-glass bottle of Loki, her favorite scent. "Like when you leave the stopper out of a perfume bottle. The essence evaporates and what's left is worthless. Well . . ." She faltered again. "D'you know what I'm trying to say? I'm not quite ready to let free some things from my life yet, and Marius is one of them. Once I tell it, some of the fragrance will be gone for me. And I want to keep that—just a little while longer." She arose now and patted the girl's hand. "When it's time to do the chapter on Marius, I'll give you all the information you'll need. But until then, he must still belong to me, alone. Can you understand that?"

"Yes, Madame, but I want you to understand something—"

"I do, I do. Marius can be a fascinating topic. And don't I know!" She laughed softly. "Oh, I was as outrageous as you are, my dear. After my first meeting with him, I was insatiable to know everything about him. Just like you, I'd sneak his name into conversations, and ask little hidden questions, and jockey people into making statements. It wasn't very satisfactory, but it was all I had. Eventually, I learned to be patient. There!" Her smile eased the tension from her face and she looked almost young. "I've gone and told you quite a bit about us, right there. For the time, that ought to content you, eh?"

"But I must make this clear to you," Elizabeth persisted. "I wasn't trying to trick you into anything. I confess I have tried before; but not just now."

"Now, now," laughed the Baroness. "I've forgiven you."

"But I want you to believe me," Elizabeth cried. "If I said anything provocative, I just stumbled onto it. I had no idea when I started talking about Kitty Leighton and the *Inferno* that it also involved Mr Wrenn."

"Oh!" The Baroness looked at her blankly. "Well, if that's true, I've made a rather foolish evening of it, eh?" She examined her fingernails, then added, "Well, I'll have to tell you all about it, one of these days. But I'm tired now. . . ."

Elizabeth, also exhausted by the scene, went to bed early that night; but Kitty Wallach's name, echoing in her mind, kept her from sleep. At last, she crept downstairs and traced it in the telephone directory. If she had hoped the sight of the name would pacify her, the opposite effect was achieved. The knowledge that in this same city, a telephone call away, was someone who might tell her of Wrenn, banished all hope of rest.

Twice more, that night, she arose from bed, determined to call Mrs Wallach; and twice more, she hesitated. She had been touched by Madame von Schillar's plea for an abandonment of trickery; and there was the promise that within a few weeks, she would give Elizabeth the entire portrait of Wrenn. "So I can wait," Elizabeth decided. "I can wait a little longer."

The following evening, however, she was waiting in the hall of an apartment house. The door, at which she had rapped, was opened by a white-haired woman.

"I'd like to see Kitty Wallach."

"Yes. I'm Mrs Wallach."

Elizabeth stared at her in surprise. She had anticipated someone restless and vivid like the Baroness, and Mrs Wallach was gentle, rather motherly, her years unfortified by artifice. Unable to summon some pat phrase to bridge the silence, Elizabeth thrust a package into the woman's hand.

"What's this?"

"A book of yours."

Mrs Wallach undid the paper and opened the copy of the *Inferno* to its flyleaf. "So it is," she mused. "My, didn't I have spectacular handwriting in those days!" She held the door open. "Where did you find this? Come on in . . ."

"I can't," Elizabeth blurted. "I just came to bring back the book . . ." But she entered the apartment.

When she left, an hour later, she carried the address of a Mrs Edith Harper.

So began a chain of interviews and letters which, meticulously indexed, Elizabeth carefully hoarded. Night after night, she pieced these fragments together, as one might a jigsaw puzzle, always hoping the next day would yield up the detail needed to complete the picture of Wrenn, and the romance which Madame von Schillar so passionately protected.

CHAPTER 3

Extracts from Elizabeth's index (in alphabetical order):

A. *Ayers, Dorothy Jefferson*

She told much the same story as her brother (See Arthur Jefferson), but added:

"Even now, I dislike discussing this part of his story, though I was too young to ever know Cousin Marius well. But, apparently, rumors began reaching the family about his conduct. Very unsavory rumors. You've probably heard them. Those dreadful Spanish girls. And that Thauly woman. And how he was evicted from his studio, and why. Finally, my mother went to see him and reproached him for his behavior. He said, 'Well, don't be afraid. We were in love, all right, but we've decided not to see each other any more.' My mother asked who he was talking about, and he said, 'Why, didn't you come here to scold me about Elizabeth Carver?' And that was the first mother knew of it. Well, she made him promise never to see Mrs

Carver again, but it did no good, because they ran away together a month later.

"I was too young then to understand what had happened, but I can still remember poor Mother and Grandma sitting alone in the parlor, day after day, with the blinds drawn. They wouldn't receive anyone or even let a newspaper inside the house. It was especially humiliating since my family was well acquainted with the Carvers. Miss Sarah Carver never spoke to Mother again, incidentally. She told mutual friends that she held Marius' family as responsible as she did him.

"I don't think the Senator was as unforgiving. Miss Sarah told this friend that when the Senator read of Marius' drowning, he left the breakfast table abruptly and went to his room. Sarah followed him and found him still staring at the newspaper, his eyes full of tears. Miss Sarah couldn't understand this, since Marius had ruined the man's marriage and, indirectly, his political career. But Senator Carver seemed to hold himself responsible for Marius' death. He felt the drastic divorce action had so shamed Marius, it had driven him to suicide. But this possibility has always seemed as doubtful to me as Sarah's statement that Marius' death was but God's just punishment."

C. *Carver, Miss Sarah*

I went several times to her Beacon Street home, but her housekeeper always said she was out. Finally, I said I'd wait, and the woman looked most uncomfortable and said, "She's always out, Miss. She hasn't received anyone for over twenty years."

D. *Dickens, Madge Laird*

"I often tell folks that Marius and I grew up together, but actually I didn't see him much. We lived next door, but our families weren't intimate. We're Unitarian, you see, and of course, they were Episcopalian. Besides, he was rather violent, you know. He and his family were in constant conflict. I actually heard him shouting at his grandmother the night before he ran away from home. This was when he was sixteen. He'd done a drawing of naked women, and old Mrs Jefferson struck him. Or so I've heard. I've often wondered if it wasn't to get back at her that made him always draw such degenerate types when he grew up.

"Of course, his work is accepted now, but Mother always said the only reason Marius painted the kind of people he did was because he couldn't draw very well, and on lower-class types it didn't show up. That's not true, of course, because I saw some of Marius' early sketches, all very tasteful and classic—statues, Greek gods and temples—his grandfather taught Latin, you know—and the drawing was just lovely. But when he turned against the Jeffersons, he turned against this kind of art too. Years later, I reproached him for changing so terribly in his work. He just laughed and denied that he'd changed so much. 'Maybe I don't draw deities any more,' he said. 'What I look for now is Deity in the faces I paint.' I don't think he meant to be profane, but that's what he said."

E. *Encyclopedia Britannica*

"Wrenn, Marius (1882–1915) American painter, was born in Boston (Mass) on March 3, 1882. He ran away from home at an early age, apparently to work on the barges and in canneries along the New England coast, although his movements were always obscure. These experiences furnished him the scenes and types of his most generally popular pictures, 'Portugee Girls', 'Wharf at Midnight', 'The Captain', and 'The Bathers'. He was little affected by European influences, his work being distinctly American. He was married in 1914 to Mrs Elizabeth Winslow Carver. He did not live to see his work recognized, meeting an untimely death in a boating accident on July 1, 1915."

The other encyclopedias state the same brief information.

Ezterhausy, Jay

Painter, critic, and close friend of Wrenn's. He was killed in the bombing of Coventry.

G. *Gow, Carlyle*

Mr Gow, now living in New Orleans, writes:

"I don't know anything about Wrenn's relationship with Josie Azores, and I never met Mrs Carver. Probably Jay Ezterhausy could give you the low-down about them, as he was Marius' roommate and best friend. As for the Thauly girl, I never believed there was anything between her and Marius. It would have been a casual affair and I don't think Marius was capable of the casual. Everything he did, he did the hard way, threw himself at it, body and soul. When he was painting, he poured all his time and loneliness and passion into it; and we all said if he ever fell in love, he'd fall hard and with that same single-eyed intensity. Only, when it happened, none of us even suspected. He was a secretive sort.

"One night, he dropped into my studio. Scarcely spoke, just chewed his pipe stem and sat cross-legged by the fire, watching me engrave. I sensed something was on his mind, but he couldn't seem to get it out and I knew better than to try and question him. Around nine, he got up suddenly. At the door, he said, 'I won't forget tonight.' I thought that strange, as it had been such a quiet evening. A few days later, when I heard he'd run off with Mrs Carver, however, I understood. He had known that this night marked the end of his student days. He knew he was entering a new phase of life—and I think he already knew his happiness would have a big price.

"I never met this Mrs Carver, but of this I am sure—Marius saw beneath her madcap reputation and found the real person. He had that power in his relationships, as in his work. To paraphrase Augustus Johns, 'He made no attempt to squeeze his subjects into the mold of beauty. He took people as he found them, and he found in them his own goodness.'"

H. *Harper, Miss Edith*

"I only met this Wrenn a few times, I'm grateful to say. My family knew his—not the Wrenns, they were nobody—but the Jeffersons, who had excellent connections. Well, old Mrs Jefferson was most distressed because all her grandson ever painted was the dregs of humanity, and she asked my mother to have me introduce Marius to some proper people, so he'd want to paint their portraits instead. Well, Mother and I made one attempt. We took him to Kitty Leighton's. That was enough. Why, we'd have been laughingstocks if we'd tried to foist him off on decent society.

"Why? Why, indeed! He was a tramp. Oh, handsome, but in an uncouth fashion. His hands were coarse, and he kept looking into people's eyes. And his shoes had specks of paint on them. He stammered, too. That is, when he talked at all. Didn't talk to me much, anyway. But, of course, I didn't have red hair and a fast reputation. But Elizabeth Carver got what she deserved. Nobody in this neck of the woods will have anything to do with her, even to this day."

When I asked her for particulars of the meeting between Wrenn and the Baroness, she repeated substantially the same story as Mrs Wallach, but added:

"Mr Wrenn was a boor, but even so, I felt responsible because it was through me that he had met Elizabeth. So I went by Mr Wrenn's studio some days later, to warn him just what kind of a woman she was. Well, I wish I hadn't bothered. Not only was he just as rude as before, but there was some female, name of Thaw [Thauly], trying to get her clothes on in back of a screen all the time we were talking. I washed my hands of everything, then and there. He and Elizabeth were made for each other. Both of them had a taste for the outlandish. Disaster was the natural outcome of such a union. . . ." As I left her, Miss Harper asked, almost eagerly, "Is Elizabeth old looking now? Her looks gone? She's getting on, you know. She's sixty-five, if she's a day!"

Hiltie, Captain

Also alluded to as "Hiller" or "Hilton." I believe Wrenn lived with him and his family for some time after the scandal, but I can find no trace of him now.

Holtzer, Irving, art agent

"I think you are doomed to disappointment," he said. "Often I have considered doing an article on Wrenn, myself. So always it ends up a critique of his work. There is nothing to say about the man. Only about his paintings.

"Yet in the old days, I saw him often. He'd sit here and I'd sit, and maybe we'd have a pipe and maybe we'd talk. I should remember all that clearly, but how can I? He was a secret, walking. Kept himself to himself. What did he give me to remember? Of himself, nothing as man to man. But his paintings! Only in his paintings did he let me know him. These, in my mind, I can see clearly any time. These told me about Wrenn, as he never could himself. He was a man in conflict. He was a puritan in rebellion against his own puritanism. But he could fight it only with paint. Only in his pictures came out the fury and power and his capacity for passion. He painted the free, animallike men and women in bold, slashing colors, and this was the self he otherwise denied. Yet however coarse the face he painted, always in it was understanding, for that was part of himself, too. This is the Wrenn I know, not the dark man I talked and smoked with.

"You know what? When Ezterhausy came here and said, 'Marius is dead,' I said, 'No!' And I pointed to his picture of the Portugee Girls on the wall. And Ezterhausy knew what I meant.

"Yet I wish he'd stayed on here. He was just beginning to find himself. The artist and the man were beginning to join hands instead of clenching fists. And the first step was letting himself fall in love. I am not being romantic, but very practical. He had to fall in love. He was aburst with the need, until even his painting couldn't hold it. He needed to express his heart with his lips and his body, not just with his paint brush.

"Oh, some say that loving Mrs Carver ruined him as an artist; that he wasted his passion and thought on her and so had nothing left for his work. They'll say an artist should not be too happy, or what is the compulsion to create? And to all this is some truth. But an artist can not stand still. He must grow. You can not forever plant in the same soil. It must lie fallow sometimes and be replenished and enriched with new elements. The artist must experience and build on his experience, and so gain greater stature. And I think that's what love was doing to Marius. But his time was cut short—" He glanced up at a space where I suspect the portrait of the Portugee Girls had once hung—"and so the walls of our homes and museums are the emptier for it."

J. *Jefferson, Arthur C.*

Mr Jefferson, principal of a high school, refused to discuss the matter until my third visit. Even then, his words were accompanied by much uneasiness.

"I didn't know until I was seventeen that my cousin had run away with the Carver woman," he said, at one point, "although I knew something untoward had happened. No one ever spoke Marius' name at home. Not openly, although I suspect there was not a day when my Grandmother Jefferson, who had raised him, did not grieve for him.

"Marius was the second disappointment in her life, you see. Her eldest child, Lydia, fell in love with a lithographer named Wrenn, Henry Willis Wrenn. He'd been doing some engravings for a book on ancient Rome written by Grandfather. Nobody realized what the situation was until Henry asked permission to marry Lydia. Naturally, Grandfather disapproved. In the first place, Henry was reputed to be an atheist. And, of course, that would just never do in a family like ours. The Jeffersons are not unreasonable people, but we've always believed in certain things, and you just can't go against them.

"Aunt Lydia did, however. Despite all family opposition, she married Henry. She pretended to be happy, but everyone saw through that! I'm not sure it wasn't a blessing that Aunt Lydia died when Marius was born, for it spared her the pain of having to live with a man she could not possibly have respected.

"Well, my grandparents just couldn't see that newborn child being brought up in the kind of home and atmosphere Henry Wrenn would supply. They reasoned with him first, and finally, very quietly, took the matter to court. They were able to prove several scandalous factors in Henry Wrenn's character, as well as his atheism, and so became legal guardians of the child. Mr Wrenn drifted on, as was his bent anyway, and finally died in Georgia or Ohio, or one of those places.

"This may sound heartless, Miss Deveny—taking a child away from its parent; but look at it understandingly, and you will see it was done with a heart full of love. My grandmother was a very fine woman. She'd give the coat off her back if anyone needed it. She had Alden blood on her maternal side, and her father was a minister, as were two of her brothers. When she was seven years old, she knew over twenty of the Psalms by heart. I might add, she also knew literally thousands of fairy stories.

"I mention this because, while she adhered very closely to what she believed, she could be wonderfully gay, too. She could make up songs out of her own head, and she'd sing them to us when we were good. She adored children. My mother told me how, when Marius was about six, he and Grandmother always got up early in the summer to water the garden. Well, one morning, to amuse Marius, my grandmother began to waltz very slowly about the flower beds, weaving the hose around her like a snake charmer. Our neighbors, the Lairds, saw this and said old Mrs Jefferson was losing her mind. Grandmother said right back that if it was sanity to judge your neighbor, but madness to make a small boy laugh, then blessed be the insane.

"So you see, for all her strictness, she was very human, and she loved Marius very much. That's why, when he began showing more and more artistic leanings, she became afraid he was taking after his father and would turn out like him—an irresponsible and godless wastrel. And that's why she did everything to discourage his painting. She disciplined him like a soldier and strengthened him with a firm foundation of love for God and truth. She showed him how a beautiful life was greater tribute to God than a beautiful painting which was, after all, only a graven image.

"Marius loved her very much, and I suppose he tried to heed her, but his father's blood won out. When he was about sixteen, they quarreled violently, and he ran away. To sea, they say, or some such. All because she found a rather too realistic Venus he'd drawn, and she burnt it.

"No, she did not strike him! Whoever told you that, lied. She never struck Marius, or anyone. It was her strong conviction that when a person erred—and knew he had erred—he would punish himself.

"Only Marius didn't. He only indulged himself the more. When he was heard of again, after several years, he'd turned completely against the ways he had been taught. You know what an artist's life is, how careless morally and socially. And you know what sort of pictures he painted, sailors and water-front trash. And then running away with a married woman and getting into the newspapers. Maybe Marius wasn't a consciously bad person, but despite what they believe today, blood tells. He was his father all over again, an irresponsible iconoclast. Death was the best thing that could have happened to him."

L. *Letters*

"If Wrenn ever wrote to me, I didn't bother saving the letters. Why would I? I never thought he'd be famous. But I don't think he wrote many letters. He hadn't the time." (Bentley Sprague)

Hitherto, a biographer could always count on the letters of his subject to furnish him clues of character, to identify his friends and tap his thoughts. In a sense, letters can be a visit over a span of time. I have found no such easy access to Wrenn, however. None of the people I have got in touch with possesses any written word from him. The villain of the piece, I fear, is the telephone. What busy man will write to anyone he can possibly telephone? This saved Wrenn much time, no doubt, but it has lost me many hours of his life. I have nothing to go on but a little secondhand information, dimmed by the years and reshaped by the teller's own personality.

Low, Marjorie Beecher

"I suppose everyone who went to high school with Marius now swears they were his best friend, but they weren't, and I wasn't either. He wasn't easy to know. Oh, nice enough, but very self-conscious about being so awkward and overgrown; and, of course, that stammer!

"Oh, yes, he stammered. When he'd have to get up and recite, he'd start stammering something awful. Sometimes in chemistry, he'd take so long getting through phrases like supersaturated solution that the rest of the class could relax for practically the rest of that period.

"No, he wasn't a good student. I sat next to him in geometry and I know. Once, during a test, he couldn't answer anything. His face was just ashen, and those big eyes practically glazed. We were on the honor system there, but he looked so pathetic, I shoved my paper nearer him, so he could copy my answers. He looked at me like I'd just healed him of leprosy or something. Well, as a result, he managed to finish the test. But he flunked it just the same. Know why? The next day, before class, he went up to the teacher and admitted that he'd cheated. Don't ask me why. That was Marius for you.

"It would be grand to say that was the beginning of a beautiful friendship, but actually, I was kind of disgusted with him. And then everyone began to kid me for helping him out. Said I was sweet on him. The only way I knew to prove I wasn't, was to laugh at him louder than anyone. Not to his face, you know, but I guess he caught on. Yet I've often thought, since he became famous, how strange that he had all that beauty in him, and none of us ever knew it."

1067 Lynn Street

Wrenn occupied the studio, fourth floor back, in this building around 1907–09. Since then, the building has twice changed hands and I can find no trace of Mrs J. R. Owens, the landlady who ordered him off the premises for alleged misconduct with Josie Azores.

M. *Morrison, Mrs Hobart*

She writes from San Francisco:

"My husband is no longer living, and yet maybe I can answer your letter. I never met Marius Wrenn, but I feel I know him. My life was long at his mercy, due to his unhappy influence over Bart.

"The maddening thing is, they so nearly didn't meet. Although they attended the same art classes in '08, Marius was too solitary, too lost in work, for camaraderie. Yet when Bart had pneumonia, it was Marius who played the Good Samaritan. Though they'd never spoken, when he learned of Bart's need, he moved over to his studio and nursed him. That opened their friendship which so nearly ruined Bart's life and, consequently, mine.

"Marius, you see, had enormous magnetism and strong convictions, while Bart was charming and impressionable—not a great artist, but his work had great style, assuring his future in advertising. Suddenly, Bart dropped this, declaring he didn't want to base his career on sham. Yet this is just what he did, becoming sham Marius Wrenn; lacking the fury, the power and insight so natural with Wrenn, he merely achieved—at great effort—mediocrity.

"Bart used to tell me how they'd share a model—only Bart's painting would be pretty, while Wrenn's was dynamic and real. He'd ask Marius the reason for this difference, and Wrenn would say, 'You go about it backwards, Bart. You make the person beautiful. It's the person who must make the portrait beautiful.' That was his creed: Look after truth, and beauty will take care of itself.

"A wonderful ideal, of course, but several sizes too large for my poor Bart. He wasted his life, measuring himself by Wrenn's impossible standards. I often wonder, incidentally, if Marius found living up to his own ideals an easy thing. How could he reconcile his statements about truth, and his being untrue with Mrs Carver? To my mind, he was a bigger failure than Bart . . ."

P. *"Portugee Girls"*

Esther and Josafina Azores. Posed for Wrenn in 1909, and for a time, his constant companions. Rumor connected him with Josie. She is now thought to be dead, and I can find no trace of Esther.

S. *Song* Popularized at the Old Howard by May Franklin, at the height of the scandal (1912)

> Now Lizzie McLee
> On a bird-watching spree
> Heard a lady bird (a shady lady bird)
> A-singing this song in a tree:
>
> Couldn't bill 'n' coo with the cuckoo
> So I flew off with a wren.
> Though I'm out on a limb
> In my love-nest with him,
> Guess I'd do it over again.
>   My perch may seem precarious,
>   My flight seem quite a plight.
>   The owl says he won't marry us
>   But some legal eagle might.
> Went nearly cuckoo with the cuckoo
> So I flew off with a wren!

Sprague, Bentley

"Wrenn? Wrenn? Yes, I knew him. Rather, he knew me. I was all the fashion then, and I expected he thought he could use me. Well, I taught him what I could, but it was wasted. He had no talent. Posterity will prove that. Daubed his paint on so thick, his pictures could be sliced thin, like cheese, into twenty copies. And he had no feeling for beauty. He rejected it, hated it. If something was beautiful, he had to defile it. Look at how he defiled every woman he loved or painted!"

Sprague indicated a sentimental portrait above his mantel—a gypsy maid coyly masking her smile with cards spread fanwise. Her plump hand was literally pocked with dimples.

"See that? I painted it. Beautiful! Know who the model was? Josephine Azores. Can you believe it? The same girl Wrenn painted in his Portugee thing, only he made her common and squat. Typical of him. He had to make everything sordid. No wonder he never sold a picture while he was alive. Then, nice people wouldn't invite a factory girl to tea, so why would they hang her portrait in their parlor? Nowadays, of course, everyone works in a factory and won't hang pictures of nice people on their walls. Anyway, I guess making Josie hideous and squalid was his revenge on her. She'd never let him touch her, you know. So he defiled her in paint."

Sprague's grandchildren raced noisily into the parlor and out again. He watched them affectionately. "At least, children insure us a kind of immortality," he mused. "Wrenn couldn't hope for that kind, anyway. He didn't leave any children."

A moment later, he added, slyly, "Although you never can tell. Not with Wrenn. Tried to pass himself off as a puritan, but if he was, it didn't keep him from sinning; just from enjoying it. He fooled some, but not me. A volcano passing itself off as Mt. Olivet, there's a portrait of him. Emma Thauly, for instance. I'll tell you a secret, but you can quote me: she was his mistress! That's why I say he was a fraud. A whited sepulchre. To moon about truth and beauty, and then consort with the scum of the earth. And the biggest hypocrisy of all, seducing Mrs Carver. I knew her. And she knew me!" Then he added, firmly, "I introduced them. I'll let you put that in your article. Bentley Sprague introduced them. I can't be blamed, though. I always disapproved of their escapade. Well, he started to do her portrait, but at a snail's pace. Very suspicious.

"'I can't seem to get the portrait right,' he'd excuse himself. 'I can't seem to catch the real quality of the woman.' (I could have told him the answer to that! Elizabeth Carver had no quality at all!)

"Well, he'd nearly finish her picture, and then he'd paint it out and begin again. It was like Penelope with her weaving. He'd destroy each night what he'd done during the day, stalling for more time with his ladylove. Of course, he never finished the picture. Gossip began, you see. It was my unhappy duty to tell him their secret was out. Then he got frightened, I expect, because he deserted her. But he went back to her eventually, because he was basically weak and attracted by ugly situations.

"After the scandal, I didn't much care about seeing him. The whole thing disgusted me. But he'd drop over occasionally, and a few weeks before he died, he came back from the Cape for a weekend. Elizabeth's house was closed for the season, so he stayed here. He and the vulgar Ezterhausy. I suspect they drank a lot that night. Found bottles in the room the next day. And they talked so loud. Kept me awake half the night. That's when I learned how low his taste for ugliness had led him. Oh, the things I could tell you—"

Sprague told me nothing more, however; merely assumed a manner most mysterious and secretive which, I suspect, was to mask the fact that actually he had nothing more to tell.

As I left, his daughter followed me down the front steps, urging me to buy some of Sprague's pictures. "I could let you have some at a real bargain, since you're a writer and must appreciate fine things . . ." But she said this with a kind of hopelessness, as if knowing in advance that I would not be interested.

T. *16 Terrace Street*

Wrenn lived at this address from 1909–12. A ponderous brick house, it is in process of being demolished. I watched the workmen throwing down shutters which Wrenn might have opened, or hacking at walls where his sketches once may have hung. The shell of the building stands enclosed by a high fence made up of discarded doors which lead nowhere—a symbol curiously pertinent to my search, so far.

Thauly, Emma

A chambermaid at the Statler. Stout, middle-aged.

"I can't think which one he was," she said, furrowing her brow.

"I posed for a lot of them fellows. I had more of a figure then. But since, I've had four kids. I got married early, you see. Ed—my husband, Ed Thauly—was a blacksmith, but horses was going out, so I started modeling. Fair money, I made, too. Always in demand. So I don't remember this Mr Wrenn, particularly. He might have been any one of them."

The next time I saw Mrs Thauly, I brought a small print of the famous "Study of Emma," which she carefully studied.

"Yes, that's me," she said. "You can tell I had a fine figure then." Still studying the picture, she added, "Maybe this was the man with the cold room. Yes. He used to hum while he was painting. Or maybe that was the other one . . ."

On my third visit, mention of the divorce scandal jogged her memory. "He liked to start work early in the day, so I'd get the kids off to school and pack my lunch in a paper bag and be at his studio with my clothes off at nine, every morning. He worked slow, and he was real unhappy, that was plain. Sometimes, he'd stop work and put his hands over his eyes, smearing paint on his face. And he didn't hum like he used to."

As delicately as possible, I asked Mrs Thauly if she had ever been intimate with Wrenn. She understood at once, without surprise or indignation.

"No," she said. "Ed wouldn't have liked that. I was just buddies with all them painters. And anyway, this Wrenn was all tied up with someone else. That's what was making him so miserable. This rich redhead. They'd just broke up, you see. No, I never seen her, except for her portrait, and he scrubbed that down with turpentine and used the canvas to paint me on over it.

"Well, one day, his buddy with the funny name [Ezterhausy] come in and give him a letter. It was from her, all right, because those two men begin talking about it. Funny-name don't even want him to read it, but my artist does, anyways. 'You going back to her?' Funny-name wants to know. 'No,' says my artist. 'That's all over.' He sets his lips tight and goes back to his easel. Only after a while, he goes back and reads the letter again. Then he just sits down and looks out the window and I go home. The next morning, he's humming again, so I know he's seen the redhead after all. Later in the week, he says he's done with the picture and won't need me, no more. Next thing I know, I see by the newspaper that he and the redhead run away together. I never seen him after. That is, if he's the one I'm thinking about. But like I say, I posed for so many gentlemen, and they was all a little strange, like that."

W. *Wallach, Kitty Leighton*

"It was Edith Harper who brought him to my house," she told me. "Edith and her mother. I think they wanted to introduce Mr Wrenn to people who might commission a portrait. I wasn't interested, myself, but it made me think of Elizabeth. Artists loved to paint her and she adored being painted. I asked her over. At that time, I lived across the little park from her.

"Well, in she swept, quite alone since the Senator was in Washington. She looked so lovely—her auburn hair and a big hat brimming with green lilacs. I thought it would be a treat for Mr Wrenn; might even stir him into conversation. He hadn't been comfortable with us that afternoon. I felt sorry for the poor man. He seemed mystified as to why he was there amongst so many chattering women. (Edith, particularly. She seemed dazzled by him; couldn't gush enough.) As I remember, however, he spoke only when spoken to, even after Elizabeth arrived.

"But do you think she helped the situation along? Not at all. She became very withdrawn, as if overwhelmed by his silence. That astonished me. Elizabeth was always the gayest in the room and was used to being the center of attention. Now, she didn't even bid for it. Just sat there, serene, attentive, but seldom speaking.

"Well, it became so awkward, I began to talk about anything, just to fill in the gaps. That's how we came to discuss the *Inferno*. I loved Doré's illustrations and asked Wrenn, as an artist, how he felt about them. Well, for a while, Marius opened up and spoke magnificently—not much in favor of Doré, but in praise of Dante. Even Elizabeth was entranced, and, of course, she hadn't much interest in literature. I thought to myself, this has finally broken the ice. But at last, he fell into silence again, and suddenly he said he must go.

"Elizabeth asked him to escort her to her house, as it was getting dark and she didn't like to walk through the park alone. Well, the next day, she dropped over, and when I asked what she thought of Mr Wrenn, she couldn't have been more indifferent. Then she asked to borrow my copy of the *Inferno*. Well, eventually, I heard he was painting her portrait, but I didn't put two and two together until I saw her in the park one day. It was so evident she was in love—she all but spelled it out every time she spoke.

"I was afraid for her, but what could I say? Elizabeth was so headstrong, so impetuous, nothing could stop her once her heart ran away with her. And when the worst did happen—the divorce—I wasn't even here to stand by her, being in Europe on my honeymoon. We were in New York, however, when Marius died, so we came here at once. Well, right after the funeral, she left for Europe. My husband and I drove her to the boat. I'll never forget that ride. She was heavily veiled, rigid, and oh, so silent. Crushed. You see, Elizabeth had always loved power—I don't mean that maliciously, for you've probably noticed it yourself. And Mr Wrenn had all but breathed power. It was quiet, but one literally felt it. Until she met him, her life had been petty and frantic; and now, with his strength taken away from her, she was lost and frightened and, once again, frantic. I think she's been looking, ever since, for that same happiness, fulfillment and power she knew with him. And I pray that, some day, she may find it again."

Winters, Scott

"His stutter? I never noticed it, except sometimes when he got excited. But then, I didn't know Marius too well. Don't think anyone really did. Ezterhausy, perhaps. But I guess all idealists are lonely people. Marius lived in his own world and by his own standards. And were they strict! The funny thing is, though, everyone thought he lived a real heller's life. That was because he was very open about everything he did. Hated undercover stuff. No wonder people misconstrued his actions. But I don't think Marius gave a damn about public opinion.

"For instance, what Ezterhausy told me, once—when Marius was living on Lynn Street, he ran into those two Portuguese sisters, Esther and Josie Azores, he used to know when he worked in a cannery. He got them to pose for him. They were kind of flashy and loud, but goodhearted enough. And I think Josie had a yen for him. Anyway, even after the painting was finished, they kept on dropping in on him any time of day or night. Cook dinner for him, mend his clothes, or just sit around and talk. Personally, I think it was because they had nowhere else to go, and no one else treated them as gallantly as Marius did. Anyway, they were always under foot, sometimes for half the night. It was innocent enough, and that's the irony of it. One night, his landlady busted into the room and got nasty about the girls' being there. She told him she ran a decent house and that he'd have to get out. Showered all kinds of abuse on him, but it apparently didn't upset him. He told Jay later, 'If my slate's clean, it doesn't matter what she thinks about me. And if it's not clean, I have to answer to myself.'

"That's why I say he lived by his own standards. If you wanted to enter his world, you had to live up to them. I never could—but apparently Esther and Josie did. I asked Jay how that was possible, because they were really quite common and uneducated. Jay said probably because Marius saw some primitive good in them, something beautiful and unfettered. Matter of fact, if you look at Wrenn's portrait of them, you catch what he must have seen. It is beautiful and unfettered and wonderful. Personally, I was only able to see their wide faces and big feet. But then, I'm not an idealist. And then, too, I'm still an unknown painter."

The index ended at W. The next page was blank except for the tab-letter X. "The unknown quantity," Elizabeth thought. That, indeed, eloquently summed up her pursuit of Wrenn. She had tracked down every clue until each was exhausted, but the little she had learned only made more monumental what she did not yet know.

Sighing, she shoved aside the index, but almost immediately opened it again, bending close over her notations as if to find between the very words some obscure reference she had not yet investigated. The distant chiming of the hour eventually roused her from study. It was midnight. She glanced at her clock. It was fast, and she turned back its hands.

Suddenly, she was overwhelmed by the mockery of this moment. She was lying on the cot where Wrenn once had slept, in the room where he had lived; and at her finger tips were incidents he had once experienced and words he had spoken. Only a trick of time separated her from him, but no sea could have separated them further. Set back the clock she might, but, however great her longing, time itself could not be turned back to those precious hours, lost before her own life had even begun.

Uneasily, she thrust the clock away. "What difference is that to me?" she muttered.

Picking up her index again, she grimly continued to study.

CHAPTER 4

Wednesday afternoons, Madame von Schillar's hairdresser came. Thursdays, exquisitely gowned and impatient, the Baroness waited by her gleaming tea service for visitors who rarely deigned to call. The balance of the week, every afternoon followed a cloistered and inflexible pattern: the two women sat in their usual chairs before the fire, Elizabeth listening intently, the Baroness chatting and teasing the indolent dog in her lap.

This Tuesday afternoon might have been one of many, except for the sudden tension in Madame von Schillar's face. Her eyes were fixed upon Worth in the doorway.

"Who?" she demanded, uneasily.

"Mr Hereford," the servant repeated.

"Our Mr Hereford?" Worth nodded. "But this isn't my afternoon to receive—"

"Shall I say you're out?"

"I don't know, I don't know." Madame von Schillar glanced at Elizabeth apprehensively and then, pushing the reluctant spaniel from her lap, crossed to her mirror. "Oh, Lordie, my hair!" she muttered, and grabbed up her comb.

"Can I help?" Elizabeth offered.

Madame von Schillar did not turn from the mirror. "Matter of fact, you can, my dear," she said. "I think you might run up to your room for a while. I have some business to discuss with—someone." She hastened toward another mirror and revolved before it. "Use the back stairs, eh? There's a dear!"

Quickly, she slipped into another gown, buckled a bracelet on her wrist and scented her throat and palms with Loki. Her heart had begun to drum a little wildly. "But that doesn't mean anything," she thought. "I can get the same effect by climbing stairs."

He was facing the fireplace, his back to her, as she entered the dim parlor.

"Quincy!" she cried.

As he turned she caught the glint of his glasses, the gleam on the dome of his head. He had a mustache now, but so grey it blended into the wasted pallor of his face.

"Quincy?" she asked.

He bowed with that inevitable correctness. "It's been a long time, Baroness."

"Alas, it has," she said, "if you've forgotten you called me by my first name." Her tone was the more gracious to hide the shock of seeing how old he had become.

"A long time," he repeated, "but it hasn't changed you—"

"Indeed?"

"Well—perhaps you've cut your hair."

She touched her coiffure self-consciously. "It looks a wreck, I know. The girl who comes to curl me isn't due till tomorrow—" Suddenly, she laughed. "Sit down, Quincy. Surely, after all these years, we have better things to discuss than my hairdresser . . ."

She chose a seat for herself far across the room where she would not have to see him so clearly. "How about a drink?" she asked. "Sherry? Highball?"

"No, thank you."

There was a pause.

"Tea?" she asked, suddenly.

"No, thank you."

"Well, I'm going to have something." She poured herself a finger of brandy. "I love sherry," she continued glibly. "It's a tonic for these cold afternoons. Cheers!" And she saluted him with her glass.

There was another appalling silence. Beneath the sweep of her skirt, her foot tapped.

He had become, she thought, the inevitable Hereford elder, who retired from society, but never from business. Lump all generations of them together, the Quincys, the Ezras, the Edwards, and they were all one man, differing in no wise. "I and my fathers are one," she mocked, silently.

"Elizabeth—"

She started at the sound of her name. In the dimness of the room, his voice with its familiar gentleness briefly conjured the image of a young man with sandy hair and clear eyes.

"Yes?" she answered, a little tenderly in spite of herself.

"I suppose you're wondering why I came."

"No, I hadn't wondered. Old friends often see each other, my dear. And sometimes even enjoy it." She studied the amber of her brandy. "But I was beginning to think you'd forgotten me, what with Eleanor and all. Her name is Eleanor, isn't it?"

"Elaine. I have two Elaines, now."

"Daughter?"

"Granddaughter. Oh, yes, I have three grandchildren."

"Oh, my God!" She drained her glass and arose. "Well, my dear, it's been sheer heaven seeing you, and we must do it often. But I'm not a free woman, just now. Every moment, I'm hard at work, so if you'll excuse me—"

"Wait!" He stood up. "It's about this work of yours that I've come. It's vital to discuss it. Please sit down again . . ."

She did not sit down, however, in order to keep him standing and so insure his brevity. "Well?"

"They say you're writing your memoirs."

"Who says so?" she demanded, in surprise.

"I'm not at liberty to say."

"Still the soul of discretion, eh? Very well, then I'm not at liberty to say if I'm doing my memoirs. Good afternoon, Quincy."

She had crossed the room, nearly to her door, before he spoke again. "All right, then. It was from Francis Westbrook. He mentioned it at the club. And Edith Harper said something about it to a friend of my wife."

"I'm not acquainted with either of them," the Baroness said, "so how would they know about my plans?"

"But is it true?"

"Yes. Is that all you want to know?" But she knew, now, it was not.

"What are you planning to say?" he asked.

"Oh—this and that. When it's published, I'll send you a copy. Autographed."

"Are you going to say anything about me?"

She tipped her head and smiled. "I don't know. I really haven't decided . . ."

He made an uneasy attempt at joviality. "I don't suppose I could persuade you to have a lapse of memory?"

"You wouldn't ask me to do that, Quincy," she taunted. "That would be so like a falsehood. And I remember how contemptuous you always were of liars."

"But this is different," he protested. "And I'd make it very worth your while."

Her shoulders stiffened. "What can you offer me that I don't already have? I'm not a chorus girl!"

"I didn't mean money. There are other things."

"In Boston?" she cried. "My dear, don't be sacrilegious!"

He began to cough, muffled by his handkerchief. She backed away from him instantly, but continued talking. "Just what other reward did you have in mind? An invitation from a full-blooded Cabot, mayhap? Or the approval of the Watch and Ward Society? Or—could it be—you were going to say something very, very sweet about 'the sake of old friendship'?"

He spoke with effort. "I ask you to forget it all just out of common decency."

"Common decency," she retorted, gleefully, for it was a remark she was fond of making, "is so uncommon as to be absolutely indecent. I learned that when I naïvely expected a little common decency from you."

"That's rather cheap!" he said, quietly.

"You may find it rather costly," she snapped. He lowered his eyes. Madame von Schillar resumed her lazy smile. "What's the matter, my poor Quincy? Afraid to be linked with shameless, wicked me?"

"It's just that I have Elaine to consider, and the family—"

"And your position! And your tradition! And the Porcellian Club! And sacred Boston! Oh, how familiar that sounds, coming from you. Well, who knows, my dear—maybe my book might give you a new tradition. A romantic tradition! Matter of fact, my sécretary came across one of your letters a few weeks ago. Very impetuous and signed Q. I think it might make interesting copy—"

"Haven't I been punished enough, all these years?" he demanded. "Why are you so determined to humiliate me more?"

"It'll be good for you," she teased. "Help develop your character."

He clasped his hands behind his back and looked down at his

feet. At last, he said, "I should know better than to try to reason with you when you're in a mood like this. I'll call again."

"There will be no need for that," she declared, cheerily. "As I said before, I haven't decided what I'll do about you. Maybe I'll tell a great deal, and maybe I'll say nothing. See for yourself when the book comes out. That ought to be within a year—"

"Am I not to know until then?" he demanded, aghast. "Must I wait a whole year?"

"I waited longer than that, once," she said, with her little smile. All indolent grace, she tugged the bell cord for Worth. "Good-bye, my dear. I won't urge you to remember me to your grand little wife. That would not be discreet, eh?"

She was thoughtful as Worth helped her dress for dinner. "He still coughs," she said, absently.

"Yes, ma'am."

"It was just to tease him, y'know. I'm not going to even mention him in my book. We'll just forget about that nonsense."

"Yes, ma'am. You want your lace shawl?"

"Stole, Worth, not shawl; no I don't want it." She eyed the mirror critically. "I haven't changed too much, have I? Just my hair being short now—"

"Yes, ma'am."

"And I'm still capable of it. Upsetting Boston, I mean." She smiled with grim triumph. "It seems my name is still good currency for the gossips. Quincy says simply everyone's talking—"

"That's a pity, ma'am."

"I think it's rather fun," said the Baroness. "Like old times, eh?"

Worth straightened her apron. "Ma'am," she said, her eyes downcast, "you want to be careful."

"Do I? Why, pray tell?"

"Suppose she hears?"

"Who? Hears what?"

"Miss Deveny. All that slander."

"How could she hear anything? She doesn't know anyone in town, and she never goes anywhere."

"Why, ma'am," said Worth, "she goes out most every night. After finishing her work, she goes out. Can't tell who she sees or talks to. Or what she hears."

"Oh, who cares!" the Baroness fumbled with the clasp of her pearls. Abruptly, she added, "It's all a pack of lies, anyway."

"Yes, ma'am," Worth continued, "but like with a cat: give them enough food at home and then they don't go out poking in garbage cans."

"Whatever are you talking about?" Madame von Schillar demanded. "Don't be tiresome. Garbage cans, indeed! And just before dinner, too!"

"Yes, ma'am." Worth headed for the door. "Anyway, she don't get nothing from me."

"What is that supposed to mean?"

"When she questions me, ma'am. She's a great one for questions. And she goes out most every night, ma'am." Worth nodded and left.

It was on the following day that Madame von Schillar's hand was forced. The shrill ring of the telephone awakened her from siesta, and for a moment she thought she was in Paris. This was a natural mistake. In Paris, the telephone was forever ringing. Eagerly, she picked up the receiver, then sat up straight. The telephone had already been answered on the upstairs extension.

"Elizabeth?" said a voice, feminine, liquid.

"Yes." It was the girl who answered.

"This you, Elizabeth? Can you guess who this is?"

"I can't imagine—"

"Well, it has been a long time. It's Lucy, dear. Lucy Denham. Lucy Clark, who was."

A wave of fury swept over the Baroness that the girl would dare accept this call. "Hello, hello," she cut in, fiercely. "Who is this, and who do you want?"

"It's me, dear. Lucy," assured the voice. "Isn't this Elizabeth Winslow, that was?"

"It is now," the Baroness said, angrily. "Hang up, Elizabeth, this is for me! She waited until she heard the click, then explained, "That was my secretary—" And now the mistake was apparent to her. "We both have the same name, you see. Who did you say you were?"

"Lucy, dear. You remember Lucy Clark?" There was a pause. "Why, Elizabeth Winslow, I was one of your bridesmaids—I mean, at the wedding to Senator Carver—"

"Yes, it is hard to keep track of all those weddings," the Baroness said, dryly. "Well?"

"Well, I just thought I'd call and say hello . . ."

"Thank you."

"We must get together soon, dear . . ."

"Oh?"

"I mean, to discuss the adventures we girls used to have . . ."

"Oh?"

"I was thinking, the other day, of that time—I don't think the Senator was along—when all of us went picnicking—"

Madame von Schillar grew pale. "What about it?" she asked, harshly.

There was a stunned silence and, at last, the woman spoke again, her voice no longer liquid. "Well, I apologize I'm sure, Elizabeth. I thought I could help. I heard you were doing your memoirs, and—"

"Did you, now!" the Baroness interrupted. "Well, Lucy, if you're so set on remembering things, just recall the time after my divorce when I needed friends so desperately, and you always happened to be out when I called!"

She hung up and shoved the telephone away. Her heart was throbbing and her palms were moist. She hastened to the door. "Elizabeth," she shouted. "Come down, at once . . ." The girl was already waiting in the parlor. "How much of that did you overhear?"

"Nothing."

"I thought you were upstairs."

"I was, but I came down to say how sorry I was. About the call, I mean. I should have known it wasn't for me—but when someone says your name, you just naturally answer—"

"In that case," said the Baroness, "I think it best that you don't answer the phone in the future."

"Very well." She turned to go.

"Heaven only knows what preposterous nonsense that Clark woman might have poured in your ears if I hadn't cut in." She drew the girl back and, smiling uncertainly, added: "You see, there are lots of people who are jealous of me, and a lot who don't want to see my memoirs published. They've always attacked me, and they're not done yet. Nothing would give them greater pleasure than to fill your head with lies and slander about me. I don't mind for myself. I've learned to dismiss it. But you haven't had that education in the world. You're too sensitive, and it would jar you terribly. Might even creep into your writing! Unintentionally corrupt it. So it wouldn't be wise to get your information from anyone but me."

Elizabeth felt the rush of blood to her face. "But, Madame," she protested, "you don't give me any information."

"Of course, I do!"

"About your childhood. And the Senator. But as for the rest . . ."

Madame von Schillar turned away. After a moment, she said, decisively, "I shall tell you about Marius tonight, then."

"I'm not busy now," Elizabeth offered, eagerly.

"But I must think first," the Baroness replied. "It is not a story one can plunge into without preparation."

It was not, indeed. Thoughtfully, restlessly, she paced back and forth, that afternoon, sometimes whispering, "Concentrate, concentrate!" She bunched her brows in thought and then quickly massaged the lines from her forehead. To prevent herself from further scowling, she found a postage stamp, licked it and pressed it between the deft black arcs of her eyebrows. Once more, she returned to the couch and assumed an attitude of deep meditation. A moment later, she was laying out a hand of solitaire; but she did not play it. Sighing, she began to pace again, the green postage stamp buckling upon her frown.

At five o'clock, Corinne, her hairdresser, arrived. Usually, Madame von Schillar enjoyed being pampered with lotions and the warm, fragrant oils, but today it was agony, and, at last, she snatched the comb from Corinne's hand and flung it across the room.

"Been dieting?" the blond woman asked, imperturbably.

"Hold your tongue!"

"Need more sleep I guess. Or how about a facial? That ought to relax you." Then she winked at the Baroness. "Or some man's been giving you trouble, I bet."

"Shut up," said Madame von Schillar, but not unkindly. Then she glanced up at Corinne. "Yes," she said, suddenly, "that's what it is. Apparently you've been listening to gossip."

"On my honor, I haven't, Baroness," Corinne protested. "I just guessed."

"I'm so weary of being gossiped about," Madame von Schillar continued, quite wistfully. "That's why I'm on edge today. It seems this new beau of mine has heard some rumors, and now he's wanting an explanation. Frankly, I'd rather not discuss it with him. Oh, I'm not afraid or ashamed, but there are some things, intensely personal and precious that you like to keep to yourself. More important, others are involved whom I feel I must protect. So I don't know what to tell him. I'd gladly lie, but I can't be sure he hasn't some inkling of the truth. And if I keep silent any longer, he'll surely go to others for their distorted information. Or, as so nearly happened today, they'll come to him—Oh, I just don't know what to do!"

"Say no more, dear!" Corinne waved a plump hand and sat down beside her. "I've been through the same thing."

"I was hoping you had," Madame von Schillar said, edging nearer. "What did you do?"

"Well, this was with my husband." Corinne's voice sank to a tone more in keeping with confidence. "Just before we got married. Someone made a crack about me, it got him thinking, so he comes to me for an explanation. Well, I was in the same boat as you. I'm afraid to lie and risk him finding me out. But he'd raise hell, maybe leave me, if I told him the truth. So first I got him sympathetic. Told him I'd been foolish once and that I'd suffered for it—you know, brave-little-woman style. Then, when he was on my side, I told him a few, unimportant details—just enough to keep him satisfied. That did the trick! Matter of fact, it made us closer than ever before, and if anyone ever makes another crack about me, my boy'll tear him to pieces with his bare hands!"

"Very interesting," the Baroness murmured.

"The important thing," Corinne continued, picking up the comb, "is not to get carried away and become confessional. Touch on things real lightly. If he's sympathetic, he'll fill in the details to suit himself."

"I'll remember that," said the Baroness. A moment later, she added, "I think you'd better fix my hair very softly about the face. . . ."

When Elizabeth came to her suite that night, Madame von Schillar was in bed. Candlelight lent authority to her gentle regret, and somewhere a little music box briefly tinkled a tune.

"My dear," she said, slowly, "this book poses a difficult problem for us both. Let us look at it in unromantic terms. I'm an adulteress. I lied and cheated, with no excuse in the world, except that I was in love and selfishly believed nothing else mattered. I couldn't see an inch beyond my heart. As a result—" she passed a weary hand over her eyes—"as a result, the world punished me and Fate punished me, and the shame and suffering still burns me." She raised imploring eyes to Elizabeth. "That's why I don't know where to begin or how to begin. There are some things that, even yet, I can't evaluate, and some things I've tried so hard to forget that now it's difficult to remember clearly. So you'll forgive me if, in discussing my love affair with Mr Wrenn, we go slowly, by degrees— Can you understand this, my dear?"

Such a question was needless. The luminosity of Elizabeth's face made clear that the Baroness had made her point. She reached over and patted the girl's hand. "Thank you, my dear," she said. "Thank you for your understanding heart. Now I can feel perfectly free . . ."

Smiling, Elizabeth took out her notebook. Madame von Schillar moistened her lips. "From the beginning?"

"From the beginning."

The Baroness had unhooked a pendant from her ear and was examining it carefully. "It was in nineteen eleven," she said, almost inaudibly. "Winter, I think, at Kitty's . . ."

"Yes?"

"I wore a green fitted suit, trimmed with velvet. Green bows on my hat . . ." She paused again.

"Green bows on your hat?"

"Yes. I don't know why I dropped in at Kitty's that day. Maybe she asked me." She held the earring up, watching the light quiver against the stones. "I don't remember."

"Was anyone else there?" Elizabeth asked, patiently.

"I think we were alone, we three. Kitty, me, and this young man. Wrenn. Oh, I thought he was a strange one, too. But Trojan! Wonderfully Trojan!"

"Trojan?"

"Yes," Madame von Schillar said, and continued without explanation. "Well, nobody said very much. I didn't either. I don't know why. I wasn't bored, but I just couldn't seem to talk. Something about him intimidated me; yet I couldn't go away. And it was funny, because Marius told me later he'd thought I was as socially inept as himself, and that's what first interested him in me . . ."

Her voice began to drone a little. She told the story badly, stumbling, gesturing abortively when a word failed her; and often, she paused cautiously, like one feeling his way in the dark. Yet Elizabeth, who had twice before heard this story, knew at what cost Madame von Schillar spoke, and thus it had for her a new and thrilling impact. She listened attentively, no longer taking notes, but staring off into nothingness, as if asleep with her eyes open.

It was not long before Madame von Schillar noted this. It was not an aspect of listening which she recognized. She broke off in the middle of a sentence and, abruptly picking up a deck of cards, began laying out the inevitable solitaire. The icy silence roused Elizabeth from her reverie, and she sat up with a start.

"I'm afraid I've been boring you," Madame von Schillar said, coldly. "Pray forgive me."

"No," Elizabeth protested. "I was listening, believe me, I was. Please go on. You said he escorted you home through the little park . . ."

It took some persuading before the Baroness consented to continue. "Well, I didn't see him again. Not right off. It wasn't that I forgot about him, but—something about him frightened me. Something dark, something magnetic. And then the Senator's ulcers happened and I was called to Washington . . ." She paused again.

"Yes?"

Madame von Schillar gathered up the cards and shuffled them briskly. "Well, I expect I was bored with nothing to do but look after that great, ailing baby, because I kept thinking about Marius. The funny, searching way he'd look into people's eyes. The way he'd gripped my arm to steer me around a mud puddle. He was strong. Not just physically, but—He knew what he wanted to do and hadn't bothered to ask permission of society. I liked that attitude! I began to want to study to be an artist, too, and maybe take a studio near his. I borrowed a copy of the *Inferno* and read it, because it was something he admired. And, oh, very carefully, I began asking the Senator little questions about Marius—their families knew each other. Somehow, I found out that he liked Daumier, and I bought an original sketch at an art auction, though I didn't give it to him till weeks after. And

I learned his grandfather had taught Greek and Latin, so I fixed my hair in a Psyche knot. Funny little things like that, though it never occurred to me that I might be falling in love . . ."

She swept the cards aside and ran her long fingers through Jabot's curly black coat. "Well, I finally brought the dear Senator back to Boston to recuperate. Then—not right away, mind you, maybe a week later—I dropped Wrenn a note. Said I wanted my portrait done, and for him to meet me on such-and-such an evening. Of course, I didn't dare bring him into the house, since the Senator didn't approve of him. Called him a wastrel. So, that evening, I waited for him, outside—"

"Where?" Elizabeth asked.

"Across the street, in the little park. That's where I always waited for him. . . ."

As Madame von Schillar continued her narration, Elizabeth sat in an attentive attitude, but the tide of her imagination had swept her far out.

It was dark where she waited, and the rustling of the dry branches might have been the manifestation of her own nervousness. It was not cold, but she shivered slightly. The threat of discovery nagged her, yet she felt too weak to leave. Then, she heard movement and, half in fear, half in hope, she arose. The next moment, he stood before her and spoke her name. In defiance of the timidity she felt, she lifted her eyes—

The vision dissolved and, involuntarily, Elizabeth uttered a low cry. The Baroness, who had been speaking, impatiently drummed her fingers on the bedside table.

"What's the matter now? Is it too close in here? You're pale."

"No," Elizabeth murmured, and her face obediently performed a smile. "Please go on."

She tried to follow Madame von Schillar's words back into that sense of excitement but without success. Even though the park had been so dark she could not have seen Wrenn's face anyway, recurrence of the vision was blocked by her realization that she did not know what he looked like.

"You *are* pale," the Baroness insisted. "Better go to bed. I haven't anything more to tell now, anyway. *C'est fini!*"

"Yes," Elizabeth said. "Yes." She arose.

"And you won't answer telephones any more, will you?" Madame von Schillar added, with mock severity. "There's no need to listen to anyone but me, y'know. I can tell you all there is to tell, and it'll be the truth instead of some ugly, distorted rumor."

Elizabeth lingered at the door. "I was wondering if—well, if maybe you'd let me see a photograph of Mr Wrenn . . ."

"A photograph? Why, I don't have one, any more," the Baroness said, thoughtfully. "I don't think I ever did. There are some existent, of course—one, I believe, at the Gardner Museum—but I never had one."

"He never gave one to you?" Elizabeth asked, incredulously.

"But why would he?" the Baroness said. "Why would I need one? We were always together, and I thought we always would be. . . ."

Elizabeth returned to her room, plagued by a sense of incompleteness. Such a mood was not new to her, yet now it was more pronounced in the way that pain can seem sharper returning after a moment of relief.

Because it was her habit, she escaped into work, expanding the notes she had taken on Wrenn that evening; but these details of the meeting now seemed like the rooms of this house—neatly laid out, but empty, lifeless. It was impossible to impart any reality when she could not accurately picture the man. Moving through her thoughts with no more substance than a shadow, he emerged with equal flatness in her writing.

"I'll go to the museum tomorrow," she finally decided. "I'll see his photograph, tomorrow."

Suddenly, she was eager for morning to come, and, to hurry it along, immediately went to bed; but this very impatience warded off sleep, and the hours of the night dragged by, little installments of eternity.

Her excitement seemed to feed on weariness, however, and such was her impatience at breakfast the following morning, she promptly overturned a tumbler of water.

"Whatever is the matter with you?" the Baroness asked, scrutinizing her. "Are you ill? You are! I knew it, last night."

"Just tired," Elizabeth explained. "I didn't sleep."

"Why then, change to another room where the bed's comfortable." She edged out of the way of the water's driblets. "You're in no condition to work, that's plain. Better take the morning off and get some rest."

"Don't have time," Elizabeth said. "I've got to go out, today."

"Go out?"

"I have to do some research."

"On what, pray?"

"Oh—Boston. The Senator. Mr Wrenn."

"Why do you have to go outside for that?" the Baroness cried, already alarmed. "I've promised to tell you all you need to know."

"But I have to see for myself," Elizabeth faltered.

"See what?"

"Well—for one thing, I—was going to a gallery and—look at Mr Wrenn's paintings. You can't tell a person about them. They have to be seen—"

"Tosh!" She swirled her spoon in the coffee, then pushed the cup away and stood up. "I'm going with you."

Elizabeth's jaw tightened. Her voice was toneless. "Very well." As the Baroness started off to fetch her furs, she added, "Madame von Schillar, is something wrong?"

The Baroness paused, pretending to inspect the silver candelabra on the sideboard. "Don't be absurd! What are you talking about?"

"Forgive me if I'm wrong," the girl continued, desperately, "but I sense, more and more, that you don't trust me."

"Oh tosh, for God's sake!" She turned on Elizabeth, her green eyes piercing. "But we do know my enemies are laying in wait, willing and able to poison your mind with all kinds of lies about me—"

Impulsively, Elizabeth reached over and took her hand. "I understand. Believe me, I do. But please remember this—I know you. I know you as I know myself. Don't you think I'd recognize it if someone were trying to hurt or slander you?" She released Madame von Schillar's hand and turned away in embarrassment. Yet, she added firmly, "You must learn to trust me as I trust you."

Evading Elizabeth's eyes, the Baroness glanced back at the sideboard. "These candelabra want shining," she murmured. Then, she added plaintively, "Another thing—what am I supposed to do with myself while you're gone?"

"Oh, I think you'll manage," Elizabeth laughed. "You did for years before I ever came here. And anyway, it's Thursday. We never work on your at-home day."

Madame von Schillar's eyes lit up. "Yes," she murmured, "now I'm someone to deal with again, I'm liable to attract rather a crew of old friends—" Then she frowned. A moment later, she added cautiously, "Maybe it would be better if you did run along to the gallery, today. . . ."

Elizabeth's release from the house had the excitement of an escape. As if afraid Madame von Schillar would suddenly decide to accompany her after all, she ran to the corner, hailed a cab and directed it, *sotto voce,* to the Gardner Museum.

When she reached the great mansion on the Fenway, however, her eagerness was so intense as to seem absurd even in her own eyes. To convince herself of the relative unimportance of seeing Wrenn's photograph, she forced herself to get a catalogue and pass from room to room, studying the paintings which covered the high, brocaded walls. At last, she came to the broad corridor, dimly lit, lined with cabinets like glass-topped coffins, where some photographs and letters of yesterday's immortals were interred.

Her whole being demanded her to hasten. It seemed as if her strength would give out before she came to his photograph, but she proceeded with the same careful pace, judging each yellowing likeness, trying to read each crabbed inscription.

Her recognition of his handwriting was accompanied by a resounding in her ears, like the vibration of faraway cannonade. She faltered, daring to lift her eyes no higher than the jagged signature: Sincerely, Marius Wrenn. Then, with the quiet decision of one surrendering to a caress long denied, she looked upon his face.

The likeness was primitive and carelessly developed, beginning to darken, as if dusk had caught the young man unaware. His pallor burned through the surrounding shadow, but his intense, wide-set eyes were in league with darkness. "A prince of the night," she thought, "in his first twilight."

She searched his face intently, impressing each detail on her mind. His forehead was cleft by a lock of black hair; his eyebrows were black, too, dark comets in danger of collision. The jaw was hard, the nose strong, slightly thickened at the bridge, as if once broken; but his lips were still boyishly soft. In his broad, ugly hands, he carried a boating cap at which Elizabeth stared, transfixed. The young man, caught in this moment of life, unknowingly clenched a symbol of his death. Although she struggled against it, her mind whispered that phrase from the encyclopedia: "He did not live to see his work recognized, meeting an untimely death in a boating accident on July 1, 1915 . . ."

It could have been but a few minutes, or it might have been many, that she stood before the cabinet, staring at the picture, as if waiting for the man to move, for his eyes to meet hers, for him to whisper, "Elizabeth, Elizabeth—" But the voice she heard spoke other words which she could not assimilate.

"What?" She whirled around. An elderly guard stood by her.

"I say, better not lean on that glass top, Miss," he repeated. "You wouldn't want to break it."

"I was looking at the pictures," Elizabeth stammered.

The guard peered into the cabinet. "Oh, Marius Wrenn." He pronounced the name so it rhymed with tin. "He was the painter."

"It wasn't him I was looking at," Elizabeth said, quickly. She left the corridor, at once. When the guard moved on, however, she cautiously returned to study and memorize Wrenn's face.

It was midafternoon when she left the museum. For several hours she wandered aimlessly around the city, seeking distraction; but thoughts of Wrenn weighed on her like an outraged conscience.

Weary at last, she turned homeward; yet her steps faltered as the great house loomed before her. It was a forbidding structure. Bow windows had been added in a futile attempt to ease its severity, and its cupola crowned with wrought-iron lace. The vines which might have masked its ugliness, however, had been torn away, leaving the grey stone stained with varicose tracery.

Unwilling to enter the house and submit to its gloom just yet, she retreated to a bench in the little park across the way. It was a silent hour and the premature dusk of winter was lowering. The trees were barren and their branches, rootlike, burrowed into the mist as if in search of nourishment. Elizabeth's body relaxed, and she found herself waiting. First in her mind, then with her lips, she began forming those words, as the letter had begged, "Marius, Marius, Marius—"

And at last, she said it aloud, because he was before her. It was twilight now, but she knew his face, knew the pallor that burned through shadow. For a time, neither spoke, but merely gazed at the other.

"I didn't know whether or not you'd come," she faltered.

"You asked me to, didn't you?" He sat down beside her. "I'd

wondered what had become of you." She detected a faint stammer on the last word.

"I had to go to Washington," she answered. "The Senator'd been quite ill, poor ailing baby . . ." There was a pause, and she met his eyes, then glanced away quickly. Presently, she murmured, "You're not a very talkative person."

"Are you?" he asked.

"When I have something to say, Mr Wrenn, I have been known to talk the ear off a hitching post."

"But you didn't talk much at Miss Leighton's, when we met."

She smiled faintly. "I know."

"Were you uncomfortable there, too?"

"No," she said.

"I thought you were. I thought, here's someone as lost as me."

"Then why didn't you try to help me out?" she cried.

"I did. I talked about Dante's *Inferno,* remember?"

"How did you know that would interest me?" she asked.

"Because of the way your face lighted up."

"It might have lighted up in exactly the same way if you had mentioned President Taft or Timbuktu." When he did not respond again, she asked, "What's the matter?"

"I don't have much knack for banter."

"I wasn't bantering," she cried. "I was telling the truth. I've never read the *Inferno*. At least, I hadn't then. My face lighted up because I knew you weren't at ease, and I wanted to encourage you to talk. You became wonderfully excited—"

"And probably stuttered like the devil."

"But you spoke like an angel."

His eyes searched hers to see if she were mocking. That same fear she had sensed when first they met stirred in her again, and she lowered her eyes. "You mustn't," she said.

"Mustn't what?"

"Look in people's eyes that way. It isn't nice!"

"But how else am I to know about them?"

"By listening to what they say," she replied.

He laughed. "And live in ignorance?"

She looked up at this. He was still watching her. They were dark, his eyes, and fierce. His face was bony, hard, and with that faint thickness at the bridge of his nose, she suddenly knew what he looked like. "You're Trojan," she mused aloud. "Oh, wonderfully Trojan." He made no comment, and she added, quickly, "That wasn't banter, you know."

"I know. But I didn't know how to answer. To say what you look like."

"Tell me. I'm very vain, y'know. I love to hear about me."

He shrugged. "I don't talk well. I stutter—"

"You talk wonderfully, and I haven't heard any stutter, scarcely at all. Go on—tell me what I look like."

"Well—not like that portrait by Sargent."

"You've seen it?"

He nodded. "In a magazine, last month."

"I've been told my portrait was a very good likeness."

"The features, perhaps. But it might be of almost any fashionable woman."

"Isn't that what I am?"

"I don't think so. Not when you forget."

"The Senator fell in love with me from seeing that picture."

He glanced at her piercingly and started to speak, but did not. Looking down, he rubbed at a spot on his shabby coat. Rain began to fall, and he noted this almost with relief. "We'd better go," he said.

She arose, stretching forth her hand, palm up, to test for rain. He mistook the gesture for one of farewell and shook her hand firmly.

"Good-bye," he said.

"Not so fast," she laughed. "You can walk me to the gate." She offered him her arm. As they walked, she continued, "And do you think you could do a better picture of me than my Mr Sargent?"

"I think I could catch what you are, better than he did. But it wouldn't be stylish."

At the entrance to the street, they paused. "You will do my portrait then?" she asked.

He did not answer at once, but stared over her shoulder into the accumulating darkness of the park. "I'm afraid it wouldn't be worth your while," he finally said.

"But it might be worth yours. I'm prepared to pay what you ask."

He only repeated, "It wouldn't be worth your while."

"But if I think it would?"

"Then you would be mistaken. Good evening." He turned and started away.

"Mr Wrenn," she cried. He stopped, glanced back. "I may convince you yet. Perhaps if you're in the park tomorrow, at this time, you'll let me try."

"Good night, Mrs Carver," he said.

"Until tomorrow, Mr Wrenn?"

He hesitated, and when at last he spoke, the stutter was very evident. "Until tomorrow."

She watched him until he was lost in the shadows. Then, slowly, she crossed the street to the great stone house.

The tea table was still immaculately laid out with untouched cups and cakes. The Baroness, sitting alone, was having a cocktail. "Mother of God, look at you!" she cried. "Soaked to the skin! If you weren't sick this morning, you will be now. You look feverish already!"

Indeed, Elizabeth's appearance was extraordinary. Her cheeks were ruddy, as if injudiciously rouged. Her breath came fast through parted lips, and her pupils, dilated, made her eyes seem larger than ever.

"We can't have you getting sick," the Baroness fretted, rising at once. "I have a thermometer around somewhere—"

"Oh, tosh," Elizabeth said, laughing. "I never felt better."

Madame von Schillar indicated the girl's wet coat. "Where have you been doing your research? In the river?"

"The museum, And then I walked for a while. It was lovely—"

"In this weather? Sounds grim."

"Haven't you ever enjoyed walking in the rain?" Elizabeth asked.

"Oh, it can be romantic enough," said the Baroness. "But not when you're alone."

Elizabeth smiled to herself.

Madame von Schillar's brows lifted. "Oh?" She eyed Elizabeth slyly, baiting her embarrassment. "Could it be that your eagerness to go out alone today was so you might meet some young man?"

Elizabeth neither blushed nor blundered. "I'd be very flattered to have you believe so," she said.

There was a hint of that cheerful irreverence in her voice which so exactly duplicated Madame von Schillar's style, that the woman could not fail to notice. She turned on Elizabeth indignantly. The girl's face, however, was so guileless, it was evident she had intended no mockery.

"You're a funny child," the Baroness mused. "But I'd like you better if you'd stop dripping on my carpets and go change for dinner. I'm getting ravenous."

"I don't think I care for any dinner," Elizabeth said. "I'm too sleepy . . ."

When she was safe in her room, and the door locked, she sank onto the cot with a drowsy smile.

"I wonder," she mused, "if he'll be in the park, tomorrow?"

Then she sat up and laughed aloud.

It was tribute to the power of her own imagination, she thought; for a moment, she had almost been persuaded that she had actually met Wrenn this afternoon.

The following morning, however, this elation seemed, in retrospect, ridiculous, almost childish, to Elizabeth. To make it worse, Madame von Schillar insisted upon being terribly roguish at breakfast.

"Well!" she declared, nodding with mandarin sagacity, arching her brows and sucking at her cheeks. "Well, have you a statement for the press?"

"About what?"

"You know," the Baroness persisted, with a sly wink.

"It was nothing."

"Nothing! Listen to the girl!" cried the Baroness, to no one in particular. "That extraordinary entrance last night, dripping with water and romance, nothing? Like a movie queen, my dear, that theatrical!"

Elizabeth glanced down at her hands. "I can't imagine what got into me," she said. "Foolishness. It won't happen again, I promise."

She worked quietly all day; yet when twilight came and the lamps in the street dimmed up in the mist, Elizabeth found herself glancing again and again out the window, toward the little park across the street. Abruptly, she arose from her desk and left the house.

Twice, she walked around the park, and then, self-consciously, entered by the gate and sat down on the bench beneath the dark elm. As the shadows deepened, enfolding her in twilight, her restlessness eased away.

And after a while, he came to her.

CHAPTER 5

Extracts from Elizabeth's notebook:

It happened again today. I cannot call it hallucination, yet it had power beyond any daydream. Never have I imagined anything so vividly. Some details were so clear, so lifelike, that even now I marvel they occurred only in my mind. I want to note down, while still fresh, the qualities of Wrenn as I pictured them, for they might be useful in the book.

Elizabeth Carver was waiting in the park—No, I'll say, rather, that I was waiting in the park, since I was putting myself in her place and trying to see it through her eyes. I was waiting uneasily, and it was twilight. At last I heard his footsteps. He takes full strides, as if knowing exactly where he is going; and neither too fast nor too slow, apparently having no intention of being early or late. He wore a most outlandishly battered boating cap, and when I laughed at it, he seemed utterly amazed to find it still on his head. There was crimson paint under his fingernails, and his hands smelled of turpentine. I pronounced him Bohemian and asked if the artist's life was as wicked as reputed to be. He replied (so seriously, it near broke my heart) that he only knew from hearsay, as he was too busy painting to be an artist.

I cannot tell what was the matter with me today. I do not fancy myself as being without experience or poise, yet I could not have behaved more like some chambermaid with her first swain. My brow was moist. I could not meet his eyes. I was afraid he wouldn't talk, and I was afraid to say anything myself—so I chattered interminably. Whatever came into my head found immediate expression.

"You profess to be an artist," I said, at one point, "and you claim to have some background in the classics, and yet you haven't noticed what I've done with my hair. It's in the Grecian style—"

On and on I prattled at a fearsome clip. I knew it bewildered or bored him, yet I dared not stop, lest he grab that opportunity to excuse himself and escape. This humiliating prospect of being abandoned grew larger in my mind as my breath grew shorter. At last, nearing nervous exhaustion, I stood up and, before he could speak, cried fiercely, "Good evening, Mr Wrenn," and started off down the path.

He came hurrying after me, and I walked faster. Then, he stepped in front of me, blocking my way. "What is it, Mrs Carver?" he asked, his stutter once again evident. "What's the matter?"

"Please to let me pass!" I cried.

He released my arm and stepped aside. "I'm dull company, I know, but I thought everyone was forewarned of that—"

"Oh, damn! Damn!" I cried. "It isn't you, at all. It's that I've been babbling like an idiot, and I hate it, and so do you, and I can't help it . . ."

He smiled—no, he grinned, and it made his sombre face like a schoolboy's. "Mrs Carver," he said, "maybe we can learn from each other. Because I get silent when I'm ill at ease, just as you become a chatterbox. Together, we might make for moderation."

I sat down again. Now, however, I could think of nothing to say. "I've run dry," I said, a little feebly.

He laughed. "Then we're lost."

I made the mistake of glancing up at him, and our eyes met—so strange a sensation. A tingling shot up my spine like the ascent of a sky rocket and burst a spray of sparks at the roots of my hair. Perhaps I blushed, although it's scarcely my habit, for he looked away suddenly, and his smile was gone.

"It's getting late," he mumbled.

"I know."

"I've still got work to do."

"Of course." I arose. "And for all my talking, I've said not one word I intended." Lest he misinterpret this as some sort of romantic confession, I quickly added, "About the portrait, I mean."

"Ah, yes." He fingered his battered cap. "I'm afraid that will be impossible, anyway—doing your portrait. I don't have much free time . . ."

"Of course." I cannot tell why I felt so relieved.

"You understand, I'm sure."

"Yes, indeed."

There was nothing more to be said, and yet we lingered, both of us, I suspect, waiting for the other to speak again. Then we both did, simultaneously.

"It's been very pleasant—" he said.

"It's been so nice—" I said.

We laughed, but it had a strained sound. "It's not likely," I added, "that we'll meet again—"

"No. Not likely."

"Although I always stroll here around five, every afternoon . . ."

"I'm always at work then."

"Yes. Of course."

He fumbled his cap, preparatory to clapping it on and departing. I could not resist a little trickery to detain him. "The Senator warned me it would turn out this way."

"What way?"

"That you wouldn't care to do my portrait."

"You've discussed me with your husband?" he asked, in surprise.

"Naturally. I discuss everything with him." A gross lie, but it seemed to relieve Mr Wrenn. "He warned me that you were very serious-minded and hated flighty people." As an additional goad, I continued, "He said you were very short on humor—"

"Perhaps," he said, gently. "Although my painting has caused a good deal of laughter."

"Banter!" I cried. "You're bantering!"

Then we were both laughing; laughing immoderately, a humorless release from tension.

"I must go," I said, at last. "This time, I really must. But you may walk me to the gate."

He did so. We paused there a moment more.

"You're wrong about one thing, however," he said.

"What?"

"It isn't in the Grecian style."

"What isn't?"

"Your hair."

"It's a Psyche knot," I cried.

"But not quite Grecian. I'd like it simpler."

I flung him a glance over my shoulder as I started away. "Then I'll wear it simpler tomorrow afternoon, see if I don't."

He did not answer, not even with a smile, to assure me he would be in the park tomorrow. Well, for all that, I'm not certain that I'll return either!

Just to see if I could repeat my feat of imagery today, I returned to the park at sundown. It was very simple. I just visualized myself as looking like Sargent's portrait of Elizabeth Carver—and suddenly, I felt beautiful, commanding. I even knew how I was dressed: a fitted green suit, a Merry Widow hat; as for my hair—well, I was really very clever. I had it knotted simply at the nape, *à Cléo de Merode.* Upon the knot, I pinned a little silver butterfly, which was too much of a muchness, but I hoped he would object to it, whereupon I would obediently remove it and so flatter his taste. I loathe using such trickery on so simple and honest a man. I would much rather be myself; but, *hélas,* a woman dare not be too frank with a man. She must advance while seeming to stand still.

In order to have something interesting to discuss—and so make up for yesterday's inanity—I brought along Kitty's copy of Dante's *Inferno.* To pass the time until he came, I studied the First Canto; but at last, the shadows in the park became so dense, I couldn't see the page. He was late, I told myself, but a sinking sensation within warned me that it was foolish to expect him at all. He had made no promise to meet me. I was about to give up and go, when he appeared through the darkness.

I nearly cried aloud with relief at seeing him—that dark, strangely antique beauty of his head. (His profile is a perfect counterfeit of the face on a Roman coin.) Determined, however, not to run amok as I did yesterday, I only smiled and indicated for him to sit down.

"You shouldn't have waited." He spoke rather roughly.

"I wasn't really waiting. Just enjoying the twilight."

He sat down uncomfortably, at last blurting, "I hadn't planned to come here, at all."

"Then you shouldn't have. I'd have understood. I know your work comes first—but I'm very grateful that you gave me precedence today."

He tapped his pipe against his shoe. "I didn't work today."

"How so?"

"I went down to the shore."

"At this time of year?"

"At any time of year."

"What did you do there? Sketch?"

"Walked. Looked."

"Alone?"

"Naturally."

"And then you got lonely, is that it?"

"By the sea? Of course not!"

"Why did you come here, then?"

He shrugged. "I was afraid you were expecting me."

I had to laugh. "Mr Wrenn," I cried, "you manage to be gracious in a way that would bring tears to a gentler woman's eyes."

(As if by tacit understanding, when I look at him, he looks elsewhere; and when he glances at me, I lower my eyes—it is a kind of visual teeter-totter.)

We were silent, and at last, he asked, still a little roughly, "What are you reading?"

"Your friend," I replied. "Not that I read much, any more. But you were so late, I even started to memorize the opening Canto." I handed him the book. "Will you prompt me?"

"If you want."

> " 'Midway upon the journey of our life
> I found myself within a forest dark
> For the straight forward pathway had been lost—' "

As I recited on, I became aware that while his eyes remained fixed on the book his thoughts were elsewhere. To prove this, I made a conscious error in recitation, and he did not correct me. I became silent.

Presently he looked up. "You recite very badly," he said.

"How would you know?" I laughed. "You weren't even listening to me."

"Wasn't I? Perhaps not."

"You were off woolgathering?" He nodded. "I'll buy that wool for a penny."

He didn't answer for a long time, and when he did, the stutter attacked his speech. "I was remembering how—when I was little—my grandfather used to read the *Inferno* aloud. Sometimes in Italian, sometimes translating . . ."

His voice drifted off, and finally I prompted, "Go on."

He shook his head. "It's not important. Besides, I've put all that away."

"Why?"

"You can't sail ahead when you're dragging anchor."

"What do you mean?"

"I know where I want to go, but—sometimes, when the going's rough, if you look back—you're almost tempted to cash in your hopes and go back. At any cost, go back—"

"And would the cost be so much?"

He studied his hands and, at last, nodded. "My people loved me very much, and I loved them, but—I always had the feeling I was—failing them. Somehow or other, I was a disappointment to them. When I tried to be the person they wanted, it was the same as telling them a lie. But when I was myself, doing what I had to do, I was made to feel profane and dishonest. I wanted to please them because I loved them, but—finally, it meant submitting entirely to their way, or striking out for what I believed in. So I left home, cut myself adrift—"

"And it's been worth it? Standing alone?"

"I keep too busy to notice."

"Notice what?"

"The vacancies. The little vacancies that—twinge and ache, like Captain Ahab's missing leg."

"I know," I whispered. "I know."

"How could you know?"

"Because I have the same problem."

His voice was gruff with disbelief. "You?"

I lost my temper. "All right, then," I cried, getting up. "Loneliness is your private property, and I won't trespass on it further—"

He grinned. "Fire, fire," he said, holding his hands before me, as if to warm them. I had to laugh. When I sat down again, he continued. "It's just that it's hard to believe you're not perfectly content with your life, just as it is."

"Being part of the tea service? Oh, it's exciting," I said. "Tremendously satisfying. Every day, new hazards to pit myself against. I go on thrilling adventures—shopping. I explore wild territories—museums. I subdue savages—guests from New York. I grapple with high finance—my budget. I am the power behind the menu and rule my garden with an iron trowel. As you can see, it's a full life to gladden and satisfy—nay—intoxicate any woman."

"What is it you want then?"

The answer dinned against my heart so rebelliously, I was almost afraid he could hear it: that like himself, I wanted to love and be loved, to cherish and be cherished. That was the vacancy that made my busiest hour empty.

I could feel his dark eyes searching my face, but I dared not look up, and, in my confusion, could think of no alternate answer to give him. The tension of the unspoken between us tightened until I thought I should scream. Mercifully, the town clock struck six then, echoing over the park, and he leaped up as if caught in some crime.

"Getting late," he said.

I arose and thanked him for coming to see me. He did not answer, but his lips tightened. I wanted to cry out, Oh, come again, tomorrow! but I did not. Just smiled and offered him my hand. As he took it, there was once again that curious shock, as if I'd touched an electric current. I left him, not looking back; but when I came to the front steps of my house, I suddenly pounded my fist upon the iron newel post. The time with him had passed so quickly, and the words I longed to speak were still within me.

All day today, I kept thinking of things to tell Marius. Could scarcely wait for twilight. I didn't even bother to powder my face. He seldom notices how I look. And yet, I had begun to feel as if, somehow, he had noticed *me*.

But perhaps not; for he did not appear today. I waited in the park for an hour. Even after returning home, I didn't really give up hope. While dressing for dinner, I kept glancing out the window toward the park to see if, perhaps, he had come after all. Once, the Senator asked me what I found so interesting outside, and I answered, very quickly, that the sunset was lovely (which was absurd, as it was already dark).

I try not to be uneasy. I'm sure no accident had befallen him, although every thought presses this suggestion. Probably he got so busy with his paints, he forgot everything else. Maybe, he suddenly realized how late it was, and . . .

Well, I was going to say that maybe he had hurried to the park anyway and was waiting for me now; but I looked out the window again, and our bench is empty in the moonlight.

He was not there again today, although I went to our bench an hour early and stayed so long I was late to dinner. I wrote him a little note; didn't send it. To be so forward might frighten him away forever. Besides, I have no claim on him. He has made it quite pointed that he has no time for friends, much less for idle women. Of course, it makes no great difference to me whether he comes or not. He is certainly gauche and difficult to talk to. Actually, it is only because I'm bored that I spent any time on him in the first place.

Later: In my heart of hearts, I know this is all for the best. He will not come back again. Ours could never be a real friendship. We have nothing in common, except possibly our rebellion and our loneliness. Yet I think of his face, of the way his eyes look into mine, of the strength of his fingers when we shake hands, of the way his hair tumbles over his brow—Well, I shall think of this no more.

Midnight: I have decided that, under no circumstances, will I meet Mr Wrenn again, even should I see him waiting in the park. It could only lead to something sordid. I think I have felt that threat from the moment we met, and perhaps that is what made me afraid of him. I can live with boredom. I will not live with fear.

My will has been likened to tempered steel (hot tempered, Father would always add) and my decrees are notoriously final. Today was the test of it. I coolly resisted every thought of Marius all morning, and even accepted an invitation to tea in the late afternoon. Yet when five o'clock came, my famous will collapsed. Even while talking to poor Major N., I kept wondering if Marius would appear today and how he would feel if I failed him. Right in the middle of a sentence, I excused myself and hastened homeward.

And how glad I am that I yielded to this urgency. For when I came into the park, Marius was waiting. I had to restrain myself from running to him. Yet it was very casual.

"I'm glad you came," I said. "I've missed our daily chats."

Without reply, he lit his pipe. Other men beg a lady's permission to smoke. He is, as always, independent. We paced up and down, he on his side of the path, I on mine, nothing linking us, neither hands nor glances. Then, once, as we passed our bench, I saw, stowed away behind the elm, his blue duffel bag. I could not help it, I stood rigid and my mouth was dry. Somehow I contrived a safe voice. "You're making a trip somewhere, Mr Wrenn?"

"No."

"Do you always take your luggage when you call on a lady?"

"I'm just returning from a trip."

"That sounds pleasant," I said. "Did you go far?"

He shook his head. "I jumped boat in New York."

"I don't know what 'jump boat' means."

"I'd signed aboard a freighter," he mumbled.

He volunteered no other explanation then, neither why he had run away nor so suddenly returned. My heart supplied me the reason, however; and that the same torment is in his heart, he soon verified.

It was when he got to discussing the clarity he worships in color.

"It must be pure," he said, intensely. "Not muddy or adulterated . . ."

This last word barely escaped his lips. He stopped on a syllable and quickly tried to substitute some other word, but his tongue seemed paralyzed.

I changed the subject at once, though I cannot swear to what sense I made, for this word disturbs me too. A hundred times a day, it slips by the guard of my mind, sometimes in the form of accusation, sometimes as longing. I confront it with all kinds of excuses—that I do no wrong in just seeing Wrenn, that I will not be ruled by other people's morality, that love needs no excuse . . .

Here, Elizabeth lowered her pen and frowned. That was true. Love needed no justification; but deception did. Yet how was she to justify it?

She brought this problem to Madame von Schillar. The Baroness looked at her in astonishment. "Justify myself? What do you mean?"

"I mean—weren't you troubled about betraying the Senator?"

"Troubled?" She laughed. "Mercy, no. I don't think I gave him a second thought."

"Oh, I can't believe that," Elizabeth cried.

"And why not, pray?"

"It makes you sound so—cold-blooded."

"Are you planning to lecture me about my past, dear?"

"No. I'm only trying to understand."

The Baroness patted her cheek. "Well, don't bother your head about this. It's not important."

"But couldn't you tell me anyway?"

"Why bother? I'm not going to include it in the book. . . ."

As Madame von Schillar would not explain her attitude, Elizabeth had no way of understanding it. Yet until she could understand and duplicate it in her own heart, the affair with Wrenn could not reach the culmination she so longed for.

CHAPTER 6

"I can't understand what's gotten into you!" Baroness von Schillar lent a charming indolence to her criticism: the words edged, but the smile lazy. "You've been strange as can be these last few weeks. Maybe you ought to see a doctor—"

"About what?"

"You know very well," the Baroness teased. "All this fidgeting and darting out for air, disrupting our work in midafternoon."

"Maybe it's just spring fever," Elizabeth laughed.

"Spring poppycock! There's snow on the ground, and you'll catch your death skipping around in it."

"I never notice the cold," Elizabeth replied. "As for stopping my work in midafternoon, I never leave until five, and as it is, we scarcely ever work at all, past four. I can't do anything unless you give me the facts."

Madame von Schillar laughed. "Oh, go take your walk!" As

Elizabeth left, however, she called out with sudden testiness, "But don't think you're getting out of anything. We'll have to work tonight and make up for it."

"I'll be ready if you will," Elizabeth said, and closed the double doors. She hastened down the hall to the hatrack, slipped on her coat and tugged on her galoshes. Already, her thoughts had lifted in anticipation of meeting Wrenn.

"Only, from now on, we've got to be careful," she thought. "If going out every day at the same time is beginning to look suspicious, we'll have to be careful." She hastened down the front steps toward the park. "Maybe I'd better ask Marius if he could meet me after dinner, from now on . . ." Night would be better for all concerned. Then her absence would be less likely noticed, since the Senator always dozed at his desk after dinner.

"Dozing, always dozing," she added, maliciously, trying to infect herself with Madame von Schillar's attitude. "Well, I won't give him a second thought." Yet the attempt was a failure. Not knowing the cause for Madame von Schillar's seeming remorselessness, she could not produce the effect with any authority.

So deeply absorbed was she in these thoughts that it was some moments before she realized a tall, freckled woman was walking alongside her, plaintively repeating, "Miss? Miss? Please?" For just a fraction of an instant, Elizabeth could not distinguish if this were part of her imagination or reality.

The woman, mistaking the confusion in her face, quickly identified herself. "It's all right, Miss. We met before. I'm Faith, Miss Carver's housekeeper. Remember, you come to ask Miss Sarah questions, and I couldn't let you in—"

Elizabeth nodded, impatiently. "Yes, yes, of course—"

"Miss Carver would like to see you now."

"I'm afraid I couldn't go way up there now. I'm late for my appointment as it is—"

"But we're right here." Faith indicated a long black car which was slowly cruising alongside them in the street. "Miss Carver never goes out, but she thought this was important enough to rent a car and come see you. We've been waiting here most all afternoon in hopes you'd come out . . ."

The automobile stopped and the door swung open. "Come in," cried a voice. "Come in, please."

"Please, Miss," Faith urged. "It's cold, and she mustn't keep that door open . . ."

Elizabeth glanced longingly at the park and then climbed into the car. It started forward, leaving the housekeeper standing on the sidewalk.

"Wait," Elizabeth called to the driver.

"It's quite all right," said the woman in the car. "Faith is following orders. I wished to speak to you alone." Her voice sank. "Kindly close the glass partition. I don't care to have the driver overhear." When Elizabeth had obeyed, she continued, "I suppose it is not necessary to introduce myself. You have been informed?"

"You're Miss Sarah Carver."

The woman nodded. "And I hope you will forgive my approaching you in this unusual manner. You must not think it is without purpose."

Such a thought could never have occurred to Elizabeth. Everything about Miss Carver bespoke purpose. Her clothes were well-made, but without style, in order to withstand the transience of fashion. Her hat was distinguished by being, first and last, something to protect the head from rain and the eyes from sun. Her shoes were practical, cobbled for service, and the cane she clutched was of oak, stout enough to withstand eternity, which seemed the woman's purpose as well. In any other city, she might have been mistaken for an impoverished school teacher. Such an illusion, however, could never have outlasted her first syllable. She spoke with authority, as if fear, poverty, or opposition had never been explained to her.

"I very much regret having been indisposed when you called

before," she said. "Since then, I have received a letter from a Miss Edith Harper, with whom I was once acquainted, saying that a book was being written which might concern my brother. Am I correct in assuming that you came to me for information about him?"

"Yes, partly."

"Very good. I will see that you are supplied with his history."

Her highhanded manner irritated Elizabeth. "I don't think I'll need it now," she said. "At this point, I'm only interested in how he concerned his wife and Mr Wrenn."

Miss Carver's arrogance fell away in the struggle to keep from betraying fear. "Is my brother to be sacrificed to them?"

"No, indeed," Elizabeth said. "I've been very careful to include his point of view."

"But how could you know it, unless I tell you?"

"Why, from what Madame von Schillar tells me."

Miss Carver dismissed this with a wave of her hand. "I'm afraid she is in no position to give you a correct summation of my brother."

"She was his wife."

"A title she repudiated. Which, I might add, she would never have done had she understood him." She clasped her hands. "Of course, it would be useless for me to talk to her about this matter—I found it difficult enough even to wait outside her house—but I must know what is being said about Theo in this book. He is gone, you see, and only I can protect him now. So I am trusting you will oblige by telling me."

"I can't be of any help," Elizabeth said. "My work is, naturally, confidential."

The woman permitted herself a smile. "I understand," she said. "I expected as much. So I came prepared." She opened her purse.

"Do you wish me to leave this car, at once?" Elizabeth cried.

Miss Carver faltered, then drew from her purse a box of comfits and, selecting one, placed it in her mouth. "I think you misunderstand me, my dear. I can see you are a young woman of an integrity rare in these days. It is on that which I am placing my hope." She snapped shut her comfit box and stowed it in her purse. "May I ask that you hear his side of the story? Then you won't be persuaded to dye him black or tolerate suggestions which might give the public wrong ideas."

Elizabeth nodded. "I always try to be fair. But I must remind you that the final word is Madame von Schillar's."

The woman gave no impression of having heard, already too intent upon her own thoughts. She leaned forward and her voice sank under the weight of confidence.

"You see, we Carvers have always been responsible people. We've had to be. You can imagine the consecration of time and thought necessary to protect such a fortune. First things first, my father always said. I am—not unaware of the sacrifices this involves. I suppose I missed many good things in life, but—I don't think of that, any more . . ."

Only this once did she falter. Thereafter she spoke without variation of tone, as if quoting from memory the case she had, for decades, argued in the solitary court of her mind. "From childhood, we were drilled in our responsibility. We were raised to be vigilant. May I give you an example? Possibly you can use it in your book. One autumn, when Theo was very young—" Her face softened. "He was such a handsome, earnest child—Father took him down to the cellar and pointed to a pile of apples on the floor. 'These are for you,' he said. 'You may have one for dessert each meal, and they must last you until Christmas. Now what are you going to do with them, first?' Well, Theo packed them all in a barrel and rolled it into a cool corner. Father didn't say anything, just nodded.

"Then one day, he noticed that Theo was not having his usual apple after lunch, and he questioned him about it. Theo, always truthful, told him that all the apples remaining in the barrel had rotted. Father became very stern and made him bring one upstairs. Then he said, 'Bite into it, sir!' It was a hideous pulp, but Father had to be obeyed, so Theo took a bite of the apple. 'Hold it in your mouth and savor all its rottenness,' my father said, 'because I do not want you to forget this.'

"My poor brother was nearly ill before Father let him spit it out. 'You see, Theo,' he said, 'you weren't careful about what you put in your barrel. Your supply became corrupted because you included one apple that was rotten. So, it's lucky you aren't forced to live on apples alone, or you'd starve.' And he said that Theo had to learn this —whether it was apples or investments or governments, the whole must never be at the mercy of the parts. Unless the rotten element was detected and removed, all was jeopardized and we would suffer.

"Well, you might say that this very thing has been the occupation of the last four generations of Carvers—to protect what we have against the rotten element—foreigners, anarchists, and their ilk. My brother's resolve to protect and conserve—for all America as well as himself—took him to the Senate. He had a splendid mind. He felt deeply, passionately, whatever he did. There was nothing he couldn't have done. . . .

"I can say this, because I knew him better than anyone else did. It was as if his mind were our joint possession, his destiny part of my heritage. I even learned to work a typewriting machine to be of use to him. And I was of use! His famous speech in nineteen hundred and nine—the 'chaff and wheat' speech against immigration—I helped him write it. His speeches were often the product of my endeavor. Why do you think I did this? For his gratitude or my own glory? No. It was for our ideal.

"Do you see this picture? Responsible people working for a better and safer country. Then you can imagine how it was when my brother married this Winslow girl. Her family had wealth, of course, but only since 1870, so the family was not able to instill in her the same sense of responsibilty as we had. She was a madcap with a mind as light as her powder puff. (She calcimined! Everyone knew that!) But she took a whim to play with these serious matters—wanted to advise Theo and be consulted in his problems and be given responsibilities. I know, for Theo asked me if he should. Well, I had to smile! I said not a word, of course, but Theo understood. And how right he was to refuse her. Because if this woman couldn't even make a success of her marriage, how could she ever have been entrusted with duties of national importance? As I say, the whole marriage was a mistake from the beginning. She was utterly unworthy of my brother, mentally, socially, and morally—"

"Please!" Elizabeth protested. "I really cannot—"

"Of course, of course," Miss Carver placated. "Please don't think I disliked Elizabeth personally. She was not only very beautiful, but she had become part of our name. Believe me, I tried to protect her when the town began to gossip. I wrote a little note—unsigned, of course, as I didn't want to be implicated—warning this Wrenn that their secret was out. It did no good. I even tried to reason with my brother when he decided to carry things to court. I told him. 'Theo, whatever the woman did, remember your position. She's not worth jeopardizing that for.' But he answered me, 'Sarah, if I keep her, I will jeopardize everything I possess—my name, my position, my integrity and my principles.' And I remembered the lesson he had learned at the apple barrel, and I knew he could do nothing but rid himself of her, whatever the cost to him."

She knotted her fists until the seams of her gloves strained. "I thought once he was free of her that he and I could resume our old way of life and work undisturbed, but—" She spoke with effort now. "They'd amended the Constitution about that time. Members of the Senate were no longer elected by the state legislature, but by public vote. Theo had always tried to protect the people, but now they turned against him for no crime but that of protecting himself." She stamped her cane on the car floor. "Oh, when I think how his future was ruined—and America left defenseless against infiltration and rottenness—just because of this woman, whose flagrant immorality was in itself a negation of the responsibility of womanhood—"

"I have told you," Elizabeth interrupted, curtly, "that I will not listen to any abuse of her—"

"Abuse? It's the truth. She was totally unscrupulous. A cold woman, incapable of loving anything but herself . . ."

This was the one accusation Elizabeth had wanted most not to hear. Indignantly, she rapped against the glass partition. "Driver! Please let me out right here."

Miss Carver placed a restraining hand on the girl's shoulder, then withdrew it quickly, as though contaminated by the contact. "Young woman," she said, "please do me the courtesy of hearing me out."

"I'm sorry," Elizabeth replied, stiffly. She opened the door. "I could no more accept an attack like that on Elizabeth Winslow than I could on myself—"

"Apparently, I have not made clear just what she did, or you mightn't care to defend her—"

"She doesn't need to be defended," Elizabeth insisted.

"Then she's corrupted you," lashed Miss Carver, "just as she corrupted everything she ever touched. She's destroyed you just as she destroyed everyone who ever gave her loyalty—"

Elizabeth slammed shut the door and hurried away. She could hear Miss Carver rapping the car window with her cane, but she did not turn back.

As she passed the park, she hesitated, then entered and sat down on the bench. For a time, she scarcely moved, her eyes clenched shut. She could not relax enough to receive Wrenn, however. Her mind still echoed with Miss Carver's angry accusations.

"Oh, you made a great many things clear," she countered, silently. "You weren't dealing with a woman, were you? No. Just another Carver possession. An investment, a chattel. You couldn't bear to think she'd ever have any hold on your brother, could you? Couldn't bear to think she could have authority as well as beauty . . ." Even now, Elizabeth's face was flushed, her dark eyes gleaming with indignation. "Well, I don't blame her for what she did.

I'd have broken free of that family vault, too. I'd have run away with a man who could give me love and the responsibility of sharing his struggle—"

This protest, however, did nothing to silence those other words: ". . . a cold woman, incapable of loving anything but herself . . ."

Elizabeth tightened her jaw. "I won't think of it, any more," she promised. "It isn't true—just that damn Carver woman judging everyone by herself."

She pressed her hands to her ears and closed her eyes again. It was no use. She could not become Elizabeth Carver while doubt still existed. Sighing, she arose and went back into the great house.

The two women sat at the dinner table, dallying over their coffee. Candlelight lent the scene a serenity entirely independent of their moods. Occasionally Madame von Schillar flicked a trouble glance at the girl. Clearly, something was disturbing Elizabeth. Her eyes were somber, her brows drawn. She had scarcely spoken all evening. It was precisely this which unnerved the Baroness. Silence portended that some major question was forming in the girl's mind. Yet if she feared the silence, Madame von Schillar feared more the moment when Elizabeth would speak, demanding some answer to her question.

Elizabeth took a breath and moistened her lips. Quickly, Madame von Schillar lugged Jabot onto her lap.

"Oh, is her a big dog?" she cooed. "Yes, her is. Big dog! Big black dog! Yes, that's what her is—big, black dog!"

Jabot passed a loose pink tongue over her hand. Involuntarily, Madame von Schillar's nostrils pinched with distaste, and she shoved the animal to the floor. A moment later, she reached down penitently to pat the dog's head, but Jabot had already slunk away.

"Come back," she ordered. "Come right back, d'you hear!"

Her command, harsh enough to rouse Elizabeth from her reverie, caused the dog to flatten in terror on its belly and wet. The Baroness sighed. Stretching forth her hand, she snapped her fingers gently. "Come back," she purred. "Black dog! Yes! She's coming back, isn't she? Yes, that's what she wants to do: come back and make up." She poured some cream into her saucer and placed it on the floor. When the spaniel crept close to investigate, she tenderly lifted it up into her arms.

Elizabeth watched curiously, although it was not the first time she had witnessed this mock crisis. It always seemed some kind of game in which personal issues were at stake. Madame von Schillar's attitude toward the dog was a strange fusion of bullying and devotion. Her distaste for Jabot's decrepitude was evident, yet she became uneasy whenever the dog was for long out of her sight. She petted it lavishly, fed it from her own plate, but shouted abuse if the animal licked her hand, and scolded if it did not immediately respond to her pampering.

Was it, Elizabeth wondered suddenly, symptomatic of what Miss Carver had insisted: that the Baroness was basically cold, wanting to be wanted, but not to be touched. All evening, echoes of this accusation had nagged her.

"Why are you staring at me that way?" the Baroness asked, laughing uncomfortably.

Startled, Elizabeth mumbled, "I—was wondering how long you'd had Jabot."

"I don't know. Eleven years. Twelve. A birthday present from Flix—the Baron, y'know. He won her in a card game." She wrapped one of the dog's ringlets around her finger. "Of course, I ought to have her put out of the way now. She's old and weak and unreliable." She said this in an injured tone, as if the dog had delibertately chosen to become old to annoy her.

"But you're really very fond of her, aren't you?" Elizabeth's voice had a hopeful note.

"I don't know," the Baroness murmured. "I can't really persuade myself that I'm mad for animals."

"But dogs are different," Elizabeth insisted. "They can be such friends. When I was little, my father had a Great Dane, and—"

"Horrors!" Madame von Schillar laughed. "Monsters with lap dog delusions. They want to pet you, instead of you petting them." She shuddered. "I hate great beasts that leap on you with their dirty paws, all slobbering with affection—"

Elizabeth studied the Baroness with anxious eyes. When at last she spoke, the tone was deliberate. "I met Miss Carver today!"

Madame von Schillar glanced up sharply. "What?"

"I met Miss Carver today."

"Where?"

"She was waiting outside. She'd heard you were doing the book."

Madame von Schillar's green eyes blazed. "What did she tell you? Damn, I thought you said you were loyal to me, and here you go listening to every crank who comes along—"

"I didn't listen long," Elizabeth replied, quietly. "The moment she started slandering, I left."

"Tell me what she said," the Baroness demanded. "Tell me exactly what she said, every last word!"

Elizabeth met her eyes. "She said you were a cold woman, incapable of loving anyone but yourself!"

The Baroness sat up, stiffly. Abruptly, she slapped the table. "How dare she judge me! Dried up old maid! Well, it's absurd, and I don't even have to discuss it."

She arose restlessly and, after a moment, cried, "How could she ever understand a woman like me? Men never gave her any trouble. But me—even from the time I was a child. Listen . . ." She dipped into a chair beside Elizabeth and seized the girl's hand. "Once when I was only twelve, I was standing with my governess in the foyer of the opera house. It was crowded, and a man—touched me. I was frightened; didn't have any explanation for a thing like that. Later, when I asked my mother about it, I think she was more distressed about my mentioning it than about the man putting his hand against me. She never answered my question until I was twenty, and by that time—believe me—I had discovered the motives of men. Naturally, I developed a certain cold attitude. I needed that protection against them. But inside, I was just like any other young girl, wanting to love and be loved.

"Well, I was sure the Senator was different. To me, he represented everything solid and high-minded and strong, the way Father was. Well, he wasn't! I don't have to go into any details about my wedding night, but he was like an insane beast. Later, he always tried to explain by saying he'd loved me so much, he'd kind of gone out of his head. But by that time, I hated him. And he didn't give me anything to do to take my mind off hating him. I could have been a great help in his career—that's one of the reasons I'd married him—but all he wanted was a concubine. God!" She arose and poured herself a generous glass from the decanter deceptively labeled sherry.

"I used to lie awake nights hating him, afraid his body might touch mine in his sleep. I'd plan ways I could humiliate him as he'd humiliated me." She was superb in her fury. The flash of the marvelous green eyes, the color that rushed to her cheeks, momentarily restored youth to her beauty. "I was glad when I got with child, so he'd leave me alone. And when the baby died, I went into mourning for a year as an excuse not to lie with him. And that time in Washington when he was sick—hear this!—I used to sit by his bed and pray he'd die. Die and leave me free. I was trapped, don't you see? I was still young, and I was beautiful, but my whole life seemed to be over . . ."

She seemed about to cry, but instead forced a short, metallic laugh. "The books you read, the songs you hear—I used to wonder, where's the kind of love they tell about? All I knew was husky breathing and ugly, moist lips—I had to find out if there was more to love than that. I *had to find out*—" She turned on Elizabeth. "Do you understand? Do you think I enjoy talking about it? But you've got to understand!" Then she waved a limp hand at the girl and laughed again. "Oh, tosh! I don't care whether you understand or not."

"But I do understand," Elizabeth said, quietly.

"Oh yes, yes," the Baroness mocked. "You understand. You've been ravished hundreds of times by a man you despised, so you know." She downed her drink, then inspected the glass. "Well, I was cold with Theo, so Sarah told you the truth. But it doesn't make any difference, because I'm not going to mention all this in my book. And yet—" She fixed her eyes on Elizabeth, and the bitterness passed from her voice—"And yet—oh, my dear, somehow, we've got to suggest what happened, so people won't condemn me for looking, searching everywhere, for the love I knew had to exist, the love I was entitled to. A gentle, quiet man, who—"

She fumbled for a phrase, and Elizabeth prompted, "—who saw more in you than just the beauty of your face."

"Perhaps."

"And you recognized him as being that man, the moment you met?"

"The moment."

"He was kind and gentle, wasn't he?"

"Wonderfully so."

"Yet all disguised behind a roughness—"

"Roughness?"

"I mean, he was blunt, abrupt. He didn't care what people thought—"

The Baroness frowned. "Who?"

"Mr Wrenn."

"Oh! Yes, I guess so."

"Almost indifferent, at first, wasn't he?" The Baroness nodded, and Elizabeth continued, softly, "Because he didn't want to love you, he was afraid to love you."

"I expect that's how it was."

"But when did you know for sure? That he loved you?"

"I don't remember. It must have been just before he started my portrait. Anyway, a month or so after we began meeting."

"And you kissed?"

"Yes," the Baroness said, a little impatiently.

"For the first time?"

"I suppose it was."

"What were you wearing?"

"What difference does it make?" cried Madame von Schillar. "It was raining, and I probably looked a sight." Then, seeing the girl was preparing to ask yet another question, she cried, "No, that's enough!" She left the table. "I'll have remembered a lot more by the time we've finished our chapter on the dear Senator . . ."

She did not leave the room, however, but lingered at the door. "The important thing," she added, anxiously, "is to make sure you're not still worried about what that fool Sarah said."

"No. I'm not worried. Not now."

"And you're sure she said nothing more?"

"She said lots more," said Elizabeth, "but what difference does it make? It was all part and parcel of the same thing. She hates you. She's still jealous of you." Then she smiled. "Still—I'm glad I met her."

"Why, for heaven's sake?"

"Because," Elizabeth answered, happily, "now that I know why you had to fall in love—and why you didn't have to justify yourself—why, there needn't be any more delay—"

"Delay?" The Baroness cocked her head. "How do you mean?"

The girl flushed. "In my work," she said, quickly.

Elizabeth hurried down the dark path. Wrenn was already waiting at the usual bench. She paused on some pretext to see if she were being followed, then sat down beside him. "Thank God, you're still here. I prayed you might be—"

"I had to come back," he said. "I was worried when you didn't show up this afternoon."

"I had to spend it with the Senator and Miss Sarah. And I don't have much time now. I said I was just going to run over to Kitty's, for a minute."

Thunder rumbled faintly, and, somewhere in the distance, someone was playing the same bars of Schumann over and over. At once restless and languorous, the two arose and began walking in silence. Words were no longer sufficient. It was the shared glance, the pressure of hands, which allowed them a higher communication.

At last, across the darkened park, above the blundering Schumann, they heard the church chimes salute the hour. Reminded once more of the transience of time, Elizabeth paused by the frozen fountain and gazed about, as if to suspend this moment in her mind forever. She realized, suddenly, that Marius was studying her face and, unflinchingly, she raised her eyes to his. Deep in her was a sensual yawning which only the strength of his arms could compress. They were standing close, but not yet touching. Her heart was hammering, yet she seemed to breathe not at all. She lifted her face, arched her back. Their hands touched, then locked together. Suddenly, he stepped away. Startled, she opened her eyes.

"Someone's passing," he said, in a harsh whisper.

They drew back deeper into the darkness, then waited breathlessly as the footsteps neared. Soon a figure, preceded by a long shadow, trudged by. Only when he was gone from sight and from sound did they release their hands. Her forehead was moist. She glanced up at him for reassurance, but his face was set, his expression, strained.

"Who did you think it was?" she whispered.

"I didn't know."

"The Senator?"

"It could have been."

"But it wasn't, so let's forget it."

"Yes."

They were standing close together again; but anticipation had changed to apprehension, and the moment was lost. She turned away with a sigh. Then, for fear silence would widen even farther the intangible breach between them, she bridged it with quick reassurance. "We mustn't be afraid . . ."

"It's no use," he said. "I am afraid. We're in the wrong—"

"No, we're not," she protested.

"Aren't we? Didn't you know that from the start? Isn't that why we meet here, rather than in your husband's house?"

"It isn't his house. It's mine."

"But he lives there."

Elizabeth tossed her head. "I don't care."

"We both care," he said.

"I'm not going to let it make any difference."

He smiled ruefully. "Oh, Elizabeth, Elizabeth—"

"It's not fair," she cried. "I see other couples holding hands right out in public, or even kissing, while we—not even this!"

The stutter, suddenly evident in his speech again, forced him to speak hesitantly. "I'll go away. Should have, long ago."

"No!"

"Why go on tormenting ourselves this way? All this guilt and stealth— You can't love and fear at the same time. Fear always wins out and kills—"

"Then we mustn't meet by stealth, any more. We must arrange to meet more in the open." She considered this, then added, quickly, "You could paint my portrait. There's a little room upstairs with a good light. You with your paints, me sitting for you. We could be together, and no one could question that."

He shook his head. "It would only be postponement. It'd only make it harder to say good-bye. And that's all the future can hold for us."

"I thought you were a rebel," she cried fiercely. "I thought you could dare and chance and fight!"

"It's not hard to fight when I see something wrong," he answered, slowly, "but when I know it's me who's wrong, I'm defenseless."

"Oh, you're so pure, so noble," she lashed. "You make me feel like some tart for even suggesting—" Then, wilting, she pressed her head against his shoulder. "I didn't mean that. Just I'm so on edge—"

"And we'd always be on edge, Elizabeth," he warned. "Don't you see that? And soon, we'd be blaming and resenting each other . . ."

She raised her head, and, looking into his eyes, knew his anguish was no less than her own. "Then is that the only way to keep what we have? To . . ."

Her voice wasted and, almost inaudibly, he supplied, "To say good-bye."

Rain began falling lightly, streaking their tense faces. Elizabeth touched his hand to let it say the farewell she could not articulate; and suddenly, magnetized by contact, they were in each other's arms. As their lips crushed together, thunder boomed above, a patriarchal reproach, but they did not heed it. The tormenting prickle of his cheek against her smooth skin made more delicious, by contrast, the hot pliancy of his mouth. So as to remember by pain, should the memory of rapture ever fade, she knotted her fist, sank the nails, like teeth, into her palm; but even this pain was ecstatic.

At last, she nestled her head against his neck and exhaled as if in weariness. "What happened to our renunciation?" she whispered.

He shook his head. "I love you," he said.

"And I . . ." She longed to spend the treasure of those words, but could not. Instead, she caught up his hand and pressed it over the tumult of her heart. Once more, he bent down, his lips on her brow, her chin, her eyes, the tip of his tongue tracing a gleaming line above her lashes; for which she quickly substituted her mouth.

Ignorant of the thunder's repeated warning, they clung together, and only when rain began to pelt them did they release each other.

"Run," he ordered, huskily; and they raced to the gate. He ducked aside into the shadows. "I'll wait here till you're gone."

"And tomorrow?"

"Yes. I'll come to you."

"But here? Must it be here?" Her eyes were pleading. "Not my house?"

His intense, warrior's face softened. "If you're not afraid, how can I be?"

"My house, then?"

He nodded. "We'll begin the portrait."

"Oh, my dearest—" She grasped his hand and, in her delight, did not make very good sense. "Hello, hello, my darling—"

He pressed her fingers to his cheek. "Until four o'clock, then?"

"Until the last hour of my life." She kissed him quickly on the lips, then hurried across the street.

When Elizabeth was in her room again, she took off her wet coat. It was nearly ten o'clock.

"But in eighteen hours," she calculated, "I can see him again."

Humming the little Schumann theme, she undressed and brushed her damp, dark hair. It would be in this room, she thought; this room that would become his studio. "And I'll sit by the window where the light is good. He'll stand over there . . ."

She slipped on her nightgown, then glanced back at the little clock on her desk. Already, it had seemed an eternity, but less than five minutes had passed. "And there are still eighteen hours, thousands of minutes, to wait," she thought.

Impatiently, she picked up the clock and turned forward the hands until they angled at four o'clock.

Blowing out the lamp, she lay down on the cot. She did not sleep, however. Her eyes were open in the moonlight, and sometimes she smiled, and sometimes her lips moved in silent speech. Eventually, she arose and lit the lamp again. The pen scratched as she wrote, but she did not notice.

"I thought four o'clock would never come; but when it did, I suddenly felt all unprepared. I was beautifully groomed, it is true, but he never notices that. The woman he does see, however, the woman within, was all unsettled, unsure, her emotions untidily gathered in, like a careless coiffure.

"Worth had already ushered him into the little room upstairs. I entered, careful to leave the door ajar. He was unpacking his portfolio, and when he saw me, his hand faltered. I said a few, foolish, meaningless words of welcome very loudly, lest someone be lurking in the corridor, and then whispered, 'My darling,' for his ears.

"Seeing he was still uneasy, I sat by the window and picked up the volume of Dante to read aloud until he was calm. Soon he sat down and began making preliminary sketches. As he worked, I read the beautiful lines about Paolo and Francesca reading together, pale, their anxious eyes meeting. How true, I kept thinking; these lovers so like ourselves. And when I came to the part where Francesca confesses, 'We read no more that day.' I put the book down.

He was watching me. He had drawn scarcely a line.

"When did you first know?" he asked, at last.

"I'm not sure. I think I knew when I first saw you. And you?"

He shook his head. "There was no one moment. It built like—a coral reef, one tiny cell upon another, until—it lifted out of the sea, a mountain—"

"And you steered onto it, wrecking yourself—"

"I wasn't going to say that," he protested.

"Well, it won't wreck us," I promised. "It'll only give us a foundation to build on. An island, all of our own."

He came over and kissed me. "I love you," he whispered.

"Why?"

"I don't know," he said. "Does anyone ever know why? It's only important to know that I do . . ."

Elizabeth wrote on. The room was silent except for the scratch of her pen, and the little clock innocently ticking away its falsified hour.

CHAPTER 7

The third week in February always found Madame von Schillar in low spirits, this ungraciously culminating on the twentieth day, when Worth reminded her with cake and candles that she was a year older.

"How old would you say I looked?" she asked Elizabeth, after dinner.

"I've never thought of it," said Elizabeth; and then, to counteract this lie, added truthfully, "Although, when you came in the door, that first day, I thought you were perhaps forty . . ."

With half-closed eyes, the Baroness studied a mirror. "I don't look too grim," she mused. "In Rome, I could still make a man look twice. Three times, if the light wasn't too good."

"I'm sure those who love you don't really know what you look like, anyway," Elizabeth comforted. "The closer you get to a person, the less perspective you have."

"May be some truth to that," the Baroness agreed. Then she laughed to herself. "Once, someone ask my Father what color poor Mother's eyes were, and he said he supposed they were brown. Well, they were green, just like mine. And, for all that, if anyone asked me the color of—well, Wrenn's eyes, for instance, I shouldn't have the faintest notion."

"They're almost black," said Elizabeth.

The Baroness fanned out her hands expressively. "That proves what I just said: the closer you get to a person, the less perspective." She moved nearer the girl, adding, intensely, "And that's why I've been so slow about giving out details of Marius. I knew him too well, I took too much for granted. I can't see the forest for the trees—"

"Like painting a portrait," Elizabeth suggested, eagerly. "Sometimes you love a person so much—the sweetness, the understanding, the fire and gentleness—the real person—that you forget the actual appearance. And that's why he could never catch the exact likeness of you—he saw too many people in you—"

The Baroness was watching her with that air of lazy mockery. "If you please, dear," she begged, "whatever might you be talking about?"

"The portrait. How Marius did it over and over again, and never could get it right. Remember?"

"Yes—but I don't recall mentioning it to you."

Elizabeth felt her face grow hot, realizing it was Bentley Sprague who had told her this. "Oh, but we discussed it," she insisted, feebly.

"Well, it doesn't matter. At all events, he never finished my picture."

"Why not?"

"People had begun to whisper about us."

"You sent him away?"

"I had no choice."

"But how could you?" Elizabeth cried. "It was only love that mattered. You told me so, yourself. What did you care what people said?"

"I didn't care! Well, maybe I did! Oh, I don't know. I couldn't think. I was afraid . . ." She looked away from Elizabeth. "I don't know. I just can't discuss that part now. It's still too painful—"

"But could I know how long you stayed apart?"

"I don't remember," said Madame von Schillar. "It seemed like a hundred years."

"And then?"

"When I couldn't stand it any more, I dropped him a note."

"He came back?"

"Yes."

"And then?"

Madame von Schillar uttered a little laugh which, being out of context of gaiety, had a frightened sound. "I'll have to think . . ." She arose and wandered restlessly around the room. When she turned back, the girl was waiting with that soft luminosity, which more than once in these past weeks had piqued Madame von Schillar's curiosity. "You know so much about me, and I know nothing of you," she said, suddenly. "Tell me about yourself."

"Myself?" Elizabeth spoke like one newly awakened. "It's not very interesting."

"How old are you? In your thirties?"

"Twenty-eight."

"You look rather older." Madame von Schillar glanced at her reflection in the pier glass, then turned away with a shrug. "But I wouldn't be twenty-eight again for anything," she said, sharply. "An ugly year."

"How do you mean?"

"That was when the Senator divorced me. Oh, and the newspapers just couldn't seem to let me alone. Needless to say, all my friends began cutting me dead. And all the filthy little people who were aching to besmirch their betters—I'd get anonymous letters calling me harlot, and worse. Once I received a lovely florist box, but in it was a dead cat—"

"But even so, you had Marius," Elizabeth said, exultantly. "You were free to marry him, after that."

Madame von Schillar examined her scarlet fingernails. "But we were talking of you," she said. "Where do you come from? Who are your people?" She was forced to repeat the question twice before Elizabeth answered.

"I was born in St. Louis," she said.

"Yes?" Sensing the girl's reticence, the Baroness leaned forward, prodding her on with attentiveness. "Go on, child. Turn about is only fair."

"My father was a broker," Elizabeth continued, clumsily. "We had a big house with a green mansard roof, and I used to play in the attic—play I was Rapunzel, or Joan of Arc, or my mother—"

"Why your mother, for mercy's sake?"

"I suppose because she was so beautiful. Everyone said so. She was like a princess—" She paused again.

"And?"

"She and my father were very much in love—not just loving companions, like most people who've been married for quite a while, but deeply in love, like two guilty people."

"And?"

Elizabeth fumbled as though she were repeating the story of a stranger. "My mother always dressed for him—beautifully, even if they were only dining alone, downstairs. She kept her hair long, even when it was unfashionable, because he liked it that way. She dressed it high, with little sparkling ornaments or pink roses. I used to think the nearest thing to heaven was to watch her get dressed for him . . .

"Well, when I was about fifteen, my father lost everything in speculation. That same year, he died. My—my mother wouldn't live without him. She took an overdose of sleeping tablets—"

"How sordid," the Baroness said. Then, more gently: "Not that elements in my own life haven't been."

"No," Elizabeth insisted, recklessly. "You gave up everything for Marius. That wasn't sordid. It was brave, it was heroic! Life has to be lived that way, whatever the cost!"

"I thought so, once," Madame von Schillar said, uncomfortably. "But one learns. You'll learn!"

"Never!"

Madame von Schillar's jaw tightened. She resented this enthusiasm, this naïveté, that made her feel, by contrast, old, cautious, outlived.

"Of course," she mused, toying with her rings, "you're in a position to make such sweeping statements. We know your vast experience with romance." She tipped her head and smiled. "So do go on with your story . . ."

The exaltation dimmed in Elizabeth's face, and her lips narrowed self-consciously. Haltingly, she continued her story until, bit by bit, she resumed the colorless dimensions which the Baroness preferred.

"I went to live with relatives. It wasn't easy for them. They'd also been hit financially. So, quick as I could get a work permit, I began taking jobs, just anything—waitress, switchboard operator; sometimes, at night, I was a baby sitter. That's when I first began writing poetry—all alone in other people's homes, with other people's children . . ." Her voice had lowered until, at last, she was speaking scarcely above a whisper.

"I gave my earnings to my aunt, and I suppose it helped her out, but I was never made to feel I belonged there. I slept in a pull-down bed in the front room. I'd get home late, when the others were already asleep, and I'd go out early before they were up, and there was no one at work to talk to. Sometimes, at the switchboard, I'd listen in on the conversations and pretend someone was talking to me—"

Beginning to be depressed herself, Madame von Schillar interrupted: "Perhaps we'd better finish our little talk another time, my dear," she said, gently. "It's getting late, and we haven't done a lick of work yet."

It was long after midnight when Madame von Schillar finally dismissed her. Dejectedly, Elizabeth trudged back to her room and lit the lamp. Too many shadows still lingered, and she lit another lamp and closed the shutters upon the dark windows. Isolated in the light, she glanced about the vacant room and sighed. She longed to fall upon the bed and cry herself free of despondency. Instead, she refilled her pen, sharpened her pencils, put on her nightgown, washed out her stockings—well-established ruts of action which might channel away her unhappiness.

Abruptly, in the midst of a task, she covered her eyes and whispered, intensely, "Marius, Marius . . ." A moment later, she peered through her fingers. Her brows drew together in perplexity, and she repeated aloud and more urgently, "Marius?"

She stood silently, waiting, the line of her mouth tensing. At last, she tugged open her desk drawer and took out the journal in which she had recorded the details of their many meetings. Intently, she studied them, often glancing up expectantly. She turned the pages faster and faster, and the pressure of her fingers left marks on the paper. At last, she cast the notes aside, and her anguished eyes searched the room.

"Don't leave me alone," she whispered, huskily. "Don't stay away when I need your strength and sweetness . . ."

She had forbidden herself to cry, but now loneliness and despondency overruled this mandate, and she began to sob, cupping her hands over her mouth lest any sound betray her. At last she hastened to the bureau in search of a handkerchief; but it was something else her blind fingers touched. She drew out a pair of men's grey socks, neatly rolled into a ball.

This was the latest acquisition to her scant hoard of Wrenn's possessions. A tape, sewn in each sock, was inked with his name. While seeking material to patch her blue dress, some days before, she had come upon these in the rag bag. Automatically now, she lifted the grey wool to her eyes and dried her tears with them. Then, on sudden impulse, she unrolled the socks and slipped her hands into them like gloves. The heel of one had been worn through. She smiled gently and took out her sewing kit. Sitting down by the window, she began to darn the sock.

Sewing was something she usually did clumsily, but now it was without effort. As she wove the needle in and out of the grey wool ladder, peace returned to her, and perspective. The color came back to her face and, smiling, she nodded to herself.

It had been her own fault, she thought. No wonder Wrenn had not responded. Love can not communicate when the mind is clamorous with insecurity, resentment and doubt. It was probably in just such a way that Elizabeth Carver had lost touch with Marius, that time early in their romance. Madame von Schillar's words echoed in her ears: "I don't know. I couldn't think. I was afraid. . . ." Again the girl nodded knowingly.

She looked up from her sewing at the man who stood before the easel. Today, however, he did not hum as he painted.

"Tired?" she asked. He shook his head. "Can you paint me while I'm sewing?"

"It doesn't matter. I'm doing your face."

"Again?"

"This may be the last time."

"Well, I'm finished with these, anyhow." She bit through the yarn and rolled up the grey socks. "Here you are," she cried. "All ready to put on. Next time, bring over that frayed shirt, and I'll mend that." She threw the socks at him, but he made no effort to catch them. In effort to cheer him, to make him smile, she said, drolly, "What a shock it would be, if people only knew."

Marius looked up, abruptly. "What?"

"If people knew the Senator's wife was a seamstress in secret."

"Oh!" His attempt to laugh made her uneasy.

"What's the matter?" she asked. "What did you think I meant?"

For a moment, Wrenn studied her over the corner of his canvas.

Then he came to her, sat down beside her. "Listen," he said, gently. "Listen, Elizabeth—" His eyes searched hers, as if he hoped to convey this visually rather than with words. "Suppose people did know? I mean, about us?"

"I'd be proud as punch," she said, mussing his hair. "Now, go paint my picture." He did not move, and her hands on his hair grew still. "What do you mean, Marius?" she asked. "Are people beginning to whisper about us?"

"Your tense is wrong," he replied. "They're not beginning. They've begun."

"Tosh!" she said. "How do you know?"

"I received a letter."

"Who from?"

"It was unsigned."

"Poof! Means nothing."

"Someone else said something, yesterday. Bentley Sprague."

"That pitiful parasite? How would he know?" A moment later, she added, "It couldn't be general knowledge anyway. My sweet friends wouldn't lose an opportunity to let me know they knew—Go on back to your painting, silly, or we'll never get that portrait done."

He returned to the easel. "Relax your face," he ordered.

"What?"

"You're smiling too much."

Her face released its aching smile, and she sat silently, except for her hands which twisted at her rings. Soon her eyes wandered back to him, and she declared, "After all, we've done nothing wrong, have we? Have we? Lots of women have their portraits done . . ."

He looked up from his work. "It is bothering you, isn't it?"

"Why should it? A lot I care about public opinion."

"I think you care a great deal," he said.

"Why do you say that?"

"Because you fight against it so hard," he replied. "And because you're used to being admired."

"As long as you admire me, let them think what they will. I don't give a fig for the whole of Boston—" She braced herself against a faint wave of nausea. Presently, she asked, "What else did he say? This Sprague?"

"Only that we were being discussed around town."

"Well, I'm not going to let it change a thing," she said, vehemently. "Matter of fact, it's a challenge, and I'll fight it, I'll fight it!" She straightened her blouse and secured a comb tighter in her back hair. When she glanced up at him again, he was still watching, and her bravado collapsed before his sad, penetrating eyes. "Are you afraid, too?" she asked, in a little voice.

"Isn't that the price of loving like this?"

She lowered her eyes to her restless hands. "People knowing about us, talking about it—makes it so—"

"I know," he comforted.

"And when it gets back to my husband—and it will—"

"Yes," he said, "it will. Tonight. I'm going to tell him, myself."

"Are you insane?" she cried. "What good will that do?"

"Put an end to all this nonsense."

"Don't be heroic!" she said, almost angrily. "Do you think confession will absolve us in his eyes?"

He shook his head. "I want him to know how things stand. It'll be kinder to him and better for us. I want to be open in loving you."

"And all that's to be achieved just by telling Theo? It'll be the end of everything."

"No the beginning, Elizabeth. I want to marry you."

"Marry!" She smiled ruefully and touched his cheek. "I seem to have a husband, already."

He spoke decisively. "Ask him for a divorce."

"Oh, my darling, don't you think I haven't asked him for that, many times before? But he won't discuss it. I'm a property, you see."

"Doesn't he know you don't love him?"

"Of course, he knows. And refusing me a divorce is just one of his ways of punishing me for not loving him. But he has other ways of punishing, too, and if he learns about us, he'd make my life a hell. And ruin yours. You don't know Theo—oh, God, I don't know what to do . . ." She bowed her head and covered her eyes with her hands.

He grasped her wrists. "Don't," he begged. "Don't." She fell forward, sobbing, and he held her tightly.

"Go on painting," she finally whispered. "Please—just until I can get hold of myself . . ." When she raised her head again, he was standing before the easel, but his hands were at his side. "Go on," she urged. "Paint! We've got to get it finished—"

"Today?"

"That isn't what I meant, you know it isn't!" she cried. "There will be other days, of course. Only—"

"Go on."

"Do I have to say it?" she implored.

"If you have the courage to do it, then you'll have the courage to tell me what you must do."

"Very well." Her voice was unsteady, but she dared to meet his eyes. "I think we must stop seeing each other. Just until this talk dies down."

"And then?"

"I'll send you word. Maybe we can meet somewhere else—"

"And begin this all over again? And stop conveniently when talk starts up again?"

"If you love me."

"It's because I love you that I don't want that!" His voice rose, and in panic Elizabeth pressed her fingers against his lips. He continued in a fierce whisper, his eyes burning. "I'll fight for you, Elizabeth. And I want you to fight alongside me. But it's got to be in the open, or not at all."

Elizabeth bowed her head. She did not answer.

"What are you thinking?" he asked, at last.

Her hand was over her mouth, making her words indistinct:

"'—I found myself within a forest dark
For the straight forward pathway had been lost—'"

She looked up at him miserably. He was pale. Their eyes met, then she quickly looked away. The long shaft of the paint brush snapped in the pressure of his hands. He glanced at the pieces in surprise, then stuck them into his pockets. Taking a deep breath, he knelt and began packing his paints.

"But we'll find our way again," she promised, tremulously.

"Let's be honest, Elizabeth," he answered, gently. "We knew from the beginning, didn't we? Knew that today would have to come."

Again she did not reply. He turned back to the easel and lifted down the wet canvas. It seemed more final than any word they had spoken. The tears came to her eyes and her lips flattened. "I can't help it"—her voice was strangled—"I'm afraid, and I can't help it . . ."

He put down the canvas and held her in his arms until she stopped trembling. "It won't change things," he whispered. "I love you. I will, if I live to be a hundred—"

She made a desperate attempt at lightness. "When you're a hundred," she said, "I'll ask you if it's still true. We'll meet in the park, and—I'll be old and grey then. How will you recognize me?"

"Wear some pink roses in your hair. I'll look for that." His intended laugh was more nearly a croak. "Banter!"

She turned from him with a little cry. When she had saved enough breath to speak again, she said, "I wish it were a hundred years from now . . ." He did not answer. "Marius?" She turned. He was gone.

She watched the door he had closed until tears blurred her vision. "You left your socks," she whispered.

It was after a long time that she went to her desk and, drawing out her journal, began to write. Her hand was unsteady, but there was no fumbling for words. How long she wrote there she could not judge, but it was terminated by a knocking at the door. Worth peered in. Guiltily, Elizabeth covered the pages of her confessional.

"Why, you're awake already," the servant cried, in surprise. "Well, whenever you're set, breakfast's on the table." She withdrew, closing the door.

"*Breakfast?*" Elizabeth murmured.

Surely, Worth had meant to say dinner.

She glanced at the clock on her desk. It had stopped. She arose and threw open the shutters. Her eyes, prepared for evening, blinked at the influx of light. Outside, the icy streets were bright, and the sharp shadows of the trees were long, lying westward.

Yet somehow, she had thought it was evening. She always posed for Marius in the late afternoon, and now it should be night.

As she turned away, she glimpsed her reflection in the windowpane. Startled, she peered at it closely. It was not a beautiful girl with red hair that she saw, but a slender, dark woman, whose startled eyes stared back at her.

The shock of recognition anchored her senses. She looked down at herself. Her feet were bare. She was standing there in her nightgown; Elizabeth Deveny, standing by her bed, and it was morning. She had just awakened, she decided, but with fragments of her dream still clinging to her in defiance of daylight. That was not unusual, she insisted. Many people awoke in the morning, momentarily believing their dreams had actually happened.

Satisfied, she thrust up the window and stretched in the chill morning air; then, humming, she quickly dressed. As she prepared to go down to breakfast, however, she discovered some freshly penned notes on her desk. They were in her own handwriting. She glanced at a paragraph, and the color drained from her face. If she had really been asleep and her parting from Marius merely a dream, when had she written about it in such detail?

She stepped back in confusion and her foot grazed something—the rolled up grey socks on the floor, just where they had landed when she had tossed them at the artist.

"Were you here, then?" she asked, tensely. "Were you really here, after all?"

Baffled, she passed her hand over her eyes, the gesture of one who has walked into a cobweb. She glanced at the socks and at her journal, and again at her reflection in the mirror. "Think, think," she whispered.

Her face was waxen, gleaming with sweat, and her chill hands clenched until the knuckles went white. Holding herself rigid against panic, she tried to remember the passage of the entire night, to identify fact, to distinguish it from fancy; but she was frightened, terribly frightened, at how far out she had drifted, and this all but paralyzed her reasoning.

"Marius Wrenn is dead," she said aloud, in desperation. "Dead before I was even born." The sound of her voice gave her courage, and she added, even more insistently, "I am not Elizabeth Carver. I am Elizabeth Deveny!"

Her mouth tightened. Striding to the desk, she ripped page after page from her journal, swept the pile of them into a drawer and turned the key. As though pressing her signet to a contract, she spoke aloud once more. "This will never happen to me again."

A second time, that morning, she sent Marius Wrenn out of her life.

Part One of Madame von Schillar's memoirs were finished and a new dread took hold of Elizabeth. Hitherto, she had been eager to finish the chapters describing the marriage to Senator Carver and commence writing in earnest the love affair with Wrenn. Now, she dared not touch it until she was calmer, safe from the threat of darkness.

"Let's postpone Mr Wrenn for a while," she urged the Baroness. "I'm not really satisfied with the first part of the book yet. It needs polishing badly."

"As you will. I leave it entirely up to you." Madame von Schillar spoke indifferently; but for the rest of the day she was inexpressively gay and co-operative.

Respite from the new chapters was brief, however. Within a week, Elizabeth no longer had any excuse to procrastinate, so lavishly detailed, so highly polished, were the early chapters. Even more conclusive, she received another letter from Harry Mellett which insisted upon seeing the first part of the book. She had no choice but to send him the manuscript.

While the mailbox was not far off—only across the park—Elizabeth preferred to take the longer route and went several blocks out of her way to the postbox by the drugstore. "It's not that I'm trying to avoid the park," she assured herself, "but I really have to buy a nail file at the drugstore anyway."

As she released the manuscript down the chute, she felt she was letting go of some protective talisman. Now her work would be entirely with Wrenn, and there would be no escaping thoughts of him.

She mopped the moisture from her brow. Abruptly, she entered the drugstore and demanded of the clerk, "How often does the train run?"

"Depends where you're going," the man replied, dryly.

"To New York. I want the next train back to New York."

"They go every hour, I think. But you better call the station and check. There's a pay phone back there."

She dialed the station number, but a moment later, hung up the telephone and lifted her chin, stubbornly. "I won't give up and be driven off like this," she thought. "I'm not afraid. Why make an issue of this?" She pushed out of the narrow booth. "I never loved Marius, anyway. I never loved him. I never loved him." She repeated the words over and over, glorying in them, until they became a kind of marching song which measured her quick pace back to the house.

Her uneasiness returned, however, the minute she entered Madame von Schillar's suite. For a moment, neither woman spoke.

"So today's the day," the Baroness finally said, a little too brightly. "Start on Marius, eh?"

"Yes."

"How do we begin?"

"That's up to you."

"I've already told you some things, haven't I?"

"Yes."

"I see." There was a long silence. "Well, then," the Baroness presently added, "it might be worth your while to study them a bit, and in the meantime, I'll be dredging up some new goodies for you."

She closed her eyes and lay back on the couch. A moment later, she was arranging the lace pillows. Then she picked up her mirror and examined her eye make-up. Casting this aside, she dragged the dog onto her lap and tied a lavender corsage ribbon to its collar. "We're going to concentrate, wee Jabsy," she assured the pet in a husky whisper. "Yes! That's what we're going to do: concentrate!"

Elizabeth set her jaw and bent closer to her shorthand notes. Sometimes, she made a notation, but this, she inevitably erased. Again and again, her eye was drawn to Madame von Schillar's restless caressing of the dog. Jabot began to wheeze and twitch in its sleep and, impatiently, the Baroness slapped it and pushed it to the floor. She lay back, scowling, and suddenly cried at Elizabeth, "For Heaven's sake, do sit still."

Elizabeth looked up from her notes, dazedly. "Pardon?"

"You're creaking your chair," the Baroness said. "See?" She paused so the girl might hear, and then realized the source of sound was not the chair, but the wind outside teasing the shutters. Obstinately, she persisted, "Get another chair and do try to sit still in it."

Elizabeth could not keep the edge from her voice. "It's not the chair," she retorted. "It's the wind."

"A creaking wind? That's something new in nature."

"I mean the wind and the shutter."

"All right, then!" cried Madame von Schillar. "Blame it on the wind. Blame it on me! But don't bother sitting still or keeping quiet just because I have a headache . . ." She shook some aspirin from her silver snuffbox and thrust them into her mouth. The dusty pellets caught in her throat and, coughing, gasping, she pounded on the table with her fist until Elizabeth rushed her a glass of water. When her breath returned, she eyed the girl vindictively. "What's gotten into you, today? Are you sick again? You are, and now I've probably caught it—" She could see Elizabeth struggling against tears, and this, even more, whetted her rage. "If you're going to start sniveling, get out! I won't have you ruining my day with your sobs and scenes. You can't bend me that way! I'm not a man—"

"I'm not going to cry," Elizabeth whispered.

"I don't care what you're not going to do, you're not going to do it here! Go up to your room. Go away!"

To be alone now was the thing Elizabeth most dreaded. Even humiliation was preferable. "Let me stay with you," she begged. "I'll be still. Just let me stay here . . ."

Madame von Schillar was too clever to labor a point beyond victory. She had reached the climax of her wrath and, unable to top it, knew the shock-value of a sudden, unconditional shift to charm. Smiling lazily, she dabbed her lace handkerchief to the girl's cheek. "Am I such good company?" she asked. "Surely you can do better than a black-tempered witch like me. Why not run and see someone more understanding? Your young man, perhaps."

"My young man?" Elizabeth's voice was toneless.

"Whoever it was you went mooning around with in the rain that day."

Elizabeth picked up her pencil and began to write again. "I have no young man," she said. "That was just your imagination. Shall we get back to work?"

"If you wish." Sighing, the Baroness gazed into a mirror and drew a red ringlet into place. "What have you put down, today?"

"Nothing. I have nothing to go on, yet." She wadded up the page on which she had been writing. "I need more, many more, facts and anecdotes that will make Mr Wrenn come alive . . ."

Madame von Schillar slipped off one of her rings and tried to force it down over the knuckle of her index finger. "He was born here in Boston. March third, I think." She spoke hesitantly. "I don't know much about his father's people. His mother's family was quite acceptable. The Jeffersons—"

"You've already told me that. See?" She pointed to a paragraph.

Having lost her temper once today, the Baroness struggled to control it now. "It's in shorthand," she said. "How am I supposed to know what it says?"

"I know about his background," Elizabeth continued. "I know how you met him, and about your trysts in the park. I know how gossip began and that you—separated. But what happened then?"

"I tried to forget him."

"Could you?"

"As I say, I tried. Went to lots of parties, cultivated new people—"

"But it's hard to forget," Elizabeth murmured.

The Baroness nodded. "Very hard. Sometimes, you have to struggle not to remember things, but it's on your mind, all the time . . ." Madame von Schillar closed her eyes. Her mouth tightened. "And there's no rest—"

"I know, I know." Elizabeth drew nearer Madame von Schillar, but the woman did not continue. "Yes?"

"Yes what?"

"More details," Elizabeth urged. "I can't make them up by myself . . ."

The Baroness concentrated on a piece of paper she held, folding it, then tearing it in two, then folding and tearing the fragments. At last, she raised her eyes to the girl.

"Once in Washington," she said, "I sat at a card table for forty-two hours and won eleven thousand dollars. A week later, I lost all that and more in two hours." She laughed. "Funny. The losing was as thrilling as the winning. I was fighting, you see, and every second was alive, full of chance and drama." She brushed the scraps onto the floor. "It's the high stakes that make a game thrilling, win or lose. If you play for nothing, why play at all? Without risk or challenge, any game becomes a bore, and then sometimes you start playing foolishly, throwing away all you have, ruining yourself, knowing you can't win, but still risking it . . ." She leaned forward, peering at the girl's face. "Do you understand what I'm trying to say?"

"Yes," Elizabeth murmured. "Yes." But she did not. She had closed the door of intuition when she had driven Wrenn from her mind, and so could interpret nothing of what the Baroness had been trying to express. "It's very interesting. But it's Mr Wrenn we really must discuss."

Madame von Schillar drew back. "It's hard for me to talk, today. My headache's coming back." She stared at the floor, then scuffed her narrow foot over the scraps of paper, urging them toward the fireplace. "I hate disorder," she murmured, "and I'm always tearing things up . . ."

Elizabeth put down her pencil, trying to hide her impatience. When she spoke again, her voice was almost clinical. "Shall we try again? Details about Mr Wrenn—"

"Yes," said the Baroness. "Of course, of course. You want details." She tapped her foot restlessly on the floor and, taking a deep breath, began again. "Marius was born on March third. In 1881, I believe, or maybe 1882 . . ."

Elizabeth did not even bother to note this down.

CHAPTER 8

It was night again. Elizabeth returned home from a walk, but despite the late hour, she felt too restless for sleep. Fearful of sitting alone and brooding, she tried to lose herself in work. Soon, however, a sigh escaped her, and she shoved aside her notes. As yet, there was nothing to work from. These last days of interview with Madame von Schillar had yielded much talk, but its concentrate was worthless—facts she had already heard, or trivia whose sum could not equal the Wrenn she had known in her locked imagination.

"But if you just wait," she told herself, "the Baroness will give you the whole story."

Yet, more and more, she began to wonder if Madame von Schillar would ever consent to share more than the superficial aspects of her romance with Wrenn. Each day her stalling became more apparent, and Elizabeth, fearful of being tempted back to the gratifying yield of unreality, grew more frantic in her need for concrete evidence.

Abruptly, she took his letter from its hiding place and studied it anxiously. "If there were only more letters, I wouldn't have to depend on Madame von Schillar," she sighed. "They could tell me the whole story, themselves."

Unconsciously at first, then with intent, she began copying his letter, word for word, upon another sheet, even trying to duplicate the slant, the loop and cross of his handwriting. Then, despairingly, she crumpled up the paper and dropped it in the empty fireplace. A moment later, she retrieved it. Even in copy, these were Wrenn's words, and she could not destroy them.

Sighing again, she turned off the lamp and stretched out on her bed; but sleep was not to be lured by these patterns of habit. To discipline her thoughts into monotony and so induce sleep, she tried to imagine the mechanism of knitting—forced her mind to focus on yarn and the maneuvering of needles, to chant the litany of purling and to count the stitches. At last, hypnotized by routine, she heedlessly worked in a strand of illusion, until her web became half consciously imagined, half dream; partly yarn, partly memory. She found herself knitting the memoirs. Then, with a silent cry, she discovered in this fabric, a dropped stitch—a sentence she had not caught up and placed correctly: "I burned his letters," the Baroness had said.

Elizabeth sat up suddenly, Madame von Schillar's words still ringing in her mind. At first, she recalled, the Baroness had flatly denied that Wrenn had ever written to her—clearly a lie. "Or if he ever did, I burned the letters." Was not that a lie, too? It had to be. This very night, Elizabeth had been unable to destroy even a copy of Wrenn's words. How much less likely, then, would the Baroness be able to burn the actual letters of the man she loved, whatever the danger? No! It was merely a device to preclude sharing these treasures with anyone.

"She hid them," Elizabeth whispered. "She didn't burn them. She hid them in this house."

Tensely, she sat on the edge of the cot, staring into the darkness.

However small the chance, her need for evidence of Wrenn was so desperate she dared overlook no opportunity. Decisively, she flung on her thin wool coat and quietly tiptoed down the steep stairs. She pressed her ear against the double door to Madame von Schillar's suite, then cautiously turned the knob and inched open the door.

It was dark inside. She crept forward stealthily, pressing her hands against her heart to muffle its tumult. Beneath her faltering foot a floor board groaned. She shrank back, tautly. There was no interruption of Madame von Schillar's husky breathing, however, nor its wheezing counterpart from the sleeping Jabot. Reassured, she sidled toward the desk. It was locked, but she knew the Baroness hid the key by sticking it in the lock of the bureau. Clearly, the letters would be concealed as obliquely. Yet when the desk was open, it was too dark to sort the contents. Blindly, she ran her fingers over the polished surfaces, into cubbyholes and little drawers, seeking some evidence of secret space. Suddenly, Madame von Schillar whimpered in her sleep, and Elizabeth stepped back, automatically hiding her hands behind her. She heard the tattoo of Jabot's claws on the parquet floor, and then the dog was on its mistress's bed. "Go 'way," the Baroness whispered drowsily. Elizabeth stood motionless, unable even to wipe away the perspiration which slid down into her eyes. When Madame von Schillar's deep breathing resumed, the girl crept from the room.

Obviously, there was no use in searching the suite now. It would be necessary to wait for some propitious moment during the day when the Baroness was out. Yet Elizabeth was too impatient to wait. And since, she reasoned, Madame von Schillar was given to cunning concealment, there was always the chance that the letters might be hidden elsewhere than in her own room.

In the wincing shadows of lamplight, she intently searched the upstairs rooms, even the locale so familiar to the Senator, he would never consider hunting for evidence there—his own bedchamber. Her nervous fingers insistently tapped the oak paneling, pinched at curtain hems and the plush upholstery. Urged on by the threat of dawn, she inspected the underside of every bureau drawer and pried loose the backing of pictures.

She found nothing.

Wearily, she returned to her own room. Within her, logic and discouragement joined voices in arguing that the letters no longer existed; but this she could not, dared not, believe. The letters were her last hope. If she failed to find them, there was no way left to reach Wrenn, but through the imaginary door which both tempted and frightened her.

Or leave. Leave this house. That was the easiest solution of all.

"But I'll find the letters," she promised herself. "Maybe tomorrow . . ."

From the moment breakfast was through, Elizabeth waited impatiently for Madame von Schillar to leave her rooms so she could search them. Gradually, however, she realized that, except for meals, the Baroness seldom left her suite. At lunch Elizabeth excused herself from the table before coffee, in hope of examining the desk again. Her time was too scant, however; and when Madame von Schillar entered, her petulance at Elizabeth's interruption of the meal made clear that this ruse could not be repeated without suspicion.

"I don't know how you ever find anything in this desk," Elizabeth said. "Why don't I put it in order while we chat?"

"As you will, I don't care," the Baroness yawned.

The desk was not large, but it held a surprising clutter of papers, amongst them insurance policies, stock certificates and currency clipped together with bobby pins. She found, however, no letters whatsoever.

Smiling tautly, Elizabeth held up one of the securities. "Don't you have some place to put valuable papers?" she asked. "A secret drawer in the desk? Or a safe . . . ?"

"No. Just put them where they are, so I can find them again." After a moment, however, she took the valuables from Elizabeth and folded them into a brown envelope. "Turn your back," she ordered.

Elizabeth obeyed, but in the reflection of a mirror, she witnessed the Baroness tucking the envelope behind the Sargent portrait; and she smiled.

"You look as if you need relaxation," she told Madame von Schillar, that night. "Why don't you and Worth go to a movie?"

The Baroness waved away the suggestion. "If I want to be bored, I don't have to go to any movie. I can stay right here."

That was true. To stay right here and be bored forever seemed Madame von Schillar's determination. She received no invitations worth accepting, and disdained calling on old friends until they had repaid her initial call. Each Thursday, she stubbornly awaited them, but as it was a rare day that brought even one guest, she usually kept Elizabeth with her for company.

"Oh, God," the girl prayed, "send the Baroness some callers, so I'll be free to search her suite . . ."

Unwilling to count on divine interception, however, Elizabeth arranged her own miracle. That night, she called on Kitty Leighton Wallach.

"I want to be frank," she told the older woman. "I want to ask why you never visit Madame von Schillar. She used to be a dear friend of yours, and I know you're above this petty idea of punishing her, like her other so-called friends."

It was not difficult to persuade Mrs Wallach. Three o'clock was the hour set for the visit, and all through the next day, Elizabeth waited impatiently. When, however, Worth announced that Mrs Wallach was waiting in the parlor, Madame von Schillar only groaned.

"People ought to remember I don't receive except on Thursdays. And I'm really too tired . . ." Elizabeth's face froze with alarm. Madame von Schillar, however, rouging her cheeks with an eagerness which belied the languor of her voice, added, "But since she's here, I suppose I'll have to see her." With elaborate reluctance, she entered the parlor. "Kitty darling," Elizabeth heard her carol. "Oh, my dear, how lovely to see you again . . ."

Quickly, Elizabeth slid her hand in back of Madame von Schillar's big portrait. The brown envelope was there, but nothing else. She hurried to the next picture, expectantly, and lifted it from its hook—

It was an hour later when Madame von Schillar returned to her suite. Everything was in order, and Elizabeth was sitting in exactly the same chair as before. She glanced up glumly.

"Have a nice visit?"

"Grim, dear. But grim! Kitty's let herself go snow-white. And so metaphysical, I all but screamed. I expected her to lead me in silent prayer any minute! Why, I remember when she was the madcap of madcaps."

She chatted on volubly, but Elizabeth, staring straight ahead, heard not a word.

If she discontinued her search of the house after that day, it was not because Elizabeth had relinquished hope of finding Wrenn's letters; merely that she was inspired by an easier plan of getting at them.

The following morning, an elevator, caged by wire pin-curls, lifted her to the elaborate loggia of the state library. Half suffocated by steam heat, she thumbed through bound copies of prominent newspapers, dated 1912. Curiously enough, the Carver divorce was mentioned only once, a brief paragraph hidden away in the foreign news where no one would notice it. An attendant supplied the reason.

"Decent papers didn't print that sort of thing," he explained. "They never catered to scandal in those days, particularly about our best families—"

"But were there no scandal sheets?"

"Oh, to be sure. The *Reveille,* for instance. Undoubtedly, they feasted on it . . ."

"And do you have any copies of the *Reveille*?"

He leaned closer. "We have," he said, with prideful intensity, "everything!"

The yellowing sheets of the *Reveille* were brittle, the edges flaking in her fingers as she turned each page. Here, the Carver divorce proceedings were generously in evidence. As she read, Elizabeth's nostrils pinched. Had there been any doubt in her mind before, none now was left as to why the Baroness feared print, and why she so stubbornly protected the memory of her life with Wrenn.

The reporting was comparable to St. Augustine's promise of heaven, where the virtuous were entertained by witnessing the torment of their erring brothers below. The paper had sanctified its relish for scandalous detail by using the case as a moral indictment. Each day's article included its sermon; and if half-truths and distortions of fact were frequently found, it could be argued that the means were justified by the uplifting purpose.

No love letters were printed as evidence, however. Since nothing in the spectacular suit was omitted which could possibly boost circulation, it was probable that the letters had not been introduced in court. Indeed, there was little need for them, since the evidence presented was damning enough. Elizabeth was not satisfied, however. It was possible, she told herself, that Carver's lawyer had withheld the letters as spare ammunition in event his case met unforseen opposition.

According to the report, the lawyer retained by Senator Carver was the renowned Lincoln McCab. Elizabeth found such a name in the telephone directory. A few minutes later, she was bound for his home on Commonwealth Avenue.

"I'd like to speak to Lincoln McCab, please."

The tall woman at the door smiled. "There are three of them, you know," she said, "but the youngest is only fifteen, so I don't suppose you want to see him. Is it about a case?" Elizabeth nodded. "Well, perhaps you'd better see my husband at his office."

"I rather think it's his father I want to see."

"Oh, but he doesn't practice law any more. Celebrates his eighty-first birthday, this month."

"But could I see him?" Elizabeth urged. "It's about a case he argued many years ago. And it's important—"

"Well . . ." Mrs McCab chewed her lip, thoughtfully. "If it were to ask him what he did yesterday, I'd say don't waste your time. But if it happened a very long time ago, he just might remember. Only don't stay long. When he gets tired, he starts to wander."

She ushered Elizabeth back into a cheerless sun porch. The old man wore a yachting cap to shield his eyes, but there was little light in the room, and the only warmth came from an electric heater near his blanketed chair. His voice, no longer the surge of sound described in the papers, cracked as he answered her question.

"Yes. I represented Theo. Theo Carver. Senator Theodore Carver. Yes. Didn't want to touch the case, but he was a friend. We studied law together. And it's too bad he went into the government where they have no use for law." He gasped out a laugh, then repeated the remark so Elizabeth might realize repetition could not dim the lustre of his favorite joke.

Geared for talk now, he utterly disregarded Elizabeth's interruptions and questions, as fifty years in court had accustomed him. Often, he would get just so far in detailing the circumstances, and then, like an ill-set machine, stop and begin over again.

"I tell you," he cried, at one point, "that Elizabeth Winslow was Venus incarnate, men around her like flies on a cherry pie. Best looking woman in Boston. But I always said, I wouldn't be in Theo Carver's shoes for a million of money. When women like that get in your blood, the only way to free yourself is to spill blood. She didn't give Theo any peace, I can tell you. No, no. Not for a million of money . . ."

His eyes wandered and his voice grew dim. For a few minutes, his lips moved silently, then abruptly, he added aloud, "Theo came to my office one day, his face all white. Voice shaking. Told me that

Mrs Carver had been at him, day and night, for a divorce, and he didn't know what to do. I told him, 'Theo,' I said, 'Theo, sit tight. Make her happy somehow, but don't give into her. By all means, avoid trouble. Avoid trouble, because in your position—' he was a United States Senator—'in your position, a scandal will do you irreparable harm!' Well, sir, he promised to take my advice. Said he'd try to win her all over again. And I think he could have. Anyway, for a few months everything seemed to go fine. Then his sister Sarah had to start hinting that his wife was seeing other men. That very day—"

"I know, I know," Elizabeth interrupted, "but what I came to find was if any love letters were—"

"That very day," McCab continued, imperturbably, "he came running to me and asked if I'd heard any rumors. Honesty forced me to admit that, in the last week, certain stories had come to my ears about Elizabeth and this painter. Well, that was the end. A man can overlook everything until others know about it. Then he must act. Theo became very businesslike. Ordered me to begin divorce proceedings against her, at once. I just shook my head. 'You don't have any case,' I told him. 'Gossip isn't acceptable evidence in court as well you know. If she's faithless, we must have facts. Give me facts, sir, and I'll give you freedom.'

"Well, he got detectives right off, set them on her trail. Only, one night he caught her sneaking out of the house in her maid's hat and cape, and he just plain lost his head. Accused her of having a lover. She snapped back, 'Well, if you won't give me a divorce, what do you expect?' That's when he let on that he was going to get the divorce.

" 'You mean let me divorce you?" she asked.

"Theo said no. She had disgraced him before the world, and now, before the world, he would disgrace her. 'You need evidence,' she said, 'and just catching me in my maid's clothes isn't enough.' Well, sir, Theo smiled and pointed out the two detectives waiting outside. She got very pale. Began to pretty up to him now, but when he wouldn't listen, she cried, even fell down on her knees.

"Well, letting the cat out of the bag, that way, could have ruined our case—put her on her guard against detection, so we'd never have gotten any evidence. Only Elizabeth got panicky. Either thought we knew more than we did, or couldn't stand the strain. Anyway, she threw caution to the wind, and ran off with him. Ran off with this Wrenn. It couldn't have been better, Miss—Miss—"

"Deveny."

"—Miss Deveny, if we'd planned it ourselves. The detectives traced them to Shilleth, on Cape Cod—she owned a cottage there—and that's where they found her. But not alone! No! She was there with this painter, so called; this intruder, this immoralist, who judges life from the gutter—" His voice began to resound and his gesture eloquently stirred the air, as if, once more, he were performing for an admiring court room. "Sitting on the sea-sand, picnicking and wading in the surf to disguise their evil purpose. No, they were not found in each other's arms. But they were sharing the same cottage on the shore. The house contained but one bed. His night clothes hung by hers in the wardrobe. And, *and,* were not that evidence enough, what were the guilty woman's words? Was she ashamed, when apprehended in her little seaside saturnalia? Was she penitent? Did she throw herself at her husband's feet, and, there, weep? No, ah, no, my friends. She smiled brazenly. She laughed in his faithful face, and these words lay like cankers on her lips: 'I'm in love with Marius Wrenn,' she sneered—"

His voice had risen excitedly. Mrs McCab appeared in the doorway. "Daddy," she cautioned. "Now, Daddy—" As he only raged the louder, she turned to Elizabeth and, almost imperceptibly, nodded toward the door. "Come back another time."

"Where are you going?" the old man cried, as the girl arose. "Come back, come back!" He reached out imploring hands to his daughter-in-law. "Don't send her away, Peggy. This is my friend, this is—" He groped for her name again. "Who?"

"Elizabeth," she laughed. "Elizabeth—"

"Winslow," he cried. "Elizabeth Winslow."

"No, Deveny," Elizabeth said, uneasily.

"Elizabeth Winslow, my friends," he roared, rising halfway in his chair, "who wronged the finest man of his hour—"

"No," Elizabeth protested. "I'm Elizabeth Deveny, can't you understand? Deveny!"

"Adulteress!" he shouted. "Harlot!"

Mrs McCab quickly led her into the dark interior of the house. Her words were a jumble of humiliation and apology, but Elizabeth scarcely heard. She was grateful when the woman hurried back to quiet old McCab, leaving her alone to recapture control of herself, to ease from the shock and, what was more alarming, the delight she had experienced.

As Elizabeth left the house, Mrs McCab momentarily returned. "Is there anything I can possibly do for you?" she begged.

"Yes," said Elizabeth. "When Mr McCab is calmer, you can ask him about the letters Mr. Wrenn sent to Elizabeth Winslow Carver. Did they figure in the divorce? The love letters of Marius Wrenn . . ."

Late that afternoon, when anticipation had been wracked into impatience, Elizabeth was finally summoned to the telephone. It was Mrs McCab. She had questioned the old man, as instructed. No letters from Wrenn were used as evidence in the case, because none had ever been found.

"Thank you," Elizabeth whispered. Despairingly, she hung up.

For a long time, she stood there, her lips tense, her brow furrowed. So deep was her preoccupation, she did not remember returning to her room for the flashlight; she only became aware that it was in her hand as she trained its beam down the narrow flight of stairs into the cellar. Gingerly, she descended into the darkness. However negative the evidence so far, she felt compelled to search the house, just once more.

A dank smell, like seeping gas and mushrooms, awaited her. She flashed the torch over a pile of grimy lumber, into the coalbin and around the white-crusted stone walls. Abruptly, she stood still. There was something in the corner which had not been there on her previous search: a large, stained canvas stretched on a wooden frame. She hastened to it, her heart hammering. Turning the picture around, she focused her light upon its dusty surface. Then she sighed. It was not one of Wrenn's paintings, as she had hoped; yet she had seen it before. A gypsy maid was depicted, coyly masking her smile with a fan of playing cards. It was the absurdly dimpled hand which reminded her. This painting had hung in the cluttered parlor of Bentley Sprague.

Her disappointment suffocated her brief flicker of curiosity and, with another sigh, she leaned the painting back against the wall and went on with her search.

Eventually, the far away clangor of the dinner bell interrupted her. She hastened upstairs. Madame von Schillar was already seated at the table. Her upraised brows questioned Elizabeth's dirty hands and smudged face.

"I was in the cellar," Elizabeth blurted. "I'll go wash—"

"The cellar! What were you doing there, pray?"

"I was—looking for something."

"Such as?"

"Well . . ." She licked her dry lips. "I thought maybe some of Mr Wrenn's—drawings might be stowed away—You don't have any on the walls, you see, so I thought possibly there'd be some around that you didn't know about, and how pleased you'd be if I could find some—"

The Baroness shook her head. "There are none around. Oh, I had an excellent portfolio of sketches, but Flix made off with most of them. Sold them to pay his debts. No, my dear, if there were any left here, they'd be on my wall, not in any damp cellar . . ."

Elizabeth laughed self-consciously. "I thought I'd stumbled on one of them today. There is a picture down there, you know. Won't the mice get at it?"

"Not if they value their digestion," the Baroness said. "Oh, what a fearful daub!"

"A Bentley Sprague, isn't it?"

The Baroness sat up. "What do you know about him?"

"Nothing."

"How did you know it was his, then?"

Only after a desperate moment did an answer come to Elizabeth. "It was signed by him," she said.

"Well, then, don't say *a* Bentley Sprague, as if it were *a* Rembrandt, or *a* Renoir. If he's to be discussed at all, let it be said he's *a* nobody, who can't even give his wretched pictures away."

"He apparently gave one to you," Elizabeth said.

"I bought it," snapped Madame von Schillar. "And for far more than his collected works is worth."

"How much?"

"I never disclose my charities." As Elizabeth glanced up at this word, the Baroness added, impatiently, "Oh, he was an acquaintance of Marius, and I knew him too, vaguely. Fool of a man. Likes boys, I've heard. Well, he's down on his luck now, with scarcely a roof over his head, to hear him talk. He tried to borrow some money from me, last week. Well, I told him I never lend, but I'd buy one of his pictures. So I gave him some money, and to my horror, he sent around that fortune-telling monstrosity—" She slapped the table, irritably. "Oh, let's forget about it!"

"But—"

"I say forget about it, Miss!" She was very pale, and her eyes were blazing. "I don't want his name mentioned in my presence again, do you understand? Ever!"

Astonished at such unwarranted fury, Elizabeth took a step backward. "Very well," she murmured.

"Now, for mercy's sake, go wash those hands," the Baroness added. "And in the future, I'll thank you to stop prying around in places where you don't belong. I've been thinking all day of canceling these memoirs, and if you provoke me any more, I most certainly shall!"

The house echoed with nine o'clock, each timepiece competing to announce the news. Elizabeth waited uneasily in her room.

"I'll just relax," she told herself, stretching out on the cot, "and if I happen to think of Marius, why then, I'll just think of him for a moment and that's all. He doesn't have to take form. It'll be impersonal as mathematics . . ."

So she reminded herself, from time to time; but with every repetition, her uneasiness sharpened. A single thought of Wrenn no more satisfied her than would a single drink an alcoholic.

Could she hold out, she wondered? Could she hold out so much as a week more, when even the course of a single day was paved with treacherous moments of weakness, of piercing need for Wrenn, which could give way, like a trap door beneath her feet, pitching her back into darkness.

Abruptly, she arose and, hastening down to the room behind the kitchen, rapped on the door. Worth peered out, in her wrapper and crimping combs.

"Yes, Miss?"

Elizabeth assumed that hauteur which betrayed rather than concealed her turbulence. "Mrs Worth, could I see you, please?"

Worth studied her pale face, then opened the door wider. "Come on in."

Although Worth made a shrine of the old house, her own room was cheerless, almost barren; except for a sewing kit and a religious picture pinned to the wallpaper, it was devoid of personal belongings. Elizabeth sat down on a raveling wicker chair, earnestly trying to think of some way to begin. Then she drew out a crushed package of cigarettes and offered one to the woman.

"I don't smoke, Miss."

Elizabeth colored and murmured an apology.

"Don't bother, Miss," Worth interrupted, brusquely. "You light up if you want. I just never got around to the habit, because in my mind's eye, I couldn't ever see our Lord smoking. 'Course," she added, after a pause, "I can't quite picture him playing cards either, but—" Not quite accidentally, her hand brushed up against a deck of cards. She watched the girl, expressionlessly. "Sometimes, some things help ease you into talk when your tongue is tied . . ."

Elizabeth's smile was timid as she moved her chair closer to the table. "What shall it be? Hearts?" Worth's mouth pinched, in disapproval. "Rummy?"

"I favor draw poker, myself," Worth said, shuffling the cards with a practised hand. "Only"—And she fixed the girl with a stern eye—"I've never played for money and I never will. We'll use matchsticks for stakes."

For a time, they played without speaking. Then Mrs Worth asked, "Work coming along?"

"Not very well." Elizabeth hoped this would provoke the servant to ask questions, but Worth made no such violation of her code. Abruptly, Elizabeth said, "Worth—" She faltered—"that is, I mean to say Mrs Worth—"

"Just Worth is quite enough, Miss. My given name's Phoebe, but till I was twelve, my people thought it was spoken Fo-eeb, and afterwards, I never got used to the new way. So now I just think of my first and last name both being Worth. What were you going to say?"

"Just that—you have to trust a person to play cards with them, don't you?"

"Yes, Miss. And not just in cards."

Elizabeth took a deep breath. "Do you trust me, Worth?"

The older woman met her eyes squarely. "I do, Miss. I didn't, but I do. See, I thought you was here looking for scandal, and there's been that a-plenty. But now I think different."

"Then, would you help me?"

"Is it about Mr Wrenn?"

"Yes."

The servant laid down her cards and looked away. "Don't know what I can honestly tell you, Miss. I didn't know him well. That's not my position. We only really talked a few times, and that was when he was sick. He'd get lonesome, now and then—none of his friends seemed to come here much, except sometimes Captain, what's-his-name, Chrysler or Crisler."

She looked back at Elizabeth now. "It was Mr Wrenn who taught me to play cards, you know. This time when he was sick and wanted company. Nothing would do but for him to teach me poker. Not that he was very good, himself. But the Lady liked cards, and she always won. I guess he wanted to practise up." She laughed silently. "Never held cards in my life, before that—didn't believe in it—but even so, I could beat him every time. He just couldn't keep his face still when his hand was good. And the worse his hand, the higher he bet. I tried to let him win sometimes, but he wouldn't have it. He had to play straight and honest, win or lose." Her face resumed its habitually sober cast. "Your deal."

Elizabeth shuffled and flicked out the cards. Worth studied her hand intently, but the girl did not even glance at hers. Moistening her dry lips, she began again, "Worth—" The woman looked up. "You know this house pretty well, don't you?"

"Every rafter and stone, I expect."

"Are there any secret panels or—hiding places?"

Worth narrowed her lips sternly. "This is a New England house, Miss. I'm sure no one would have thought of putting in a thing like that. But if there was one here, I'd have found it, the way I've searched this house, top to bottom—"

"Searched it?" Elizabeth blurted. "For letters . . . ?"

"For a drawing, Miss. Mr Wrenn done a drawing of me, once. Started it, anyway, and when he died, I felt I'd like to have it for a keepsake. Only I never found it in all these years. It's been a long time—"

"You must have been just a girl, then," Elizabeth mused.

"Yes, Miss, so I was, not that it made much difference. I never was a beauty. Always solid fleshed, you know, with this brown spot on my cheek. I used to pat flour over it to make it passable, but when he drew my likeness, he made me wash the flour off. That was like him, you see. He never liked things hid. He drew that brown spot in my picture and didn't spare me nothing. All I was, was in that drawing, but it wasn't ugly. He had to have the whole truth, you see. And I guess the whole truth is, I wasn't ugly clear through, and he saw it." She shuffled her cards absently. "I'd rather have that picture now than twenty-thousand mirrors."

For a time, they sat in silence, toying with the cards. Then Elizabeth spoke. "I don't suppose, in your searches, you ever came across a packet of his letters."

"Mr Wrenn's? No, Miss."

"If you have, please tell me," Elizabeth begged.

"He used to write her pretty often before they were married, I know. None of my business, of course, but I got to know his handwriting on the envelopes."

"How often did he write?" Elizabeth demanded.

"Couldn't say, Miss. Often enough."

"Then they must be somewhere," Elizabeth said, intensely.

"I wouldn't think so, Miss. The Lady burned everything, you know—"

"She couldn't have!" Elizabeth protested.

"But she did, Miss. I helped her. We took a shoe box full of letters and I don't know what all out into the back yard and set it afire. It was me who put water on the ashes—"

"But surely she saved some!" Her voice was rising.

"I shouldn't think so, Miss."

"You're lying!" Elizabeth cried. "She told you to say that, didn't she!" Worth stood up, and Elizabeth jumped up, too. "Didn't she!" All vestige of calm had vanished now. She grabbed the woman's fleshy arm. "Tell me!"

Mrs Worth studied her as if squinting and then, with barely perceptible pressure, withdrew her arm from Elizabeth's grasp. "I'm sure I don't know, Miss," she said, tonelessly.

Shocked by her own outburst, Elizabeth lowered her eyes. "I beg your pardon. I didn't mean to offend you."

"No matter if you did, Miss. Good night."

With head bowed, Elizabeth left. The door closed behind her and she knew it would not admit her again. She leaned against the wall, her hands covering her face. "She was lying. The Baroness made her say that. The letters must be somewhere . . ." But though she said this aloud, her words did not convince her. In her heart, there was no doubt: the letters no longer existed.

With dragging footsteps, she returned to her room. Numbly, with little awareness of what she did, she undressed. She did not go to bed, however, but to her desk. After a long time, she tried to write out the stories Worth had related; but every page she began was soon crumpled in her fist.

She mopped the perspiration from her brow. Why, she asked herself, why seal the imagination when it was all she had to work with? It was in the mind that conception began. Had Wrenn, for instance, denied himself visions of the ocean, he never could have endowed his seascapes with such passion and life.

"Give in," she whispered. "Let him come back to you. Give in . . ."

She sank her teeth into her lip and bent back to her work. After writing only a few words, however, she flung aside her pen. She felt cheated, bitterly so. She had turned from fantasy to find Marius, but it was in fact that she had lost him. Self-denial had rewarded her with nothing but a more aching loneliness and an inability to create; so if love and understanding were to be found in illusion, then to insist upon reality was madness.

"Give in," she whispered. "Give in." Her moist brow gleamed in the lamplight and her fists were knotted. The dark doorway would open again easily enough, but, once she had entered, might lock forever behind her. Yet for all her fear of that, the words continued to din in her mind, "Give in, give in." It seemed to be Wrenn's voice, instructing, pleading. Her little clock ticked out the same command, "Give in, give in, give in . . ."

She leaped to her feet, pressing her hands against her ears. A moment later, she dragged her suitcase out from under the cot and began flinging her clothes into it.

She snapped shut the clasp and turned the key. Her breath still came fast and her hand was unsteady, as she wrote a note of good-bye to Madame von Schillar.

Yet as she reread it, the words seemed unreasoning, hysterical, and this flight off into the night absurdly theatrical. With a sniff of wry amusement, she crumpled the note. After all, her suitcase was packed, a symbol of her decision, a promise that she would soon be far away. This certified, her breath came more easily, and the color returned to her face. "I can just as easily wait for morning to say good-bye," she decided. "I'm calm now—out of danger . . ."

Even so, in falling asleep that night, she reached out and gripped the handle of her suitcase for reassurance.

Either she awoke or dreamed she did. It was still dark. Although the room was chilly, her nightgown was damp with perspiration, and she slipped it off. The moonlight, edging through the louvers, slashed her bare skin with stripes of light and shadow. Drowsily, she pushed aside the shutters and glanced out at the silent, ice-polished park. It was empty. Of course, it was empty. The bench where she had always awaited Wrenn was crusted with dirty snow. Her throat constricted and she turned away.

In crossing back to her bed, she stumbled against something. It was a suitcase. She had put it there, she remembered; but why?

"Maybe I was going to run away with Marius," she mumbled.

She pondered this, then sadly shook her head. Marius did not even know she still longed to see him. Marius. Perhaps at this very moment, he was awake too, thinking of her, summoning her, conjuring her. "Sometimes, when I say your name enough, I can bring your face to my mind." He had said that, once. "I suppose this should be enough for me, but it isn't. I want to see you, talk to you. A letter, Elizabeth . . ."

The tears had come to her eyes, and suddenly, she picked up a pen. The moon provided scarcely enough light to write.

"Marius—Forgive me. I hadn't the courage to go on before, but now I haven't the strength to go on without you. It's too late to think of cost now. And nothing could be worse than the torment of these last weeks. There must be a way for us somehow. I'll be in the park tomorrow night at nine. Be there, I implore you. Elizabeth."

She sealed this into an envelope and was scarcely aware of the time it took her to find a stamp or to finish the addressing. Pulling on her light wool coat, she crept, seemed to float, down the stairs. The front door creaked as she opened it, but above caution and without haste, she slipped out and across the silent park to the mailbox.

Whether this had been a dream or fact, Elizabeth could not distinguish when the morning light awoke her. More substantial was her knowledge of surrender. Humming softly, she unpacked her suitcase.

Her work with the Baroness, that day, was shot through with nervous excitement. Every time Madame von Schillar mentioned Marius, Elizabeth's breath caught in the tightening of her throat. Yet, because guilt had a delicious place in her game of anticipation, Elizabeth brought up Wrenn's name recklessly and spoke of the park as if it meant nothing at all. Laughter had been too long an exile from her life, and she literally flaunted its return.

"Happy today, aren't we?" the Baroness drawled.

"Within an inch of my life," said Elizabeth, gaily.

"And so gloomy yesterday! Really, my dear, one could get quite seasick trying to follow your emotional ups and downs."

Dinner was at seven. Elizabeth barely touched her food. She was aware that Worth avoided meeting her eyes, but she did not care. Continually, she eyed the clock which seemed to be in conspiracy against her eagerness for nine o'clock.

She dressed, that night, with infinite care; but only when viewing herself in the mirror did she realize the most important detail was missing. For a moment, she stood paralyzed. It was March and the garden snow-filled. Nor was there time to run out and buy them. Then, blessed by inspiration, she hastened up into the attic and forced open a trunk of outmoded elegance. Within a few minutes, she found the bonnet she remembered and, from it, wrenched a small bunch of pink velvet roses. These she pinned in her hair, as he had bid. Her heart was thudding painfully, ordering her to hurry to the park; but Elizabeth did not yet heed this mandate. Something was still missing.

"Oh, of course. My perfume."

As casually as though this were part of her everyday job, she went down to Madame von Schillar's suite. She could hear the Baroness splashing in the bathtub. Quickly, Elizabeth picked up the cut-glass bottle of Loki and dabbed the scent on her hair and ears. Then she revolved slowly and faced the Sargent portrait. Unconsciously, she assumed the attitude of the girl there, and, gazing into her lovely, proud face as one might examine a mirror, she smoothed her hair, smoothed her burning cheeks. A phrase she had once heard in this room came to her mind, and she obeyed it: "Bite your lips and lick them before entering a room or a romance."

She let herself out of the house. Taking a deep breath, she crossed the street into the little park. After brushing the snow from the bench beneath the familiar elm, she sat down. Several times, she glanced at her watch; several times adjusted her high lace collar. No confusion of sound could have tautened her nerves more than this silence, and to dispel it, she hummed to herself. Abruptly, she straightened, hearing the crunch of hard snow beneath his decisive steps. Then he was beside her, his warrior's face aglow. "Elizabeth," he whispered. "Elizabeth. . . ."

"Thank God," she gasped. His lips were warm against her icy hand. She lifted his head away, studied his face, then pressed her mouth against his. At last, she whispered, "How long has it been?"

"A hundred years."

"No. It's been a hundred years just while I've been waiting here, tonight."

The corners of his mouth tipped up in a smile. "Time will go faster, now."

"But not too fast," she urged. "I want to know every moment with you." She glided her finger tips over the hard curve of his cheek. "We won't be apart again, ever, will we?"

"Doesn't that depend on you?"

"Then we will be together. I don't know how yet, but we will be, even if—"

"Even if what?"

"We have to go away together."

"Have you the courage for that?" he asked.

Her smile was wistful. "I don't seem to have much courage at all, any more. That's why I need you so."

"Then we'll find a way," he promised. "Somehow, we'll find a way. . . ."

It was an hour later when Elizabeth returned home. As she hurried toward the stairs, the Baroness appeared at her door.

"You flounced out without a good-bye and pop back in without saying hello," she accused in an injured tone. Elizabeth whirled around, startled. "I don't know why it is, that people I'm fond of care nothing whatsoever for me! I've been calling for you this past hour."

"Can I do something for you now?" Elizabeth asked.

"Nothing! Nothing! Don't bother about me. It doesn't matter if I get lonesome," said the Baroness, wearily. "Where've you been, pray?"

"Out walking."

The Baroness snorted, and, as the girl came forward into the light, appraised her more carefully. Elizabeth stood proudly, her delicate skin glowing and her dark eyes incandescent. It lent her a beauty which made the Baroness curiously uneasy. Without quite knowing why, she immediately sought to devaluate it. "Aren't we rather overdoing it?" she asked, silkily. "Or are you planning to go to a masquerade?"

"Pardon?"

"Why the big blossoms in the hair?"

They might have been bloodstains, the way Elizabeth's hand guiltily covered them. Quickly, she recaptured her smile, and with it, a self-confidence which was almost impertinent. "I think they're pretty, don't you?"

"That," said the Baroness, "would depend on who wears them."

"Or possibly," Elizabeth replied, gaily, "on who looks at them. No?" She nodded graciously and swept upstairs.

Within a week, the chapter on Wrenn was well in progress. No longer able to discriminate between what was fact and what was fancy, Elizabeth blindly included both in her narration of the romance. Never once did she question this, for her identities of Elizabeth Deveny and Elizabeth Winslow Carver were not separate viewpoints, but, as two eyes, blended a singleness of vision.

CHAPTER 9

"You're mad!" cried the Baroness. "Absolutely mad!"

She co-ordinated this statement with decorative laughter, qualified it with phrases like "too sweet" and "simply celestial." Even though this was only a telephone conversation and she was unseen by the other speaker, her face was alive with smiles and her eyes practised a subtle coquetry. This persisted even when she hung up and turned back to Elizabeth.

"Harry Mellett," she stated.

"Was it?"

"He's in town on business and wants to take us to Symphony, tonight."

"That'll be nice."

Elizabeth's absence of excitement did not sap Madame von Schillar's. She dipped into a chair before her mirror and peered into the glass. "You'd better call my hairdresser. Tell her to drop everything and get over here. And tell Worth I'll need her to do some pressing." Thoughtfully, she tapped the marble tabletop. "The Schiaperelli," she murmured. "Haven't worn it for ten years. But its cut will be daring a century from now. It ought to make the Back Bay boil!" She smiled at her mirror and studied the reflection with half-lidded eyes. "Lots of people I used to know may be there, and—well, Mellett *is* good-looking."

"I had no idea," said Elizabeth, gently, "that you were so fond of music."

The Baroness swiveled around. "What are you wearing, incidentally?"

"I don't have much choice. My long black skirt and a white blouse."

"Nonsense!" the Baroness cried, gaily. "Go look in my closet. Pick out something. I can't have you tagging along, looking like our chaperon."

Indifferently, Elizabeth selected a heroic drapery of smokey chiffon, stippled with silver. As the bodice was too large, she was forced to alter it, her needle the clumsier because she resented taking time from the book to prepare for an evening which did not interest her. She tried to dream while sewing, but was continually distracted by the heavy sweetness of henna and unguents, and by the chatter of the Baroness and her hairdresser.

"Wish my boy'd take me to hear some good music sometime," Corinne was saying. "I really love it. Tschaikovsky," she added, and began to hum a theme by Ravel.

"Tosh!" cried Madame von Schillar, at the risk of cracking her mask of hard white paste. "You like a jig, and so do I. Oh, the other kind is divine, and all that, but I've just had too much of it. Poor Mother was a patroness of the opera, and Flix moaned *lieder* from morn till night. Even Marius! Simply doted on the stuff. Fact is, the first time we ever appeared together openly was because there was some symphony he wanted to hear. I don't think anyone present that night heard a note but him . . ."

Elizabeth's needle was idle. She was leaning forward, listening intently. Then she glanced down at the gown she held. Suddenly, she began to sew again, eagerly, but very carefully.

Watching the girl try on the dress before a mirror, Madame von Schillar judged, "You look a little more human now, my dear." She stretched comfortably. Her hair was pinned flat against her scalp in moist, red rosettes, and her skin felt tight, tingling from massage. Such expert pampering always left her refreshed, aglow with expectancy; she felt self-confident and, consequently, generous. "Now if you'd only let Corinne do something with that hank of hair, we might even marry you off to a Cabot."

Elizabeth submitted without much protest. Corinne trimmed the ends of her hair, but it was evident she longed to do more. Hers was a Pygmalion art, and the enemy of caution. She cast an eloquently despairing glance at the Baroness and indicated Elizabeth's high forehead. Madame von Schillar raised two fingers and pantomimed scissors. The next moment, a heavy lock of hair fell onto Elizabeth's hands.

She looked up in alarm. "What have you done?"

Both women answered at once. "A fringe," explained the Baroness. "Bangs," answered Corinne. "A woman should always look smart, but only a fool would want to look intellectual." She nudged Elizabeth and chuckled. "Did you hear that? I ought to be writing a book, myself."

Mellett was due for dinner at seven. By six, the women had transformed Elizabeth. She stood before them in the grey and silver gown. Soft curls hid her forehead, while her back hair swerved high, exposing the nape of her slender neck. Her skin was evenly dusted a shade more compatible to a peach, and a new, scarlet mouth was imposed upon her lips.

"Pretty as a picture," said Corinne. "Don't you think so, Baroness?"

"I suppose so," Madame von Schillar murmured. She glanced at her own reflection, then asked, "What color powder has she got on?"

The artist in Corinne was instantly displaced by the salesman. "It's called 'Ginger-gilt,'" she said, producing a large package from her case, "and honestly, Baroness, it's made for miracles."

Deftly, Madame von Schillar applied some to her face and neck, then stood back from the mirror. Her eyes darted sharply from her reflection to Elizabeth, then back to the glass. Her mouth tightened. Abruptly, she opened her jewel case and clasped a sinewy emerald bracelet on her wrist. Once again, she eyed Elizabeth, then sank into a chair. "You kept me under the drier too long," she snapped at Corinne. "I think I'm going to have a headache." Then her eye was caught by Elizabeth slowly revolving before the long mirror. "For mercy's sake, stand still! You'll have that dress torn to shreds in ten minutes. And slick up your back hair—"

The criticism did not end there and, as quickly as possible, Elizabeth withdrew. She edged up the stairs stiffly, fearful of stepping through the hem or snagging the delicate tissue of the gown. Her head and shoulders were rigid, lest some accustomed awkwardness bring her hair tumbling down. Nor was there respite in her room. She dared not sit down and risk wrinkling the dress. Consequently, she stood. Not knowing what to do with her hands, she held them winged out at her side like a kewpie doll's. Under this added strain, her brow grew damp, but she dared not mop it and risk smudging her make-up. A stay tormented the delicate flesh beneath her breast, and in her stomach was that clammy vacancy which always accompanied the wearing of clothes not her own. Although she was sewn into one of Madame von Schillar's gowns, and her face colored with the same cosmetics, never had she felt less like Elizabeth Winslow. Pinioned by self-consciousness, she could rise no higher than her own being.

A drop of perspiration slid down her brow into her blackened lashes.

Mellett arrived shortly after seven. The Baroness timed her own appearance a few minutes later, and was not pleased to find Elizabeth had not yet come down. "The eternal feminine," she said, with rather too bright a laugh. "I suppose she wants to build up an entrance . . ."

They had begun cocktails when Elizabeth came downstairs. Both watched her descent with wonder. The girl's face had been scrubbed until it gleamed like polished bone. She wore a white blouse and long black skirt. Although her bangs had presented an irrevocable problem, a wet comb had eased out the curls, and her dark hair swung free and shining to her shoulders. She advanced, smiling with perfect poise, holding out her hand to Mellett.

"Elizabeth," he cried, admiringly, "you look positively sinful!"

The Baroness slipped an arm around Elizabeth's waist. "Much, much better, my dear," she whispered.

"Put on a few pounds too, haven't you?" Mellett continued.

"If that's meant to be flattering," Elizabeth laughed, "I'll admit I have."

At dinner, Madame von Schillar invested the brightest treasure of her charm in conversation. Her adroitness, her lazy laughter, the animation of her still beautiful face, rescued even the passing of a plate from the commonplace.

In the shadow of this gaiety, Elizabeth sat silently, content to listen. Mellett, too, sat in silence, watching Elizabeth—the fragile curve of her lips, the shadow cast over her eyes by the burnished bangs. Once, as he watched, her eyes lifted to his. Always before, she would wrench away her glance with a shyness allied to hostility. Now, her brief attention was casual; pleasant, but without emphasis. He cocked his head wonderingly, and his face held both smile and frown.

They were late to Symphony Hall, and the entrance Madame von Schillar had awaited all afternoon was lost in the darkened auditorium. No sooner were they seated than she whisked out her opera glasses and surveyed the audience. She had not forgotten that, in Boston, it is fashionable to be dowdy; but to her horror, the audience's dowdiness was strictly informal. Uncomfortably, she inched her furs up over her bare shoulders, then glanced at Mellett to make sure he had not witnessed this retreat; but his eyes were turned toward Elizabeth. The Baroness dropped her bag so he would have to pick it up.

"Isn't the music heavenly?" she whispered, as he bent down.

Mellett nodded and smiled vaguely. Soon, he was watching Elizabeth again.

Only the girl appeared to be engrossed by the music. Her eyes were gleaming, her lips half parted, and her head, majestically erect. Yet the symphony was not the focus of her thoughts; only the stimulus of them. If she remained oblivious of Madame von Schillar's restlessness and Mellett's silent inquiry, it was because she was entirely absorbed by Wrenn's nearness. She never turned her head toward Marius, or otherwise indicated that she knew he was beside her, but when the music would soar, she would feel the pressure of his arm next to hers, and the blood would throb in her head, an unpremeditated accompaniment to the orchestra.

When the program had concluded and they had, somehow, captured a cab, Mellett said, "We've still got business to discuss, you know. Let's find us a nice, quiet little café—"

"Whatever for?" cried Madame von Schillar. "When I've a perfectly good kitchen at home?"

"Lady," he said, "don't tell me you can boil water!"

"Dear man," she drawled, "I make soufflés and blintzes lighter than an angel's conscience. But scrambled eggs is what you're going to get!"

No sooner had she reached the kitchen, however, than she regretted her offer. The responsibility of fixing the supper exiled her to the stove, far across the room from Mellett's quiet conversation with Elizabeth.

"Dearest," she called, at last, "that headache's coming back, and this heat is stifling. Would you be a dream and do the eggs . . . ?"

Even in an apron, with a skillet in her hand, Elizabeth retained the quality of unconscious elegance. Mellett tried discussing the merits and faults of the first chapters with Madame von Schillar, but he was consistently distracted by the girl's movements. "Actually, she isn't beautiful," he suddenly told the Baroness, "but damned if she doesn't act as if she were."

"Who?"

"Elizabeth," he said. "You've been a wonderful influence on her."

"Really?" Madame von Schillar's smile was a little tight. When Elizabeth brought over the plates, she arose with a yawn. "My darlings," she said, "I've sad news. I'm not hungry now." She slung her furs over her shoulder and crossed to the door. There, she glanced back, her smile at Mellett tinged with mockery. He would see just how long Elizabeth's "beauty" lasted once the "wonderful influence" had withdrawn. "It's been heaven, my dears," she cried. "Good night."

While it is true, the brighter force of conversation left with the Baroness, a more leisurely pace gave Mellett the opportunity he'd awaited. "You've changed," he announced.

"Ah?"

"Well, haven't you?"

"We live," Elizabeth said, smiling, "in a state of flux." Then: "Is there enough salt on your eggs?"

"Yes, damn it! Now, be serious."

"Very well." She arranged him a face of long-drawn solemnity. "I'm serious."

"Stop it," he ordered.

"Stop what?"

"All this dam fiddle-faddle!"

"Why don't you stop your damn fiddle-faddle and eat your eggs before they get cold," she laughed. When he began to eat again, she added, "As for changing, Harry, have you considered it might be you who's changed?"

"Me?"

"You. I don't recall your ever being so abrupt before. You didn't demand answers to silly questions. You took me as I was. And it was very pleasant that way." She held out a crushed package of cigarettes.

"Well, one thing hasn't changed," he growled, accepting one. "You still smoke the most beat-up cigarettes in the world."

He left shortly after, but returned the next day, prior to leaving Boston, on pretext of discussing the unfinished business. His frown, when told that Elizabeth was not home, was scarcely flattering to Madame von Schillar.

She sharpened her words against her smile. "Elizabeth isn't always to be accounted for, any more. The way she goes mooning about—"

"I hadn't noticed the mooning."

"How could you miss it? And you miss very little, Mellett. Plain as the nose on your face: she's in love!"

"Bull!"

"Well, my dear," the Baroness laughed, "it's that, or she's taken to secret drinking."

"Who is he?"

"I thought it might be you, at first. But quite obviously, she isn't interested, eh?" She examined the clasp of her bracelet. "Anyway, it's been going on for weeks. She keeps denying she has a young man in one breath, and in the next, she hints she has."

"So that's it!"

"What?"

He reached for his hat. "The reason for the change in her."

The Baroness nodded. "That is very much it," she declared, pleasantly. "I know you're as glad for her as I am."

"Yes," he said. "Of course."

Madame von Schillar had only suggested the romance to punish

Mellett for his attentiveness to Elizabeth, but now that the words had been spoken, she began to wonder if she had not hit upon the truth.

When the girl returned that afternoon, the Baroness watched her carefully. As Mellett had pointed out, there was a decided change in her manner; romance could easily have been the catalyst. She remembered the signs from her own experience—the secret smile, the gentleness, the sleepwalker's preoccupation. It put her in mind of the early days of her own great affair: the way, for instance, that Elizabeth sneaked out of the house every night at nine, returning an hour later in a state of exaltation which transcended all her efforts of concealment. Elizabeth in love! Madame von Schillar tugged at her pearls, not knowing whether to laugh or frown.

It was the frown she settled for. As she discussed her affair with Wrenn, that afternoon, her aggravation grew. Although Elizabeth was listening attentively, taking copious notes, the Baroness suspected an attitude of superiority, as if the girl claimed to know better than anyone what love was.

"Could you explain something to me?" the Baroness finally cried. "Why you must smile so smugly? Can you explain that to me?"

"Was I smiling? I'm sorry."

"I suppose my romance must seem pretty pallid alongside your own affair."

"You imagine things, Madame," Elizabeth said, sweetly.

Yes, it was that, the sweetness, which Madame von Schillar especially resented. Once she had sensed longing and envy in Elizabeth whenever romance was discussed. All that had vanished now, and, with it, Madame von Schillar's sense of proportion. Without Elizabeth's envy, she had no way of knowing what in her experience was important.

In the days that followed, the Baroness no longer meted out the small change of her hoarded memories, but began unearthing the brighter treasure to dazzle the girl and reclaim her envy. But Elizabeth, hiding behind an enigmatical smile, merely noted down the passionate events as if such things might happen to anyone.

Because it had worked before, the Baroness again sought to collapse Elizabeth's exaltation by a reminder of her dismal past.

"If I seem to harp on your love affair, my dear," she said, gracefully, one afternoon, "it's because you've never been in love before, I dare say, and I feel I must assume the responsibility of a mother, since your own is dead." She smoothed Elizabeth's hair. "Didn't you say she committed suicide when your father was ruined?"

"After he died, Madame. Not when he was ruined," Elizabeth replied, gravely.

"And how did she kill herself? Poison, didn't you say?"

"Sleeping tablets."

"But how could she bear to leave you alone and starving?" the Baroness persisted, all sympathy. "Or was it, my poor darling, that she just didn't care what happened to you?"

Elizabeth studied her hands. "I don't think she had any thought of me, Madame von Schillar. I don't think she had any thought, except for my father." There was an understanding, a compassion, in her voice, new even to her own ears. "She was so beautiful, and so was he. Her love for him was the strongest thing in her life. But it wasn't strong enough, was it? Because she didn't have the courage or imagination to know that love can endure even beyond death."

"Poppycock!" the Baroness cried. "Let me hear you say that when your young man is run over by a truck or dies of tuberculosis. Or drowns!"

The gentle smile and assurance had not dimmed from the girl's face. Indeed, her radiance seemed to intensify as she repeated softly, "Love is stronger than death—"

But this, too, was to change in Elizabeth.

The Baroness sat at the piano, her rings clacking against the ivory keys as she fumbled out a waltz whose great popularity had coincided with her own. Then, abruptly, someone spoke her name and, startled, her fingers jammed out a discord.

"Merciful God," she cried, glancing up at Elizabeth. "Scare a person to death! Creeping in here like a ghost . . ." She eyed the girl critically. "Can't say I really adore that hat, my dear."

"Just borrowed it," Elizabeth mumbled.

"From whom? Worth?" She began to play the piano again.

"Madame von Schillar—"

"I've been playing some old tunes tonight," the Baroness interrupted, gaily. "Here's something you won't hear at Symphony Hall. Called 'That Red Rose Rag.' Absurd title, but it used to be all the rage . . ."

Ill at ease, Elizabeth twisted at her coat belt. "I'd love to listen another time, but I've still got work to do tonight, and—"

"*Und zo?*" She pounced out the chords with even more abandon. "Speak up, my girl."

"You asked the Senator for a divorce again before you and Marius ran off, didn't you?"

"Yes." Her hands withdrew from the keys. "On bended knees."

"And he refused again."

"Yes." Her face hardened. "That was part of his plan. To force me into some desperate act, so he could disgrace me, publicly." She tapped a bass key slowly. "Why do you ask?"

"I just had to be sure." She took off the hat. When she spoke again, her voice was clear, decisive. "It's time for me to go to Cape Cod."

Madame von Schillar glanced up at her, quickly. The girl was extremely pale. "What do you mean, it's time for you? Do you mean tonight?"

"I mean—I've written everything up to the time you and Mr Wrenn eloped to the Cape."

"So why do you have to go there, pray?" Madame von Schillar asked, with her deceptive indolence. "To check up on me? Well, there wasn't a soul there who knew me well enough to tell you a blessed thing—"

"It's not the people I want to see, but—to know what the wind feels like there, and the air, and how the clouds look—"

"Is she writing my autobiography or a weather report?" the Baroness asked of no one in particular.

"And I ought to see your cottage there."

"A fat lot there is to see!"

"—and learn about the town, so I can write about it. It's important to get all these details right, particularly in this chapter. It's—that I must see it as you saw it."

Madame von Schillar strummed the keys idly. "Suppose I said no?"

Elizabeth smiled. "Did you let anyone stop you when you wanted to go there? I might just follow your example and go anyway."

"Might you?" The Baroness smiled, too. "Well, go along then, if you must. But I don't think you'll stay long. It's a dull place."

"You didn't always think so," Elizabeth teased.

"No." Softly, she resumed her playing. "Maybe not. But then, you see, dear, I wasn't alone."

Elizabeth continued to smile.

Although April had arrived, the weather was sharp that morning; yet she stood outside on the deck of the ferry, delighting in the whip of the wind, the sting of the rain. The bay was dark, restive, as in so many of his paintings. It was Wrenn's sea, and as of this day, it was hers, too.

"You're not sorry, are you?" he asked.

She looked up at him, then covered his hand with hers. "No. But even if I were, what else could we have done? Only I'm not sorry, and I never will be, no matter what happens."

"Don't tempt fate."

She read his lips rather than heard him, for the wind carried away his voice. "Oh, listen, Marius," she cried, thrusting her arm through his, "I don't know what will happen. But if anything does, I have this moment, anyway. And that's worth everything I've ever known before. To be with you, to know our life is before us—for better or for worse—but, at least, for us, together."

He could not hear her, but it did not matter. These words were for the wind to carry over all immensity, to inform the elements—the sky, the earth, the sea—that on this day, before God, she had contracted herself to obey and love this man beside her.

"That's the higher law," she told herself. "That's the only one that counts."

He was watching her, and she turned to him smiling, though no smile was capable of expressing all the happiness she felt.

Shilleth was a drowsy little town, needlessly patrolled by gulls and fruitlessly searched by sea breezes. Laden with groceries, and with the key from the real estate man in her pocket, Elizabeth trudged along the single street, out beyond town to the silver-shingled cottage by the shore. It had been closed since September and smelled of oilcloth and kerosene. A ridge of sand sealed anew each shuttered window, and a lone fly buzzed in insane wonderment at the glass panes. By the time she had unpacked her bag and made up the bed, it had grown darker. Although the summer tenants had left the lamps filled with oil, she did not light them, finding more pleasant these shadows. All afternoon she lounged lazily on the couch, smiling to herself. Picking up a large pink-lipped shell, she pressed it against her ear and listened to its murmurous memoir of the sea. Content, like nothing she had known before, stirred and yawned within her.

"But you fool, it can't last," some voice warned her.

"I know, I know," she whispered. "When Theo finds I'm gone, he'll tear the world apart till he finds us."

"I don't mean that. This can't last, and you know what I mean!"

She flung away the sea shell as if it were responsible for this warning. "It will last," she declared, aloud. "As long as I live, this happiness will last."

The door rattled, and she sat up with a gasp. Then she laughed. It was not Theo and his detectives—only the wind.

She fed the driftwood fire in the hearth and let it illumine her solitary dinner. And when the dishes were washed and the doors locked, they sat before the embers, holding hands and whispering, though there was none to hear them.

At nine o'clock, she arose and lit the lamp. "It's growing late," she told him.

"Then why light the lamp?"

She shrugged and smiled lazily. "Perhaps so we can turn it off, later."

Still smiling, she went into the bedroom. Her mood was languorous, yet she did not tarry long in washing or undressing. She took down her long hair, let it hang, red and magnificent, against the whiteness of her body. So clad, she slipped into the bed.

She waited. At last, above the pounding of her heart, she heard Wrenn approaching. As he entered, she turned off the lamp. The darkness of the room isolated the rustle of his clothes as he took them off. Then silence. She sat up in the bed and opened her arms to him.

Outside, the tormented surf flung forward, enfolding the shore; surging, pulsing with rhythms too subtle to distinguish, sweeping back with a gasp only to thrust forward again. All through the night, haunting Elizabeth's dreams and her wakefulness, the ocean's thunder and whisper warned her, and there was no escape from it; the sea, Wrenn's beloved sea, would one day take him from her arms.

The storm passed, taking winter with it. The sand was left smooth and clean, stitched with long, dry grass stalks. Although the sun was still dim, the weather was pleasant, and Elizabeth took advantage of this. Except for those encounters necessary to marketing, she avoided everyone. The townsfolk, however, always suspicious of alien intrusion, were highly aware of her. It was not that they cared—but they kept their eyes open and competed in speculation about this proud, slender girl who walked alone by the outer flounce of low tide, whispering to herself.

Too often for chance, Elizabeth began to encounter self-conscious villagers on the hitherto deserted beaches. Too often for comfort, she felt unseen eyes upon her; yet she did nothing to escape it. Uneasiness and being spied on were an integral part of this pattern. Its culmination was inevitable, and, however she dreaded it, was necessary to her.

It was on her fourth day at Shilleth. She took her lunch in a basket down near the surf. For a time, they paced up the beach, pausing to heap up sand castles or gather driftwood; and when the fire was built, they lay down before it, their finger tips touching. Today, however, Elizabeth could not smile. A dark undertow of expectancy surged through her. Once more, she felt they were being watched.

"What is it, dear?" Marius finally asked.

"Nothing," she insisted. "Nothing, really."

At last, however, unable to endure the waiting, she swiftly turned around. Three men were coming over the dunes.

She jerked her hand way from Wrenn's. "It's him," she whispered. "It's Theo . . ."

He took her hand again, pressed it tightly. "We're not going to let it make any difference to all that we've decided on. We have what we want most."

The intruders were only some village men soothing their curiosity by asking directions which they already knew. Elizabeth answered their questions, but like a sleepwalker anguished by dreams. The three men glanced at each other uncomfortably, shrugged, and ambled on down the beach.

Elizabeth, scarcely aware that they were gone, sat on the shore, staring into the fire until it dimmed. After shoveling some sand onto the embers, she stumbled back to the cottage. Although she felt ill from the experience just undergone, and her hand was unsteady, she wrote until long after dark. When, at last, she fell into an exhausted slumber, she had completed in rich detail the chapter describing the flight to Shilleth, the idyllic days alone with Wrenn, and, at last, the grimly polite apprehension by Senator Carver and his henchmen. The words she had flung at them still echoed in her sleep: "I'm in love with Marius Wrenn."

She was awakened by the pound of waves. The morning sunlight, reflecting in a mirror, shone in her eyes. She drew up the covers, burrowed into the pillows, as if to hide; longing already for these days which had just passed, afraid of the days awaiting her in Boston.

Not bothering with breakfast, she packed her clothes and bolted the shutters. Before she left, she revolved slowly by the door, impressing every detail of the room on her mind. "But we'll be coming back here again, my dear," she assured him, tenderly.

Carrying their shoes, they trudged along the sifting shore towards town. Knowing her trepidation, he held her hand the tighter. "Don't worry about me," she told him, trying to hide her discomfort with the lazy smile. "I'm not afraid. Not while you're with me."

"And I'll always be with you," he assured.

"Always?"

"Always."

An incoming wave raced up the shore and lashed at his bare feet. Elizabeth shuddered. "Someone walk over your grave?" he laughed.

"No. Just that—the water's cold."

"Didn't even touch you."

Her smile was bleak. "But it touched you. Maybe I was shivering for you . . ." She looked out at the ocean, pleadingly. "I'm not afraid." Her own words returned to her. "Not while you're with me." But the time was so short until that day, one July, when the sea would claim him, and she would be alone again. Alone, and once more afraid.

"Beautiful, isn't it?" he mused.

"Beautiful?"

"The sea, today."

"It—frightens me."

Reaching down to the inrushing surf, he scooped up a handful and held it out to her. She looked up at him wonderingly, then cupped her hands, and he poured the glistening water into them. "This is your wedding present," he said. "The ocean. So you mustn't be afraid of it."

She gripped her fingers together, but the water seeped out between them. She glanced up at him, ruefully. "I couldn't hold it," she said. "It slipped away. . . ."

He laughed. "Why try to hold just that little part? The whole infinity of it—out to the horizon, and beyond—all of it is yours now."

She leaned her head against his shoulder. His arm slipped around her waist and, silently, they stood there. No need to think of July now, she thought. When the time came, she would know what to do. If the earth could not afford them an eternity together, the sea could. When he was gone, she would follow him. The buoys would not knell then, but ring out joyously. Sea lace would be her gown, and coral, her cathedral.

She stepped forward, suddenly, and let the tide swirl about her bare feet; reached down and cupped the chill water in her hands. July was not to be dreaded now. There would be no parting. Infinity—out to the horizon, and beyond—belonged to them.

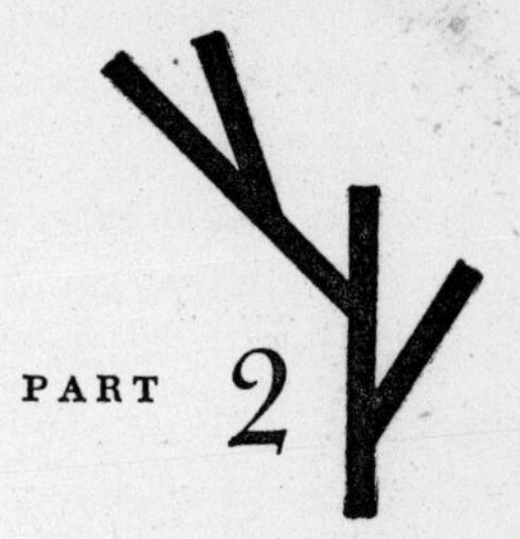

PART 2

Elizabeth von Schillar

CHAPTER 1

The day Elizabeth left for Cape Cod, Madame von Schillar had a visitor. She glanced at the card Worth gave her and sighed. First removing her rings and the pearls, she swept into the parlor where he waited.

"Well, Bentley, this is unexpected!"

The old artist bowed with seedy grandeur. "*Madame la Baronne*," he said; and would have kissed her hand had she not snatched it away.

"What can I do for you, Bentley?" she demanded. "As you know, I'm a busy woman, these days."

"Ah, to be busy!" Sprague sighed. "Still, I mustn't complain. I still have my memories." His smile put an edge on this last word. "Not spectacular memories like yours, perhaps—just little things—but all has its value."

"All right, all right," she said, impatiently. "You made that quite clear on your last visit. But you promised not to bother me again, when I helped you out."

"Helped me out! Please, my dear! I wouldn't have taken a penny, unless I had thought it was purely a business transaction—"

"Then you're not living up to your end of the bargain," she interrupted. "You promised to stay away from here."

"Circumstances force me," he sighed. "My beloved grandchildren—"

"Starving again, no doubt!"

"But absolutely starving!" He flicked a speck of lint from his lapel. He was old, a dapper wraith, whose spare, ascetic features were contradicted by the folly of a curled toupee. "After all, my dear, your name may go down to posterity, thanks to dear Marius. But my grandchildren are my only hope for immortality. So I must insure their welfare as best I can—selling such treasures as I have . . ."

The Baroness remained expressionless. "How you must hate Marius," she mused.

"Hate poor Marius?"

"Because he became great, and you didn't! Listen, my friend, your grandchildren aren't starving. You're merely trying to punish Marius through me, and paper your pockets, as well."

"Before God," he cried, raising his hands in mock horror, "that's an injustice! I adored Marius. Adored him! But after all, when your book comes out, people will naturally want to know even more about him. I dare say some magazine or newspaper would pay me a pretty penny for my recollections of him. Of course, I should hate revealing those things. It would be so messy. Ungentlemanly. Paint is my forte, not words. I want to be remembered as an artist, not a raconteur. But a man must live. I couldn't afford to pass up some tabloid's offer—unless, of course, I was able to make a good living selling my pictures."

"If you published a word, I'd sue," she said, struggling to remain calm. "And I'd win. You have no letters, no evidence, to back up your fool statements."

"Do you," he asked, "have any evidence to prove that my story is false? Of course, you don't. Because what I will be telling is the truth, just as I heard it from Marius, himself."

She flicked him a contemptuous glance. "I can just picture Marius telling you anything! Even if there were anything to tell."

"Oh, he didn't confide in me, directly. Not directly, dear lady. But the night he stayed at my place, that last spring—he and some other chaps, Ezterhausy was one, I believe—the walls were thin. I overheard. So did my daughter. And I dare say, we could find a few others who knew the real facts, too." He yawned to effect an air of complacency. "It should make very good reading. But not for children."

"It seems a pity to me," the Baroness said, slowly, "that you never concentrated your cleverness into your painting, instead of your intrigues. Maybe, then, you wouldn't be reduced to blackmailing old friends."

"Temper," he warned, coldly, "is infectious. I beg you, don't make me loose mine, too." He waited until she sat down, then added more genially, "As for blackmail, my dear, that's such a melodramatic phrase. All I'm asking is that you buy a picture so I can afford to live in quiet seclusion from this ugly age, as a gentleman should."

"And what pictures are you offering up this time?" she asked. "Another of those clever satires you do on nineteenth century art? Another fortune teller? Or perhaps Lillian Russell ascending to heaven?"

His smile stiffened. "Art," he said, "is the prettier part of truth—as you, writing your memoirs, obviously realize. If one wants the stark truth, then buy a photograph. Or a tabloid!" He unwrapped, and held up for the Baroness to admire, a portrait of some nymphs daintily sampling a bunch of grapes. "I call it, 'Afternoon in Paradise.' "

"How much?" she demanded.

"Five thousand dollars."

"Tosh! It's not worth a nickel!"

"Shall we let posterity decide? Posterity, you know, must judge us both."

Madame von Schillar met his pale, unblinking eyes. Then, shrugging, she arose. "I'll get my checkbook."

"Bless you, my dear," he said.

Yet as she made out the check, her eyes narrowed. A moment later, she smiled faintly, this persisting as she handed him the bank draft.

He glanced at it in surprise. "Haven't you made a mistake?"

"No. I believe it's made out for ten cents. That's for carfare home."

"Then," he said, regretfully, "I have nothing left to sell but the truth."

"You won't get even a nickel for that," Madame von Schillar said, pleasantly. "It'll be old-hat, already. You see, you've convinced me that all this might make sensational reading. So now I think perhaps I may include everything in my own book."

"I doubt it," he replied.

"Why, pray tell?"

"It's not the kind of thing a lady discusses. It's only a wonder that, looking back on that part of your life, you haven't turned to a pillar of salt." He tried not to smile at this drollery, but failed. "No, no, my dear," he continued, quickly, "I know you. You've already suffered too much abuse from the public. You won't go courting any more scandal."

"Oh, Bentley, Bentley, how naïve you are!" She laughed to hide the tremble of desperation in her voice. "Do you think I can be hurt any more? Do you think I care what people say now? Let the public roar, I'm deaf to it now. What can they take away from me? My reputation? Good God, if people screamed loud enough, I may have a best seller. So, I'd just as soon print the whole business myself, and be done with it. And done with you." She stood up and flicked him with her handkerchief. "Now, pray, what will you do?"

"Wait," he answered. "I'll wait for your book, to see if you had the courage to tell about it. And if you didn't, I will have that courage, and you will read my story." He tossed her check onto the table. "Or would you care to reconsider my oil painting?"

She stood close to him, ran her fingers up his arm. "Now, Bentley," she pouted, "don't be inhuman. It's not that I don't want to help you; it's that I can't. I'm almost stony now. And terribly, terribly in debt. Look!" She held up her bare hands. "I've even had to sell my rings—"

"But you're going to have a best seller," he reminded her, cheerfully.

She slapped her hand against the table top. "Well, you're not going to get a cent of it, be sure of that!"

He met her hard, green eyes. Then, shrugging, he picked up his coat. "Then I must write a best seller of my own."

"It'll never reach the light of day."

"No? Who'll stop it?"

"Can't you guess?"

Their eyes met.

Madame von Schillar continued. "That's why I've had to keep quiet, myself. An open threat from him, and many veiled threats from his lawyers—that if I so much as mentioned his name in the book—"

"But could he stop it?" Sprague demanded. "Stop the publication?" She nodded. "That would be very expensive, I should think."

"Very."

"I wonder . . ." Sprague said, thoughtfully. "I wonder, if instead of putting him to all that trouble, I could persuade him to become a patron of the arts."

"He could afford it better than I," said the Baroness. "And who knows—he might even enjoy your little paintings. He's so fond of the conventional."

He bowed. "Let me congratulate you, dear. Your genius for passing the buck, at least, has not deteriorated with age."

"Nor your avarice, my dear. I only hope it will not be too taxing for even his fortune."

"If it is," Sprague said, going to the door, "he can borrow."

"Of course. He has strong connections everywhere." She spoke casually, but carefully. "Everywhere. The banks, the city hall, the police force, the District Attorney's office—"

Sprague halted at the door. "How's that?"

"I said, he has lots of influential friends, if he needs help. Undoubtedly, they'll see you're well taken care of."

Sprague touched his handkerchief to his lips. "I see," he murmured. A little uncertainly now, he came back to her. "Elizabeth," he said, "give me a hundred dollars for the picture, and we'll forget about everything." She shook her head. "Fifty, then. Oh, it's true, the children aren't starving, but they need things terribly, and—I'm old now. I don't have too much time left to dicker around with Quincy—" She smiled, but again shook her head. "Then give me whatever you want and keep the picture. It's really not bad—"

"No, not bad," the Baroness said, pleasantly, "but even with my 'deteriorations of age,' I've no need yet for laxatives. Good afternoon, Bentley."

Her triumph at outbluffing Sprague buoyed her well into the next day, but when this wore thin, she found herself spoiled for less challenging occupations. To stimulate the original elation, she summoned to mind all her old enemies and pitted herself against them, vanquishing them just as she had Sprague. Rather than relieving her, however, it only made her feel the more unwanted.

"I should go out more," she told herself. "I should entertain."

But go out where? Entertain whom? Her former friends, never having forgiven the divorce which had betrayed their code, still refused to acknowlege her; and even if they would, they were old now, and she despised age. It was the new generation she wanted to know, the bright young set in which she had always traveled; but in Boston, they had not sought her out. The trouble with being a legend, she fretted, is that young people always take it for granted you're dead; or if these knew she was living, they didn't much care. It took youth to attract youth spontaneously. Their indifference made her conscious that she was not as young as she felt. Ignored by the old, forgotten by the young, and too proud to receive the *parvenus*, she sat alone in her suite, superbly gowned, with the cheerless impatience of a hostess waiting for her party to begin.

"And it will begin soon," she reminded herself. Youth, itself, could not be regained, perhaps, but the book would recapture for her the powers synonymous with youth: the attentions, the flattering and prestige, the right to pick and choose, even the ability to excite envy. This last had always been particularly important to Madame von Schillar. Success had come so early and so easily, she'd had no way of evaluating a thing until someone else coveted it. And with the memoirs published, people would envy the richness, the scope, the romance of her life; the parties, the beaux, the glamour; and again she would be a public figure they would stand on their chairs to see.

But the promise of all this, rather than sustaining her, only soured each moment with growing impatience.

By nightfall, she had drunk too much from the decanter labeled sherry, and was literally praying for Elizabeth's return. In these last months, without realizing it, she had come to depend on the sympathetic audience which the girl provided. Missing her sorely for the one virtue of listening, Madame von Schillar soon attributed to her all the other virtues—charm, wit, intelligence and good taste. "So it's a pity you chose this time to be away," she said, aloud. "Oh, the things I could tell you now . . ."

She sat up, self-consciously, glancing right and left, to make sure no one had overheard her talking to herself like some old woman. Then she bent over and shook her finger at the sleeping Jabot.

"Yes! I talking to black dog, and her don't even listen!" The beast opened a moist eye, then, with difficulty, arose and climbed onto Madame von Schillar's lap. "Her isn't going to desert me, anyway, is her?" the Baroness said, gently rocking the animal. "No! Black dog wants to be with me, don't her? Yes! That's what her wants most: to be with me. . . ."

On the third day, the Baroness saw no possible way to face another hour by herself. She loathed being alone, loathed this enforced idleness, and before long she was blaming Elizabeth for it all. What right, she demanded, had the girl to run off to Cape Cod? For research, Elizabeth had said, but the more the Baroness considered this, the less likely it seemed. The Cape was synonymous in her mind with deception. It occurred to her that Elizabeth had gone there for a few quiet days with her lover.

Immediately, she was attacking the girl's duplicity, and wrung nearly an hour's entertainment out of it. The thing which most vexed her was that Elizabeth had not confided in her. "Good God," she exclaimed, "I tell her all my innermost secrets, but she won't trust me with anything. Me, who could be the most understanding about such things!"

Was the girl afraid of derision, she wondered; or ashamed of the man she loved? "Oh, but itsy-me has no lover, Madame," she mimicked, savagely.

She arose, abruptly. It was time to put an end to this nonsense. Elizabeth's room was empty, now. "And it won't be as if I'm really spying," she told herself. "After all, this is my house, and since she's my responsibility, I ought to know what's going on." She hurried into the hall. There would be letters, perhaps, or some such token to betray the wretched intrigue, once and for all.

She mounted the stairs, stiffly. With the years, she climbed stairs less and less often, blaming her reluctance on that interesting heart condition which, for years, had excused her from doing whatever she was too lazy to do. Now, just in case someone might be watching, she clutched her breast, bravely, and made great show of biting her lip, until she was safe in the room which had once been Wrenn's.

It had changed little, she thought, painfully; the narrow cot, the austere white walls, the window seat where she had posed for him. Her step faltered and abruptly, she clasped hands over her ears as if to deafen herself to memory. "Why, oh God, why?" ran through her mind. "*Why, oh God, why*?"

She glimpsed her contorted face in the mirror and immediately straightened up; her lips curved languidly, her eyes became impassive. Elegantly aloof, she began sorting through Elizabeth's possessions. They were scant—the drab clothes in the wardrobe, the neat, inexpensive cosmetics on the washstand, the small bottle of scent—it was Loki, she noticed. Her narrow nose pinched with contempt, and she turned to the desk. There were no letters in the drawer; only the carefully penned manuscript. As the Baroness had not yet read this, she brought it near the light and, flipping open the pages, idly scanned one.

A moment later, she sniffed and reached for a pencil. The girl had made a mistake, a very obvious mistake, that must not go uncorrected. Then her fumbling for the pencil ceased as her eye traveled further down the page. "Impossible!" she snorted. "I never said such a thing in my life!"

With mounting fury, she read on until the blood pounded in her temples and her hands shook. Motives were misconstrued, events which had never occurred were included, and the depiction of herself was an unbelievable travesty, guaranteed to make her a laughing stock the world over. "How dare she?" the Baroness cried out. "Just how dare she!"

Gasping for breath, she hastened downstairs more rapidly than was discreet and, in trying to avoid a fall, spilled the papers over the stairs. Not pausing to pick them up, she tramped over the pages and, hurrying into her suite, put through a call to New York.

"Mr. Mellett," she said, coldly, when he was connected, "I want you to come here, at once."

"But, my dear woman," he said, in amazement, "I'm not sure I can. Perhaps at the end of the week—"

"If you are no longer interested in publishing my book," she interrupted, "then, by all means, don't bother coming today."

"Is something wrong? Something serious?"

"Of course, it is. That's why I must see you immediately."

"Couldn't you tell me over the phone?"

"I certainly could not!" The Baroness recognized no drama without a visible audience. "I hope I may expect you some time tonight. Otherwise, we'll simply have to forget about my book."

Without giving him opportunity to reply, she hung up the phone and tugged the bell cord for Worth. "I want you to gather up the papers on the stairs and bring them here," she ordered, when the servant appeared. "I have a few hours to kill, and I think I'll get in a little reading. . . ."

Harry Mellett arrived shortly after ten. A rough trip by air, added to Madame von Schillar's imperious command, left him in no mood to toy with social amenities. He came to the point, at once. "Now then, what's the trouble?" he demanded.

The Baroness was not to be rushed. This man was not going to make a mere curtain raiser out of the spectacle for which she had so carefully set the stage. Candles burning on silver branches lighted her advantageously. She had contrived her scarlet hair into soft clusters above the brow, and wore her famous pearls. Advancing slowly, she studied Mellett. She had always felt his charm deeply, but now, in defense against it, she picked out all his faults: he looked tired, his hair had been cut too short, a small scar hyphenated his eyebrows.

"Well?" he said.

"That girl is an idiot!"

"Not entirely, Baroness," Mellett smiled. "Just a writer—a lesser degree of idiocy. Is she around, incidentally?"

"Naturally not!" This was another debt she was not willing to absolve—Mellett's apparent attraction to Elizabeth. "She's hiding out on the Cape for a week. For research, she said, but I rather fancy she is not researching alone." She watched his face for some sign, but he merely shifted his gaze. "Her private life does not concern me. But my private life does." She indicated the manuscript. "Read this. I think it will speak for itself."

He eyed the pile of papers with alarm. "Read all that, now?"

"Just a few paragraphs should suffice."

Reluctantly, he picked up the manuscript and settled back in a chair. Apparently a few paragraphs did not suffice, for he continued to read, intently.

Impatiently, Madame von Schillar drummed her red nails on the table top. "Well?" she said, at last.

He looked up from a page. "I should say it does speak for itself," he said. "Eloquently."

His remark took her by surprise and, before she could recover, he was reading again. She eyed Mellett uneasily. By all rights, he should be apologetic by now, and she bullying him. But that would come. Postponement would only add savor to her recriminations. While the young man skimmed rapidly over the sentences, she silently rehearsed her grievances.

When, at last, Mellett put down the final page, Madame von Schillar was ready. She spoke quietly, for gentleness would allow her a wider basis from which to rise. "Now do you see?"

"Yes." His voice was strange, and he blew his nose.

"What are you going to do about it?"

"Congratulate you. It's a remarkable work. All I'd hoped it would be."

"You don't see at all!" she snapped.

"Then maybe I don't know what you wanted me to see," he answered. "All I know is, it moved me very much. I saw every episode, just as if it were myself involved. Every page came alive. Believe me, you and Elizabeth have done a superb, a really superb job."

"Wouldn't creation be a better word?" she began, bitterly. "Or invention," she meant to add, but he interrupted her, enthusiastically.

"Creation is a better word, by God!" He came forward and took her unwilling hands. "Over the phone, you had me scared, but now I can understand your impatience to have me read it." Mellett was by no means persuaded this was Madame von Schillar's motive in summoning him, but he knew her vanity and hoped, by playing on it, to calm her a little. "How soon can you get your book finished?"

"I don't think it's likely to be finished, ever!" She waited for his explosive reaction, and was not disappointed.

"Not finished!" he cried.

"No."

"Now, listen," he said, tensely, but with surprising steadyness, "I know how hard it must be for you to open your heart to the public. I know every sentence must cost you much anguish—for there is anguish in that writing. The anguish and—fierceness, rapture and culmination to be found in a great love. But whatever the pain was and is, I beg you, don't deny us this story."

"Us?"

"The whole world of us." His sincerity was no less, but if he gradually became more florid, it was because he was first a salesman, and he was desperate. "What famous lovers has America produced? We're a nation with a great capacity for love, and yet we've produced no great, true love story. Even the romance of Ann Rutledge and Lincoln doesn't fill the bill. But here we have one, at last—the tragic love story of a great artist and a famous beauty, wonderfully remembered, alive, intimate, poetic, and burning, burning—"

Mellett, arch enemy of purple prose, indulged its easier excesses when he became excited. Since his bombast seemed to have impressed the Baroness not at all, however, he dropped his hands to his side and concluded in a simpler voice. "Marius Wrenn has been a great inspiration for artists. Let Marius and Elizabeth Wrenn be the same for lovers."

She studied his flushed face to see if he were mocking; but there was no laughter in him. "You're an educated man, I presume," she finally said. "At all events, not naïve. Yet you found this treatment—convincing?"

"Yes. Don't you?"

"No."

"Why not?"

"I know my opinion, Mr Mellett. It's yours, I'm interested in, now."

"Very well, then. I found it most convincing. I'm an outsider, you see, while you're too close to the story. You have no perspective on it; every detail seems of equal importance. To you, ten volumes couldn't do your story justice. Shakespeare, himself, could never make it entirely convincing to you, because he couldn't include everything you felt, every color and shading you saw." He laughed. "Though, as it is, certain parts of your book come very close to total recall."

"Total what?"

"The past utterly recaptured. Thought and conversations too complete, impressions too vivid—details which would ordinarily be forgotten over the years. Usually, I find this highly suspect in autobiography, but here—well, it reads as if it were torn from an inspired diary. I tell you, there are moments—as when you describe your reunion in the park—when I could almost feel your breath and see the way you looked—"

"Pink roses!" she scoffed. "Can you picture that?"

"Why not?" he asked. "Only a great beauty would have the audacity to wear pink roses in red hair."

She turned from him and peered out a window, rattling her long nails against the pane. It was hard for her to put aside the drama of wrath, but this demanded immediate revaluation. Suppose, she thought, suppose she allowed this astonishing galaxy of lies to be published? Surely, it was prettier than the truth, and more expert than any lies she could devise. And it was safe enough, since few were left capable of exposing it as fabrication. For years, she had encysted that part of her life with apology, but no one reading this version would demand excuses. There would be no more ugliness to hide from; there would be only understanding. "Marius and Elizabeth Wrenn," she murmured. "Elizabeth and Marius . . ."

When she turned back to the anxious Mellett, her voice was gracious, her manner already that of a legendary heroine. "Perhaps, then," she said, "I will try to finish my book."

When she was alone again, that night, the Baroness carefully reread the memoirs. This time, they seemed less shocking, somehow less distorted than she had thought on her first reading. Possibly she had acted just so, spoken exactly such words, but had forgotten. It was not impossible that time had warped her recollections and that the girl, somehow divining these discrepencies, had restored the rightful color and proportion. At last, she yielded entirely to Elizabeth's version. It was true, she decided, every word of it, true.

As she undressed for bed, she paused before a mirror and held a pink powder puff against her vivid hair. The effect of the pink against the red was startling, but not impossible. "I probably did wear pink roses in my hair," she mused. But, for the life of her, she could not remember mentioning it to Elizabeth.

CHAPTER 2

"I suppose it rained the whole time you were there," the Baroness said, when Elizabeth returned from Cape Cod.

"Only the first night."

"Cottage still holding together?"

"It was lovely. I had a wonderful time."

"Now, now," reproved the other, slyly. "It couldn't have been all that wonderful. There's nothing to do there."

"But I had my work—finished the chapter on the elopement."

"And that's all you did? Just worked?" Madame von Schillar's smile was knowing, but without malice.

"Well, I'd go walking or shopping. And one day, we had a picnic on the shore—"

Madame von Schillar's eyes brightened. "We?"

Elizabeth laughed. "I suppose I was using the editorial we," she said.

The Baroness gave Elizabeth's arm a gentle poke, but she did not follow up the matter. She was content, for the moment, to let the girl keep her little romance as secret as she pleased.

As the week progressed, Madame von Schillar refused to become annoyed by Elizabeth's air of preoccupation. This, she interpreted as the manner natural to the artist at work. She felt not a little awe and respect for this young woman who could so rightfully mirror her life. No one had ever before been so understanding of her, and the Baroness rewarded her accordingly. She gave her a flower-shaped coral pin. She suggested that Elizabeth invite her young man to dinner and did not protest when the girl declined with an abstracted smile. She insisted that Elizabeth bundle up well on going outside every night at nine. There was no patronizing, no conscious bounty in her manner. She was simply acting with the grace and understanding which the memoirs had portrayed as her rightful nature.

Such a mood was not to last. Monday brought a strange letter. It was addressed to Marius Wrenn, and the envelope heavily annotated by the hieroglyphics dear to postal bureaucracy. Madame von Schillar smiled. "From the dead-letter office to a dead man," she mused.

Her smile faded, however, as she read the contents. If this was a joke, she thought, it was in appalling taste. The urgent appeal, addressed to her late husband and signed by her own name, was like some mockery out of the past. The postmark, however, was of recent date.

> Marius—Forgive me. I hadn't the courage to go on before, but now I haven't the strength to go on without you. It's too late to think of cost now. And nothing could be worse than the torment of these last weeks. There must be a way for us, somehow. I'll be in the park tomorrow night at nine. Be there, I implore you. Elizabeth.

First bewildered, next indignant, she reread the message and then, crumpling it, cast it aside. It was not so easy, however, to cast it from her mind. This was not the first time in her life that she had received a crank letter. Usually they were so abusive as to amuse her or inspire a brief attitude of martyrdom. This one, however, with all its oblique simplicity, touched a yet unsheathed nerve. It was too near, too painfully near, that note she had once sent Marius which had so changed the course of their lives. Uneasily, she picked up the crumpled letter and, smoothing it out, again studied the lines.

The handwriting seemed familiar. Yes, she thought, the letter would have to be from someone who knew her, for no stranger could so closely parallel the actuality.

Now she gave the envelope careful scrutiny. Having been addressed merely, "Marius Wrenn, Boston," an official notation had been appended: insufficient address. Below, someone had scrawled in pencil: deceased; and next to this, stamped in purple: return to sender. Frowning, she glanced at the back flap for the sender's name, and new vexation pinched her lips. Under the initials, E. W. C. her own address was written.

"Someone's playing a joke," she insisted, aloud; but the sound of these words did not heal the dread beginning to stir deep within her. This was no mere mockery. Whoever wrote this letter had in mind something more concrete than malice.

Her eyes narrowed. Abruptly, she went to the telephone.

It was a half-hour of eternity before her door opened to admit Bentley Sprague. "I came as quickly as I could," he said, fanning himself with his Homburg. "You sounded most mysterious, dear lady. Irresistibly mysterious!"

She merely stared at him.

The old artist fumbled with his cravat and faltered. "But what is it, Elizabeth?"

Her voice was accusing. "It won't do, Bentley!"

"How's that?"

"If it's revenge, it's pretty poor stuff," she continued, balefully, "and if it's another subtle prelude to extortion, you'd better watch your step. Maybe I can't do much myself to stop this annoyance, but you know who can—and won't hesitate to. Don't start things you can't finish, my friend!"

He held out his hands. "For God's sake, Elizabeth, what is it? What have I done now?"

She pointed to the letter. "I spotted your fine Italian hand in this, right off. All the malice and intricacy of it. Oh, I know you! Never walk a straight line when you can use a labyrinth. Sending it in that roundabout way to cover your tracks!"

"My tracks?"

"Because you knew the steps I'd immediately take against you. That's why you sent it in this tricky fashion. To try and scare me, and then send around someone else to collect."

He snatched up the letter and, holding it close to his eyes, quickly read it. Then he shrugged. "It's charming," he said, "but how does it concern me?"

"Don't bother play-acting," she snapped. "You sent it!"

"I did not," he protested. "I didn't, Elizabeth. On my honor."

Her smile marked down this oath.

"But I didn't," he cried. "And anyway"—he tried his jaunty laugh—"even if I had sent it, what's blackmailable about that letter? Undoubtedly you wrote him often, no one doubts that."

"But *this* letter . . ." She turned her anguished face from his gaze.

"I see," he said, at last. "Whoever knew enough to write that letter would obviously know everything else too, is that it?" He smiled now. "Believe me, dear lady, I'm not the only one who knows the truth. There were others. Ezterhausy, for instance—"

"He's dead!"

"Yes. But you and I were never deceived by his air of trustworthiness. Undoubtedly, he told others. Strangers."

She shook her head. "This was from no stranger. It was from you. With all your motives showing, too!"

"Listen, Elizabeth . . ." Thoughtfully, he peered again at the letter.

"Well?"

"Blackmail isn't the only possible motive, you know."

"What then?"

"Couldn't it be, dear lady, a warning?"

"What are you talking about?" she demanded.

"Think," he urged. "A warning that your secret is no secret. A weapon, as it were, to discourage you from continuing with the memoirs. A hint that, if you persist with them, this information will be used to your disadvantage."

"Rot!"

"Is it? Surely there must be rather a pack of people who don't want that book published. Oh, not just those directly involved. There are others—"

"Such as?"

"I don't know their names. But I can think of their reasons."

There were those, he explained, who bore her a grudge. And those who were afraid she'd tell the truth about Wrenn; and those who were afraid she would not! And those who had earned her enmity and were afraid of her printed reprisals. And those related to the Senator or Wrenn or even von Schillar, who didn't want her affairs opened to the public, lest they suffer by reflection. "Oh," he concluded, with an air of profound regret, "their name is legion!"

Madame von Schillar sank down into a chair. "Give me a cigarette," she murmured.

He produced a dented silver case. "I didn't know you smoked."

"Haven't in years . . ." She watched the curling drift of smoke for a time, finally asking, "What's to be done?"

"Wait."

"Wait?"

"Wait," he repeated, fully enjoying his command of the situation.

"Whoever sent the letter will show up before long—they always do—to make his demand known while the impact of fear is still fresh—"

"But I can't just wait," she cried.

"What else can you do?"

"If I only knew who sent it, I could map out some defense. I could be all prepared, ready to bargain or fight—"

"Fight?"

"Yes." She turned glittering green eyes upon him. "Oh, don't think I'm just going to sit back and take this! Let them try what they will, I'm not going to give up my book!" Her hand clenched. "I've staked too much on it. Nothing's going to stop it!"

"The cost may be high." Noticing her hands now, and the rings she had claimed were pawned, his voice became sharp. "Very high!"

"So? I've always played for high stakes!"

"And when you can't bluff, I dare say you've learned other ways of winning." She did not answer, but sat there, her brows drawn, her hands restless. At last, he shrugged. "Well, if I can be of further aid, you know where to find me."

"Yes. My pocketbook's on the table."

"Only carfare," he said, opening her purse. Preoccupied, she did not watch him. He smiled. "Taxi fare," he corrected.

For a long time after Sprague had left, Madame von Schillar sat at her desk, intently sifting and listing the names of those who might benefit by suppression of the book. Quincy? She shook her head. Much as he dreaded implication, it was not in his character to block her so deviously. Hyltie? It was doubtful that he knew anything, and besides, he was not clever enough, or his handwriting that good—

She glanced at the peculiar handwriting of the letter, and then quickly rang for Worth. When her hamper of old correspondence had been brought down from the attic, she busied herself studying and contrasting the penmanship of the dusty letters to that of this new and threatening note. By noon, however, she had found nothing to identify her enemy.

As she tossed the last paper back into the box, she noticed Elizabeth's copybook lying on the table. Idly, she flicked open the pages. While these were mostly in shorthand, there were a few written words which she mechanically compared to those in the letter. In this last, the pressure of the pen was heavier, often puncturing the page; and the writing was large, carelessly formed, slanting like an armada of sailboats in high wind—this, in contrast to Elizabeth's precise, almost vertical script. In both specimens, however, the o's and a's were tightly sealed, and the t's reached up for their cross bars. It was precious little to go on, for, the Baroness realized, she crossed her own t's in much the same way.

"And if she wrote this," she added, "why would she write it? What motive?" Although she shod the question with a hundred explanations, none seemed to fit. She could see no way Elizabeth could benefit by discouraging their work. Besides, the letter had to come from someone with accurate information.

There was a tap at the door. It was the girl. "I can't do a thing right now," Madame von Schillar cried, guiltily pushing away the notebook. "I've got something on my mind."

"Can I help?"

"No, you can't. You don't have to share all my thoughts, you know."

Elizabeth looked so startled, the Baroness had to laugh at her own vehemence. "Oh dear, oh dear, I am in a state today, aren't I?"

"Find anything in the letterbox?"

Madame von Schillar stiffened. "What?"

She indicated the hamper. "Any letters we can use in the book?"

"No. Nothing."

"Well, when you want to work, just ring for me."

The Baroness glanced at the clock, then spoke defiantly. "I've changed my mind. Let's get on with the book, right this minute. Might as well work as wait—"

"Wait?" asked Elizabeth, sitting down.

"Never mind," said Madame von Schillar. "Where did we leave off, yesterday?"

"Where the Senator had begun his divorce proceedings." She opened her notebook and tonelessly read: " '—and one by one, all my friends began to drop me as if I had leprosy. Oh, what utter bitches they were—' "

"Go on," ordered the Baroness.

"That's all. You got mad there and sent me off."

"And no wonder! Now Lucy Denham, for instance. She crossed the street once, so as not to acknowledge me. I crossed right after her and was sweet as honey. But that afternoon, I bought a hat just like one she'd been wearing and put it on Worth, then sent her over to Lucy's on some pretext. Very petty of me, of course, but I had no defense left. I was so horribly alone—"

"There was Marius."

"Yes, of course. But only in the evenings, when we could meet in the park . . ." Her voice faded away, and then she spoke again, almost fiercely. "It was the most sickening period of my life. Did I ever tell you of the letters I'd get? Usually unsigned, and always cruel. Calling me filthy names or threatening—"

As she spoke, she watched Elizabeth intently, letting no flicker of expression pass without first testing it as an unconscious confession. It was not that she actually suspected Elizabeth, but the girl was handy. One could not deal with a letter; could not threaten, argue or bargain with a piece of paper. Madame von Schillar's desperate need, at this moment, was someone tangible to blame.

Impatiently, she turned her eyes back to the pensive girl. "Where were we? What was I saying?"

"I don't know," Elizabeth answered. "I'm afraid I was off thinking, too—"

"About what, pray?"

Elizabeth shrugged. "Nothing important.'

"I see," the Baroness said, irritably. "I'm supposed to tell you every little thing that pops to my mind, but you're a little too fine, I notice, ever to tell me what you're thinking."

"Very well," said Elizabeth. "I was trying to imagine how I'd feel if I got abusive letters through the mail."

"And why were you trying to imagine such a thing?"

"Because I have to describe how you felt, in the book," Elizabeth explained.

"Well, I can tell you how it feels!" Madame von Schillar's voice was unhesitating. "It's ghastly and humiliating. And when I get my hands on whoever sent it, believe me, he'll rue the day!" Her eyes narrowed. "I learned a lesson then, and it's still so, today—whatever you want to do, there's always someone who'll try to stop you. But you go on, just the same! By hook or by crook, and whatever the cost, *you go on*!"

Elizabeth noted down this last, her face luminous with pride. "But one thing isn't quite clear," she added, glancing up. "Why did—"

But the Baroness was not listening to her. She had risen, was standing tensely, as if ready to spring. "Was that the doorbell?"

"I didn't hear anything."

Madame von Schillar shrugged and sank down. "What were you saying?"

"Why did you and Marius keep meeting in the park? Why not in the house? The Senator had moved out, hadn't he?"

"Yes, but . . ." Her voice drifted off.

"Maybe it was because the park was your own," Elizabeth suggested. "There were no memories there of anything except each other and your love."

"Yes, that was probably it," decided the Baroness, inattentively.

"And then?" She waited for the Baroness to speak, and finally said, "Yes?"

The Baroness sighed and fanned out her hands. Although no

threat could force her to abandon the memoirs, that curious sense of waiting for a trap to spring, of girding for an unknown battle, prohibited the concentration necessary to the book's progress.

"Give me time to think," she murmured, and waved the girl away. "Come back, later. . . ."

She shoved open her windows, left her door ajar, and paced about restlessly, often glancing at the clock, often and fruitlessly hastening to the front door. "Be patient," she instructed herself. "Don't waste your energy. Nothing can be done till he calls . . ."

But it was not in her nature to wait passively. Challenge had always forced her to act swiftly, to attack, to gain the advantage of the first move. Impulsively, she pocketed her list of suspects and had a taxi summoned.

Lucy Denham was not only at home to Madame von Schillar, but effusively gracious. She began, at once, to reminisce about "you and Marius and me," eulogizing every inadequate incident like a peddler his wares, and assuring the Baroness that each *belonged* in her book.

"Once you were deathly afraid of being mentioned in the same breath with Marius and me," the Baroness finally interrupted. "Why are you so eager for it now?"

Mrs Denham glanced away. "My grandson," she admitted. "He's studying art. A great admirer of Marius. And if he could see, in print, that I—well, it would give me *some* way of reaching him. . . ."

Satisfied that Lucy Denham was not implicated, Madame von Schillar continued her search. Unwilling to climb the four flights to Morley Magoffin's apartment, she sent a child up with a message requesting him to come down. The note was returned, across the bottom of which was scrawled, "I'm sick. If important, please phone." Quickly, the Baroness compared his writing to that of the letter, then sighed with relief; not so much because he was innocent, as because it had spared her the ordeal of talking to him and rehearsing the horror of those days. She hurried on.

She had never before met Ezterhausy's sister, Ada, but she could see the resemblance: the wide cheekbones, the direct eyes. Even the crisp, curly hair, although grey, was cut short like his.

"I was sorry to hear of Jay's death," the Baroness began.

"Were you?" The woman returned to the copper plate she had been engraving.

"Of course, I was. Deeply grieved."

"Why?"

"I liked him. He was one of the few who stuck by us."

"He stuck by Marius," Ada corrected, bluntly. "I don't think Jay cared about you."

"Indeed? I was the intruder, eh? He resented me, resented my influence?"

"That may have been it."

"Don't you know? Surely, Jay never left off trying to turn people against me. Even Marius."

"Did you ever stop working against Jay? His influence?"

"Is that what he told you?"

"I can't remember that he ever discussed you."

"Well, now, that's a blow to the ego," the Baroness laughed. "Incidentally, if you're concerned about it, I'm not going to mention Jay in my book."

"I would imagine not," his sister said, dryly.

"Do you object then? To the omission?"

She looked up from her work now. "You can put Jay in your book or leave him out. It doesn't change facts!"

Madame von Schillar drew her furs close and arose. She was satisfied. Unfriendly, Ada Ezterhausy might be, but she was too straightforward to have sent so circuitous a threat.

Her search continued. One by one, she crossed the names off her list, and, at last, returned home in a curious conflict of victory and despair.

She slept ill that night, and her dread was justified, the following day, by a letter in the mailbox, addressed in the same heavy, sloping hand. It was, however, for Elizabeth.

Squinting, the Baroness held the envelope up to the light. Failing to determine the message within, she hurried to the kitchen and steamed open the flap. The paper she pulled out bore just one word: harlot.

She bit back her breath. Was the entire house being terrorized, then? Elizabeth, too? This narrowed the field of suspects considerably. The culprit would have to be someone familiar to the girl as well. "And we have no acquaintances in common!" Then, she added aloud, "Sarah Carver!"

She tensed the muscles of her jaw. Sarah, of course. Sarah hated them both. And she was famous for her poison pen. The motive was clear too. Sarah had tried to interfere with the book once before. Now, to suppress publication and so protect her brother, she was not above blackmail.

Angrily, Madame von Schillar shouted for Worth. "Come in and help me dress," she cried. "I've got a little visit to pay this morning. And a little debt to pay back."

Miss Sarah Carver's house, on the correct side of Beacon Street, had an uninhabited look, and the Baroness kept her gloved finger on the doorbell much longer than was necessary. The door flung open and the housekeeper thrust her head out.

"We're not deaf, you know!" she cried, indignantly.

"Indeed?" Madame von Schillar took a step forward, but the servant did not move out of her way. "I wish to see Miss Carver."

"She don't see people any more."

"I'm not people," the other replied, grandly. "Advise her that Baroness von Schillar is here."

Faith glanced at her face in surprise. Then she spoke gently. "I'm sorry, ma'am. I know she won't see you."

"Get out of my way!" The Baroness shoved by her and strode into the house. "Sarah," she called. "Sarah Carver, where are you?"

As she passed the parlor entrance, she glimpsed a figure seated by the fire, bundled in shawls and a brown sealskin cape. Madame von Schillar sauntered in with an indolence designed to madden the old woman. "Well, my dear," she said, "I decided to answer your sweet note in person." She paused to indicate the fur cape. "Funny what happens to sable after a few decades. Gets to look like old seal pelt."

Faith was pulling at her arm. "She can't see anyone, I tell you," she whispered, fiercely. "She's been ill—"

Tugging off her gloves, the Baroness continued, imperturbably. "I want to chat with you, Sarah, if you'll call off your dog."

"I couldn't help it, Miss Sarah," Faith protested. "She pushed right in here—"

"Always did! Always pushed her way in." Miss Carver's voice was strange, slurred, and the effort to speak cost her face much distortion. Her eyes, however, unrestricted, flashed their bitter resentment, as of old.

"She's had a stroke," Faith whispered. "Now, go away."

In her revulsion for sickness and age, Madame von Schillar edged back. "I'll be brief then, Sarah. It's about these letters. They've got to stop!" She awaited some reaction from the old woman, but Miss Carver merely stared at her. The Baroness produced the letters. "Didn't you write these? I know you did, so don't pretend."

"Wouldn't waste paper on you."

"She can't write," Faith whispered. "Her writing hand's paralyzed. Now, come away—"

"Didn't write it," Miss Carver said, arduously. "Can't write now. But can still talk, thank God. Can dictate. And am! Theo's story. Tell the truth!"

"You wouldn't dare!" Her gloves fell from her nerveless fingers. "You don't have any proof! Nobody does." By the time she had picked up her gloves, she had again contrived the careless manner. "And, anyway, it's far from the truth!"

"Don't know what you mean. Not even mentioning your name, anyway. Beneath me!" Her face attempted the nuance of contempt. "This, decent book!" Avoiding every unnecessary word she saved her strength for fury. "About Theo's accomplishment. Speeches. Great work. Ideals. Let world judge him on that. Then won't believe lies you'll tell—"

"Not bothering with lies, m'dear. The truth will vindicate me quite adequately—"

"Couldn't ruin Theo then, you won't now," Miss Carver interrupted. "He sterner stuff. Even dead, he's stronger—"

"Oh, yes, yes," mocked the Baroness. "He was so much stronger. He had to show me that all the time, so he'd believe it, himself. He had to take me by force on my wedding night, rape me—that made him stronger, didn't it? I was just a weak woman. Well, we'll see who ends with the upper hand." She spoke swiftly now, angrily. "And you, too, Sarah, dear. A pillar of strength. A tower! But with a leaning, eh? A weakness for brother! Oh, my book's a decent one, too, or I might tell a few things. Like why you tried so hard to wreck my marriage. Take over my responsibilities. Keep me under your thumb. Well, now you can't even do this—" And she snapped her fingers.

In the ensuing silence, the sound lingered in her ears like a rifle crack. Suddenly, she was appalled at the gesture in the face of the helpless old woman. She reached out impulsively, touched Sarah's inert hand. "Forgive me. I didn't mean that—"

Miss Carver sat rigidly. Her face was drawn with a grimace of triumph. Madame von Schillar's mouth tightened. Then, indolently, she placed her hand directly before the old woman's eyes, and, once more, snapped her fingers.

She returned home, her head aching. The visit to Miss Carver's had only added the scourge of memory to her uneasiness. She summoned Elizabeth at once. Never had the book seemed more important; once published, it would exonerate everything, erase forever the old torment. Yet when the girl sat before her, waiting, Madame von Schillar became so overwhelmed with distrust, she feared to confide anything. Not knowing just who was against her, the whole world seemed in conspiracy against her.

Her headache intensified and, instead of dinner, she took a sleeping tablet. It was not until nearly nine that she awakened. As a gesture of defiance, she put on the gayest of her Paris gowns and situated a newly acquired pink rose in her red hair. A game of cards with Elizabeth would be fun, she decided, would distract her enough to later permit continuance with the work.

As she entered the parlor, however, Elizabeth was just opening the front door. "You're not going out!" the Baroness cried.

"Just for a while."

The door closed. Madame von Schillar slumped into a chair and morosely picked at the settings of her rings. Then, slowly, she sat upright. Suppose, she thought, this man that Elizabeth met every night was an enemy, taking advantages of the girl's loveless existence to trick secrets from her? Perhaps, unwittingly, the girl was an accomplice to this pressure against the book.

She stood up and, sweeping aside the velvet portiers, peered out of the window. Elizabeth was disappearing into the shadows of the park. Speculatively, Madame von Schillar gnawed at her lip. She hastened to a curio cabinet across the room, and when she returned to the window, a pair of opera glasses was in her hand.

"Now," she thought, focusing the lens on the park, "we'll just see who this man is."

It was not easy to see anything. The park was densely shadowed. Now and then, some wind herded the lazy clouds from the face of the moon, and she could glimpse Elizabeth. The girl sat as one moonstruck, her face gleaming, her lips parted, her eyes closed. No one joined her, however. Shortly before ten, the Baroness slung aside her opera glasses. What Elizabeth had insisted all along was true, then. She met no one on her nocturnal escapades.

Abruptly, the Baroness returned to her suite. This matter had become too nerve-wracking, and worse, was interfering with the book's progress. Decisively, she tore the strange letter to Wrenn into bits.

"I'll just pretend it never happened," she declared, flinging the scraps into the fire. "And if another letter comes, I'll call the police."

Even with the letter destroyed, however, uneasiness continued to nag her the following day. The postman's familiar ring twice stabbed her, and her tongue duplicated the taste of metal. Fearfully, she hurried to the mailbox. It held only a magazine. She sighed with exaggerated relief, to persuade herself that the ordeal was over; yet the dark expectancy persisted.

After lunch, she sent Elizabeth upstairs on some pretext, and, herself, stayed on for another demitasse. "Worth," she said, as the maid refilled her cup, "can you think of anyone who'd be bothering me with letters to Mr Wrenn?"

Worth stared at her. "Oh, ma'am, she's not up to that, again!"

"Who?" demanded the Baroness, sharply.

"Miss Deveny."

"What do you mean?"

"About those letters. She come to me once, asking and asking if I knew where the letters from Mr Wrenn was hidden—"

"No, no," sighed the Baroness. "Not letters from Wrenn, but *to* him."

"To him?" the servant echoed.

"I know it sounds silly, but that's what I received, yesterday. A rather strange letter to Marius and signed Elizabeth."

"Oh, I'm sure she wouldn't try to forge nothing ma'am, strange as she is. Unless she's got the brain fever. Or spiritualism."

"Spiritualism?"

"Like in a trance. Automatic writing. The spirits guide your hand, and you just write—"

"Tosh! And anyway, I'm not accusing Miss Deveny of anything. It's likely from someone who hates me."

Worth bent closer. "To be forward, ma'am—what did this letter say?"

Pressing her finger tips to her temples, the Baroness tried to reconstruct it from memory. A moment of lucidity illuminated an entire phrase from the letter, and with a shiver, she repeated it aloud. " 'I'll be in the park tomorrow night at nine. Be there, I implore you. Elizabeth.' "

And Elizabeth had been in the park at nine o'clock!

She stared into Worth's face, then burst into delighted laughter. Was that what Elizabeth had been doing in the park by herself, each night? Holding séances and communing with the spirit world? Did she interview Wrenn's ghost there? Ask it terribly intimate questions? Guided by his spectral hand, had she written that letter?

Of course, of course, she giggled. Wasn't Elizabeth a ghost-writer?

She laughed again, turning her merriment away from Worth's bewildered eyes. The idea of the whole thing was delicious, and already she had resolved to, one day, pass it off as the truth to amuse her dinner guests.

The weight and worry of expectation returned with afternoon, but despite the intrusive ticking of the clock and the thudding of her heart, Madame von Schillar made a heroic effort to push the book forward. At times, she was almost successful, but the pressure which sharpened her voice and wits took heavy toll of her energy. By five, she sank back on the couch, exhausted.

"That ought to keep you busy for a while," she said, in dismissing the girl. "And after dinner maybe we can even squeeze out a few words more."

"I don't mind, if you don't." Elizabeth opened the door. "We can work until nine o'clock, at least."

Suddenly, Madame von Schillar asked, "Have a nice time out, last night?"

"Very pleasant."

"Where did you go, dear?"

"Just out walking."

Madame von Schillar raised her brows. "Where to?"

"Oh—the drug store. And then over to the library."

"I thought it closed at nine."

"It does. I just walked over there for exercise," said Elizabeth. "Will you excuse me now?" She closed the double doors.

The Baroness frowned. Why had Elizabeth lied? Why would she lie unless she were ashamed of something? And why should anyone be ashamed of sitting alone in the park? Something was wrong here.

She followed Elizabeth into the park, that night; crept up behind the bench where her long shadow would not betray her presence. It was chilly, and she hugged her furs closer. Her shoes were tight, and she shifted from foot to foot, feeling the more foolish because there was so little to see. The girl was sitting erect, her hands folded. There was no movement to her at all, except for the deep rise and fall of her breast. The Baroness inched into the shadows of the tree to afford a glimpse of Elizabeth's face. A dry twig crackled beneath her foot. Convulsively, she pressed so close to the tree, its rough bark engraved the palms of her hands.

Alertly, Elizabeth arose and glanced up the path. Her face in the moonlight was ecstatic. "Is that you?" she whispered.

Rather than admit it was, Madame von Schillar decided to simulate a heart attack, which would exempt her from explaining why she was here. Just as she was about to sink to the ground, she heard Elizabeth whisper, "I thought you'd never come." The Baroness sucked in her breath. Someone had actually arrived, after all. She peered around the tree to identify Elizabeth's suitor.

The girl was standing alone in the moonlight, moving her lips in a conversation too hushed to hear. Nor could Madame von Schillar catch the words when, once again, Elizabeth returned to the bench; not until she arose suddenly and whispered, pleadingly, "You don't have to go so soon, Marius. You just got here . . ."

She seemed to listen, and then she smiled. Slowly, she promenaded up the path, escorted by her shadow.

Something like a smile crossed Madame von Schillar's face. Not until she had stolen back home, however, did the release of laughter come. She leaned back against the double doors and cupped her hands over her mouth. "You don't have to go so soon," she gasped, and smothered another surge of hilarity. It was not wholly scornful, this laughter; there was relief, too, in knowing that the letter had not been written by some dangerously informed outsider, but only by this blundering, amateur mystic.

"Automatic writing!" she giggled. "Trances! What next?"

When Worth came in to turn down the bed and take the dog out for its walk, Madame von Schillar was pouring herself a pony of brandy. "I'm celebrating," she cried, gaily. "Care to join me in a little toast?"

"Thank you, kindly, ma'am, and I would," said Worth, "only I don't indulge in spirits."

The statement had a peculiar effect on Madame von Schillar. The laughter came bubbling up just as she swallowed down; these united in a sputtering cough and issued in a forceful spray of brandy. "Oh, my dear," she gasped, when she had caught her breath, "oh, my dear, the things you say!"

She filled the glass again and viewed its amber against the light. "Well, there's nothing wrong with it, I guess," she added, more soberly. "After all, once in London, I paid ten pounds for some medium to come entertain my guests. The lights went off and she moaned something terrible, and an apparition of General Kitchner kissed me on the brow; so it's not as if it were something unnatural."

Worth wrinkled her brow and cocked her head.

"Well, I'm just trying to show you," Madame von Schillar explained. "And now that you know, let's have no more nonsense about it."

Shortly after ten, she heard the front door creak open. "That you, Elizabeth?" she called.

"Yes, Madame."

"Well, good night. Sleep well. I've a feeling that tomorrow we're going to get a great load of work done."

That was the important thing: the book. Putting up with the girl's eccentricity was a small price for the treasure she was turning out. After all, the evenings were her own and did not interfere with the day's work. Where it mattered, Elizabeth had proven her ability to deal with reality—the truth about the romance with Wrenn.

Her jaw tightened. "It is the truth," she assured herself.

As she undressed and cleansed her face, she kept whispering this. "It is true! It is!" Yet it was no longer possible to delude herself so easily. The letter was to blame. It had brought too many long-buried admissions to the surface of her mind. Fear that someone else knew the facts had forced her to acknowlege them, too. And now, with all anxiety about the letter gone, there was nothing to distract her from her own awareness.

"I just won't think of it," she resolved. "I won't remember."

Her face was stern, cold, that of a puritan resisting temptation. At last, she clenched shut her eyes, crushed her hands over her ears, but those words seeped like water through her fingers:—*why, oh God, why?*

This echoed in her mind, usher to other memories of ugly and degrading scenes. As in a flash of lightning, she saw Marius, that hideous day in the garden pergola, his white face contorted, his arm swinging up to strike her.

"That isn't true," Madame von Schillar protested. "That's not the way it was! It was beautiful, just as she wrote it. It was beautiful, always beautiful . . ."

But the memories persisted.

CHAPTER 3

The Baroness was still too unnerved to begin work the following morning. Despite her pressure to get on with the book, she dared not yet, lest the unsteadiness of her manner instill some doubt in Elizabeth's mind.

She was seated before the hearth, morosely watching the flames, when Worth came in to air the room.

"I don't suppose any of Mr Wrenn's letters are still about," Madame von Schillar asked.

Worth stared at her with such astonishment, she quickly added, "I suppose it's this writing about him, day after day, but—I get to remembering." She cleared her throat and continued with difficulty, "So I'd like to reread something sweet he sent me . . ."

"I think we burned 'em all, ma'am," Worth said. "That was years ago, of course, but I don't think I'm mistaken. Remember, we went through the house and collected 'em all in a shoe box and burned it in—"

"Yes, of course, I remember. But he must have sent me more letters after that."

Worth puckered her brow. "But, ma'am, we didn't burn them letters till after Mr Wrenn was dead. Just before you set off for Europe."

"Nonsense," cried the Baroness. "I destroyed them just before the divorce. When the Senator was poking around for evidence. Ask Elizabeth if that isn't so—"

Worth shook her head. "No, ma'am. It was just after Mr Wrenn drowned. Oh, I remember well. You was all in black, with a long veil—"

Madame von Schillar met her eyes fiercely. "That'll be all!"

The door closed, but she continued to glare at it. "Worth will have to go," she decided. "Getting old. Can't remember things straight, any more. It's ridiculous!"

At noon, Worth brought in her lunch. As she handed it to the Baroness, their fingers touched beneath the tray. Madame von Schillar jerked away her hand, then laughed nervously.

"You know what that reminds me of?" she said, as Worth crossed toward the door. "The first day I met Marius. At Kitty's, y'know. He was so dark, so intense, so Trojan! I fell in love with him in a flash. I honestly did! Once, when I passed him a cup of tea, I purposefully let my hand touch his beneath the saucer, just as ours did now. He looked at me—surprised, I suppose, but not really curious." She kept laughing as she spoke, sometimes pausing as if exhausted by merriment. "Just fancy—every swain in town begging me with his eyes, and this one, absolutely indifferent. Well, I made my mind up right then to win him over. I found out what qualities he admired in women, and then schooled myself in them. And that's why, eventually, he fell in love with me. Oh, it wasn't simple! I had to work harder than I ever did before, but it was worth it, my dear, because Marius was a great man, and he loved me very, very much, and I worshiped him. That's all true, absolutely true—"

"Of course, ma'am," Worth interrupted. "But if you could tell me another time. I'm serving lunch now and got things on the stove."

Left alone, the Baroness rehearsed once more the episode she had just related; but eventually she was forced to stop, for what followed was not compatible with her need to remember happiness. At last, she buried her head in her arms and tried to refashion those ugly events into what might have been; but without Elizabeth's instruction, her imagination was not equal to budging the facts. Inevitably, she was reduced to telling herself the scenes the girl had depicted in the book, re-establishing from Elizabeth's descriptions the awkward gentleness of his hands or the sound of his laughter. If this brought some comfort, it brought also a curious sense of inadequacy; somehow, Elizabeth, who had not even been born at the time of his death, knew Marius better than did she, who had been his wife.

During the late afternoon, Elizabeth dropped in. "—just to see if you felt like some talk," she said.

"Don't rush me," said Madame von Schillar. "I'm as eager to get on with the book as you are. It's all I think of—when I can think. So let me think a while longer. Until after dinner, anyway." As Elizabeth opened the door, she added, "Incidentally—I don't fancy you've dug up the names of anyone who knew Mr Wrenn . . . ?"

"No." Elizabeth spoke cautiously. "Although there's Worth."

"Pooh! How would she know him, except to make his bed?" She sank back in her chair. "That's all. Run along."

Elizabeth had not been gone two minutes before the Baroness was wishing her back. It was better to talk about Wrenn than to be alone and think of him. Yet what could she tell Elizabeth? The important issues Madame von Schillar could not bring herself to discuss, while the things she could safely mention, the rewarding little details and anecdotes—these had completely escaped her.

In her desperation to stimulate these memories, she tried to follow Elizabeth's example. She did not know by what magic the girl summoned Wrenn's spirit to her nightly séances, but she closed her eyes tightly as she had seen Elizabeth do in the park, and sat silently, tensely. Nothing happened. Worse, under this stress, she could scarcely remember what he had looked like; and when, with effort, she finally assembled his face, feature by feature, she could not sustain the picture or make it speak.

What she really needed, she thought, was to find someone who had known Wrenn well, but only well enough to be safely ignorant; not merely to garner material for the book, but to see Marius anew through their eyes.

Abruptly, she arose and tugged the bell cord. "Call Kitty Wallach," she ordered, when Worth entered. "Tell her to come, at once."

She was lying back on her couch when Mrs Wallach was ushered in. "Kitty," she said, sitting up, "I've got to talk to someone. Someone who knew us both—me and Marius—oh, for God's sake, take off that hat and sit down."

When her friend was seated, however, the Baroness could not focus her courage on the subject at hand. "How've you been?" she asked, in a trivial voice.

"Busy, Elizabeth."

"Me, too. I'm always busy. Such a whirl!"

"How nice that you enjoy it."

"Oh, I do. Invitations, and all . . ." Madame von Schillar lapsed into silence, then lowered her eyes. "It was at your home, y'know," she finally murmured. "You brought us together, so you've got to help me now."

"I'll do anything I can, my dear. You know that," said the white-haired woman.

"I loved him very much."

"I know you did."

"And he loved me just as much. He was such a gentle person, such a—" At a loss for words, she gestured sweepingly.

"What is it, Elizabeth? If you'll just tell me."

"It's that I don't feel well, and I have to keep work, work, working, all the time. Talking and remembering. Only"—she uttered a sharp little laugh—"sometimes I can't. Even Marius. Things I can't remember about him. Little cute things. Do you? Remember things about him?"

"Not cute things, dear."

"You know what I mean. Any endearing stories or—just anything."

"Well, of course, there was that day you met him—"

"Oh, I've got all that! Tell me something else."

Mrs Wallach examined her gloves. Then her face brightened. "Why, of course! Remember that time we all took the trolley out to—"

"Yes, I remember." Her face hardened. "But that story won't do."

"Why not? It's fairly amusing, isn't it? The way it rained, and we all tried to bundle up in newspaper, and Marius—"

"It won't do!" the Baroness said, sharply. "Try and think of something else."

"Very well." After a time, she said, "How about the story of how you and Marius ran into each other at Barbara's—"

"Oh, *no,* Kitty, for God's sake! It's not even interesting. And anyway—well, try to think of something else."

Mrs Wallach tried. Her every utterance, however, met with Madame von Schillar's instant rejection. The trouble was that few of these incidents were independent of each other. Like sprigs of devil grass, each was linked beneath the surface to others. It was impossible to uproot one without inadvertently dragging from burial the entire tangled network.

"Then there was the time I dropped over—that last spring, before his death," Mrs Wallach was saying, "and you were being fitted for a riding habit, and when I asked—"

"Never mind!" The Baroness waved her hands impatiently. "It's plain to see you don't remember much at all, Kitty. I was rather counting on you, but if you don't care to help me out, maybe you'd just better run on."

Mrs Wallach had not reached the door before Madame von Schillar called to her. "Come back, Kitty. Please. Here—sit on the couch beside me." She reached out for her friend's hand. "I'm cross as two sticks, I know, but I feel sickish, and—well, this book is such a heavy load, and I've got to get on with it."

"I wish I could help, my dear."

"Wish you could, too. But it's not your fault. You probably just don't remember things like that."

"Oh, but I do, Elizabeth," Kitty said, softly. "Not about Marius, perhaps; I never knew him that well. But of Dave, my own husband—oh, many, many things."

"Tell me," the Baroness begged. "Something charming . . ."

"Well . . ." She smiled to herself. "There's the oatmeal story, one of my favorites. You see, Dave was from very simple, unpretentious people. Even after his great success in business, he retained that simplicity. I remember once, we were entertaining clients from abroad, and—"

Heads together, the two women sat until the room was quite dark. When Mrs Wallach finally left, the Baroness called for Elizabeth, at once. "I'm ready to work now, dear," she said, in her legendary heroine manner.

Elizabeth glanced at the silver clock on the mantel. It was nearly nine. She fumbled with her purse. "Shouldn't we wait until you're feeling better? Or I could come back in an hour . . ."

Madame von Schillar smiled faintly. "You have a previous engagement? A young man waiting outside?"

Elizabeth shifted her gaze, and her answer was almost inaudible. "No, Madame."

"Then, let's not be silly, my dear. We'll have our little talk, and then you can take your little walk."

"I've thought of some wonderful stories about Marius," she continued, when Elizabeth had opened her notebook. "One, I'm particularly fond of—the corn-meal mush story. You see, Marius was from simple, unpretentious folk, and he kept that simplicity all his life. Once, we were entertaining friends from Europe, and—"

The Baroness had quite a tale to spin.

Unfortunately, it took but a few minutes to tell; occupied only a few lines of Elizabeth's notebook, and already the girl was waiting for further incident, no more satisfied, thought the Baroness, than the Sahara would be by a glass of water.

—a glass of lemonade—

The thought went racing through her mind and, involuntarily, Madame von Schillar winced.

"What is it?" Elizabeth asked.

"Nothing. I just remembered something."

"Good. What?"

"Nothing," said the Baroness, uncomfortably. "Nothing important."

The girl's voice became hard. "Curious, then, that you haven't mentioned it before."

"What do you mean?"

"You've told me everything else that's unimportant." She threw down her pencil. "Corn-meal mush!"

Madame von Schillar stared at her in astonishment. Elizabeth, gentle Elizabeth, was actually angry. "My dear girl—" she started to say.

"Days ago," the girl persisted, "we finished with your divorce and were ready for the marriage with Wrenn, but instead of telling me about it, you keep serving up trivial bits and pieces that I could fill in with my eyes closed. Am I supposed to make a book out of that? Or do you want a book?"

"Of course, I do," the Baroness said, passionately. "More than anything in the world!"

"Then give me what I need. I can't go on until you do."

Madame von Schillar glanced away. "I've tried, but—I forget things."

"Your wedding?" Elizabeth cried. "Your life together?"

"No, but . . ." Her voice sank. "I'll try again. I swear I will."

Suddenly Elizabeth knelt by her. "I know. I know it's painful for you. It's painful for me, too. When you suffer, I suffer. But if you want this book, you've got to remember, and I've got to know." In her voice, too, there was anguish. "I've got to know!"

When Elizabeth left, Madame von Schillar sat no less tensely. The pendulum of the clock chopped at the silence of the room. Again and again, she moistened her lips, and her fingers pinched at her lap robe. Remember, the girl had ordered; and that was just the trouble! There seemed to be no respite from memory. With a groan, she thrust herself up from her chair and began pacing. It was hot in the room, feverishly hot, and she hastened to shove the window ajar.

The window resisted her efforts. No moon was visible outside, yet she could see the little vine-covered pergola in the garden. She turned from it quickly. A sigh almost drained her of strength, and she pressed against the wall for support.

"Sleep, sleep," she begged herself.

The memory of the scene in the pergola had lain dormant in her mind all day, but now, as if invigorated by its rest, it charged back, again and again, to torment her. Helplessly, she saw the goblet shattered by the fury of that moment, saw the pool of lemonade on the table, and the flies already gathering.

"I won't think of it," she whispered. "I won't think of that part. I'll just remember the good things . . ." She spoke quickly now, and aloud: "I was wearing a white silk dress. China silk, with a pale green sash, because it was springtime, early May—"

But the other words persisted beneath the rush of her words.

Why, oh God, why?

"—and Marius was wearing a blazer coat, I forget what color, a blazer coat, they were all the rage, that year. And the sky was so blue, not a cloud in sight—"

I didn't want you to know, but now that you do, we'll just have to make the best of it . . .

In desperation, Madame von Schillar unscrewed a cut-glass bottle and shook out two pink sleeping tablets and washed them down with a gulp of brandy.

"What's the matter with me?" she demanded. "Overwrought and hysterical, like this. Mustn't think of these things . . ."

Mercifully, the drowsiness soon began, the gentle, relentless spiral down into darkness where regret could follow only in disguise. She welcomed the descent—yet she would awaken again she knew, and the memories would still be there to pain her. Nor was there any possible escape from them if the book was to be written.

"Then forget the book," she muttered, thickly. "Not worth it. Can't go on like this. Got to get away. Forget. Can't go on like this—"

Even though half-paralyzed with sleep, she caught herself up short and forced open her eyes. Her protest thundered through her being. There would be no giving up of the book! Not even for her own comfort and peace of mind would she surrender the book. However painful, the past would have to be faced and endured; and when the memoirs were finished, she would finally be free of the past. "Remember that tomorrow . . ."

So resolved, she hastened on into slumber, and the dancers stood on their chairs to see her pass. "Marius and Elizabeth," they whispered, excitedly. "Elizabeth and Marius—"

The clocks chiming the noon hour awakened her. Briefly she thought she was in Rome and it was August—that hideous pressure of heat, the buzzing as of a hundred flies, the dry barb of breath catching in her lungs. She mopped the moisture from her brow and, with effort sat up; then she fell back. Uneasily, she tried to take her own pulse.

"Shall I call a doctor?" Worth asked.

"I'll be all right," she whispered. "Don't need any doctor." Nor would she allow herself the cut-glass bottle and its passports to oblivion. Her mind had to be clear for work.

By night, however, she still felt too ill to see Elizabeth. "Tell her to go out for her walk," she advised Worth, weakly. "I'll see her when she comes in—"

"Shouldn't you ought just rest?" Worth asked.

"Yes, I ought," Madame von Schillar said, "but I've got to get the book finished—and then, *then,* I can rest!" As the servant was leaving, she added, "Worth, you don't happen to recall the names of any of Mr Wrenn's cronies, do you?"

"Don't recall him receiving many visitors, ma'am. Not here, anyway. Except, sometimes, that Mr Ezterhausy. Never rang the bell, or come in. Just whistled under the window. Him and the sailor."

"Who?"

"Name of Chrysler or Crisler. The sea captain. You remember."

"Yes. I remember." The Baroness chipped the scarlet lacquer from her nails. Indeed, she remembered Hyltie. Ignorant hulk of a man. He and Marius used to go fishing together. And it was Hyltie who had called her when Wrenn's body had been found on the shore. She used to tease Marius about his friend's crude manners; and yet now, she longed to see him, to hear him tell about Marius, to let the brightness of his devotion light up the past with new colors. "I wonder what's become of poor Hyltie," she sighed.

"Couldn't say, ma'am."

"He used to have a boat called—called the *Rosalie*—something. A tug, I think. Maybe the Maritime Service might know what's become of him." She jotted down a reminder to have Elizabeth check this. "Do you remember anyone else he knew?"

"No one that comes to mind, ma'am."

"Are you sure?" The Baroness attempted her careless smile.

"Why, Miss Deveny suggested that you were quite the friend to my poor darling."

"I admired him, ma'am," Worth answered, stolidly, "but the young lady oughtn't have told."

The Baroness glanced at her rings as if they had just occurred on her fingers. "Tell me what you thought of Marius. What you remember of him."

"He was honest, ma'am." Worth looked down, discreetly. "That's about all I told her. I figured the rest was our business."

"The rest?" Madame von Schillar looked up, sharply. "What else was there? He was honest and fine and we loved each other very much."

"Just as you say, ma'am."

"What do you mean by that?" the Baroness demanded.

"Nothing at all, ma'am. Just a form of speech."

Too weak to sustain her anger, she dismissed the servant and lay back in bed. Soon her face was gleaming with perspiration. She groaned and pressed her hands to her ears. At last, she hammered a spoon against the table until Worth came running in.

"Sit down awhile," she begged. "No fun to be alone when you're sick." Worth seated herself self-consciously. "No, not way over there. Nearer. So we can chat. And if I lose my temper again, I give you leave to strike me with an axe . . ."

Conversation with Worth was not easy. The two women were but a few years apart in age, and the same roof had long sheltered them both; yet their only bond of communication was the bell cord. Inevitably, they turned to double solitaire. Madame von Schillar's interest soon paled, however, even though she was winning.

"I could read to you, ma'am. Get a book from the liberry—"

"No. I don't care much for—" She rolled over and contemplated Worth. "Yes, you could! Maybe read aloud from my memoirs."

Worth did not read aloud with ease or the slightest variance of expression, yet it satisfied the Baroness. From time to time, she nodded to herself, smiling, and once, surreptitiously, brushed at her eyes.

This comfort was soon jolted, however, by a scene the girl had recently added where Wrenn joined Elizabeth Carver in the park.

"How's that?" the Baroness interrupted. "Read that over again."

"The whole page?"

"Just what you finished reading. What I say to Marius."

Worth traced her finger down the page, then read: " 'You don't have to go so soon, Marius. You just got here.' "

Madame von Schillar frowned. Her mind illumined Elizabeth Deveny's ecstatic face as she addressed the empty park: "You don't have to go so soon, Marius . . ."

"Funny," the Baroness murmured. "Don't understand, at all—"

"There's lots not to understand here," Worth said.

Madame von Schillar shrugged. "But it doesn't matter. Go on reading." Worth did not continue. "Go on," the Baroness repeated, urgently.

The servant looked at her with troubled eyes. "Ma'am, it's been on my mind to ask, while I been reading—Is this the work Miss Deveny's been at?"

"Yes, of course."

"But, ma'am—"

"Hush," said the Baroness. "Just read."

"But all this—Why, ma'am, it's falsity!"

"It certainly is not," Madame von Schillar protested. "I met Marius in the park, I posed for him, we ran away to the Cape—all that really happened."

Worth put aside the manuscript. "But there's other things, ma'am. Where she writes how Senator Carver catches you sneaking out in my hat and coat—"

"Yes. And didn't that actually happen?'

"It did, I remember. But, ma'am—one night, just before Miss Deveny went off to Cape Cod, I come on her standing in the upstairs hall, and it's my brown hat and coat she has on, whispering to herself. I said, 'Why, Miss!' and she says, 'I'm just going over to Kitty's!' Then she startles, like she'd just woke up—"

Madame von Schillar's face was as impassive as if she had just been dealt a low card. "It doesn't mean anything," she said. "I saw her in the hat, myself, that night. Maybe it was me who told her to try it on—" Then, sharply, she drew in her breath. "Pink roses!"

"Ma'am?"

The Baroness did not answer, at once. "Nothing," she finally said. "It's all the truth, I tell you. Besides, in the book, she describes pink roses in *red* hair, not black, so it's not as if she's imagining herself involved. It's always me. She's specific on that. Look . . ." She picked up a page and read aloud, at random, " 'He spoke very softly now. "We mustn't lose this chance, Elizabeth—" ' Elizabeth! *My* name!"

"Hers, too."

"That means nothing. This is about me, and it's the truth."

"If you say so, ma'am."

"Don't you believe me?"

"I don't know what to believe. There's something funny about how she always talks to a person about Mr Wrenn. Like he was a religion. Or her sweetheart. And some things are here in black and white."

"No!" the Baroness cried. "I won't have you saying such things. I'm too sick, I tell you. I mustn't think of it."

Yet she could think of nothing else. Details, uncomprehendingly accumulated, now fused into an unmistakable design: the way Elizabeth had acquired her indolent laugh, her crisp way of talking, her choice of words; even the perfume she affected was Loki, the scent as individual to Madame von Schillar as her signature. Then there was that passionate letter the girl had sent to Marius; and the initials on the envelope were E. W. C.—Elizabeth Winslow Carver. "I want to know you as you know yourself," Elizabeth had once said. "I want to remember what you remember—"

"She thinks she's me!" the Baroness whispered. "The fool thinks she's me. Those séances . . ."

Grabbing up the manuscript, she leafed through the pages, hoping to find something to contradict this, but the more she read, the stronger became her conviction. Elizabeth was not only in love with Marius, but had usurped the Baroness's identity to make it possible.

It was a feeble sound, but she laughed, as she had always laughed when she could not fully comprehend.

"What should we do, ma'am?"

"I don't know."

"Ma'am, you ought to set her straight."

The Baroness gnawed at her thumbnail. "Yes, I'll have to think about this . . ." When she glanced up again, Worth was still waiting, watching her intently. Madame von Schillar waved her away, impatiently. "That's all. I've got to think."

She sat motionlessly, her face impassive. The hands of the clock inched around, the glass curtains stirred in a draft, the candles in the crystal sconces flickered; but Madame von Schillar did not move. She might have been posing for her portrait, except for the unfashionable intensity of her eyes. At last her hand clenched. A moment later, she rang for Worth. The servant entered instantly, as if she had been waiting outside for this summons. Madame von Schillar did not face her, being suddenly busy with her nail file.

"Worth, I think we'll just forget about all this. It's for the best." She viewed her fingernails. "That's all, my dear." From the corner of her eyes, she could see Worth had not moved. "That'll be all, I say!"

"Ma'am, I don't think that girl's a conscious liar," the servant said, slowly, "or that she means to covet and bear false witness. But if we let her go on, we're the guilty ones. She's put too much stock on all this. For good or for bad, she ought to know the truth about Mr Wrenn."

Madame von Schillar sat up. "She does know the truth. That's what she's been writing. I'll vouch for that in any court of law. It's my history, and I ought to know."

"But what you said about the pink roses and her thinking—"

"Well, I'm not to be heeded today," the Baroness interrupted. "When I don't feel well, I'm liable to say anything." She slung aside the nail file. "Besides, things like that don't really happen. She's quite all right."

"I think she needs a rest, ma'am."

"And stop our work? Stop the book?"

"Someone else could take over her job, do it just as well."

"Another year of waiting and remembering . . . I couldn't bear it," Madame von Schillar declared. "Besides, she's getting into it just exactly what I want."

"Ma'am," Worth persisted, "for her own good—"

"I'll think about it, I tell you."

The servant arose. "Can I bring her in, then?"

"What for?"

"So you can tell her what really happened."

Madame von Schillar lifted her eyes slowly. "What did happen?"

"You know!"

"Indeed, I do not! And I'd be no little intrigued to learn what you think actually happened."

"I don't know, fact for fact. But I know it ain't like she believes it is."

"Perhaps you'll tell her that, yourself," the Baroness said, silkily. "Perhaps you'll tell her 'the truth.' "

Worth did not answer.

"Well, I warn you, if you so much as put a doubt in her mind, you're finished with me!" The servant's hands tightened. Taking her cue from this, Madame von Schillar continued, sternly. "You've been here most of your life. Here in this house. My father entrusted you with it. And with me. To look out for us both. This has been like your own house, hasn't it? Your home. Could you leave it?"

"I'm ready to turn in my keys whenever you say, ma'am," Worth said, quietly.

"Where'll you go now? Think you could find another job? You're old."

"I've saved."

"Of course. Enough for a hall bedroom in some dingy boarding-house. Not like practically owning this place—polishing the crystal, shining the silver, feeling the fine woods beneath your cloth. Oh, I've watched. I know what all that means to you." She waited for Worth to sink down in a chair, but the servant remained standing, implacably. "As my friend, all this is yours to cherish. As my enemy—" her lips softened—"but I can't think of you as my enemy—You grew up with me. You know, you understand! And this means so much to me. I've suffered so terribly—"

"But her, Miss Elizabeth—".

"You haven't called me that, in years," the Baroness said, softly.

Now, Worth sat down beside Madame von Schillar. "But her—think how she'll suffer."

"She won't suffer if she never knows."

"But ma'am, it's dangerous, this living in make-believe."

"Dear friend, I know, I know. Yet it's my suffering you must consider first." The Baroness took her hand. "You know all I went through, all that horror. But what you may not know is the aftermath—after it was all over, here—flying from city to city, from Paris to Rome to Berlin, and never able to forget. Pounding at me, tormenting—people never realize that. They think you can just go your own way, quite merrily, quite free." She shook her head. "I've been through hell. Paid the piper to the last farthing, and beyond. Oh, not just what the world thought of me, but what *I* thought of me! Only now—now, I can start over, don't you see? That's why this book means so much to me. It can give me back all I had: my place in the world, my self-respect, my peace of mind. And—it can erase all the rest."

She turned from Worth's searching eyes. "No, no—I'm sorry for the girl. I like her, admire her. But I can't do a thing to interfere with her finishing the book in just the way she's doing it now. And you mustn't interfere, either. The book comes first! When it's done, we'll tell her everything—tell her the truth, just as you wish." She smiled at Worth and patted her hand. "Is that a bargain?"

Worth did not look up. At last, she said, "I'm sorry, ma'am. Even if it means me leaving here tomorrow. Before it's too late for her, she's got to be woken up." She lifted her face now, looked straight at Madame von Schillar. "I can't bargain about a person's immortal soul."

"And have I none?" the Baroness cried. "Am I to be left in hell?"

Worth shook her head. "No, ma'am. Tell her. Get it all out of your heart. Free yourself."

"Not that way." Madame von Schillar's face hardened. "So I expect you'll have to tell her yourself. Well, try it! That's calling your bluff, eh? Because you don't really know anything, do you? Not enough to make it convincing. And even if you did know, d'you think she'd believe you? *You*?" She smiled. "This is as important to Miss Deveny as it is to me. You haven't convinced me of anything. You won't convince her. And all you'll gain for your trouble is instant dismissal. You'll be gone, but we'll still be here, just as before, writing my book. So think it over, my dear, before wasting your time."

Worth's plainness yielded somewhat to the gentleness of her eyes. "Ma'am," she said, "it's you who'll tell her. You'll want to do that, for your own soul's sake. That's the chance you've got to have, and that I've got to give to you."

Madame von Schillar gazed at her in astonishment, and then, very quickly, nodded. "As you say, my dear," she promised, brightly. "I'll think about it, I swear. But I must have time." She lay back in bed. "Open the window before you leave, eh? Oh, and better put the manuscript back in Miss Deveny's room before she returns. She mustn't get suspicious . . ."

Worth turned slowly, looked at Madame von Schillar, and the

gentleness dulled in her eyes. Silently, she inched up the window, then took the manuscript to Elizabeth's room.

She put it, not in the drawer, but on the top of the desk, purposefully disarranged, so it would appear tampered with. A moment later, however, she returned the papers to the drawer, just as she had found them, and hurried back down to Madame von Schillar's suite. Without knocking, she burst in.

"Did you call, ma'am?"

The Baroness sat up with a gasp. "What? What?"

"Did you call?"

"No. What do you mean, breaking in, like that!"

"It's just that I thought I heard you cry out, and—well, you can understand!" Worth was not a very good actress, but being out of breath from the stairs lent authority to her portrayal of alarm.

"Understand what?"

"Well, ma'am—with her like she is. Miss Deveny, I mean."

"What about her?"

"Well, ma'am, she *is* sick, and you never can tell—"

"Oh, for mercy's sake," the Baroness cried, "it's not as if the girl's a maniac."

"No, ma'am, but sick. Sick in her mind. And you never can tell. She might get in this too deep, and—Well, anyway, don't you worry. I'll always be near."

"What are you trying to do?" the Baroness demanded, angrily. "Frighten me? Does it occur to you I'm not well, and shouldn't be upset—"

"You just lie back, ma'am, and don't worry. I'll sit outside your door, just in case—"

"I see!" Madame von Schillar smiled grimly. "You don't trust me, is that it?"

"Ma'am?"

"That I'll tell Elizabeth the truth. So now you're trying to frighten me into dismissing her."

"No, ma'am. But she is sick." She watched the Baroness carefully. Knowing Madame von Schillar's revulsion for debility of any sort, she again stressed the word. "Very sick."

The Baroness yawned. "She's nothing of the kind. In much better shape than you or I. Now go along, before you collapse." She began humming cheerfully and picked up her nail file.

Her control lasted only until Worth left the suite; then, she slumped back amongst her pillows, weak from the effort. Breath rushed in and out of her slack mouth too quickly, forcing her to gulp and swallow for air. Eventually, the spell passed, but her fists remained clenched.

Elizabeth. She shuddered faintly. Crawling from bed, she hastened to the double doors and turned the key in the lock. After a moment, she sighed and unlocked the doors again.

"Nothing to be afraid of," she told herself. "It's not as Worth said. Only those silly séances. Mustn't let things like that bother me. Too much at stake . . ."

Yet she shivered again. "Cold," she murmured. Quickly she shut the window, closing her eyes so as not to see the pergola outside. The chill persisted, however, even when she drew the green comforter about her like an opera cloak and sank down before the fire.

"Nothing to worry about," she told herself. "No need to say anything. It would only embarrass her. Upset her work . . ."

She realized she had been speaking aloud and glanced over her shoulder to make sure she had not been overheard. The room was empty. The rooms were always empty now; yet she could remember crushes of people in this house, with bits of laughter briefly hoisted above their murmur, like gay banners. So it would be again, she promised herself, when the book was published.

Worth would have to go, of course. Maybe tomorrow. With the threat of exposure removed, she and Elizabeth could continue work, alone.

Involuntarily, her throat tightened. She feared the idea of being alone with the girl now. Feared her, hated her, loathed her.

"I do not!" She tried to sit up straight, and spoke patiently, as if to an unreasonable child. "I like her, admire her . . ."

Dragging herself up, she fumbled around the room. Elizabeth must have some token to prove this esteem. Her unwilling hand crept up to her earrings. But that was foolish! So lavish a gift would only prompt suspicion. Trust and affection could not be shown by presents; only by acts of thoughtfulness.

Bracing herself, she made her way to the kitchen. Elizabeth would be cold when she came in. A cup of tea would be just the thing! A cup of hot tea waiting for her . . .

The kitchen seemed unbearably hot, a linoleum-laid inferno. "Inferno, inferno," she muttered. "Dante's *Inferno.* That part really happened anyway . . ." Dizzied by the kitchen smells, she thrust open a window. The curtain bellied inward, licked by a breeze, but she felt no cooler. Waiting for the water to boil, she clenched shut her eyes to keep the darkness from blotting her vision.

"Let her borrow my past," she muttered. "Future I'm interested in . . ."

But these words, even committed to sound, did not quiet the soundless surge of resentment. In Madame von Schillar's own life, the romance had led only to grief; and here was Elizabeth, immune from the cost, deriving only the rapture. She had succeeded where the Baroness had failed. But the truth, once spoken, could equalize all that.

"No," she mumbled. "No, I mustn't. Not worth it. Only the book . . ."

As if generated by her conflict, darkness came seeping up. She fought against the desire to hide in it. "Got to keep fresh . . ."

The kettle began to whistle, but she did not hear it; yet when a key grated in the front door lock way out in the foyer, she immediately struggled to her feet. Half-blinded by the stabbing lights, she stumbled into the parlor. Elizabeth had closed the door, was starting toward the stairs. The Baroness took another step forward. "Wait!" she ordered; then feebly added, "dear."

Elizabeth turned, came into the parlor. Madame von Schillar waved vaguely at a chair. "Sit down. Back to work . . ."

The girl looked at her strangely and came closer. Involuntarily, Madame von Schillar inched away.

"Hurry," she whispered. "We must work. Get your notebook." Elizabeth did not move. "Your book, girl!"

Her words came echoing back to her ears. "No," she said, thickly. "Not your book. Mine! My book."

The blood was pounding in her head. She clutched a chair, trying to steady herself. Elizabeth reached out quickly, caught her arm. With a gasp of alarm, Madame von Schillar wrenched herself free, and, as if in self-defense, whipped her hand across the girl's face. Elizabeth did not move. It was the Baroness who retreated. Raising her stinging palm to her own cheek, she stared at Elizabeth as if at some stranger. "Get out," she whispered. "Get out of here!"

The threatening darkness was edging in on her again. Unsteadily, she turned and lurched back into her suite. It was hot, terribly hot. "Go outside," she mumbled. "Cool, outside—"

"Cool, outside," she heard him say.

"Nonsense, it's spring." This was her own voice, but multiple with echo as if spoken in a tomb. Only it was not a tomb, but, sharply outlined by fever, the garden, and there was a pitcher of lemonade on the pergola table.

"No, no, no," she whimpered. "No—"

He had slipped his arm through hers, was leading her toward the pergola, and once they were seated in the shade, they would talk, and she knew how it would end—with the lemonade upset on the table, and his hand swinging upward to strike—

Madame von Schillar flinched. "No," she screamed. "Elizabeth! Elizabeth, help me . . ."

It wasn't until later that she remembered. Not until she had been put into bed, and the girl sat close by, tightly holding her hand.

"Don't go," the Baroness begged. "I need you. It's me who's sick. Me . . ." She began sobbing again. "I can't face it alone. Not yet . . ."

She clung to Elizabeth's hand as if, by physical force, to drag her along into the swirling darkness and delirium.

CHAPTER 4

The shutters were closed, the portieres drawn. There was no light in the suite except for the flicker from the fireplace. The room was hot, and the unlit candles had softened and curved over like wilted stalks. Madame von Schillar raised her head from the pillow. Without quite knowing why, she sensed Elizabeth was near. "Is it morning, yet?" she whispered.

"Afternoon," Elizabeth said, rising.

"I overslept."

"Yes. It's all right." She moved over to the bedside.

"My face gets puffy when I sleep too long."

"Everyone's does."

The Baroness dabbed at her face, listlessly. At length, she said, "I don't remember much about last night—"

"It was two nights ago. But we don't have to talk about it now. Just rest. That's the important thing."

"I struck you, didn't I?"

"Not hard. I scarcely felt it."

"Didn't feel it?"

"I was thinking about something else."

"Something troubling you?"

"Yes."

"Tell me about it," urged the Baroness. Evasively, Elizabeth began to straighten the cluttered bedside table. "Come along, dear girl. We're both lone women. We've only got each other to depend upon, you know."

"We'll talk about it when you're feeling better," Elizabeth promised.

Madame von Schillar sighed and lay back in bed. "The doctor came to see me, didn't he?" she finally remarked.

"Yes. You remember. Dr. Campbell."

"Did he see me looking like this? Without a trace of make-up?"

"Don't worry. You look fine."

"What—did he decide was wrong with me?"

"He didn't tell me. But as soon as you're strong enough, he wants you to have a thorough examination."

"Nonsense! I'm fit as a fiddle." A moment later, she added, fiercely, "If he drops by again, send him packing. I'm not going to have any quack persuade me I'm ailing. It's just that I've been overdoing it, rather. I could get up this minute, if I wanted . . ." But she made not attempt to rise from her bed. Only when Elizabeth crossed to open a window, did she push herself up again. "You're not going to leave me alone—"

"No."

"I don't want to be alone. Not just now. It's such a bore—"

"Would you like to play cards?" Elizabeth asked.

Her answer was listless. "Not just now."

"Would you rather sleep?"

"Suppose you just sat here and talked to me?"

Elizabeth sat down. "About anything in particular?"

Madame von Schillar moistened her pale lips. "I'm always talking to you about Marius. Why don't you talk to me about him?"

The girl smiled. "What can I say that you don't already know?"

"That doesn't matter. I just want to hear about him. I want to be like some stranger who's never heard of him, and you'll tell me all you know, so clearly I can see it happen." Elizabeth hesitated, and the Baroness prompted, "Go on, dear, please. Please! Once upon a time . . ."

After Elizabeth had begun talking, her self-consciousness vanished, for these reminiscences of the romance helped alleviate her own distress. She described Wrenn's appearance, his manner, the pictures he had painted, and the idyllic days at Shilleth. Her eyes shone as she spoke, and Madame von Schillar's face relaxed as she listened.

"And did he love her very much?" the Baroness would interrupt, from time to time. Or she would inch closer to Elizabeth, urging, "Say that again—the part about the tenderness and understanding that—how did you say it?"

"Bound them together like each other's arms—"

Eventually, however, the details became sparse, the narrative more disjointed. Elizabeth's voice grew louder, more precise, like a child bluffing through an unlearned lesson. Then she fumbled into silence.

"Go on," the Baroness urged.

"I can't," Elizabeth blurted. "That's my trouble. That's what's been worrying me, lately. I don't know any more. You haven't told me what happened after the divorce case, and—Well, I've got to know. I've just got to, if I'm to go on writing."

Madame von Schillar turned her head away. "I can't tell you now. I still feel too weak to talk much. So you go on."

"But I don't know. I don't know."

"Then make up something."

Elizabeth sat silently, and the Baroness persisted, urgently, "That's not asking very much. You're a writer. You have imagination—"

"But I need facts first," Elizabeth protested. "If you could just tell me this—did you and Marius stop meeting after the divorce?"

"Of course not!" the Baroness cried. "Why would we?"

"What did happen then?" the girl demanded.

"Well—maybe we did stop for a while," Madame von Schillar said, tautly. "Yes, of course. We didn't dare meet as often."

"Then that's the reason," Elizabeth murmured.

"Reason for what?"

"Nothing," the girl said, quickly; and as quickly, added, "But it must have been agony, not being able to see him."

"Tell me about it," begged Madame von Schillar.

"Well—I'm just guessing, of course—but when night would come, and loneliness would well up in you, then you'd go across the street to the park and wait—knowing he wouldn't be there, and yet you couldn't stay away. There was always the chance that he might show up, and you sat there, hoping he would, praying—and the night would get cooler, and you could hear the birds twittering in the darkness. Every time someone would pass on the sidewalk, your heart would thunder and your head would swim. Only the footsteps were never his, and they passed by. And soon you'd hear the clock in the church strike ten, and then ten thirty—"

"Go on," the Baroness urged, not opening her eyes.

"That's all. He didn't come back. There was only loneliness, and you walked back to the house in a daze. And all through the next day, you'd wait, with your heart timed for nine o'clock, because, this time, he might come to you—"

"Yes," the Baroness said. "That's how it was. I loved him, but I just didn't dare see him yet. Not till it was safe. That's the way it had to be—" She lolled her head from side to side on the pillow, murmuring, "That's just how it was. More desperately in love than ever, but we didn't dare meet yet . . ." Presently she rolled over and held out a pale hand to Elizabeth. "You've been such a help to me, today. I won't ever forget it—"

"You just get well, that's all," Elizabeth said. "Get well, so we can go on with the book. Everything must be finished by the first of July."

"Why July?"

"I'm going away, then," Elizabeth said, softly.

"Going away?"

"I have an engagement," the girl replied. "A very important one."

"And leave me alone?"

"Alone? You?" She laughed.

"All my life," the Baroness whispered. "Always alone."

"But the book will be coming out, soon, and then you'll be very sought after. So you won't be alone, any more." She smiled to herself. "And neither will I."

Elizabeth went out about nine. The Baroness made no protest. "If I'm still awake when you come back," she said, "we'll have that cup of tea."

For a time, she dozed fitfully. At last, she became conscious of someone sitting near by in the dim room. "Back so soon, dear?" she asked.

"It's me, ma'am."

"Worth?"

"Yes."

The Baroness sighed. "Better start some tea," she finally bade.

"You be all right alone?"

"Yes. Anyway, it'll be coming out soon, and I won't be alone."

"Ma'am?"

"The book."

Worth hesitated. "Have you spoke to her yet, Miss Elizabeth?"

The answer was so ready, Madame von Schillar must have anticipated the question. "I've been too sick."

"She must know, ma'am. As soon as possible."

"Yes, yes, of course. Very soon, now."

"Tonight, maybe?"

"I'm too sick," the Baroness whispered.

"So is she, ma'am."

"But to tell her now! Now, when I'm not strong enough to help her over it. Like taking away a person's coat and shoving her out in the cold. To leave her alone—"

"She won't be alone, ma'am."

"And neither will I," the Baroness echoed, dimly. "The book will be coming out. She says I'll be very sought after . . ."

Worth sighed and stood up.

The Baroness reached out a pleading hand to her. "I need her, don't you see? I'm sick. I need her just as she is, till it's all over. Anyway, she's going away July first. I'll tell her then."

"May be too late, ma'am." Worth went to the door.

Madame von Schillar pushed herself up in bed. "Where are you going?"

"To fix the tea."

"Or see the girl? She won't believe you, remember. Even if there were anything to tell. Don't waste your time interfering, and"—she covered her face—"don't torture me like this, when I'm so weak."

Worth turned at the door. "It's truth, ma'am, that'll give you the only strength you can have. Once more, I beg you—"

"Get the tea," the Baroness whispered, lying back. "We'll see, about the rest. We'll see, we'll see."

The night was warm, and spring had stippled the trees in the park with buds; but Elizabeth had no eye for this. She sat on the usual bench in the shadows, but only because there was no other place to go. From habit she murmured his name over and over, even knowing it would be as fruitless as on the two previous nights.

"But he's got to," she whispered, desperately. "He must come back tonight."

That was impossible, of course. They had sworn not to meet each other until it was safe again. Even so, she waited there translating every whisper of foliage, each chirp of a cricket, as a sign of his approach. A car passed in the street, cleaving the darkness with its light, and involuntarily she grew tense; but the car did not stop. She tried to laugh. Marius would not be coming in a car, anyway. Yet, needing to keep up her courage, she made a pact with herself; if another car passed before she had counted one hundred, that would mean Marius was coming to her this night.

Although she carefully prolonged the counting, she reached the hundred mark and still the streets remained empty.

"What is it?" she demanded, fiercely. What was holding up the unfoldment? Was it that some vital fact was missing? Was the Baroness keeping something from her? And what had she meant by "safe"? What danger could there be to keep apart two people who loved and needed each other so desperately?

When the faraway clock struck ten, she suddenly knuckled her hands and pressed them against her eyes. Her jaw was tense, and her body stiff. "Come to me," she whispered. "Now! Come to me, now! *You must!*"

The sparks before her eyes were like flying spindrift, and she felt a rocking motion as if the current deep below the surface of the sea were guiding her; and she rejoiced in this, for when the sea had taken them both, there would be no more of this separation, no more agonized waiting and longing and fear.

She opened her eyes. A shadow lay across the moonlit path. She arose with a cry and reached out to him, but he did not come any nearer, did not take her in his arms. "Marius?" she whispered. It was dark, and suddenly, she could not be sure it was he. "Marius?"

"You must go away! Go now!"

For a moment, she could not tell whether it was his command or her own.

"Go away from here. Leave while you still have a chance—"

"Marius!" she cried.

"Do you hear? Leave Boston before it's too late—"

"But why? Why?"

"Go away. Go, at once!"

"Marius," she cried. "Marius . . ."

There was no answer. After a moment, she advanced, her hands outstretched, fumbling in the darkness like a sleepwalker. The path was now empty, however, and she could not be sure he had even been there, or if it had been only a warning from her own heart, a rebuke for summoning him when he should not have come.

Despite her confusion as she fled home, she knew she could not come back again to the park. It was finished there. Without looking back, she entered the house, slammed the door behind her.

Someone was standing in the darkness of the hall.

"Who is it?" Elizabeth whispered.

"Just me, Miss. Worth." She flicked on the lights and picked up a tray from the table. "Fixed some tea for you, but now it's cold. If you want, I'll make some more—"

Elizabeth only stared at her uncomprehendingly. "Was it—were you outside, just now?"

"Miss?"

"Nothing," Elizabeth said, uneasily. "Nothing important." Crossing to Madame von Schillar's door, she tapped, then entered the suite.

A lamp was lit, armament against the terrors of night, and in its glow the Baroness lay sleeping, her mouth agape. Elizabeth cleared her throat, but the woman did not stir. Recklessly, Elizabeth brushed a little silver frame from the table, and it thudded on the carpet. Madame von Schillar sat up with a cry of fear.

"Who's there?" she cried.

"Me. Elizabeth. I—came in to see if you needed anything, and I stumbled . . ."

The Baroness rubbed her eyes. "Bring me a glass of water," she murmured. "Mouth tastes funny."

Elizabeth hurriedly followed instructions, but when she returned with the water, Madame von Schillar was lying back in that drowsy borderline state which has neither the defense of consciousness nor the secrecy of slumber. Recognizing this, the girl bent over her and asked, cautiously, "Why didn't you and Marius see each other, after the divorce?"

The Baroness stirred and muttered faintly, as if under hypnosis, "I'd gone to France—"

"How soon after the case?"

"Week."

"Did Marius urge you to leave town?"

The woman opened her eyes, then sat up, quickly. "What? What's this?"

"You just said you went to France right after the divorce."

"Well, why shouldn't I? Nothing wrong with it."

"And was it Marius who suggested you go away?"

"Of course he didn't. He wanted me to stay. He adored me, why wouldn't he want me to stay?"

"Then why didn't you? How could you bear to leave him then?"

"What is this?" Madame von Schillar demanded. "More cross-examination? I'm too sick—"

"But I've got to know, if I'm to go ahead. Unless you don't care about finishing the book . . ."

The Baroness sank back, uneasily. At last, she said, "It was my lawyer, I expect. He advised me to go. Said it might cause more trouble—not just public indignation, but with the law—if I kept seeing Marius before my decree was final."

"And Marius? Did he stay here?"

"No."

"Where then?"

"He went to Maine. Lived on Hyltie's tugboat."

"And you're sure he never asked you to leave Boston?"

"Of course, I'm sure." The Baroness raised herself on her elbows. "I want you to trace Hyltie, incidentally," she added. "The Maritime Service might help. Hyltie Crisler. Captain of the *Rosalie C. Wade*—"

Elizabeth nodded, impatiently. "And how long did you stay abroad?"

"Years, it seemed. Just a blur of waiting, that's all I can remember. Anyway, until my decree was final. Then, I came running back—"

"And married Marius."

"Yes."

"And then you came here to live."

"I'm getting sleepy," the Baroness murmured.

"But you did live here, didn't you?"

"Yes."

"And he carried you over the threshold?"

The Baroness nodded. Watching the girl with stricken eyes, she cried out, "It was the most beautiful night, the happiest of my life—"

"I know, I know."

"He loved me and I loved him—"

"I know."

"We had a bottle of champagne."

"Yes."

"Marius was afraid he would get drunk. He never learned how to drink, you see—"

"But he didn't get drunk this night," Elizabeth said.

"No."

"It was like meeting all over again, wasn't it?"

"Yes," agreed the Baroness. "Almost like two strangers."

"But the eagerness—it wasn't a stranger's eagerness."

"No. We sat on the piano bench. Drank our wine. Whispered, although no one was near. Worth was gone for the week. She could tell you nothing—"

"Go on."

"I remember—there was a button off his vest. And—"

"Yes?"

"We went upstairs. Up to the room where I'd posed for him—"

"Go on," Elizabeth whispered.

"I—forget. Oh, what does happen, for heaven's sake, when two people who love each other and are free—"

"He took you in his arms," Elizabeth said. "Told you he loved you."

"Yes! Yes, and—remember once, I told you I'd never said 'I love you' to any man? Well—I think I said it to Marius, that night. It's true, I did! And it didn't mean I was weak and female and subservient to admit it. That's why I could say it to him. The happiest moment of my life. And the happiest of his. You believe that, don't you?"

"Oh, I do, I do."

"It's hard to talk about such moments. You see that, don't you?"

"Yes," Elizabeth said, softly. "I see everything." Her face was exultant, her eyes, burning.

When, at last, the girl left the room, Madame von Schillar listened for her tread on the stairs, but there was no sound. Soon, however, she heard a soft laugh in the parlor. With difficulty, she climbed out of bed, turned off the lamp, and, inching open the door, peered into the parlor.

A prickling sensation crawled through her scalp. Elizabeth was sitting alone on the piano bench, her eyes closed, her lips parted in a smile. She lifted her hand, her fingers curved as though around the stem of a champagne glass.

It was a gesture so triumphant that Madame von Schillar recoiled as if slapped. She bit her lip and her hand tightened on the doorknob; but she did not enter the parlor. Edging closer to the crack of the door, she watched Elizabeth wistfully, letting no movement escape her.

With more than usual care, Worth ran her dust rag over the furniture in Elizabeth's room. "Very fair outside, Miss," she said.

"Umm," Elizabeth agreed, checking a word in the dictionary.

"But a nice breeze. Sailing weather. That's what *he'd* say." She waited for the focus of Elizabeth's attention.

The girl only bent nearer the page. "I know," she murmured.

"You do, Miss?" Her brow lifted. "Did she say so?"

"I imagine she must have."

"Strange that she'd recall such a thing."

"But she remembers every moment of her life with him."

"Yes, Miss, I'm sure. But—" she glanced over her shoulder, then lowered her voice—"sometimes I wonder if she tells it all."

Elizabeth looked up. "Why not?"

"Some things, Miss—maybe she feels are better left unsaid."

"Like what?"

"Well, it's not my place to say, Miss, but—well, for instance—certain trouble between them."

"I know about it. The time when he was doing her portrait, and gossip started—"

"But other times."

Elizabeth spoke with assurance. "There were no other times."

"That last spring, there was. Certain trouble—"

"About what?"

Worth sighed. "I don't have facts, Miss."

"I'm sure you don't," Elizabeth laughed.

"Miss, a man on the sidewalk don't always know about the roots of the trees, but he can tell something by the foliage."

"What do you mean?"

"I can't give facts, ma'am. Just the same, it wasn't like you think."

"How do you know what I think?" Elizabeth asked, returning to the dictionary. "Have I said? Have you read what I've written?"

"Yes, Miss."

Elizabeth looked up, sharply. "You have? When?"

"Aloud to the Lady, once."

"And she said I'd made some mistakes?"

"Not that she'd admit to, Miss."

"Then, it's not very likely that I made any, is it? Wouldn't she be the best judge of that?" She turned a page of the dictionary.

"Unless she wanted to forget."

Elizabeth smiled and shook her head. "That doesn't seem likely, does it? You don't forget things like that. Oh, I know they undoubtedly had their differences. She, so high-strung, and he . . ." She grew silent, but her eyes were luminous.

"It wasn't like you think, Miss," Worth insisted.

Elizabeth's smile did not dim. "Madame von Schillar would have said something. And besides, I know . . ."

Worth sighed, but she did not linger.

"Did you and Mr Wrenn ever quarrel?" Elizabeth asked the Baroness, that afternoon.

"Never," said Madame von Schillar, without an instant's thought.

"Most married people do."

The Baroness's hands were restless. "I suppose we had our differences, sometimes. But—as you said—a bond like two arms—you know."

"That's what I thought."

Madame von Schillar bedecked her tension with infinite languor. "Whatever could have put such an idea in your funny, funny head?"

"Nothing."

"No one's been muttering around? Worth, or someone?"

"Why would she? How would she know about such things, even if they had happened?"

"Exactly," said the Baroness. "But you know how some religious people can be. Feel we must pay for our sins right now. Cash and carry. Please don't ask for credit."

"Pardon?"

"I mean, suffer now, and not wait for hell. I fancy she always felt Marius and I ought to have felt so guilty that we'd get on each other's nerves all the time. Only it was just the other way, wasn't it? Only laced us tighter to each other. We were all we had to depend on. God knows the rest of the world had deserted us." She drew Jabot closer and restlessly entwined the black ringlets around her fingers. "Well, if she starts preaching, just let me know. I don't want you to be bothered while you're working so hard."

"She doesn't bother me," Elizabeth laughed.

She did, however, bother Madame von Schillar. With the threat of Worth's interference rising darkly on each day's horizon, the Baroness found no rest. She scarcely let Elizabeth out of her sight; and when the girl went out, Madame von Schillar instantly summoned the servant, in order that the two might never be alone together. She would have gladly discharged Worth at once, except for fear that so drastic a move would propel the servant into immediate action.

"Only what could she say? What does the fool creature know?"

So the Baroness consoled herself, again and again. Yet the threat was ever there, and she was not yet well enough to resist dwelling on it.

"Dear," she said to Elizabeth, Wednesday morning, "it occurs to me that I need fresh air and rest, and—since the cottage is so handy and . . . Anyway, it might give you all kinds of local color, since Marius and I were there, near this time, that year—"

"Cape Cod?"

"Yes."

Elizabeth's face lit up. "Go there?"

"Yes, just the two of us."

"Not Worth?"

"No. We'll run off alone and work our heads off, with no one to interfere and make us eat meals when we're not hungry . . ." She looked away from the girl. "Maybe Kitty could go with us, so I won't be alone—I mean, when you're working. Only, it won't be all work, if you don't want. Getting warmer now, and you can sun and swim."

"Maybe even get a little boat."

The Baroness frowned. "No. I must forbid that. No little boats. But you won't miss it, I swear. We'll have such fun."

Elizabeth pressed her cheek next to Madame von Schillar's hand. "How long can we stay?"

"Long as you want. Till the book's done."

"July?"

"If you wish. If it takes us that long."

"Oh, it will," Elizabeth cried. She leaped up. "How soon can we go?"

"Not so loud," the Baroness cautioned. "This must be our secret. We won't even tell Worth. You know how she worries about me. Might not even let me go till she's decided I'm well. Or she'd insist on coming along and spoil our lovely time with her clucking. So—not a word, not a whisper."

"Silent as the tomb," Elizabeth promised.

Madame von Schillar smiled wryly. "Silent as something a little more cheerful, dear, please."

"I didn't mean—" Elizabeth studied the woman with concern. "Are you sure you're well enough to travel yet?"

"Strong as an ox," Madame von Schillar assured her. In proof, she tried to get out of bed. It cost her much breath, and she had to steady herself against the bedpost.

"There, there," said Elizabeth. Gently, she aided the Baroness back into bed and spread the blankets over her.

"Don't treat me like a child," Madame von Schillar cried. "I'm all right now, I tell you."

"Of course you are," Elizabeth comforted, "but don't you think we'd better wait a few days more before we start?"

"Why?"

"Work," Elizabeth decided to say. "It's not because of you, but me. I've still got some pages to finish here, but the minute they're through—off we go."

"Off we go!" The Baroness lay back. "Is it 'the wide blue yonder'?" she mused, "or 'the wild blue yonder'? That off we go into?"

But Elizabeth, smiling to herself, was no longer listening.

It was afternoon again. The doorbell's ringing startled Madame von Schillar from her reverie. "Who is it?" she asked, when Worth entered.

"Mr Hereford again, ma'am."

The Baroness glanced at a mirror, then grimaced. "I can't see him."

"That's what I told him, ma'am. I said you was sick—"

"I'm not sick. Just tired."

"That's what I told him. But he's insistent, ma'am."

Madame von Schillar sighed and ran her hand through her uncurled red hair. "Wouldn't you think he'd know he's not welcome here?" She pushed herself upright. "Well, if I must . . . Draw the curtains. Make it dark. He can't see me looking so *negligee*—" As Worth obeyed, she added, "But bring me the perfume."

"How's that?"

"My Loki. If he can't see me, at least I can smell beautiful."

As Quincy Hereford was ushered into the darkness, she briefly glimpsed his silhouette against the parlor light. "There's a chair in front of you," she warned. "Sit down, if you must."

She heard the creak of the chair, and then his voice. "I'm sorry you're not well, Elizabeth."

"I'm perfectly well. Just weary. I play too hard, y'know."

"Might I light a lamp?"

"No!" She cringed back in bed, her hands raised, ready to mask her face; but no light came to betray her and she relaxed again. "So many visitors, these days," she said, brightly. "You'd think I was a national monument. Saw Kitty last week. Kitty Leighton, remember?"

"I never knew her well."

"Oh, you wouldn't, would you?" she retorted, suddenly caustic. "After all, Kitty married a Jew, and one has to be so select!"

"Don't, Elizabeth."

"Don't, Elizabeth, don't, Elizabeth," she mocked. "You sound just like my father."

"Must we begin this way?" he asked, after a pause.

"Need we talk at all?" she asked, echoing his inflection.

"I'm afraid so."

"Well, then?" As he did not begin at once, she repeated, "Well? Well?"

"I can't go on this way, Elizabeth."

"That sounds familiar," she said. "Are you considering making me an honest woman?"

"You know what I mean. I can't go on being tortured every day, wondering if you're going to tell everything in your book."

"Everything about what, pray? What is there to tell?"

"You know."

"I assure you, I do not."

"Now, Elizabeth, let's not be absurd!"

"I have no intention of being, my dear Quincy, and I'm trying very hard to keep you from being. I'm afraid you've been carrying a rather distorted impression, all these years."

"Distorted? That we were in love?"

"Were we in love? Did I ever tell you so?" She laughed, softly. "Oh, my dear, you were charming, but—I've only loved one man in my life, and that, of course, was Marius. What I felt for you was something quite else again."

"Was it?"

"Yes. It was nothing but pity." She listened in the darkness for his reaction. "Does that hurt you?"

"Is that what you want?"

"I don't want anything from you, poor dear. I—" The rest was ruptured by his coughing. "Same old cough," she murmured.

"It's just a cold. I've been over the other for years."

"I used to wonder if you'd live past your twenty-fifth year," she mused. "You were so—I guess that was it: so helpless. You needed someone. The others never did. Didn't really need me. They could stand alone. Dominant, self-sufficient men." She peered through the darkness, trying to see him. "Do you still play the piano?"

"I haven't for years. I don't have much free time . . ."

"You were playing the piano the first time I ever saw you," she recalled. "Chopin, I think. Your hair was all sunny, and you were so pale, so delicate. Lucy whispered that you had T.B. and suddenly—Oh well, it's unimportant."

"Tell me, anyway," he begged.

"Suddenly, I wanted to hold you to my heart, as if you were my child—only you wouldn't even look in my direction, remember?"

"But I was aware of you."

"And I asked you to play a silly ragtime tune, just to make you angry. Only you played it, remember? 'That Red-Rose Rag,' it was called. I still play it, sometimes . . ." She hummed a few bars, then laughed again. "I expect you thought I was some kind of monster."

"I thought you were beautiful."

"But a Hereford is cautious, eh? After all, a married woman! The wife of a pure United States Senator!"

"And the mistress of an artist!" he added, sharply.

"And glad to be!" she retorted.

After a while, she added, "I wish we'd never met, Quincy. Or anyway, I wish our friendship had been worth while. I could have turned you into something so magnificent, if only you'd let me."

"If only I'd let you . . ." He laughed faintly. "You'd have thrown me aside, my dear, just as soon as you'd proved yourself."

"Proved myself?"

"Gotten the whip hand."

"That's not true."

"I wonder if it isn't," he said. "You always had to show you were stronger than the man, didn't you? You had to prove yourself the dominant one, whatever the cost, and wherever it led you."

"Is that what you always thought?"

"Not then. But I see it clearly enough now."

"Well, it's not true," she said, so vehemently that she was forced to rest a moment before continuing. "I was looking for someone as strong as myself. And I found him—Marius. He wasn't afraid of all these little things. He didn't let the world dictate to him. He thought for himself, and had the strength to endure anything." Her voice came more strongly now. "He was a great man. Worth twenty of you. Oh, not just as a person, my dear, but as a lover, too!"

"Don't," he begged. "Must you make it more painful? Haven't I suffered enough?"

"You?" she cried. "How have you suffered?"

"I loved you, Elizabeth."

"Did you? You chose a curious way to prove it."

"I didn't love her. I do now, but I didn't then."

"But she was clean, is that it? Socially acceptable. She hadn't figured in any scandal."

"I married her because it was what my family particularly wished," he said, with effort.

"Oh, Christ!" she cried, contemptuously. "How can any mortal be so weak?"

"But wasn't it that which attracted you to me? My weakness? You say so yourself."

"Did I? Well, I don't find it endearing any more."

"And another thing," he continued, stiffly, "I dare say you wouldn't have wanted me without the mills. You'd like to have guided their destiny too, I'll wager. Well, if I'd married you, I should have been disinherited."

"I wouldn't have cared. I have money."

"Yes, exactly. You would have had the money. The whip hand. I'd have been just your poodle. A sick poodle you could fuss over until you got tired of seeing it jump through its hoop—"

"I'm afraid that sick poodles never held my interest, at all." She laughed, not unkindly. "I tended more toward lions. One lion. That's all that ever mattered. Read my book, and you'll see."

"Then you're not going to mention me?"

"Mention you?" She spoke with some astonishment. "Of course not. Why should I? Dear boy, do understand, once and for all—you mattered very little in my life."

His sigh was of relief. "Then, thank you very much."

"For what?"

"I've reproached myself all these years. But if you never loved me, then I have nothing to be ashamed of, have I?"

"Nothing," she agreed.

There was a pause as he fumbled in the darkness for the door-knob. "Then good-bye, Elizabeth."

"Yes," she answered. "This time, I expect it is good-bye."

As the door opened, she saw him outlined against the light, and once more she shrank back in the shadows. "Good-bye," she repeated.

"Oh, Elizabeth," he murmured, turning back to her, "what horrible things we've done to our lives. Here in the darkness, it was as if we were young again, and had all our decisions before us—"

"I'd change nothing." She spoke quite matter-of-factly. "I loved Marius. I married him. That's how I wanted it. That's how it was. The one perfect thing in my life. And in his."

"I wish I had been as fortunate," he said. "Ignorance is bliss."

"What is that supposed to mean, pray?"

"This much touted strength of his—I'm sure you were careful never to put it to test."

"My poor Quincy!" she sighed. "You'd like to tear him down, wouldn't you? It would make you feel much better if you could,

I'm sure. Well, hear me—we were always honest and open with each other about everything. Everything." Her voice was tremulous with emotion. "Strength? Oh, but that wasn't all he had. There was understanding. Compassion." After a pause, she added quietly, "I learned a lot from Wrenn. Understanding. Forgiveness. That's why I can offer it to you, now." She held out her hand, although in the darkness he could not see it. "Good-bye, Quincy."

He closed the door behind him. Madame von Schillar waited for the sound of the front door latch and then turned on a lamp. From under her green comforter, she eagerly withdrew a sheaf of papers—the new portion of the book, describing her homecoming with Marius after their wedding. It was in this she had been steeping herself when Quincy had been announced.

She read slowly, carefully, sometimes staring into space, gently smiling, sometimes forming the words with silent lips. " 'There is no past, my dearest dear.' " These were words she spoke in the new chapter. " 'Only this to remember—that I love you—' "

There was a tap at the door.

"I'm resting," she called, softly.

Worth peered in. "Didn't realize he'd gone, ma'am. I didn't mean to leave you alone."

"But why not alone?" Madame von Schillar asked, in surprise.

"It's just that—often, when you get left alone, you—get upset."

"I'm quite all right," said the Baroness.

Her surprise intensified as she considered it; surprise at herself. It was true: she had been left alone after an interview which should have guaranteed her hysteria; had uttered tabu words, had tempted forbidden subjects, and yet none of these had set off the usual chain reaction of fear and despair. Indeed, in the end, she had been quite gracious to Quincy; had unthinkingly behaved like the Elizabeth in the book.

"It's that I'm still weak," she thought.

Or was it something else? Was it the effect of studying the book so much? Like the leaven the woman hid in three measures of meal till the whole was leavened, was the concept of herself which Elizabeth had instilled in her mind gradually transforming her to its likeness?

"Tosh!" she whispered. Yet an admonition of her father's echoed in her mind. "—worn long enough, the mask becomes the face."

She sighed. It would be nice to be like the Elizabeth in the book. Standing between her and that person, however, were too many unleavened memories—memories she was resolved never to divulge. Yet, she realized, if she left them locked in her heart, they would continue to fester, poisoning her life, while if she revealed but the vaguest outline, the girl would fill it in with her love and understanding, and this, rather than ugliness, would soon dictate her life.

"Tosh!" she said again, and picked up the manuscript. She did not read, however. Her eyes kept turning toward the shrouded window, beyond which lay the garden. To be free of this memory in particular, she thought, was that not worth the chance? To be free like the Elizabeth in the book! Suddenly, she struggled out of bed and tugged the bell cord. "God give me strength," she whispered.

"My dear," she said, when Elizabeth had been summoned, "I told you once that Marius and I had never quarreled. Now I want you to know the truth. We did quarrel! Oh, it may not sound important—and it wasn't!—yet, I wish you'd write it up . . ."

She had spoken almost joyously, but now the incident was to be mentioned, however fragmentarily, it became more difficult.

"It was in May," she said, moistening her dry lips. "The last May before he—before he died. It was a lovely day, though still cool, and we were in the garden. In the pergola—"

"Yes?"

The Baroness folded her hands to keep them still. "We were having some lemonade and—just chatting. Nothing important. And then—somehow the subject came up—we began to talk about truth." She faltered.

"Go on."

"I believe I said the truth wasn't always to be looked at too closely. Well, that set him off. So—just to tease him—I asked if everything in his life bore close inspection, and I ribbed him about some Portugese women he used to talk about. Well—one thing led to another, and suddenly, we were in the midst of the most hideous quarrel, saying things that bore no relation to the truth, until finally—"

"Finally?"

"I'm trying to think." She moistened her lips again. "Finally, I must have driven him too far. Something I said or accused him of. Because suddenly, he stood up, overturning the lemonade and"—her voice broke—"raised his arm as if to strike me. Only he didn't. Just stared at me. Then he walked off—"

"Are you sure?" Elizabeth cried. "He just walked away? Didn't say anything first?"

Madame von Schillar's face was expressionless. "I don't remember—"

"Try," Elizabeth urged. "It wouldn't be like him to just walk away. Not after that. Oh, I know he had a temper. There was violence in him, but there was forgiveness, too—"

"Yes," the Baroness said, thoughtfully. "Yes, of course. Now, I begin to remember more clearly. He didn't walk away. Instead he looked at me for a long time, a strange look—"

"Almost like a smile—"

Madame von Schillar nodded. "And then . . . If I can just recall—" She glanced at Elizabeth expectantly.

"He took you in his arms?"

"Exactly," cried the Baroness. "He took me in his arms—"

When, eventually, Elizabeth left, Madame von Schillar turned slowly and gazed at the curtained window, as if to see the garden outside.

"If it had only been that simple," she sighed.

CHAPTER 5

"Some folks in the parlor to see you," Worth told the Baroness. "You feel up to seeing anyone yet?"

"Is it Hyltie Crisler?"

Worth nodded. "So he says." Her eyes darted to the suitcases half concealed behind a portiere.

"Good. I'm expecting him." Her voice betrayed a note of excitement. "Miss Deveny has gone out?"

Worth hesitated, then said, decisively, "Yes."

Madame von Schillar smiled to herself. She had calmly dismissed the news when Elizabeth had succeeded in tracing Captain Crisler. "We'll have to ask him over, one of these days," she had said. Promptly, however, she had dispatched an invitation to the man, naming an hour when Elizabeth was always out. This was not so much discretion or possessiveness as the desire for a really heart-to-heart talk with Hyltie.

Quickly she touched her ears and throat with perfume. Never before had she shown any eagerness to see Crisler, having found him clumsy and commonplace, despite his superb figure. He had idolized Wrenn, however, and it was through the eyes of his love that she wished to see Marius.

"Is the Captain old now, Worth?" she asked.

"Yes, ma'am."

She smiled sadly. "Just as I thought. Well, it's better to know in advance, and then you're not so shocked, eh?" She sleeked her back hair, meticulously. "They all grow old. All the young men."

"Don't we all, ma'am," Worth said, dryly.

The Baroness put down her brush. "What do you mean by that, pray?"

"Nothing unnatural. Everything changes, ma'am. Everything, except truth."

"Now, don't start that again," murmured the Baroness. She peered more closely at the mirror, smoothing her cheeks and neck. She powdered her face again and brightened her lips; but she found no cosmetic for doubt. Even with prejudiced eyes, she could read the postscript that illness had added to the message of time in her face.

"Worth," she directed, abruptly, "go in and light the candles in the parlor. We'll have only candles tonight. My eyes still ache a bit, so—not too much light."

Worth obeyed, silently. When the candles were lit, she hesitated at the foot of the stairs, then climbed up to the second floor and tapped at Elizabeth's door.

"Come in."

She entered. As she expected, Elizabeth's suitcase lay open on the cot, half packed. The servant's voice was as expressionless as her face. "I made some gingerbread," she said. "Nice and hot. Come down and sample some, if you like. But come down quiet. The Lady's got a visitor. One of Mr Wrenn's old buddies." She opened the door again. "It ought to be done in a few minutes. The gingerbrea[illegible]

By force of habit, Madame von Schillar bit and licked her scarlet lips, then whispered "crush" to form her smile, as she swept into the parlor.

Crisler was not alone. A woman was with him. The Baroness frowned. She had not counted on this. Men were easier to handle when alone. He stood up as the doors clicked shut and stared in her direction, but without recognition. Her uneasiness swept back over her. Advancing, she cried far too gaily, "Don't look at me, Hyltie, don't look. I've changed."

The woman, who had also arisen, pointed to her eyes, and her lips silently formed a word.

"She's saying I'm blind," Crisler rumbled. "Trying to keep it a secret from me, you'd think." He turned his massive head as the Baroness passed before him. "But you smell the same. That perfumery!"

Her relief that he could not see her was quickly supplanted by her habitual distaste for any kind of debility. Although she addressed her words to him, the Baroness did not again look his way, but only at the woman, as if expecting her to interpret everything to the old man.

"Can I serve anyone a drink? Just a wee one?"

"Not for me," said the woman, "and I guess not for him, either." She was of mediocre appearance, plump and greying, clad in a cheap brown coat. From her constant attention, half-nagging, half-tender, Madame von Schillar itemized her as the Captain's nurse or daughter.

"Well, Hyltie," she cried, with forced gaiety, "it's been a long time since that last summer at the Cape. Or do you still remember?"

"It's my sight, not my mind, that's gone," he growled. "Yes, I remember, ma'am."

"What glorious, what golden days those were," she prompted. Although unwilling to look at him directly, she watched for his reaction from the corner of her eye.

Crisler sat motionless as if considering her words. At last he nodded. "Golden days," he repeated.

"The sun was always shining then, remember? And Lord, how I'd freckle if I so much as poked my nose outside. That's why you didn't see much of me, I suppose. But I used to be so envious of you men—out in your little sailboat every day, getting positively *noir*—"

"It wasn't every day," Crisler corrected. "Only on Sundays, when I didn't work." He turned ponderously to the other woman. "We used to fish together on Sunday. Marius and me. As if I didn't get enough fish every other day of the week . . ."

This set him off on descriptions of the fishing jaunts he and Wrenn had taken; and how, once, the artist had swum out in the bay to retrieve a bottle, hoping it might contain a message; and how they had walked along the beach at midnight, in search of phosphorescent driftwood. "And once he draws a picture of me on the table cloth at Ezterhausy's boardinghouse, and the landlady is fit to be tied, and if she hadn't washed it out, might be in some picture gallery now. And another time . . ."

The Baroness sighed. She had expected to find new sustenance and comfort in these memories of Marius, but instead was only irritated by the old man's appearance and the way he spoke. His stories were disconnected, seldom reaching the point, and nearly always narrated in the present tense, as if they were somehow occurring at that moment. With neither challenge nor curiosity to buoy her, the Baroness began to fight her yawns; and while she smiled and agreed and prompted Crisler when he fumbled for a word, she kept glancing from the clock to the woman's face with pointed regularity.

"Father," the woman said, at last, "it's time to go."

"Must you?" the Baroness said, rising quickly.

"I'm afraid so," the woman replied. "You probably remember all these things, anyway. Come on, Daddy."

"Why do we have to go so soon?" he demanded. "I haven't blatted out anything—"

"Hush," said his daughter.

"What does he mean?" Madame von Schillar asked.

"Nothing, really. Only he always gets talking too much about Marius, and I said if he didn't behave himself, this time—"

"She figured you wouldn't want to be reminded," the Captain rumbled.

"Why not, Hyltie?" Madame von Schillar inquired. "It was the most beautiful—and most terrible part of my life. But I remember the beauty best." She smiled sadly at the Captain's daughter. "Marius and I had been married such a short time. Or so it seemed. But fate had its own designs, I suppose, and doesn't care how madly you're in love—" Crisler snorted. Madame von Schillar wheeled around in surprise. "What's the matter?"

"Madly in love!"

"We were, Hyltie. You, of all people, should know that."

"I don't know any such thing," he retorted, slowly.

"Father!" the woman warned.

"You've forgotten," the Baroness said. "Maybe you're past the age when love means much."

"I reached that age early, where love matters, and I never let go, not yet anyways," he said. "I don't forget those things. Nor anything else. That's the only sight I got now, the things I can remember. Why, I can bring to mind the color dress you're wearing the day Marius drowned himself—"

"He didn't drown himself," the Baroness corrected, carefully. "It was an accident."

"Yes, an accident. He'd been looking for one pretty hard. Swimming out too far when the tide was strong. Diving into the shallows with only luck to keep him alive. Sailing out in that little boat in fool's weather—"

"Father," the other woman protested. "After all . . . !"

"It was an accident, I swear," the Baroness protested, turning to his daughter. "I can't imagine where he got such an idea. You don't believe him, do you, Miss . . . ?"

"Mrs Sullivan," the woman prompted. "I understand, ma'am. Father shouldn't be upsetting you by talking about it now. What ever reasons made Mr Wrenn not care about living, it's over and done with now."

"But he didn't want to die," Madame von Schillar insisted. "Why would he want to die? We were so much in love. But he went out in his skiff, and it got stormy. I can't be blamed for that. I wasn't even there, that day—" She caught herself, then added, quickly, "Anyway, it was fate, and he couldn't help it, and neither could I!"

"You could if you tried," Crisler boomed. "You shouldn't led him on that way, if you never meant it. You shouldn't pretend to be fine and good, getting him to think you was an angel, if you didn't have any notion to keep it up."

"I didn't pretend anything," the Baroness cried. "I was fine and good, and loved him right to the end. But no one could live up to his idea of what I was. The Mother of God couldn't have lived up to his ideal of what I was. I tried, heaven knows, I tried!"

"Then why was that foreigner always hanging around you? Marius knew about him, too. And why was you carrying on with that other puppy, if you was so fine and good, with Marius eating his heart out? You was living a lie, and making him live one, too—"

"Really, what a fascinating repertory of clichés," purred the Baroness, hiding her tension with the indolent smile. "I must remember that one. Too amusing. Living a lie—"

"And so you did, and made him live one, too," Crisler repeated, fiercely. "Like he was always saying about drawing pictures, 'Let's have the truth first, and the beauty'll take care of itself.' Only, you give him the beauty first, and then make it a lie." From somewhere, a draft stirred, and he turned toward it. "Well, he must've been blinder than me now, not to have seen through you right from the start. Oh,

I know all about it! Me and Jay Ezterhausy, we got him drunk once, at old Sprague's house, so he'd talk and get it out of his blood before he done something dangerous to himself. We knew something was wrong. And we found out, the whole shame of it, just as he'd got it from your own lips—"

"Father," said Mrs Sullivan, uneasily, "we just must go—"

He turned to her, excitedly. "She never loved Marius—"

"I don't even have to answer that!" The Baroness spoke coldly, but a nerve began twitching under her eye. "Why would I marry him if I didn't love him?"

"*Why, oh God, why?*" dinned in her mind.

"I loved him very much," she cried, as if in answer. "I loved him from the moment we met."

"But for how long after? A week? A month? Until folks' whispering gets you scared, and you send him packing." He addressed the room as though he believed someone new had just entered who must not be left out of the conversation. "Sent him packing! Then she meets this Quincy and starts cheating with him. Only old Senator Carver, he's suspicious now, so to find out who she's cheating with, he sets detectives on her—"

"Father, if you don't come on, I'm going without you!" Mrs Sullivan threatened. As the Captain persisted, she too continued talking, trying to drown out his accusations. Crisler only boomed the louder, explaining to an empty corner:

"Then she gets more scared. Don't know how much them detectives already know. But she does know if delicate Quincy gets dirtied up in any scandal, she'll lose him. It's too late to save herself, but to throw her husband off Quincy's scent, she quick sends Marius this note, all sweet and sorry. Sees him again a few times, then gets him to run off with her. So it's him she don't even love gets caught and blamed. She throws him to the wolves to save delicate Quincy's hide—"

"That's a lie!" the Baroness shouted. "Get out! Get out of here!"

"But it didn't help, did it, lady?" he persisted. "Didn't tie that Quincy to you out of gratitude, as it should. No, he's too fine, too delicate, to want any divorced woman. He marries a decent girl and leaves you holding the bag, high and dry and ruined. And that's why you married Marius. Just to save face, so people wouldn't think no one wanted you, not even him—"

"It's a lie, a filthy lie!" the Baroness cried, pounding the table, her face livid with fury. "A lie, a lie, a lie—"

"No, it ain't," Crisler shouted back. "It's just what you told Marius yourself, to spite him, out in the pergola that day—"

"Damn you," Madame von Schillar lashed. "I loved him, I always loved him." Feverishly, she faced Mrs Sullivan. "Can't you make him understand that? You understand, don't you?"

"Yes, ma'am, I understand." She met Madame von Schillar's eyes. "I knew Mr Wrenn when I was little. He lived with us on Daddy's tug for a year before he married you. He idolized you, ma'am. And loving him, myself, I know how much his love was worth." She helped the Captain to his feet. "I can't hate you like Daddy does. I did once, but now I just feel sorry for you."

Madame von Schillar spoke scornfully. "You sorry for *me?*"

"Yes, ma'am. Because you had to go so fast, you never got anywhere. I wouldn't like to be old and alone with memories like you got. Nothing but ashes that nothing ever grew out of." She took the old man's hand. "Come on, Daddy. We'll treat ourselves to a taxi."

As Crisler reached the hall, he paused. "Why'd you ever have to tell him?" he reproached. "Why'd you have to let him know?"

"He was always wanting the truth," the Baroness cried, defensively. "He was always saying so. Well, finally I gave it to him!"

"Why? Why, when you knew how he believed in you? Why tell him he'd sold himself out for a pack of lies? Why'd he want to go on living when he couldn't believe in himself or you, no more? Better you should let him keep his dream."

It took all her strength, but Madame von Schillar spoke. "A strong man shouldn't need dreams. If he can't face the truth, then he's not really strong."

"And that's what you had to prove," Crisler challenged. "That you was the stronger. You was the Delilah cutting away his strength. You had to punish him for being stronger in ways you never could be. That's the only reason you told him the truth." He shook his head and, holding his daughter's arm, went out.

When the front door had closed, Madame von Schillar had barely strength enough to pour herself some brandy. All through her being was the quivering promise of vertigo. "But I'm all right now," she kept telling herself. "It's over with now, and there's nothing to fear." The old man was senile, and even if he lived much longer, who would heed his words? As for the Sullivan woman, she had no proof of anything; only hearsay. Quincy would never talk, Ezterhausy was dead, and Bentley Sprague's silence could be bought. There was nothing to fear, no one to expose her. She sipped her brandy slowly, pressing her hand against her breast to reassure her pounding heart.

At last, she arose. She still felt weak, but to deceive herself, she hummed a tune and waltzed across the room to blow out some candles. Then, as she revolved slowly, gracefully, she glimpsed someone standing in the shadows of the hall. It was Elizabeth.

"When did you come in?" Madame von Schillar demanded, a trifle shrilly.

"I didn't go out," Elizabeth murmured. "I don't go out, any more."

The Baroness twisted at her pearls. "Where were you, then?"

"In my room, working. Then I started downstairs—"

"I had visitors . . ." the Baroness faltered.

"I know."

"Old friends of mine. You remember, we discussed Captain Crisler . . ." There was a silence. "Why do you just stand there, gawking?" the Baroness cried, uneasily. "Either go on back to your room or come out here, I don't care which."

Elizabeth advanced slowly. Her face was white, dazed, in the candlelight.

"Get much work done tonight?" Madame von Schillar asked.

Elizabeth did not answer; merely stared at her, stupidly.

The Baroness clenched her fists. "You listened in on us!" she accused. "You were eavesdropping!"

Still the girl was silent.

"Well, he was lying," Madame von Schillar persisted. "He scarcely knew Marius and never knew me at all. He was just making it all up—"

"And so did I," Elizabeth murmured. "I didn't know Marius, either, and I was just making it up . . ."

Her pallor and stunned eyes frightened the Baroness. She touched Elizabeth's arm, gently. "Of course, you know us," she soothed, "or how could you have written about it so beautifully?" As Elizabeth made no response, she continued impatiently, "Well, it needn't make any difference with the book. Just go on writing it the way you have been."

"Writing lies?" Elizabeth cried, stepping back. "Go on violating everything he tried to live by? That's what I've been doing—" She covered her face. "That's what I've been doing. Looking for beauty, and—not the truth—"

"Don't worry about that," the Baroness interrupted. "I'll tell you what to write. I'll tell you how it was."

"How could you?" Elizabeth whispered. "How could you tell me how it was? You never knew him. Never really understood him. You never loved him."

"But you did, eh?" Madame von Schillar said, scornfully. "You love him, you understand him! Oh, yes, I know! I've read all your sentimental tosh. I know about your pitiful daydreams and séances in the park. Pink roses and honeymoons! But could you ever stretch your fine imagination to believe he would ever love *you?* He looked for beauty. Well, look at yourself. Look in the mirror!"

Automatically, Elizabeth matched glances with her reflection in the pier glass. She saw a tall, slender girl with restless hands and straight, dark hair. She saw the pale, boney face with its stupefied eyes. She saw the Elizabeth whose face she washed and made up every day, and yet had almost forgotten.

"What did you expect to see there?" jeered the Baroness. "A beautiful girl with red hair and green eyes? Of course, you did. Because even in your imagination, Marius wouldn't look at you until you became me. So he never loved you, did he? Always me!"

She turned abruptly, as if weary of a game too often won. "I think we needn't meet again." She tugged at the garnet pendant hanging from her ear, then removed it, jingled it in her hand. "Mr Mellett can send me someone else to finish up my book the way I want it. Maybe it won't be the truth, but it will become the truth when it is published."

Knowing she was watched, she crossed the room slowly, paused to break a dead flower from its stem, then opened the doors to her suite. "Good night," she mocked, without turning. "And needless to say—sweet dreams."

The anguish which had dammed up in Elizabeth suddenly spilled over in words. She spoke them so quickly, so mechanically, there was neither the pleasure of malice nor the solace of revenge.

"Yes, Marius looked for beauty, but he wanting a lasting sort," she said. "Do you think that kind of beauty is to be found in a mirror? Does the beauty in a looking glass last? Ask your mirror if it does. Look at yourself and see!" The Baroness flicked a glance at the mirror. "What did you expect to see there?" Elizabeth cried. "A beautiful, young girl?"

The Baroness whipped around with a gesture of rage, then checked herself. She had long ago learned that a lazy, superior smile was her best protection.

"I don't need a mirror," she said. "I have a book now. When I want to see myself, I shall read it." Still smiling, woodenly, painfully, able to feel every wrinkle and wretched crease in her face—but smiling still, she turned and left the room.

Once safe in her suite, however, she stumbled to a chair, gasping for breath. "I won't think of it," she kept telling herself. "I won't."

Actually, she could think clearly of nothing. To the throbbing of her heart, thoughts spiraled about her mind until she was dizzied. "Light," she whispered. "Light!" Yet, when she had lit every lamp in the room, she found new tortures awaiting her. Now, she saw her hands before her clearly, and they were corded, stippled with brown. And everywhere about her were mirrors, ready to humiliate her if only she would raise her eyes to them; ready to show her an old woman with withered face and dyed hair.

Stifling a cry, she slid down on her knees beside the bed, searching her whirling mind for some prayer. Although no words came to her, the very posture of prayer soon set the pattern for relief and hope. At last she was able to whisper, "You forgive me, don't you, Marius? You forgive me because you know I never meant to hurt you—"

"It's all right, it's all right, Elizabeth . . ." The words came to her indistinctly, like a friend approaching through the mist. Marius had spoken thus, soothing her, she recalled, once early in their marriage, when she had awakened from a nightmare. Now she clung to these words as, then, she had clung to his arm.

"It's all right, it's all right, Elizabeth," she echoed, seeking in these words his full pardon, "it's all right, Elizabeth . . ."

How long she had knelt there beside the bed, she could not determine, but when she arose again, her pulse was steadier and her thoughts coherent. She experimented with her laugh, and it rang clear. In relief, she turned down the blazing lamps. It had been a foolish evening, she thought, an ugly nightmare; but she had wakened now and need never think of these things again. The past was obliterated, forgiven; and with the girl gone there would not even be a reminder of it. The memoirs would soon be published and, once again, her life would be full.

"I don't need a mirror," she repeated triumphantly. "I have a book."

Yet as the last word formed on her lips, it froze there. Abruptly, she yanked the bell cord, and then, with growing alarm, hastened into the parlor, calling for Worth.

"Tell Deveny to come here, at once," she ordered.

"She's already gone, ma'am," Worth replied, uneasily.

"But she gave you my manuscript, of course—" Expectantly, the Baroness held out her hands.

"Your what?"

"Manuscript, you fool! The book. The memoirs."

"No, ma'am. She didn't leave me anything. I went upstairs a minute ago to see if she was all right, but she'd already gone, bag and baggage—"

"But she couldn't have taken the book with her," the Baroness protested. "It doesn't belong to her. It's mine—"

"Yes, ma'am. But she didn't leave it with me."

"Go after her," Madame von Schillar ordered. "Get a cab and go after her. Try both stations." She pushed the servant toward the door. "Hurry! Hurry, I say!"

When the door slammed shut, the Baroness made a tempestuous circuit of the parlor. The manuscript, however, had not been left there. It would be upstairs, then. Desperately, she glanced up the steep flight; then, gritting her teeth, clutching the bannister, dragged herself up, pausing breathlessly every few steps.

Elizabeth's room was stripped of personal belongings. As if left in great haste, everything was open, the drawers, the wardrobe doors, the window. The acrid air seered her lungs as she gasped for breath. Feverishly, she rifled the desk. It was empty, except for a cast-off tissue carton, which she flung to the floor. The wardrobe cabinet held nothing. The bureau, too, was empty.

"Then she took it with her," Madame von Schillar groaned.

As she hastened toward the door, however, she suddenly understood the significance of the open window and the sharp odor. Smoke had been caught in this room. There had been a fire on the hearth. Her breath stilled in her as she looked back at the fireplace. The heap of ashes there, teased by crosscurrents, agitated restlessly. Unbelievingly, she knelt down and thrust her hands amongst them. The ashes were still warm.

"But this can't be it," she murmured. "It's only newspaper or something . . ." But one of the fragile black fragments she picked up bore the spectral writing, "Marius did not find . . ."

Her face was chalky, bringing into more garish contrast the black tracing about her eyes, the jagged red of her mouth. Stupidly, she gazed at the handful of ashes. "No, no," she whispered.

Slowly at first, then frantically, she began sifting the dusty heap, hoping to find one unburned page; but the fire had been thorough. A moment later, she realized she had shouted for help. But help from whom? The memoirs, the dreams of renewed glory, the opiate to her guilt—these were ashes now, and who could help?

Again she cried out, a broken, strangled sound, and stumbled across the room. Her toe grazed the paper carton she had flung from the desk, and, as if this were some effigy of Elizabeth, she shook her fist at it, crushed it with her foot, ground it to the floor.

Half-blinded by the exertion, she tottered toward the stairs. As she tried to descend, a sickening dizziness swirled up at her, and the tightening stricture in her breast dared her to breathe. She dragged up her left hand and clenched it over her heart.

"I'm just fooling," she gasped. "Just pretended all that about heart trouble. Really feel fine . . ."

To convince herself of this, she smiled and took another step. Then the smile peeled back over her teeth and, grabbing convulsively for the bannister, she plunged downward.

When Worth returned, she found her crumpled on the landing. In the remaining two days, Madame von Schillar drifted back toward consciousness only once, and then to ask for Philip.

CHAPTER 6

It was nearly a week before Mellett learned of Madame von Schillar's death. The news magazine, open on his desk, summed up the sixty-eight years of her life in approximately as many words; of these years, Mellett had hoped to build a book.

"Died: Baroness Elizabeth Winslow Carver Wrenn von Schillar, 68; old-time glamour girl, once wife of Boston's late, great Marius Wrenn; of a heart attack; in Boston. Thrice-married heiress to the Winslow glass fortune, her elopement with painter Wrenn and consequent divorce by her Senator husband pushed politics off the front page for a season. An expatriate since Wrenn's death (1915), she returned to the U.S. last year, forgotten, nearly broke ('—down to my last pane of glass.')"

Shocked by this news and exasperated by Elizabeth's failure to inform him of it at once, he put through a call to Boston.

"Miss Deveny, please."

"She's not here, sir. No one here now, but me, the housekeeper. I'm closing the place up."

"Miss Deveny's left, already?"

"Oh, yes, sir. Last Friday, just before the occurrence."

"But that's absurd," he cried. "If she left Friday, she'd be back here by now."

Worth's voice was troubled. "Is this the book gentleman?"

"Yes. Mellett."

"And she's not showed up there, yet?"

"No. Did she say where she was going? Leave a forwarding address?"

"No, sir."

Frowning, Mellett hung up and glanced at his calendar. It was Thursday. Abruptly, he rang for his secretary. "Are you certain Elizabeth Deveny hasn't called me, this past week?"

"Deveny? No, sir, I don't think so. But I'll check at the switchboard."

"And you might ring up that place where she used to have a room," he instructed. "She might be there. Resting or finishing up the book. . . ."

A moment later, he strode into the waiting room to see if, by some chance, Elizabeth had left a message at the front desk. There was nothing there for him. Impatiently, he lit a cigarette, and then, almost immediately, crushed it out. "Well?" he demanded, as his secretary returned.

"She's not there, Mr Mellett. Matter of fact, the landlord didn't remember her at all."

"Of course, he does!" Mellett retorted. "Call again. Describe her to him." And he tried to depict Elizabeth, her fragile beauty, her proud stance, the radiance of her eyes.

"Is this our Miss Deveny?" the secretary interrupted, in surprise.

Mellett glanced up. "See for yourself, when she comes back," he said. "And if she doesn't check in here by tomorrow, maybe we'd better drag the river."

"Yes, sir."

"I was just kidding, for God's sake," he said, irritably. "She's all right. Only why doesn't she get here?"

"It might be in the mail right now, Mr Mellett," said the secretary, who was eager to be indispensable.

"What might be?"

"Her manuscript."

"Manuscript?" He drummed his fingers on the desk and eyed her with new annoyance. "That'll be all," he said.

When, by Monday, neither telephone nor mail had brought word from Elizabeth, Mellett once more put through a call to Boston. Eventually, Worth answered.

"See here," he said, "this is Mellett, again. Any news, yet?"

"Of Miss Deveny? No, sir." It was apparently a bad connection, for her voice was faint.

"And she didn't come to the funeral?"

"There was no funeral, sir, not in the real sense. Just words over the grave. Only me and Mrs Wallach and Mr Hereford was there. Like I say, it's not likely Miss Deveny'd have come back even for that. She and the Lady had words, you know."

"Quarreled?"

"I'd say so, sir. Raised voices, and afterwards, she left."

"And you're sure she didn't mention where she was going?"

"No, sir. I didn't see her again. When I went up to see if she was all right, she was gone, sir. Like into thin air."

"Damn!" After a moment, he added, "She was in love with someone, I've heard. Could she have gone to him?"

"Oh no, sir," Worth assured, fervently. "Oh, I hope not, any-ways—"

"But if there's a chance, we ought to follow it up. Who was he, do you know?"

Worth hesitated so long, he finally barked, "Hello—"

"It wasn't anyone, sir," Worth said.

"Must have been!"

"And anyway, sir, the way I figure, she couldn't have gone to him. She took her suitcase, you see."

Mellett cocked his head. "I don't follow that."

"Well, a person wouldn't bother to take a suitcase, if they had plans to—"

"To what?"

"I don't know, sir. But I'm sure she's all right. Better than she was here. She needed a rest, and probably that's what she's taking.

"Where? That's what I want to know."

"I just don't . . ." Worth paused, then added abruptly, "They was going away, sir, her and the Lady. They didn't mean me to know, but Miss Deveny's suitcase was packed, even before they had words, and so was the Lady's. I seen it behind a drape."

"What was in it?" Mellett demanded. "Maybe plane tickets, or something like that?"

"I haven't opened her bags yet, sir. I'm not supposed to touch personal sort of things, you see. Just clean up. The place has been impounded-like until after the will. She had debts, you see. Thousands of 'em—"

"Look in the suitcases," Mellett ordered.

"If you say so, sir."

Mellett tried to wait patiently, drawing elaborately embossed question marks on his memo pad. At last, he heard the servant pick up the telephone again.

"I'm talking from downstairs now, sir. The Lady's suite. There was just clothes in her suitcase. Three bags, sir. Just clothes."

"But what kind? I mean, clothes that she might wear on a ship, or in New York, or what?"

"Well, sir, I—did come across a bottle of sun lotion, and a pair of them high cork clogs, and some dark glasses—"

"The beach!"

Worth did not answer.

"If she went to the beach, which one would she be likely to choose?"

The servant's voice was faint. "The Cape, sir. Shilleth. She had a cottage there."

"Might she have gone to Shilleth, anyway? Miss Deveny? Alone, I mean."

"Sir," said Worth in great agitation, "I'll go there now, myself."

"We could phone—"

"Yes, phone, sir. Right off. But I'm going there, anyway. It's my responsibility!"

"Your responsibility?"

But she hung up without answering.

Mellett's call to Shilleth proved fruitless. Yes, the real-estate agent had received word from the Baroness that she was going to open the house there, only she was dead now. Yes, he remembered Miss Deveny, the dark, slender girl. She had been here once, a month or so earlier, but she had not returned since. If she had, someone would have mentioned it. Shilleth wasn't large enough that a stranger could come and go without people knowing. Particularly, a girl like Miss Deveny. She was not likely to be forgotten, not in Shilleth.

On Thursday, when Mellett returned from lunch, there was a notation on his desk that Mrs Worth had telephoned. Immediately, he put through a long distance call to her. There was no answer. Several more times that day he tried to reach her, but without success. Nor did Worth again call him. On Friday, when he tried phoning Madame von Schillar's, the operator informed him that this number had been disconnected.

Trying to curb his impatience, he flew to Boston that afternoon. The windows of the great stone house were shuttered. He rang the doorbell. No one answered, and he pushed the button again, his ear pressed against the door panel. There was only silence within. The electricity had been shut off. The house was deserted. In the darkened rooms, the furniture would be sheeted, the mirrors covered, the clocks silenced. Time had stopped here.

Unable to locate the servant even through Madame von Schillar's lawyer, Mellett returned to New York. A memo was waiting on his desk. Mrs Worth had telephoned again and left word that he was not to worry.

May merged into June, and there was neither another call from Worth nor word from Elizabeth. June passed, and July became August. Regretfully, Mellett shelved plans for publishing the book.

"You've given her up, then?" his secretary asked.

"No," he said, wearily. "She'll come back."

If she was in New York, however, he had not been able to find her, and there had been no report of her appearance in either Boston or St. Louis. In Worth's words, she might as well have turned into thin air.

Mellett was not a man to dwell on thin air, and his knowledge of Elizabeth—how she thought, how she spoke, how she laughed—was not extensive enough to sustain him indefinitely. Yet the persistence of doubt kept her in his mind. Some nights, when the telephone would waken him, his first thought would be that, at last, Elizabeth was calling. Or a phrase of music over the radio would bring close to him their night at the symphony, and he would glimpse the proud radiance of her face as she had listened. Or on the street, or in a café, someone would pass with that same graceful assurance he remembered from their last meeting, and the poignancy of the unfulfilled would sweep over him.

It was in mid-September that he received a note from Worth. It was brief, enclosing a name and address where, she said, information concerning Elizabeth could be obtained.

Mellett needed no more elaborate invitation. He went to Boston at once.

The address was that of a shabby building in view of the harbor, where breezes brought the smell of oil and the cry of gulls. He climbed the creaking stairs to the top floor. A neat sign by the door read, "Sullivan. Bell out of order." He knocked. Soon, the door was flung open, and a plump, ruddy-faced woman looked out.

"Mrs Sullivan?"

She smiled. "You must be Mr Mellett. Come right on in." She pressed back against the wall to let him pass. The room was neither large nor well furnished, but it was cool and spotlessly clean. Above the stove hung a print of a Wrenn seascape, framed in sea shells.

Without preface, he demanded, "Do you know where she is then?"

Mrs Sullivan indicated a chair for him and drew up a rocker for herself. Only when he was seated, did she nod. Yes, she knew.

He freed himself of a sigh of relief and knew how long it had been welling up in him. "Where is she?"

"Here."

She arose and he followed, expectantly; but she went no further than the stove to pour out two cups of coffee. "I'll take you in to her, directly," she said. "But first, we ought to talk."

"She's all right, isn't she?" he asked, uneasily.

"She is now." Mrs Sullivan handed him a cup.

"But she's been ill?"

Mrs Sullivan nodded.

"Has she had care?"

"The best we could give her, sir. Daddy's doctor come for a while, but like he said, mostly it was rest and affection she was in need of. Now, she's fit as a fiddle and twice as tuneful."

"If she was sick," he reproached, "you should have let me know, at once."

"But how could I, sir?" Mrs Sullivan asked. "When she come here, we didn't know where she was from, or who her friends were."

He frowned. "But—aren't you an old friend of hers, yourself?"

"Never set eyes on her before she come knocking at our door

that night, last May. She seemed to know all about us, but— No, she was a stranger to us. But she needed help. That's all we had to know."

"And she never mentioned any of her friends, or— Well, for instance, me?"

"No. Not for a long time, anyway. Not till after Mrs Worth came searching for her. Come in, one afternoon, on a hunch, she said. Right off, I wanted to write you, so you wouldn't worry. But the girl just wouldn't have it."

"Why not?"

"She wanted time to pull herself together. She'd been through quite a shock, you see."

"But now she's all right, she wants to see me, is that it?"

"She don't know you're coming, Mr Mellett. It was a measure me and Mrs Worth decided was best to take."

"What is it?" he cried. "What's been wrong? Has she told you?"

"No, sir." She rocked her chair, frowning slightly. "I learned somewhat from Mrs Worth. But from herself, not a word. Oh, she's cheerful and bright now, fair talks our arms off about everything else; but not that one thing. Just freezes up when we try to draw it out. And that ain't right. You're not really over a heartbreak till you can talk about it without fear or shame. And she can't bring herself to discuss it. So that's why we called you." She leaned toward him. "The girl sets great store by you, Mr Mellett. Maybe she'll open up her heart to you."

Mellett stood up. "Could you take me to her now?"

She led him down a dark, shelf-lined hall and opened a door to the narrow back room. A window looked out over the roofs onto the cluttered harbor, and the pale radiance of sun beautified the white-washed walls. Mrs Sullivan glanced in. "Someone to see you, Betty." She slipped away, leaving Mellett alone on the threshold.

Elizabeth had turned from her impromptu desk. She was thin, and her hair was too long, but the delight which lit up her face when she saw him was all he noticed.

"Harry! Harry Mellett!" She grasped his hands, and when, impulsively, he kissed her, she kissed him back. Still gripping hands, they looked at each other, their smiles almost too big for their faces.

"Here! Sit down. Let me take your hat," she cried, abruptly.

"Is it Betty they call you here?" he asked. "Our Elizabeth just plain Betty?"

"Not too plain, I hope," she mocked, gaily.

"Well, whatever the name," he decided, "it's good to see you're the same as ever."

"I do hope not," she laughed. "I pray I've made a little improvement." She hung up his hat. "Did you meet my sailor?"

"Your sailor? No, I didn't."

"You will," she promised. "He's a dear."

"Is he your anonymous beau?" he asked, gently.

"No," she replied. "Do sit down, Harry, and tell me what you've been up to."

"Oh, we're going to be mysterious, are we?"

"About what?"

"The man in your life."

She smiled. "You're the only man in my life; you know that."

"Then who's the sailor friend?"

"Why, Captain Crisler. Mrs Sullivan's father. They've been such friends to me. So kind, so patient."

"If patience is the mark of friendship," he mused, "then I've been your closest friend. I've waited for you for months."

"For the manuscript?"

"Well, for that, too."

"I burnt it, Harry."

He studied her face to see if she were joking. "Did you really?" She nodded. "I'm sorry. I liked it."

"I'm afraid it wasn't worth much," she said. "Just a lot of words, meaning nothing. All . . ." She fumbled for the right phrase.

"Sound and fury?" he prompted.

"At all events," she laughed, "a tale told by an idiot."

He did not smile, but only searched her face. She lowered her eyes. Presently, he said, "Where've you been all this time, Elizabeth?"

"Here."

"You came right here from Madame von Schillar's."

"I guess so."

"But why here?"

"I had no other place to go."

"To your friends."

"And so I did. I came here," she replied, obstinately.

"But Mrs Sullivan said she'd never seen you before you came here. Is that true?"

"Oh, Harry, do let's talk about something else!"

"But I have to know. Why didn't you come to me? Or let anyone tell me where you were. I've looked everywhere for you."

"And I was doing the same thing," she replied. "Looking high and low."

"For whom?"

"Me. I had to find me. That's why I came here. To be alone and—find myself. And I think I have, Harry. Almost for the first time in my life."

"Find yourself?" he asked. "How do you mean?"

"I don't much want to talk about it," she said, glancing away.

He moved around until he faced her. "Are we such strangers, Elizabeth?"

"You know we're not." Her voice was affectionate, but her lips were firm.

"Well then?"

"Well then, what?"

"Why can't we talk about it?"

"Because it's all over now, Harry." She picked up a pen from her desk and examined it. "Let's not open up old wounds."

"If it's all over, then it can't hurt to discuss it." She did not answer, and he took the pen from her restless fingers. "It can't hurt to look at the truth, you know."

"Oh, yes, it can," she murmured. "Believe me, it can!"

"It only hurts," he continued, "when you've looked at the truth and haven't the courage to build on it."

She turned on him, indignantly. "I have that courage! I'm still alive, aren't I? That took courage."

"Did it?"

As he expected, the lightness of his tone piqued her. "Yes, it did," she said, sharply. "But you wouldn't know!"

"No, no," he mocked. "Confusion and fear are entirely unique to your experience. Me, I've never suffered. Never ever."

"Not this way," she retorted. "Not deserted by everyone and everything you trusted and loved—"

He chanced it. "So you wanted to forget—"

"Yes, forget and be me again. But I didn't know how. Couldn't see how I'd ever recover peace of mind. I couldn't go back to the old way. But there was another way out. I'd destroyed the book because it was a lie; so why not my life?"

"Go on," he urged. "When you left her house . . . ?"

"I must have headed down here to the bay front," she said, slowly, as if assembling the fragments of a dream. "Then I saw the name of this street. It was familiar. I tried to recall who lived here. It was hard to think. By the time I remembered it was Captain Crisler, I'd realized that death wasn't the solution. I'd been submerged for too long already. That wouldn't help me find myself. Only by living. It took courage to know that. I remembered the Captain had tried to help Marius. I felt he could help me now. So, apparently, I climbed the stairs here, and . . ." She faltered, then shrugged. "*Voila!*"

Still his face did not relax. Though his voice was gentle, he met her eyes unyieldingly. "*Voila?*"

"Yes. And now we can, please, talk about something else?"

"But I only know what you did after you ran away from Madame von Schillar's," he said. "You haven't told me *why* you ran away."

"She discharged me."

"And that made you want to die?"

"It's just that I don't remember. It was all so hazy—"

"You remember, Elizabeth." He took her by the shoulders. "Can't you tell me what it was? It means a lot to me, you know."

She lifted startled eyes. "Why?"

"We'll go into that, some other time," he said. "For the moment, what you have to tell me is more important."

"Important!" she scoffed. "I tell you it's nothing. Just foolishness."

"Then let's laugh at it together."

"It's nothing, I tell you," she repeated, twisting free of his grasp. "There's nothing to tell."

"I want to hear you say it," he said. "Dare to put it into words, Elizabeth. Talk about it. Free yourself, once and for all."

"Leave me alone," she cried, turning away.

"Won't you let me help you?" he begged.

"I don't need help," she retorted.

"Elizabeth . . ." But she did not answer; only gazed out the window at the harbor. He sighed. "All right, then. Sorry I intruded."

"You didn't, Harry. And I'm glad you came." She turned back to him with a smile. "You'll come again, won't you? Often. We'll still be friends."

He reached for his hat. "I often wonder," he said, "if people can ever be friends with a wall between them."

"What wall?"

"A silence, a secret, keeping them apart. A truth that can't be uttered because it can't be faced."

She put her hands over her ears, not to blot out his words, but as if to recapture in silence words once spoken. "As he used to say . . ." she murmured.

"Who?"

"Marius . . . The Captain tells of him saying that. 'I don't want any secrets to keep us apart . . .'" She sank onto the bed and stared at her hands. Presently, she whispered, "All right."

He knelt beside her, his head close to hers, for her voice was very low.

"Harry, I—fell into the same trap as Marius. He fell in love with an ideal, an illusion. Something he wanted to exist, but which wasn't there at all. And when he found out his ideal was based on nothing but lies, he couldn't survive it. And when I found out that the love I was in love with had never existed—that I'd been in love with dreams and lies—I felt betrayed and shamed and frightened—had nothing to count on any more. And I wanted to die, the same as he did— And I suppose, the same as my mother did when she lost her love. . . ." She lifted her white face to him. "That's all. I've said it all, now."

He offered her his handkerchief, but she shook her head. "I'm not crying."

"Then it's really over now," he comforted. "You don't have to think of him any more."

"No. Not any more." She glanced at the desk, then stood up, the uncertainty in her face gone now. "Although—I'm not afraid to, you know. I think I still want to do our book on Wrenn. I've all kinds of new material about him from the Captain and some of his cronies—" Smiling thoughtfully, she sifted the papers on her desk. "I can go ahead with it now. There's nothing to stop me any more, is there?"

"Nothing," he agreed. "This time, you'll have no excuse if you let me down."

She drew a letter from her bureau and handed it to him. "As a pledge," she said.

"What is it?" he asked, opening the envelope.

"It used to be my passport," she said, "but I don't need it any more."

It was an old letter which began, "Elizabeth, Elizabeth—"